I0562036

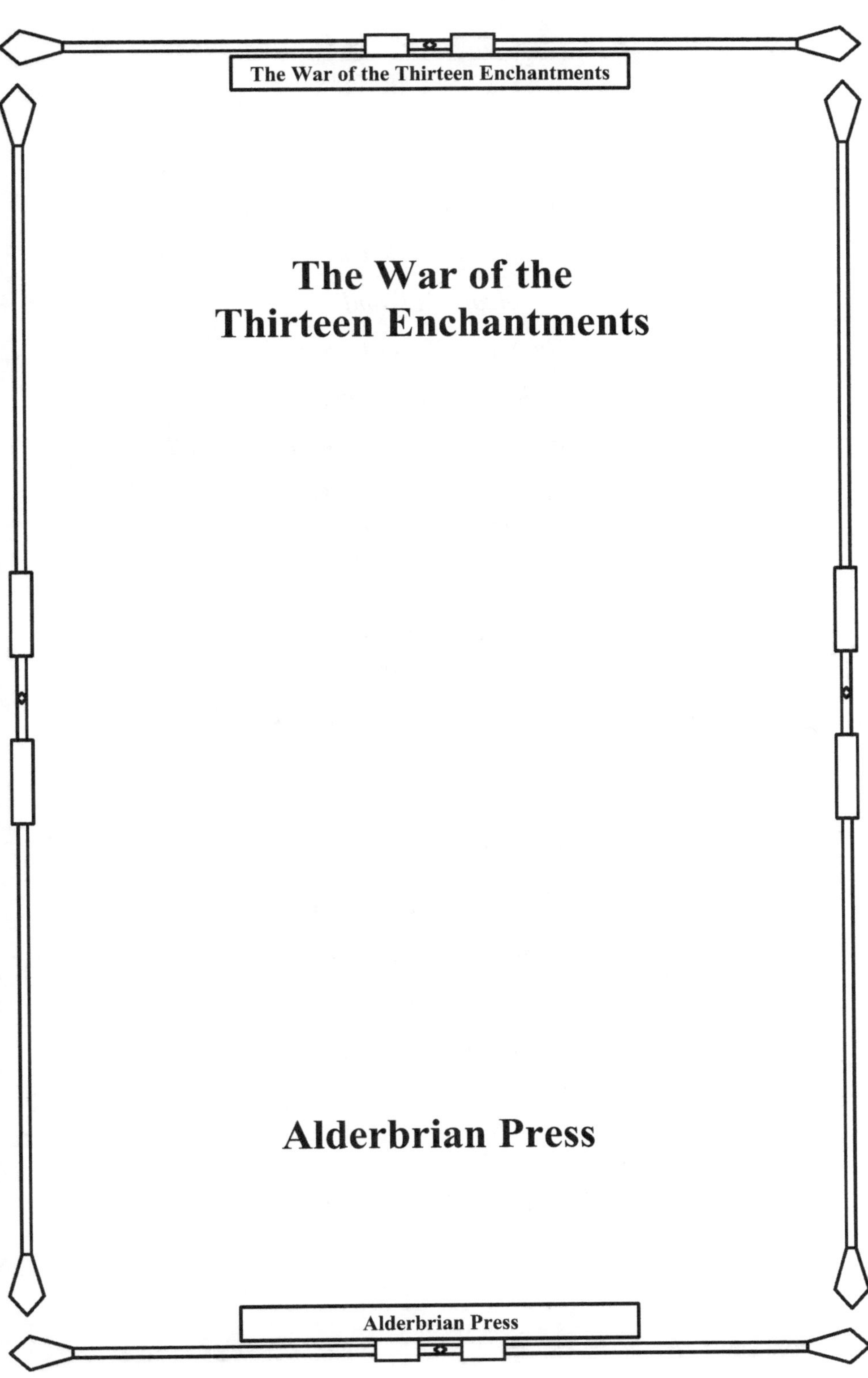

The War of the Thirteen Enchantments

Alderbrian Press

Other books by Philip Raymond Sadler:

Asblin's Magic Cave

Azophi's Wand

The Sweet Void of Space

The Yarrow Enigma

Wild Wilkenson and The Man in the Moon Prophecy

Suggestions of Stained Glass
Flower Window Art
A coloring book.

Suggestions of Stained Glass
Abstract Art
A coloring book.

Books by Philip Raymond Sadler and T. D. Sadler:

Never Trust a Cricket

Wizards War

Published by Alderbrian Press.

Books by T. D. Sadler:

The House of Other Worlds

Wherever the Road Leads

The Reluctant Hero

Published by Famulus Press.

Alderbrian Press

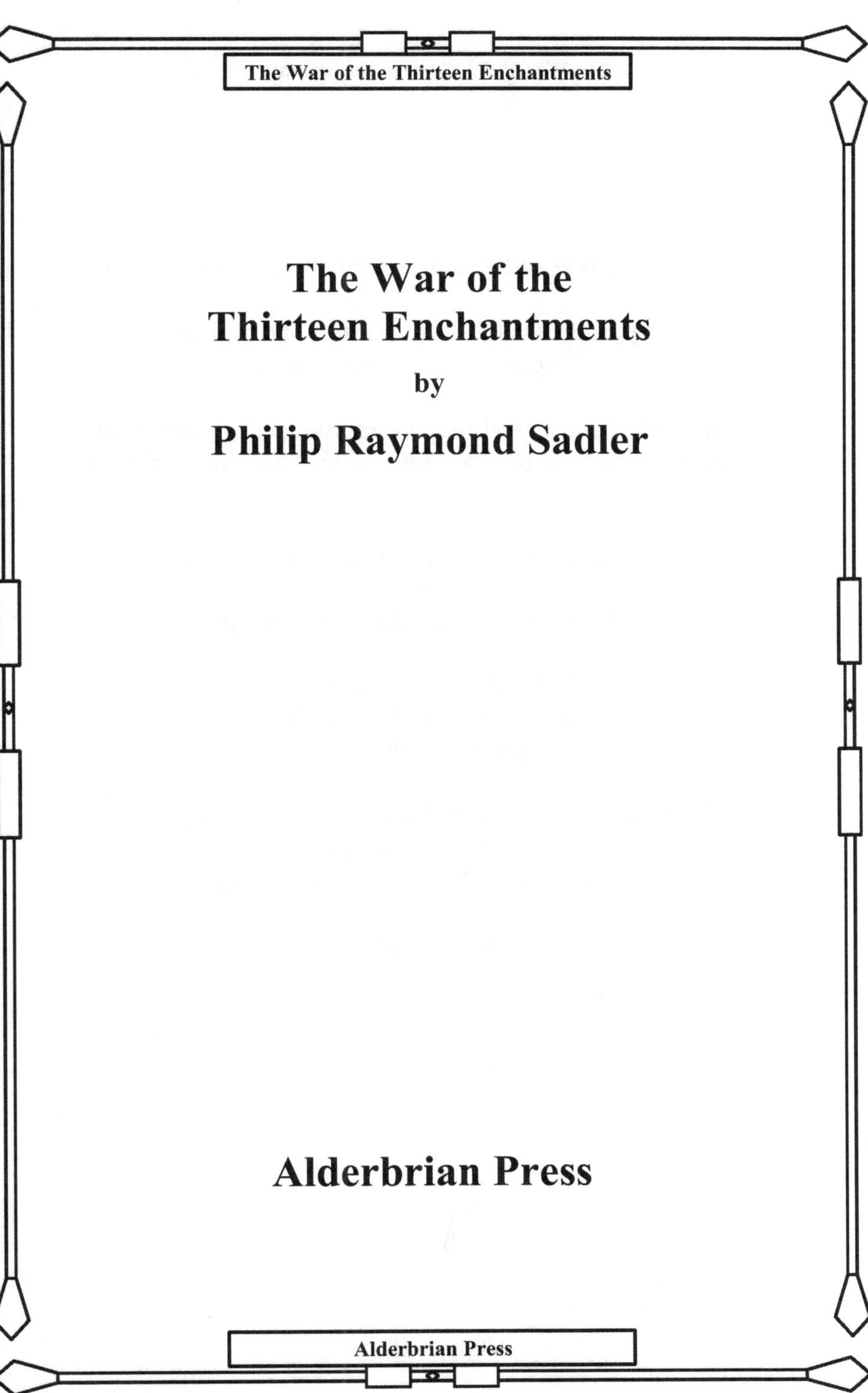

The War of the Thirteen Enchantments

by

Philip Raymond Sadler

Alderbrian Press

The War of the Thirteen Enchantments

Published in the United States of America
by
Alderbrian Press, Adrian, Michigan.

ISBN-10 0-934370-46-X
ISBN-13 978-0-934370-46-2
EAN 9780934370462

ISBN-10 0-934370-54-0 (6x9 hard-cover)
ISBN-13 978-0-934370-54-7 (6x9 hard-cover)
EAN 9780934370547 (6x9 hard-cover)

SAN 222-8238

Characters

Alaric	----------	Ruler of All
Aldora	----------	Winged Gift
Angela	----------	Saintly
Arden	----------	Fervent, Eager, Sincere
Aubrey	----------	Elf Ruler
Avery	----------	Ruler of the Elves
Bildron	----------	Of the Hammer
Brendan	----------	From the Fiery Hill
Brougher	----------	Fortress Resident
Calder	----------	From the River of Stones
Crandall	----------	Caretaker of the Cranes
Doyle	----------	Dark Stranger, Negator
Durward	----------	Keeper of the Door
Elatiella	----------	Joy of the Elves
Galen	----------	Healer
Guthrie	----------	War Serpent
Hilliard	----------	Battle-brave, War Guard
Inessa	----------	From the Island
Joelib	----------	Cautious Fighter
Kelsey	----------	Cloud Bright
Lara	----------	Noble Nurse
Lartrel	----------	Wise Warrior
Luana	----------	Graceful Battle Maid
Lynn	----------	From the Waterfall
Marsden	----------	From the Marshy Valley
Monrow	----------	From the Red Swamp
Nigel	----------	Dark Black
Perlon	----------	Quick Witted, Forge Tender
Ryley	----------	Valiant One
SaCee	----------	Radiant Ageless Seer
Sanborn	----------	Of the Sandy Beach
Sumner	----------	One who Summons

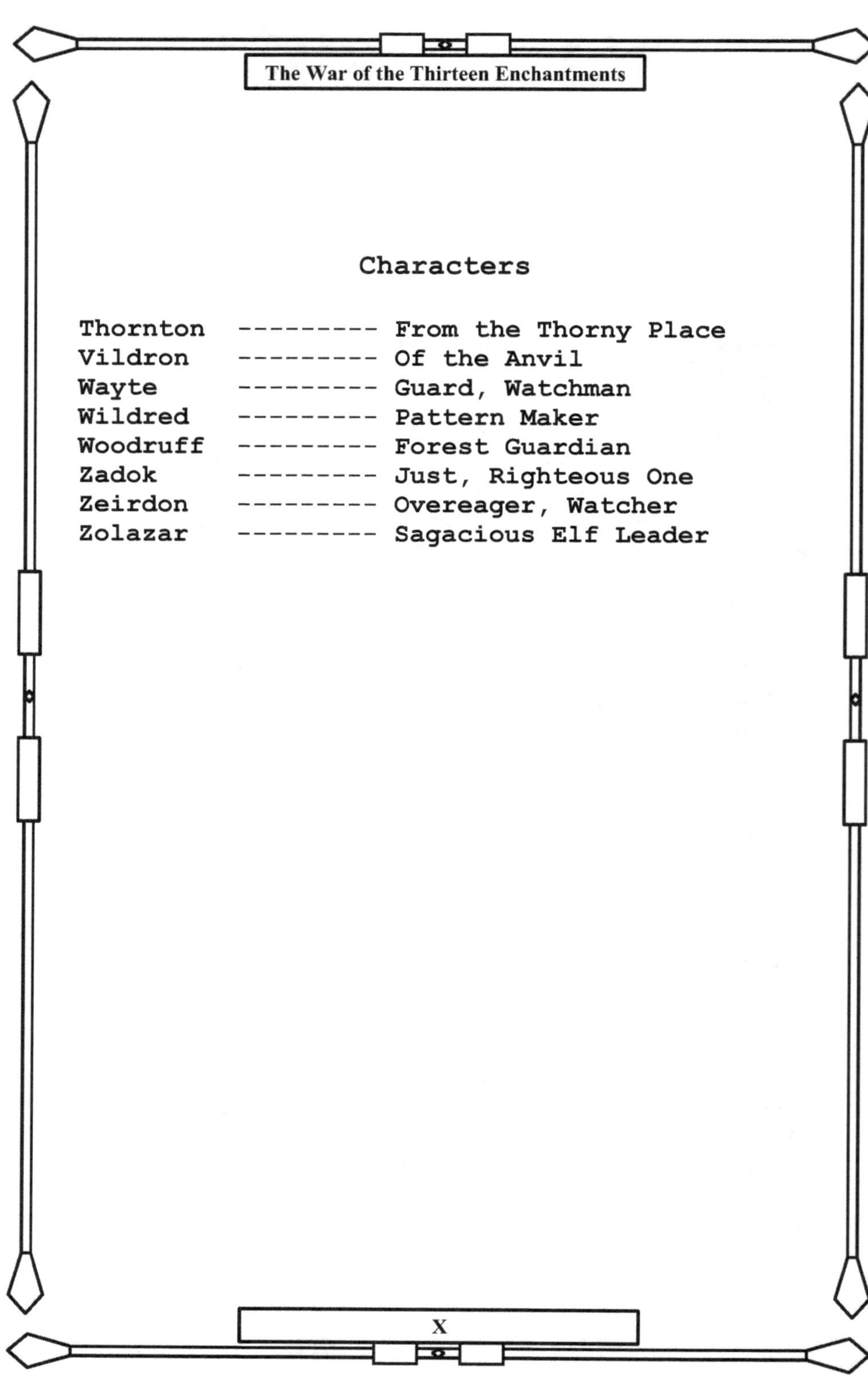

Characters

Thornton	----------	From the Thorny Place
Vildron	----------	Of the Anvil
Wayte	----------	Guard, Watchman
Wildred	----------	Pattern Maker
Woodruff	----------	Forest Guardian
Zadok	----------	Just, Righteous One
Zeirdon	----------	Overeager, Watcher
Zolazar	----------	Sagacious Elf Leader

Table of Illustrations

Table of Contents

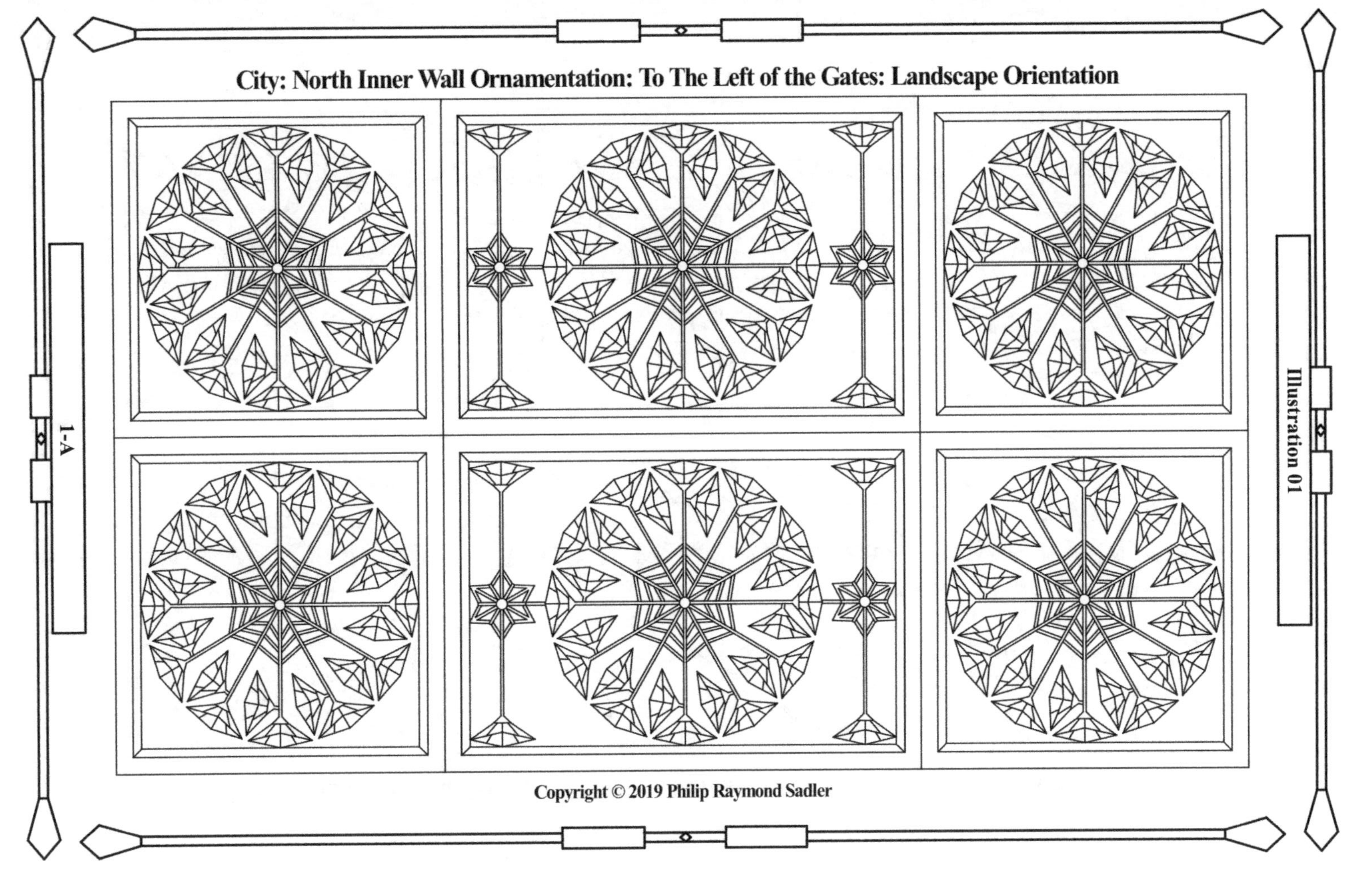
City: North Inner Wall Ornamentation: To The Left of the Gates: Landscape Orientation
Illustration 01
1-A
Copyright © 2019 Philip Raymond Sadler

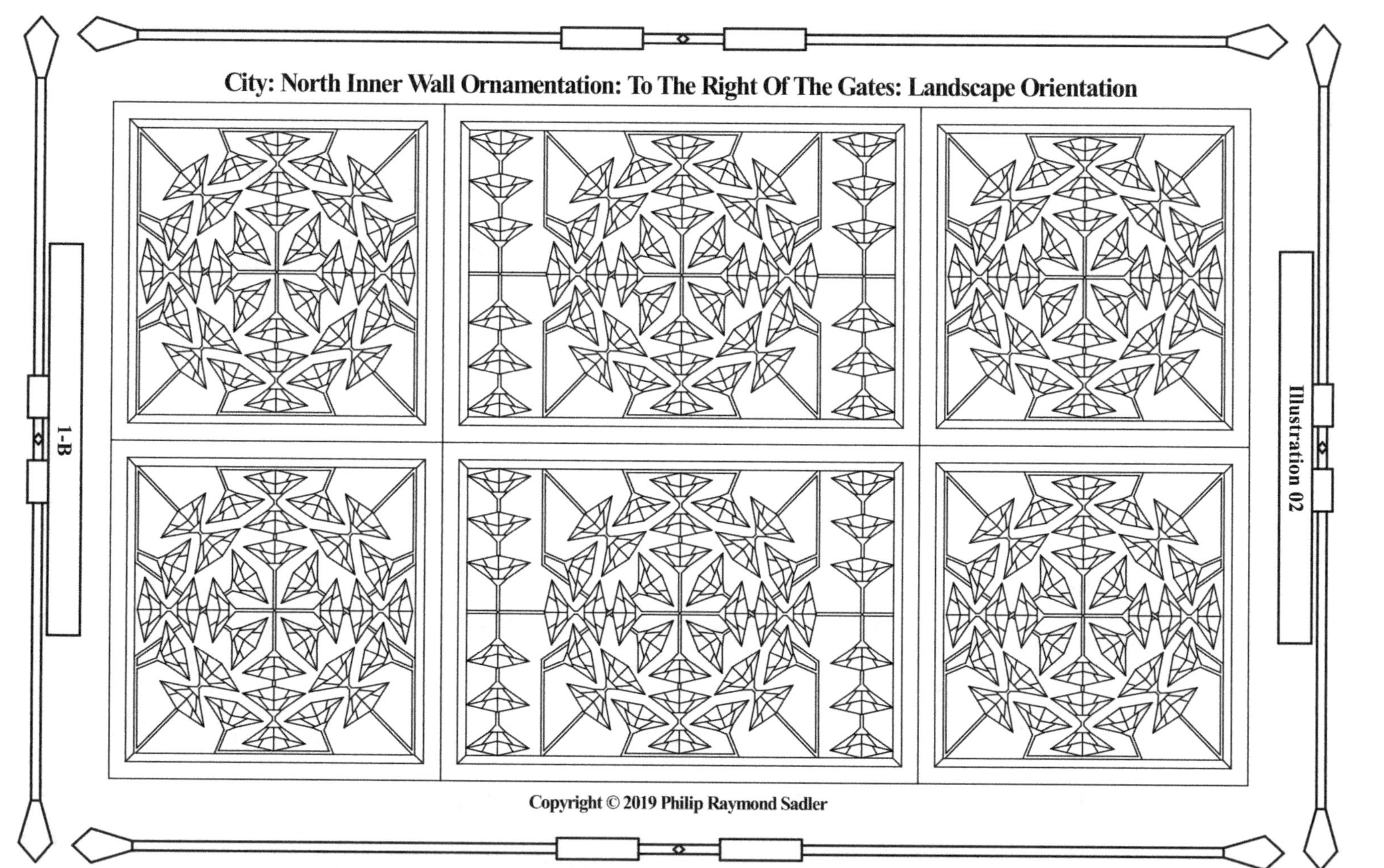
City: North Inner Wall Ornamentation: To The Right Of The Gates: Landscape Orientation
Illustration 02
1-B
Copyright © 2019 Philip Raymond Sadler

Chapter 1
A Gauntlet Down

"Lord Durward, how stand matters with your son?" King Alaric asked. Short, dark, hair caused his stern gray eyes and strong, responsibility-creased face to appear forbidding, but his wise countenance became softened by his deep sympathy for his life long friend.

Alaric was of medium build, yet possessed unusual strength and quickness of reflexes. He was dressed in blue velvet tunic and slacks, and brown sandals. He was seated on his ornately carved, pink marble throne which stood flush against the rear wall of the square, coral marble throne room.

Beside the King, in her elaborate throne, sat Queen Angela. Long, black, lustrous hair highlighted her beautiful face which held a slight resemblance to their daughter Aldora. Green happy eyes showed shrewdness. A blue velvet gown, trimmed with white lace, hid the blue velvet slippers that warmed her feet.

The graceful Castle was comfortingly illuminated by a special white paint, devised by Durward, which coated the ceilings.

During the erection of the Castle, Durward mind melded with various artisans. He used the energy of his Mind Magic to etch into the walls, floors, doors and thrones, thousands of their beautiful, elaborate designs.

To Alaric's right, a doorway led to a corridor. A long, high, rectangular window in the wall opposite him was filled with thick, clear glass. This showcased the farmlands between the Citadel and the Wind Barrier Forest which had been planted to block the strong spring winds from the crops and farmhouses. Beyond this, and unseen from the Citadel, lay more farmlands, the Zelam River, and the greenery of the Windy Hills Orchards, which acted as a natural wind barrier for the second tract of farmlands.

Durward had fashioned irrigation channels which led away from, and back into, the River, enriching the farmlands adjacent to the Citadel and bringing fresh, running water into the Citadel and the Castle. The territory viewable from the throne room was bathed in the soothing red sunlight of late afternoon.

The Court Magician approached the thrones, with his head hung. The bald spot reflected the shine of the ceiling. His gray hair was thinning rapidly, due, in recent years, to his son. He looked, sadly, at King Alaric, and shook his head. His square face was lined with worry and his broad shoulders were slumped. He wore blue velvet tunic, slacks, and tan sandals.

"Nigel has severed every tie with us, Alaric, and has gone to reside in the Gray Fort," he said. "When I told him of your refusal to wed Aldora to him, he became incensed. There was no reasoning with him. Even *Inessa* failed to calm him.

"This is not what troubles me most. He acted as though he no longer views my Mind Magic as a halter to him. I fear he has increased his psychic power capacity and intends to—" He disliked the words. "—fight for Aldora, in some manner. I do not know what he would have done had I told him of her marriage, next week, to Arden."

Durward shook his head. "When Nigel was born, Galen found no defects to indicate he would fall prey to the warping tendencies of Mind Magic. Now, we can only surmise the power he has developed has intensified and twisted his unrequited love for Aldora and driven him to insanity.

"Galen is unable to dampen Nigel's Mind Magic, or mitigate his mental and emotional distress. With his latest outburst, I have less hope of finding a sanative for him. I fear I shall have to journey to the Gray Fort and place him into a trance. To keep him thus, until Galen and I can discover the cause of this malady and muster enough energy to heal him, or until the years threaten my life. If my Nigel still ails then—" He was determined, now, as well as forlorn. "—I shall take him with me into Afterlife, to spare Indwin his insanity."

Urgently, Queen Angela whispered into Alaric's ear.

"Lady Inessa," Alaric said, warmly.

Durward snapped his head up and looked to the doorway.

Inessa paused, as though deep in thought. Long, shiny raven hair was drawn back with a black bow. Oval, pale, delicate, beautiful face was lined with sadness. She saw Durward and her blue eyes blazed momentarily. She plucked at the lace on her ebony velvet dress with trembling fingers. Without a word, she walked to Durward and anxiously searched his solemn face for signs of a happy solution for their tragedy.

Durward embraced her tenderly.

The King's Knight strode into the room. Brown hair was close-cropped. Rough face, honed by sun and wind, looked fierce. Usually jovial red eyes were deadly serious. Tall, broad, and well muscled due to daily weapons training with the Palace Guard. Brilliant red tunic, slacks, and brown boots were spotless. A sheathed sword was buckled around his waist.

Lord Guthrie was followed by his wife, Lady Luana, almost his height. Long brown hair was tied, with a leather thong, into a pony tail. Stocky, browned by wind and sun, and attractive, with a slight resemblance to their son, Arden. Guard outfit was similar to the one her Knight husband wore. A sword was sheathed at her left hip. A physically powerful woman, mainly due to constant weapons training with Guthrie and Arden.

Guthrie and Luana knelt on one knee, then stood up.

"What *news* have you, Guthrie?" Alaric asked. "*Ill* news, I perceive."

"I am sorry, Durward, Inessa," Guthrie said, self-consciously, "It is of your son. The farmers report he has spoiled the grapes on the vines and the vegetables and grains in the fields, on both sides of the Zelam River, for as far as they could see, in all directions.

"The water in the irrigation channels was drawn toward the River, and he has turned the River to stone, from The West Shield to The East Shield Mountain Ranges, apparently channeling the River along the far side of the West Shield Range, beyond our use."

Alaric, Angela, Durward and Inessa were stunned for some time.

The South Shield Mountains sheltered Indwin from the Spring Storms, the East Shield Mountains blunted the hurricanes engendered by the Briney Sea, the West Shield Mountains muted the great sandstorms of the Alkali Desert, and the North Shield Mountains reduced the bitter winter blizzards of the Polar Expanse.

"So much *power*," Durward finally whispered. "*Too* much for me to *entrance* him, *now*," he told Alaric.

"This is not all," Guthrie said. "When Nigel cursed the crops and the River, the farmers say he was in the company of *Elves*."

"*Elves*!" Alaric said, with dismay. "*But*, they are our *oldest* allies!"

"*Were,* our allies," Guthrie said. "*Aubrey* was at Nigel's side."

"The *Pretender*!" Alaric said, with distaste. "Then, Avery is *dethroned*! Nigel must have *overcome* Avery's Mind Magic and *gifted* the Elf Caverns to *Aubrey*!"

Lord Galen entered the Audience Room. Short brown hair. Stern faced, but soft-spoken. Tall, and burly, but gentle. Green tunic and slacks, and tan boots. Galen spread good spirits and vitality wherever he passed.

Alaric smiled. "Our Psychic Healer's timing in impeccable, as always," he said, "our minds and hearts are in need of succor."

"*Look*!" Guthrie shouted. He pointed to the huge window in the pink marble.

"*Fire*!" Alaric said.

"It is *far* beyond the Wind Barrier Forest, and *even* the River. It is the *Windy Hills Orchards*!" Guthrie said, with disbelief. "*Every inch*! From the *West Shield*, to The *East Shield*, Mountain Ranges!"

"A *week* seems a *far* long time," Aldora said. Long, black, silky hair gloried her lovely face and wise, happy, green eyes. Slim and graceful. An amused smile danced on her lips. Crimson, velvet, full length dress, gaily trimmed with white lace, hid red slippers. Alaric's only child.

"It *is* an *eternity*!" Arden agreed. Black haired, handsome, intense, slender, and firm from daily arms exercise with Guthrie and Luana. Blue tunic, slacks, and brown boots. Arden was the Crown Prince Designate.

They were in the Royal Gardens, on the east side of the gates. They sat in a large seashell Durward had mind sculpted out of coral marble. The vermilion sun caused the pink walls of the Citadel to shimmer behind the enchanting greenery of the plants, making the flower beds appear fairy like.

Behind them, and beside the castle, was the great silver dome of the Royal Reservoir.

Aldora caressed Arden's cheek.

There was a tower battlement at the sides of the great

iron gates. A sentry was posted atop each.

"Do you *see* them?" the left guard shouted, with fear, to his fellow watchman. "Do you *see* them?"

"Aye!" the right sentry averred. "What *new* curse can cause such *haste* in so *many*?"

"What is it?" Arden called up.

"A horde of people are, *again,* fleeing this way, Prince Arden," the left guard said. "And they are, *again,* bearing their *children*, and *most* of their belongings!"

Aldora frowned. "What could cause the country folk to abandon their farms?" she said. "It is not the stormy season."

"What do you mean by, *again*?" Arden shouted, to the sentry.

"Not two hours past, scores of *terrified* families arrived, seeking entry," the guard replied.

"It is *Nigel*," Aldora said, with sad realization. "He has heard of our betrothal and has brought some type of magical misery down upon our people, in revenge."

"I *fear* so," Arden said, "Why did the first group flee their homes?" he shouted, at the sentry.

"Lord Guthrie said Nigel pronounced a curse that rotted the crops and turned the Zelam river to stone, then commanded the farm folk to flee, or die," the guard replied.

Arden's shoulders slumped, with despair, for his boyhood friend.

"Oh, Nigel," Aldora said, as though his actions were her fault, "why *must* you be *so* unforgiving?"

"Open the gates!" shouted the sentry in the left tower, "the King's standing order is to protect those in peril!"

"I must speak with these country folk to discover why *they* have fled their homes," Arden said. "Then, I must report to your father. He will be *forced* to take action against Nigel for his heartless deeds. Nigel *leaves* him no choice."

"I shall accompany you," Aldora said, taking his arm for comfort.

Arden and Aldora rushed into the Audience Room to find their friends and relatives staring out the long window at the malignant scarlet scar stretching across the horizon behind the Wind Barrier Forest. When they saw Durward and Inessa, they became hesitant.

"Report," Alaric bade the Crown Prince Designate.

"I am sorry, Durward, Inessa," Arden said, soberly. "Sire, we have just come from the gates. The Orchard workers, the shepherds, the herders, and their families, say Nigel ordered them to flee, but grudged them little time to do so before he ignited the Orchards with blinding lightning from his hands.

"Most of the sheep and cattle were killed, and the Honey Apple Orchards are but charred skeletons of trees."

Alaric glanced through the window. "You say the Orchards are *consumed*, yet the fire *rages* with *undiminished* fury?"

"As they fled, our people watched Nigel cause the foul occult fire to grow ever greater, until it was, apparently, burning of its own accord," Arden said. "Many of the farmers tried spading dirt into the flames, but this would not smother them.

They gave it up as futile. To reach the Citadel, they crossed the River along a narrow path they say *Aubrey* and his Elf soldiers ordered them to use."

Alaric raised a hand. "The harvests were just beginning, therefore, the Royal Grain Bins are almost empty. The only water, now, is in the Royal Reservoir." he said. "Depending on the final number of people to be fed, even at the most austere rations, we shall face thirst and starvation in, perhaps, fourteen days."

Durward was pale, and appeared desperate. "Nigel *must* have *discovered* some *agent*, probably a *liquid*, or a group of *powders*, which steadily enhances his might," he said. "There is no *other* way he could perform such psychic feats, *across* the land, so *swiftly*. There is little chance I can muster enough force to *negate* his might, altogether. But, I may be able to *reverse*, or *destroy*, his malevolent Enchantments, *separately*.

"The rotting of the crops, and the stoning of the River, are one Enchantment. The fire on the Hills, is a second. If I can reverse the first, the River will become normal, and the crops will return to edibility. We will, then, not have to fear that our populace will starve." He could not look at Inessa and speak in more direct terms. "Then, I will have to cancel the threat Nigel poses, even though his might is enhanced. I have no choice, but to so endeavor."

"There is *one* way to *avoid* war."

They looked at Aldora.

Her sadness and the determination in her voice, plus her words, led each person to the next logical sentence.

Arden threw an arm around Aldora's waist. "*I* will *not*

allow it!" he said, firmly.

"Nor will *I*," Inessa said, with tearing eyes, "though it would *bring* my Nigel *back* to me."

"Is *war* better?" Aldora said, avoiding Arden's eyes. "If I marry poor Nigel, he will have no reason to war. He will lift his vile curses and our people will not suffer."

"Well reasoned," Alaric said.

"*Alaric*!" Arden said, with disbelief. "You cannot *sanction* such an *act*! A *loveless* marriage for your *own* daughter!"

"Aye!" Angela, Inessa and Luana agreed.

"Well *reasoned*, Aldora," Alaric said. "But, not *taken* far *enough*, for you have not the *full* facts. Lord Durward."

The magician sighed with the burden of reality. "In his madness, Nigel believes Aldora loves him as obsessively as he does her, and that Alaric and Arden, against her wishes, prevent her from joining him. He believes sweet Inessa conspires with all of us against *him* and *Aldora*, and has threatened to *slay*, Inessa, in *revenge*."

Inessa gasped in horror, her stricken expression revealing she had been ignorant of this tragic matter.

"Nigel dares not attack the castle with Mind Magic," Durward continued, "for fear he will strike, and slay Aldora. Nigel knows *nothing*, but *threat* of *death* to our *people*, will *force* Alaric to *allow* him and Aldora to wed. He will *abide*, until Alaric *capitulates* to redeem the populace. *Yet*, Aldora, if you *reached*, and *married* Nigel, *today*, he would *destroy* us *all*, to *preserve* your *union*."

Inessa groaned, in dread, at her husband's words.

Durward gazed at her, with intense sorrow, then looked at Aldora. "Nigel's insanity begets our reality, and we dare not sit idle, for we would surely perish. This is why *your* noble *sacrifice* would be in *vain*, and why war *is* inevitable. Were it not *so*," he added, sadly.

"Were it not *so*," they each said, with equal somberness.

Inessa said nothing. She stood, with a hopeless expression, clenching the front of Durward's tunic, and staring out the great window.

A guardsman appeared at the throne room doorway. He gestured to Guthrie.

"Sire," Guthrie said, "Zadok beckons. Wisdom says we must all be present to hear his news."

"Receive his intelligence and report," Alaric said.

The Knight and the guardsman spoke, briefly.

Guthrie returned, with a shocked expression. "Alaric, SaCee approaches!" was all he could say, as he pointed to the long window.

Even Durward and Inessa were distracted from their grief.

The Lords and Ladies, and Queen Angela, rushed to the window.

In the inky darkness beyond the outer wall of the Citadel a roughly Humanoid white light was approaching the towering iron gates with the slow and deliberate pace of an unhurried and dignified person traveling on foot.

Alaric closed his eyes and rubbed them. "Durward, Galen," the King said, softly, "*verify* this *is* our *SaCee* and *not* some magical *horror* which has been *convened* and *dispatched* by *Nigel* to *challenge* us or to *assault* our Citadel."

Guthrie pushed the center of the top of the frame, and the great window moved forward, then downward, on hinges, allowing the cold night air into the throne room.

Durward and Galen held their hands toward the glimmering light.

"I have never seen SaCee," Aldora said.

"Nor have I," Arden said. "Though we have tried," he whispered to Aldora.

"Thirty years have elapsed since SaCee returned to her Clear Crystal Mountain to seek solace and communion with the Ethereal," Queen Angela told them. "This was five years before the two of you, and poor Nigel, were born."

"It is only logical that Seer SaCee returns during this time of tragedy," Guthrie whispered to Luana.

"Will SaCee bear news of the future, to Alaric as, she has in the past?" Luana whispered.

"Of our coming war with Nigel?" Arden said, with wonder. "Of who shall prevail?"

"Of whether my Nigel will return to me?" Inessa whispered.

Guthrie laid one hand on his son's shoulder, to calm him, and the other on Inessa's shoulder, to comfort her. "Perhaps," the Knight said.

"There is no doubt, Alaric," Durward said.

"No doubt, indeed," Galen agreed.

A horn sounded at the gate battlements signifying the

great metal portal was being opened to allow in a person of revered importance.

Although the hour was late, there were many sad, worried people moving, restlessly, in the Citadel. They began to mass toward the gates, forming a cheering human corridor for the white light as it made its way, resolutely, down the long, cobblestone thoroughfare leading to the rosy Castle.

Alaric held out his hand. "Angela," he said.

The Queen, eagerly, returned to her throne.

The Lords and Ladies stood to the left of the Queen.

It was well-known that SaCee did not enjoy pomp and circumstance. Therefore, there would be no escort provided, and no chamberlain to announce her arrival.

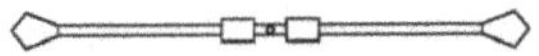

A white glow illuminated the pink floor tiles and doorway as SaCee stepped into the throne room; an almost ghostly presence.

Arden and Aldora gasped.

"She is so beautiful!" Arden whispered.

"More than words have been able to convey!" Aldora said.

SaCee paused, looking out the long window as though checking to see if someone, or some, thing, had been following her across the somber, night-enshrouded, countryside. Her aura spread a feeling of peace and warmth. Golden fine hair cascaded halfway down her back. Her blue eyes were unlike anything in nature and sparkled like jewels in sunlight. Her skin was translucent. She wore a flowing yellow dress which held no pattern or adornments. It swept the floor like a whisper of affection yet showed no signs of soiling or wear. In her left hand, she held her long, green marble staff which had been burnished to a reflective sheen. She turned from the window and approached the thrones.

"Revered SaCee, viewer of the past, present, future, and speaker of our holy beliefs, we, and the people of Indwin, gratefully welcome you unto our midst," Alaric said, with affection.

SaCee began to kneel.

"No," Alaric proclaimed, "one such as SaCee must not *kneel* to *this* or to any *other* monarch!"

Durward and Galen started forth, to take SaCee by her elbows, to prevent her from genuflecting.

"Beware!" SaCee whispered, with a soft feminine voice, which held deep love, and obvious, regretful, threat. "I have earned the protection of the Ethereal and it is merciless in its devotion to its duties."

Durward and Galen drew their hands away and stepped back to where they had been standing near their Ladies.

SaCee's hand slid down her staff as she knelt on both knees. She bowed her head.

King Alaric gripped the arms of his throne, to quell his fear. "We are *lost*?" he asked.

Durward turned pale, ran to the Seer, and knelt beside her. "*Speak* to us, *SaCee*!" he pleaded. "*Proclaim* that the *destruction* of *Indwin* is not *fated*!"

SaCee did not lift her head, as though she lacked the strength. "A great darkness has gathered around Indwin," she said. "None like it has been known within the two hundred years since my first seeing. This ebony force blinds my inner eyes. Dulls my inner ears. Muffles my inner voice. It terrifies me, and draws upon my vitality like the winter draws upon the body heat of the animals residing on the frozen slopes of the Leban Mountains." She looked at Alaric. "This did I see and hear, before the darkness befell me, and I failed in my purpose to oversee the safety of Indwin.

"Nigel has conjured five Enchantments, five colossal magical barriers between the Citadel, and the Gray Fort.

"King Avery and Queen Elatiella have vanished, and they appear, to me, to be dead."

Durward paled, trembled, and his eyelids fluttered. It seemed as though he was about to die, in shock, from the thought that his demented son had slain two of the most loving, gentle, and otherwise, immortal beings, who had lived.

Inessa was chilled, with deep despair. "Nigel," she pleaded, "come, and swear to me, that these savage words, are not true!" She grew faint, and sagged against Luana.

Galen rushed to his friend, knelt beside him, and pressed his healing hands to the Magician's forehead, invigorating Durward, and allowing him to begin to deal with the horror. Galen then provided Inessa with the same care.

SaCee continued her heart-rending lament. "Nigel, and his possessed Elves, mass in the North, to attack Indwin. Nigel tells the Elves his victory is at hand."

"Be this *Fate*?" Alaric whispered, his voice betraying his fear, for the first time.

SaCee vented a cry of despair so chilling it elicited fright and tears from everyone. "*This* I am unable to foresee!" she said. "The *blackness* is so *cold* and *thick*! I *recoil*, in *horror*, that it will *defile* me, *consume* me, *include* me *within* its *noisome* self, as if it is a *living* demon." She stood up, with a blinding flash of her aura momentarily washing the throne room with her determination. "*If* it will *save* Indwin, I *shall* hurl myself *into* this engendered *evil*, and *fight* to *divine* the future, *until* there is no *more* of me!"

"*This* you will *not* do!" King Alaric commanded. His voice was invigorated with the essence within him which caused all who dealt with him to yield to his authority. "*If* our War Party *fails*! *If* Indwin *falls*, we, and our people who *survive*, shall require your *strength*, and *wisdom*, to be a *beacon* to our *constructing* a *new* Indwin! You *shall* maintain your life and safety, at all costs! In this *matter*, shall I *not* be *disobeyed*!"

SaCee drew a long, deep breath, as if to refresh herself. A sad smile touched her lovely face. "In *this* matter, neither *man*, nor *woman*, nor *King* may *interfere*," she whispered. "I can answer, *only*, to the *Ethereal* in this, *however* much I wish to *obey*, and to *respect* my *King*."

The tragic Seer turned to leave.

"*Perhaps*, if we *link* with you, good SaCee," Galen said, quickly, "our combined minds, and energies, might blast through the blackness, and unveil the future."

"Aye," Durward said, although he was still shaken.

SaCee faced them. "You would *risk* this?" she whispered.

Chills traveled down Galen's spine.

Durward appeared surprised. "What hazard can there be?" he asked. "My magic is not Dark Magic. Galen's talents are, sun warm, and pure. What peril can there be?"

"Soul meld," SaCee whispered.

Even Alaric gasped with wonder.

"I have removed myself from worldly matters for thirty years and have basked in the presence of the Ethereal. I am become more of the Other Life than of the World Life. To join with me may meld your souls to mine with a finality that not even the Ethereal can reverse, and it will also precipitate the death of each of us." She stepped toward the Healer, and the Magician. "*I* shall *risk* this, for *I* have *naught* to lose, and much to *gain*. Will *you*?"

Galen nodded without hesitation.

Durward straightened his back with resolve.

"Durward! Do not leave me!" Inessa begged.

"*Galen*! *Durward*! Do *not* do this *thing*!" Guthrie warned. "*If* you cannot *pierce* the *evil* magic *darkness*, and *see* the *future*, without your *talents* and *Mind Magic* we will *lose* all *hope* of *defeating* Nigel! It is better *not* to know the *future*, and to be able to offer *defense* against whatever the future *holds*, than it is to *know* the future and have *no* defense! Do *not* do this *reckless* thing!"

"Wise and correct!" Alaric concurred, sternly. "This melding of your souls may be the tragic act which allows Nigel to vanquish us!"

SaCee closed her eyes and tilted her head back.

"What, good Seer," Alaric asked, with intense concern.

"It *is* Nigel!" she exclaimed, softly, in realization. "The darkness *is* his mind! Since *he* cannot *divine* the Future, Nigel *moves*, and *swells*, and *eddies* the *darkness* of his mind, much more thickly around all of Indwin, to *prevent* others from *seeing* portents. He cannot control *me* for his evil plans. I cannot *dim* his mind, nor *read* his thoughts, nor wrest *control* of him, for his magic is *too* potent. My mind communion with Lord Durward and Lord Galen would be a *waste* of effort, power, lives, and souls." She waved Durward and Galen away. "Now, I can only do as our sage King commands," she whispered. She turned to the doorway.

"Where do you go?" Alaric asked.

Everyone was frightened she would return to her Clear Crystal Mountain, leaving them bereft of her love and grace.

"From this *time*, until the nation either *prevails* against Dark Nigel, or *falls*, I must be a *beacon* of *hope* to all who *seek* comfort," SaCee said. "I shall *hold* the high place where all may see me and heed this fact: *Indwin* and its *people* shall not *flee* from any *danger* at *any* time." She, and her warm, loving glow, vanished into the hallway.

"SaCee will station herself atop the Castle, directly over our heads, in our Observation Tower," Alaric said. "She will neither eat, nor sleep, nor flee from weather, until the War has ended. Our people will be calmed and heartened by her vitality which she shall flow upon them." He motioned to Guthrie, "Tell our Palace guards to lock up the Royal Grain

Bins, and patrol the Royal Reservoir. Instruct the rest of our Royal Guard to ready themselves. They shall march, tomorrow."

When Guthrie left the Audience Room, he was met by a member of the Palace Guard. They conversed, briefly.

"I ask a boon," Arden said.

Alaric nodded. The King knew what Arden desired, and that Sir Guthrie would approve. "Speak," he said.

"Allow me escort Durward. Give me *command* of the War Party," Arden said.

"Granted."

Through the open window, faint, angry voices were demanding food.

Guthrie strode to the King. "Alaric," he said, soberly. "The Palace Guard cannot march against Nigel. The word of Nigel's plagues has spread throughout the Citadel. The people are panicking. I have ordered the Palace Guard into the streets to preserve peace. Only, I, and four of my men, can be spared against Nigel."

Angela whispered into Alaric's ear and he smiled. Her beautiful, determined face rekindled his love for her and her words reminded him of her value as an adviser. "You have devised a way in which half our Palace Guard can march with Arden and Guthrie against Nigel," he said.

Angela nodded, the light glistening off her long, dark hair. "Of the thousands within our Citadel, only a few dozen are known rabble-rousers. Sweep the streets of these malcontents and lodge them in the great Meeting Hall where they can pose no danger to those of our people who are calmer of temperament and wiser of mind. Fewer of our Guard will be required to contain them."

Alaric nodded at his wife, with appreciation. "The metal doors and shutters of the Hall were built to protect the people in times of siege. They can also protect the people from the panic purveyors," he agreed.

"I am sure you will find many volunteers among our people who will take up arms in defense of Indwin," Angela said. "There are the reservists, as well, whom you can set to the task of crowd control. They have been trained and can act as squad leaders for the volunteers, with the regular guard as commanders. Surely, this will free up more than half your guardsmen to follow you, Guthrie."

Luana and Guthrie exchanged glances of admiration for Queen Angela.

"Aye, my Queen," Guthrie said. "We have forgotten these matters, in the shock of the news. Luana can be in over all command of your royal forces, so that I might serve with Prince Arden."

"You shall join Arden and Durward, of course," Alaric said. "It is *fitting* that the War Serpent should go forth."

Arden and Luana smiled, proudly.

Guthrie bowed. "My birth trick is ever at your command," he said.

"And, Galen, our Psychic Healer, shall go," Alaric said.

"As my King commands," Galen said, with gusto.

"I have given this much thought," Durward said. "If we fail against my son, your guardsmen, your reservists, and your volunteers, will be vital to the defense of the Citadel against the Elves, especially, if Nigel sets them upon you sooner than SaCee has foreseen. Now that he has blocked good SaCee from divining the future, Nigel may change his time schedule for the assault." Durward nodded, as though agreeing with himself, and said:

"This will be a war, not of arms and attrition, but of Magic to Magic. The fewer people I have to shepherd, to protect against my son's conjured threats, the more likely I am to succeed in controlling him. I fear a larger compliment will result only in the needless deaths of those who would better serve your Majesty here. I fear events, of which we have not yet had time to think, will make it even more imperative your army be held in reserve. I respectfully advise keeping your troops, and potential troops in the Citadel."

There were no objections voiced.

"So it shall be, for your wise council has never been in error in all of our long past," Alaric said. He patted Angela on her hand. "There are matters to which we must all attend, before we can seek our slumber," he said.

The Lords and Ladies filed out of the throne room, followed by Alaric and Angela.

Arden paced, angrily, back and forth in front of the pink seashell bench in the Royal Gardens.

The moon and weak starlight illuminated Aldora and the pink flowers. "If I go with you," she said, "when you finally face Nigel, I can distract him, so Durward and Galen can surmount him, in whatever way they intend."

Arden was unmoved by her argument.

"Besides, if I am *with* you, Nigel is less likely to strike at *you*, for fear he will harm me with his magic."

"And, if Nigel uses his magic to separate you from us? What then? We can not protect you, if we cannot see you. If Nigel were to magically whisk you away from us, that would be the end of the war, and Nigel would win. All Indwin would lose, because Durward would be unable to strike at Nigel, for fear of killing you; his goddaughter; the Princess of the Realm." He stopped, crossed his arms, and stared into her eyes.

Aldora was furious that he had used her argument against her. She tried to stare back, defiantly, but could not. She realized he was correct. "All right, I *shall* remain here. But, you *must* return to me. You must *not* perish. If you do, I shall end my life to join you. This I vow, upon my soul!"

Arden turned pale, in horror, and pain throbbed his heart. He grasped her shoulders. "*Recant* this oath!" he demanded. "Say you have spoken in *jest*, only! I will be unable to battle for Indwin if I know each threat to my life is an equal threat to your priceless life by your *own* hand! Not even Durward's, or Nigel's, Mind Magic, can protect you from the wrath of your *own* hand. *Recant*!"

Aldora smiled, but crossed her fingers at her sides. "It was, of course, my beloved, only an expression of my abiding love for you, not an actual intent."

"This you swear, by your soul?" Arden insisted.

Aldora threw her arms around his neck, with her fingers still crossed. "This I swear, by my soul," she whispered into his ear. But, her mind was set. She had felt this way since childhood. There was no point to life, without him.

The Castle stood in the middle of the great Citadel. The throne room was in a high tower in the center of the Castle, and its pink roof provided the best vantage point for observing the countryside. There were thirteen merlons along the four walls.

SaCee stood, with her pale arms crossed, just in front of the seventh embrasure of the south wall. The comforting white radiance of her warm spiritual essence bathed the Citadel, like bright moonlight, under the weak stars. Her staff leaned against the merlon to her left.

A guardsman stood at the embrasure to the left of the staff. He was awash with SaCee's invigorating glow. There were three other sentries stationed on the roof; one at the seventh embrasure of each wall.

Alaric and Angela were at the embrasure to the right of SaCee. They were gazing beyond the greenness of the Wind Barrier Forest at the cerise conflagration which had charred the Windy Hills Orchards.

Someone rapped on the ornate door of the tower. The guardsman stationed at the east wall turned to respond. Alaric motioned him back to his post and drew the portal open.

"Sire, Queen Angela," Guthrie said, "a problem brews in the night at the area between the Wind Barrier Forest and the Citadel. It is one of those events of which prescient Durward warned we should have predicted, my King."

Alaric and Angela frowned, with worry.

"I shall clarify," SaCee said, softly. She withdrew her comforting light from the inner confines of the great Citadel and cast it forth, like a white spotlight, moving it from left to right over the vast fields between the Wind Barrier Forest and the Citadel.

Farmers, herders, traders, trappers, and the members of their families, were, resolutely, bearing their prized belongings, toward the great iron gates.

"Nigel opened a wide tunnel through his occult fire, so Aubrey and his Elf soldiers could herd our people to the path which crosses the accursed River," Guthrie said.

SaCee withdrew her light from the fields, and cast it around the inner confines of the Citadel.

Angela turned to the King and Knight."We must allow them sanctuary," she said.

"There is no question of this," Alaric agreed. "Their need for our protection would have negated our chance of dispatching half the Guard with our War Party. After we sweep the malcontents into the Great Hall, the Guard will be *hard-pressed* to ward these new arrivals, and those thousands of our people who are already here, even *with* the *help* of the *reservists* and any *volunteers*."

"If you provide succor to those who approach, you *halve* the rations of *food* and *water*, and you *shorten* the *time* each will *last*," Guthrie warned, "putting an *impossible* time constraint on the War Party; on *Durward*, for it is *his* skills which shall *win* or *lose* this war."

Alaric grasped the Knight's shoulders and stared into his eyes. "You shall not *speak* of these *matters* to Durward, nor Arden, nor Galen, *unless* they broach these *matters*, themselves," the King said. "Once you are upon the path of war, you *shall* forget the needs of Indwin, the King, the Queen, and our people. You will battle for as *short* or as *long* as is *required* to *defeat* Nigel. *This*, and only *this*, will you *set* your mind to."

Guthrie averted his eyes. His primary duty, since early childhood, had been the preservation of his King, his Queen, and his people. Now, they asked him to abdicate this duty.

Alaric and Angela comprehended Guthrie's thoughts. Angela placed her hand atop Alaric's on Guthrie's shoulder. "Sir Knight," she said, firmly, "*acknowledge* the orders of your King!"

Guthrie looked into Angela's eyes, then Alaric's. "I have never *disobeyed* nor *failed* you," the Knight said. "I shall not *disobey* nor *fail* you *now*." The Knight knelt on one knee, stood up, and swiftly exited the great tower, shutting the ornate wooden door.

Guthrie turned into the small hallway which led to his chambers. He stopped short, with surprise.

Luana stood before the ornate wooden door of their lodgings. She crossed her arms and gave the Knight the look he had grown to know, only too well, throughout their years as man and wife.

"Soldier," Guthrie said, gruffly, "our discussion is over."

"Pulling rank in this matter is worth less than the sweat off an old earthworm," Luana said, just as gruffly. "You and I have trained four sub-Commanders to take our place if we fall in battle. Any of them can follow the King's orders, for he will leave nothing to chance once he has had time to properly analyze his resources. There is no excuse to prevent me from marching alongside you."

Guthrie fought to maintain his anger, and his practiced sternness, and not to laugh at his wife's earthworm remark. "The country folk from beyond the dead Orchards are even now streaming through the gates of the Citadel seeking the succor which shall not be denied them by King Alaric. They will almost overwhelm all of our control plans."

"I know that I cannot doubt your words, my husband," Luana said, "but, these facts do not preclude my attending, my Knight, and my Prince, in the midst of war."

Guthrie smiled, warmly, and held his hands out.

Luana stiffened and did not uncross her arms. "Whatever trick this be, sly Knight," she said, "this maiden will not fool for it. I have been wed to you too long to remain so artless. I will accept no denial of my desire to travel with you. You know, full well, I am as capable at arms as any of your guardsmen. That I have, sorely, defeated you, and our much younger Arden, on more than one, red-faced, occasion."

Guthrie broadened his smile, and wiggled his hands, to invite her into his arms. "All this is well-known," he said, affectionately, "Still, must you remain behind."

"*No*!"

"With our King, our Queen, our Princess, and the other Ladies of the Court," Guthrie said.

Luana raised an eyebrow, for her husband's words warned her that some matter of importance, of which she was ignorant, had transpired.

"Luana, please," Guthrie implored, with exasperation.

Luana uncrossed her arms and allowed Guthrie to embrace her. "What do I *not* know?" she asked. "On penalty of a drubbing of you by me if you deceive me through misguided notions of loyalty and thoughts of my protection from harm!"

"The increased number of people within the Citadel, halves all rations, and shortens the time we have to defeat Nigel. *If* we *fail*—"

Luana tried to pull away, but Guthrie would not allow it.

"—and none of us *survive* against Nigel, to *whom* can our King and Queen turn, other than *you*? From *whom*, can they seek *advice*, if the Elves *attack*? If *Nigel* arrives to *commit* battle? *Yours*, would be the *final* chance, at *victory*, against Dark Nigel."

Luana stared at her husband with a mixture of anger and gratitude.

"All this was I prepared to impart to you before we embarked upon the morrow. No one else, would I *trust*, with the safety of the Royal Family. This is why you *must* remain, *steadfast*, within the Citadel." He caressed her cheek.

"*Must* I be called upon, by my *husband*, to abandon, and perhaps, lose *him*, and my *son*, for the sake of my *King*?" Luana said.

"Was this not *my* solemn *oath*, in childhood? Was this not *your* oath, freely given, when we wed?" Guthrie said. He gazed at his wife, with admiration, then sadness.

Luana shook her head, with anger and frustration. "*Unacceptable*," she said. "So *unacceptable*, and so *unfair*."

"*Will* you, then, *honor* our *oath*, my beloved?" Guthrie asked, gently.

Luana gazed at him, with tears in her eyes. This was the only reply she could offer.

This was the only reply Guthrie required. He smiled, with pride for his wife, then kissed her tenderly.

Durward paused outside the adorned wooden door to his son's former chambers. He thought of the child who used to run, gleefully, to him to see new feats of Mind Magic. To hug his neck, and squeal with delight, as Durward spun around in a circle, to allow Nigel to fly.

The door snapped open.

Durward startled. Wild, foolish, hope raced through every fiber of his being, only to painfully fade away from disappointment.

Inessa glanced up at him, with equal surprise. Her blue eyes blazed, momentarily. She straightened her ebony velvet dress with her nervous hands. "*What* do you *seek* here?" she demanded, her voice trembling with anger.

Durward stood speechless, deeply concerned for his

wife's suffering.

She stepped out of the room and slammed the door shut. She moved, threateningly, toward her husband and glared into his tragic, loving eyes. "*If* you *cannot* return my *child* to me *alive* and *well*, do not *bother* yourself to *return* to *me*!" she whispered, fiercely.

Durward moved back as though she had struck him.

Inessa saw the expression of grief, despair, and desolation her words etched on her husband's haggard face. "*Ethereal*! What have I *said*! My *sweet* Durward! I *meant* it *not*! It was *only* my *fear*! My *frustration*!" She threw her arms around his neck and hugged him close with all her strength. "*Forgive* me! *Can* you *forgive* me?"

Durward, gratefully, returned the embrace. He pressed his cheek against hers and whispered:

"By *all* that we hold *holy*, by *all* that *powers* the *Universe*, by *all* the *Mind skills* at my *command*, my *sweet* Inessa, I *shall* find *some* way to *heal* our son and *return* him to *you*, though it *requires* the *surrender* of my own *life*!"

Inessa took his face in her hands and stared into his eyes. Tears streamed down her cheeks with sudden, unwanted, realization. "Not *both* of *you*! I *cannot* lose *both* of you! Oh, *Ethereal*, Durward, tell me there is *no* chance, I shall lose, *both* of you!"

The poor Magician desperately wanted to assure his beloved wife that this horrible event could not occur. But, this, he could not promise. They gazed, forlornly, into each others eyes, with tears falling to the pink tiles of the castle floor.

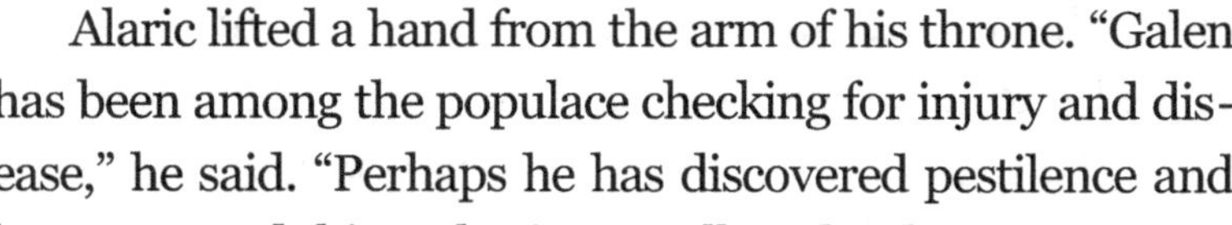

Alaric lifted a hand from the arm of his throne. "Galen has been among the populace checking for injury and disease," he said. "Perhaps he has discovered pestilence and has requested this gathering to tell us that he cannot journey with the War Party."

Guthrie and Durward frowned at this thought.

Angela leaned forward in her throne and whispered to Inessa.

"When Queens and Ladies whisper confidences, Kings cringe," Alaric said.

Aldora pulled away from Arden's embrace and went to her mother.

Inessa, Angela and Aldora exchanged soft words.

"Go on," Guthrie said to Luana. "Join into the secret. We may as well cringe alongside our King."

Luana bumped the Knight's shoulder with her shoulder and joined the other ladies of the Court.

Arden, Guthrie and Durward approached the King.

"Shall we engage in sly whispers, also?" Durward said, wryly.

"Have we anything about which to whisper?" Alaric said.

"We could discourse upon how rudely certain Ladies are behaving in the presence of certain men," Arden said.

"*Only* if we were *brave* enough," Guthrie said.

Alaric laughed, heartily. Everyone's apprehension lightened a bit. The King had seldom expressed humor, of late.

"I offer my apologies for requesting a Court gathering so far into the night," Galen said, with his usual cordial enthusiasm.

A woman of about thirty walked next to Galen with her arm laid on the Healer's strong arm. Long blond hair shone in the light from the ceiling like straw in sunlight. Blue eyes, and pretty tanned face gave her a motherly appearance. Flowing brown dress hid her sandals.

The men looked at each other with bewilderment.

The Ladies appeared smug.

"This is Lara, of the old Village of Ventier," Galen said, with obvious affection. "She has, graciously, consented to be my wife."

The Ladies appeared as surprised as the men.

"We had hoped to announce our betrothal under happier circumstances," Galen said. "But, time and wind, bow to no one."

Alaric leaned toward his wife. "You were *aware* of *this*?" he said.

"*Only* that she had been seen at his side several times," Angela said, "*not*, that they were *intended*."

"I had hoped, with your permission, Alaric, that Lara could stay in my lodgings, here in the Castle, while I journey with the War Party."

Alaric tilted his head, and his face showed sternness. His eyes seemed to sparkle, and a smile played on his lips. "It is high time, Healer, that you allowed yourself to be civilized," he said, jovially. "You, my dear, are more than welcome unto our midst. I have no doubt that you can hone down Galen's rougher nature into finer qualities."

"No offense, Sire," Lara said, her voice sounding like a soft song, "but I have found nothing about Lord Galen that I would, or could, change."

"Well spoken," Angela said. "Let us welcome Lara, Ladies. Let us, also, properly chaperon her. You will lodge with Aldora, until the War Party has embarked, then, we shall assist you in taking over Galen's chambers."

The Ladies laughed and swarmed around Lara.

Alaric shook a finger at Galen. "This is *only* the beginning," the King said, "and, you have brought it upon your *own* miserable self."

"Gladly, Sire, and, I welcome the mysterious changes that will be rained upon me by our sweet attuning!" Galen avowed.

Lara looked around at the smiling, friendly faces. "I am, already, overwhelmed," she said.

"Wait until you *see* Aldora's *lodgings*," Arden said. "You will be, *truly,* speechless, then."

"*So*," Alaric said, "the Crown Prince has *lounged* in my daughter's chambers?"

Arden blushed.

Aldora and Angela laughed.

"He was *allowed* to *peek* in, like a *puppy*," Aldora said.

"Much better for him," Alaric said, with a smile.

However, everyone knew the King was serious. Propriety, and tradition, were never ignored in his Kingdom.

Guthrie motioned Luana to him. "Lady Lara shall be included among those whom you shall protect, *if* our war fails," Guthrie whispered. "The same holds *true*, for good SaCee."

"This I already vowed to myself, and the Ethereal," Luana said.

Guthrie proudly hugged his wife to him.

"Let us pray these tragic events will never be, lover," Luana said.

"This is all I have done since Nigel left the Citadel," the Knight said, sadly.

"Such gay news, at any other time, would require immediate, Kingdom wide celebration," Alaric said, "Tonight, we must all retire. Our War Party needs sleep, and we all have much to do upon the morrow."

Guthrie and Luana followed the weary monarch, and the Lords and Ladies, out of the solemn throne room. There was not much time for slumber. Assuming sleep, for any of the distressed nobles, was possible.

Alaric allowed Angela and the others to pass him by, then returned to his throne room. As he neared the guards at either side of the entry way, he paused. "Summon our Officer of the Watch, soldier," he said. "He shall receive new orders in our throne room."

"Aye, Sire," the guard said, with a smart salute and a swift gait away from the King.

Alaric turned to the remaining sentry and said: "You shall keep your King company, until the Officer of the Watch arrives."

The soldier was surprised, and a bit frightened.

They passed into the deserted throne room.

"You are Zadok"

"Yes, Sire," the soldier said, surprised the King knew his name.

"Of the sharp tongue, I hear," Alaric said.

"Only when warranted, Sire," Zadok said, with wry hesitance.

"Your King requires only your strong, silent companionship, for a short while," Alaric said, tiredly.

"That will be easy, Sire, for I am scared, speechless, in your royal presence."

"How sad, for I am comforted, in your noble presence," Alaric said.

The weary King sat down in his pink throne and stared out the long window at the night, the pale stars, and the ugly red fire flickering across the misty horizon.

Zadok stood, steadfast and proud, to Alaric's right, between his King and the entry way, and any danger that might arise.

Alaric opened the ornate wooden door that allowed access to the great tower's roof. He paused, for a moment, with affection and awe.

Throughout the chilly night, SaCee had stood, unmoving, with her arms crossed, in front of the seventh embrasure of the wall that faced due North. The comforting white glow of her warm spiritual essence had bathed the Citadel like moonlight beneath the weak stars and was still evident under the harsh light of the morning sun. SaCee's staff leaned against the merlon to her left.

A guardsman was stationed at the center embrasure of each of the remaining three walls. The forth sentry stood at the embrasure to the left of SaCee, awash in her warm, inspiriting aura.

Alaric led the Ladies of his Court onto the old pink stones of the roof.

The guardsmen turned, saluted, then returned to their surveillance.

SaCee did not pay heed to the King, the Queen or the Ladies.

Alaric, Angela and Aldora took places at the embrasures to the right of SaCee. Inessa, Luana and Lara stood at the embrasures to the left of the Guardsman and SaCee.

Lara left her embrasure, went to SaCee, and wrapped her arms around the Seer.

Everyone gasped.

"No one in the Universe expects you to be strong, one hundred percent of the time, dear Lady," Lara said. "Decrease your shine, and rest. Save your beacon for the nighttime when we all so dearly need and appreciate it."

SaCee was distracted from her mission. She looked at Lara. Glistening tears traced down the Seer's beautiful face. "Two hundred years ago, when I was twenty," she whispered, "I accepted what I believed was a gift from the Ethereal. The price I must pay for this, is eternal vigilance. I was apprised of this, at that time. This, I freely accepted."

"I am told that Galen accepted Healing, Durward accepted Mind Magic, and that their price, also, is eternal vigilance against evil. But, they rest, they join in with companionship. The Ethereal does not chide, or punish them. It will not do so, to you, if you rest during the day. I am sure you can rest, and also remain vigilant."

Aldora came over to them. "The least you can do is share our rations with us," she said.

SaCee laughed; a sound as pretty as the giggles of children. "I draw vitality from the Ethereal, and need neither food, nor water, and I do not tire," she said. "But, I have been lonely, many times."

"Then, take a respite, and spend some merry time with us," Aldora said, with affection.

"You should *see* Aldora's *lodgings*," Lara said.

"They are not *that* lavish!" Aldora said, with exasperation.

SaCee laughed, then snapped her head up, and stared, intently, into the North. "The War Party has passed into the Wind Barrier Forest," she announced.

"We must join in a meditation circle and offer them our spiritual support," Alaric said.

"Great King, such a circle of love and faith would be futile," SaCee said. "Nigel's blackness will block all the hope you would seek to dispatch to our War Party. He bars even my Inner Sight and my light from penetrating beyond the Wind Barrier Forest. Your noble efforts would be best served with your daily duties to the people."

SaCee returned her attention to the North.

Lara reluctantly ended her embrace of the Seer.

Those were not half spirit, turned to their embrasures, with bated breath and troubled minds. They stood there, for a few moments, in silent prayer for their loved ones.

Alaric stood away from his embrasure. "As Good SaCee advises, we must see to our duties," he said, sternly.

Sad, they followed King Alaric into the Castle.

The Royal Grain Bins stood midway between the Palace and the West wall of the Citadel. There was a loading dock before each of the great marble silos. The members of the court were stationed on their assigned loading dock. With the aid of a granary worker, they were handing out portions of flour, rye and barley.

Aldora dipped a measuring scoop into a barrel of rye and stepped to the edge of her dock to dump the ground grain into the basket of a child.

"These rations are not enough!" a large, bearded trapper said, angrily.

"Aye!" his three rough looking friends agreed.

The first trapper reached up, grabbed Aldora by her hips, and lifted her off the dock. He wrapped his sinewy arm around her waist and placed a hand over her mouth, before she could cry out, with rage.

"I reckon we'll receive *real* portions, if we have the King's haughty *wench*, to *trade* for them," he said.

The horrified granary worker reached for the Princess.

One of the other trappers punched the man in the stomach, knocking him to his back on the grain dust covered loading dock.

"*Well* struck," another of the trappers said. "We'll just have them *give* us the *keys* to the *bins*, in *return* for her *highness*."

Alaric raced across his loading dock and leaped the wide gap between it, and Aldora's, as though he had wings. When he jumped to the cobble stones of the street, it almost seemed as though he had appeared from nowhere. A frightening hardness etched the King's face as he drew his blade.

The trappers, except for the one who held Aldora, drew their swords.

A beam of white light illuminated the trappers. They startled, and looked up at the Castle, to where SaCee stood.

"There is no match for the King, in, or, outside of Indwin," SaCee's soft voice spoke around the trappers. "If you persist in this selfish, unmannerly, behavior, today is the day you shall perish."

"Better to *die* like *men* than to be fed *foul* scraps like pet *rats*," the bearded trapper said. He was having difficulty working against Aldora's struggles to free herself.

"While the royal *pigs* feast behind the Castle walls," the armed trapper who was nearest to the King, said.

"The King sups on no more than he allots to each of his subjects," SaCee spoke around them.

The nearest trapper moved to attack the King.

Alaric's blade swept so quickly it was almost impossible for the eye to follow it.

The trapper's sword flew from his hand and landed on Aldora's loading dock with a thud.

One of the other trappers grabbed his startled friend by the shoulder and yanked him out of harms way of Alaric's blade.

"*SaCee* does not *lie*!" the trapper shouted, at his friend. "If *she* says the King sups *as* we *do*, it *is* the *truth*. You *know* SaCee does not *lie*! We *all* know *SaCee* does not *lie*!"

Luana and a band of guardsmen rushed down the street, through the mass of hungry people, to the site of the discord.

Alaric sheathed his sword, shoved the trappers aside, drew Aldora away from the bearded man, and stared into his eyes.

The trapper, looking like a cornered animal, drew back, two long steps.

The King's rage was almost a physical presence. "For assaulting our daughter, today, have you, and your criminal allies, earned death!" he avowed.

The man who had attacked the King, turned pale, fell to his knees, and started shaking. "Sire, please, *forgive* me! *Banish* me! But, do not have me *slain*!"

"I intercede," SaCee said, around them.

Queen Angela leaped from her loading dock and ran to embrace Alaric. "I, too, must intercede for these men," She said. "Place them, instead, into the locked Hall, where they can be of no further bother to us. After Nigel is defeated, they will return to the wilds, and their hunts men's lives."

Alaric looked at Aldora. "What say you?" he asked.

Aldora glared at the bearded trapper. "SaCee?" she said.

"Yes," the Seer said, around them.

"Has this man, or any of his friends, learned their wrong, and earned their mercy; their freedom?" Aldora asked.

SaCee remained silent and her beam of light vanished from around the trappers.

"SaCee can find no good in these men," Aldora said, to Angela. "Do you *still* intercede for them?"

Angela appeared horrified. "I must," she said, "for the consequences of not doing so are too ugly for my soul to bear."

Alaric glanced at the hungry people waiting for their meager rations. "Note this," he warned the trappers, "the only reason you shall leave our Citadel alive, is the mercy of Queen Angela. After our war with Nigel has ended, you shall be banished from our Citadel for the remaining days of your lives. To set foot within its walls will earn you your death. I can waste no more time on you. Take away their weapons and lodge them in the old Hall with the other rabble-rousers," he ordered Luana and the guardsmen.

The trappers could no longer meet the King's enraged eyes.

"*Bless* you, my Queen!" the kneeling trapper said, fervently. "Thank you for your *mercy*!"

Luana waved a hand. The guardsmen disarmed the trappers and started to hustle the miscreants away.

"Wait!" SaCee said, softly, around them. She sounded concerned.

"What troubles you, SaCee?" Alaric asked.

The seer did not reply. She projected her spiritual beam on the four trappers. She brightened it, almost to the point of blinding everyone. A ghostly gray form was revealed around each huntsman. It shimmered and swirled, much like a mist in a breeze.

Alaric motioned everyone to draw back from the trappers. “What means this, SaCee?” the King asked.

“Great King,” SaCee said, “I have been *deceived*. I mistook what you see for evil intent in these men. But, they are blameless for their behavior. They deserve our intervention, not our judgment. This noisome presence which is revealed upon them is the tell-tale sign of Nigel’s power of possession.”

SaCee spoke only to Alaric: “Demand of them, as only you can, their true intent in taking control of your Aldora.”

With undisguised menace, Alaric advanced upon the trapper who had manhandled his beloved daughter. The King already suspected the answer he would elicit. He spoke with that special essence within him that inspired respect and obedience: “Was your true intent to slay your King and bear your Princess to Nigel’s waiting arms?”

The huntsman tensed like an animal cornered by a superior predator. His eyes were wild. Nigel’s possession force fought to keep the man silent, but was no match for the powerful will of the King.

“Speak!” Alaric commanded. His voice was so forceful, it shocked and frightened all who bore witness.

“Yes!” The trapper wailed. “*Not* as *I* want, but as *he* desires! He will *slay* me, now that I have *failed* his will!” He dropped to his knees and placed his fists to the sides of his head. “*Please*! *Free* me of *his* voice! It *never* ceases! It allows *no* rest and *haunts* me in my *dreams*! *Please*,

Majesty!"

Alaric was moved to cautious compassion. "SaCee," he said, "can you exorcise Nigel's essence from these men?"

There was a silence which horrified Angela and frightened Alaric. Finally, SaCee spoke with regret: "*This* is *not* within *my* power, for Nigel's Mind Magic is *too* potent. Short of ending their lives, there is only one way in which I can offer them solace; peace."

The kneeling tapper looked, wildly, up at SaCee. "*Anything*!" he shouted. "I will accept *anything,* to *end* this *horror*!"

The other huntsmen agreed, with equal desperation.

"As you request," SaCee whispered. Her ethereal light turned to mimic the color of the marble from which her staff was fashioned. The trappers sparkled. They lost all signs of life, and appeared to be men of stone.

Angela gasped, with dismay. "SaCee, what have you done?" she cried out."You promised they would not die!"

SaCee's light retained its clarity, and became less bright around them. "Fear not, merciful Queen," the Seer reassured, "they only sleep in the guise of pseudo stone. When Nigel is defeated, I shall return them to their natural state, no worse for the experience, and freed of Nigel's unkind influence."

"Are you *certain* Nigel cannot *free* them?" Aldora said.

"They are under the watch of the Ethereal. Just as he cannot control me, nor can he affect them. Be at peace, in this matter," SaCee said, soothingly.

Angela's wise mind moved her to speak. "My King," she said, "where and when Nigel may have applied his dark arts to these trappers is unknown to us. Shall we be wise to assume these are *not* the *only* members of our vast populace who have been *cursed* thus, by Nigel?"

Alaric nodded his head, in admiration.

SaCee acted before her King could frame his request. She flared her light to its almost blinding intensity and swept it across the huddled masses within the great Citadel.

"How can this *be* so?" Alaric said, with a mixture of astonishment and rage.

For as far as the dismayed royalty could see, there were people of all ages shimmering with the gray ghosts of Nigel's possessive power. Hundreds. Perhaps, half their subjects.

SaCee widened her illumination to the throngs of people outside the walls. Only she and the sentries atop outer walls could see the hundreds snared in Nigel's power.

"Great King," SaCee said, "twice the number that you behold, are possessed outside your Citadel."

Alaric motioned to the guardsmen with Luana. "All those within lodgings, whoever they be, shall present themselves to their King for SaCee's magical test. We will brook no more surprises from Nigel!" he said.

Time seemed to stand still as the Citadel was searched and those found were added to the assemblage of the people of Indwin. This included the rabble-rousers who had been locked in the Old Hall.

"SaCee," Alaric instructed, "reveal, to us, the extent

of Nigel's threat among these people."

SaCee cast her dazzling light over the two hundred subjects the soldiers had herded forth. Half were cloaked with the gray of Nigel's evil force.

Alaric was greatly saddened by the number of his people afflicted by Nigel. "SaCee," he said, wearily, "preserve these people from the curse of Nigel and the harm they might be impelled, by him, to commit against our people, or themselves."

SaCee shone forth her green light, sweeping it over every afflicted man, woman, and child, in, and outside of, the Citadel. They became as statues, transferring into pseudo-stone in the midst of all manner of movements and positions. SaCee spoke to the minds of the people who were free of Nigel's dark magic, explaining the necessity of her actions, how the condition of their loved ones was temporary, and calming their fears, anger, and resentment.

"My King," SaCee cautioned, "there may be stragglers bound for the Citadel. I shall remain vigilant on this matter of possession, checking all who arrive. With your permission, Sire, I shall audit the royalty for signs of Nigel's influence."

Alaric turned and stared up at SaCee. "Have you *not* already included *us* in your test?" he demanded.

"I would not so presume," SaCee replied.

"Your King commands you to so presume, from this day forward," Alaric said. "We shall, in fact, assemble on the Observation Tower for just such a presumptive assay, once we have finished rationing."

"As my King wishes," SaCee said.

Alaric motioned to Luana. "Though I love SaCee, *dearly*, and trust her *implicitly*, she cannot be in *all* places, at *all* times, or aware of *all* events. Nigel may slip someone passed her vigilance. From this point, forward, Luana, you shall station two guards with each member of the court when they are among the people."

"By your command, Sire," Luana said. She hesitated. "Sire, may I speak of strategy?"

"Always," Alaric bade her. "This, I required of Guthrie, and it shall be so, with you."

Luana said, "Since statues cannot eat or drink, SaCee has almost *halved* the number of mouths we must feed, freeing up food and water. If she were to place more of our people into this magic state *as* our supplies grow lower, we could *withstand* Nigel's war far *longer* than we might, *otherwise*, hope. If she worked this wonder on *all* nonessential people, would we not fare *best*?"

"Well reasoned," Alaric commended her.

Angela and Aldora were heartened by the hope they saw on Alaric's face.

"My king," SaCee said. The regret in her voice caused them to feel sad. "The Ethereal limits my actions. It will not supply the incredible power necessary to immobilize thousands more of our people. It will assist with controlling only those who are possessed by Nigel."

"Not *even* to prevent them from *starving*?" Luana said, with anger.

"The Ethereal does not share *all* of its secrets with me, nor does it *explain*, or *justify*, its *decisions* or *actions*, to me," SaCee said. The usual warmth was, chillingly, absent from her voice.

"I meant no disrespect, great SaCee," Luana said, earnestly. "I spoke from *frustration*."

"I spoke, with anger, at the *Ethereal*," SaCee said, warmly. "Not with you."

Luana wiped away tears of relief. Alaric, Aldora and Angela were reassured by SaCee's tone.

Luana turned to gather the necessary men to carry out Alaric's prior order of protection.

"We must finish our work," Alaric said, to Aldora and Angela. He waved to the granary man who had tried to protect Aldora. "You have our thanks, and shall be promoted," he said.

"*I* was of *little* use," the granary man said, bitterly, "*I* deserve no reward."

"Would you argue with your King?" Alaric said.

"Not upon my life!" the granary man avowed. "And, I will do as my King bids."

Alaric helped Angela and Aldora climb onto their loading docks, then returned to his loading dock and resumed meting out rations to his people.

The Granary loading docks were connected by narrow catwalks at the bases of the great silos. The granary man who had tried to intervene on Aldora's behalf was the Master of the Royal Granaries. He noticed, with annoyance, that his workers were gathering around him, rather than performing their work. Before he could chastise them, they began speaking to him, with excitement, and obvious concern.

Aldora observed this when she turned to scoop more grain from a barrel. She handed her scoop to one of her guards. "Take my place," she ordered, and approached the gathering.

The second soldier shadowed his Princess.

The Master ran forward to meet them. He bowed. "My Princess," he said, with urgency, "my men hear sounds of work beneath the silos. It is faint, as if to prevent notice, but it *is* there. They have heard footsteps, and heavy objects being dragged about. Unless his Majesty has ordered repair, or construction, there is no reason for anyone to be in the maintenance tunnels. They are usually kept padlocked until new harvest time. We fear this might be of Nigel's doing!"

Aldora nodded. "First," she said to the Master, "assign someone to take my place meting out rations so my other protector can return to my side. Then, tell the King what you have relayed to me. Let him know that I, and my guards, are investigating the matter, and will report as soon as events dictate."

The Master bowed, and spoke to one of his men.

Aldora motioned to the soldier scooping grain.

The Guard dropped the scoop and hastened to his Princess.

At the base of the silo, on the right edge of the loading dock, Aldora led them down a steep flight of steps, into a narrow passage which ran to the rear of the silos where the entrances to the maintenance tunnels waited.

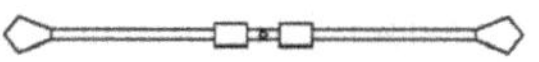

"Sire!"

Alaric looked up in surprise.

Luana's expression spoke of misfortune.

Alaric motioned to one of the granary workers who had returned to the loading dock, indicating for the man to mete out the grain.

Alaric drew Luana some distance toward the center of the dock, for more privacy.

"*Most* of the *explosive* powder in the armory has gone *missing*!" Luana said. "Our sentries were rendered *unconscious* with the padded arrows Durward devised for non-lethal animal control. They *saw* nothing."

The granary Master, respectfully, approached them. "Forgive me, Sire," he said, earnestly, "but, I have a message from the Princess."

Alaric looked at the dock where Aldora should have been. When he saw the granary worker handing out the rations, he frowned. "What *is* this message?" he asked, sourly.

"My people have noted sounds of activity in the tunnels beneath the silos. Princess Aldora has taken her guards to investigate. She said she would report, as appropriate."

Alaric and Luana reached the same, threatening, conclusion.

"Where away?" Alaric demanded.

The Granary Foremen pointed toward the tunnel on the right side of Aldora's loading dock.

"Granary Master," Alaric said, in a calm and reassuring

way, "remove your people from the granary. Luana, escort Angela, Inessa and Lara to safety in the Old Hall. Gather our guard and have them herd our people as distant from the silos as possible. If necessary, send them out of the Citadel. I, and my soldiers, shall seek Aldora. Dispatch troops around the first and fifth silos to reinforce us!"

The King raced to the back of his loading dock, and across the catwalk to Aldora's loading dock. He bounded down the steps that led to the corridor which Aldora had taken. His soldiers were hard-pressed to keep, even, five feet behind him.

Luana made special gestures to the guards protecting Angela, Inessa and Lara on their respective loading docks. This code passed on the King's specific instructions, the information about the missing explosive powder, and its probable location and intended usage. She descended the steps on the left side of the middle loading dock and met with some of her soldiers.

Angela was well versed in this code, and understood the danger. When she realized Aldora was nowhere to be seen, she further comprehended her husband's urgent departure. She noted Luana headed her way, on the ground, in front of the loading docks, with four additional sentries in tow. She saw two-thirds of the King's army shepherding the people toward the gates of the Citadel. Many citizens were reluctant to leave behind the loved ones and friends SaCee had stilled with the essence of the Ethereal. They were offering resistance, delaying the exodus. The people camped outside the walls were attempting to force their way into the Citadel for their rations. Soldiers were outnumbered, ten to one, and were losing control over both groups. The kingdom was on the verge of chaos. With a stern expression, she stared down into Luana's eyes and commanded:

"*Close* the gates, then form your troops into a wall around the granary, and *sweep* everyone, *breathing* or *not*, away from the silos! *Carry* them, *push* them, *drag* them! *Whatever* is required! *If* you *line* them *against* the Citadel *walls*, they will be *safe* from *concussion* and *debris*!"

Luana did not argue. She was aware Angela had assisted Durward in developing the explosive powders and knew their limits better than anyone, other than Durward.

Luana conveyed the orders, with hand gestures, to her guards, near the first and fifth silos. They passed the message down their ranks. When the soldiers at the massive gates received their command, a great rush of them slowly, but inexorably, forced the portal closed, with a startling clang. There were screams of rage from those inside and outside the Citadel.

SaCee cast her comforting illumination in a circle, bathing all those within and without the Citadel with a sense of calm and trust which none could rebuff with any emotion.

The Citadel fell into an eerie silence.

"My Queen," SaCee said. Her words sounded as though she were standing beside the Queen. "How may I explain our actions to our people? This calm is of limited duration. Their collective will is to scale the walls and confiscate the food and water. They will commit any act to preserve their lives and the lives of their loved ones. You know, full well, that *I* will not *allow* the *infants* and *children* to *suffer*."

Angela and Luana were shocked, cold, from SaCee's veiled threat against the Kingdom and the Royalty.

Angela stood speechless. She made a slight gesture of acceptance. "Good SaCee," she said, "our stores of explosive powders have been stolen. There are signs someone has planted these urns beneath the silos. It is reasonable to assume some of our people, still possessed by Nigel, have committed this act. We know not how long we have before fuses are lit. Most of our people are outside the Citadel, and are safe. *What* would *you* have us *say* to *our* people?"

SaCee flashed from the roof of the observation tower, to within a foot of Queen Angela. There was an eerie gray glow, of intense anger, in the Seer's eyes. In spite of this, SaCee's comforting shine still bathed everyone, on both sides of the walls.

Queen Angela gasped, and took one step back.

"*Truth*," SaCee said, with a coldness which chilled Angela, Luana, and the soldiers guarding them. "*I* will speak, to them, the *truth*. I will *seek* their *cooperation*, in *vacating* the Citadel with their stilled loved ones and friends, *before* fuse meets match. *I* have prepared them for this for you. *What* say *you*, wise Queen? *Time* is *fleeting*."

Angela was frightened by SaCee's demeanor, and angry. "*You* have *power*, of which, no *other*, not even *Durward*, can *dream*," she said, sternly, "can you not *prevent*, match from meeting *fuse*, with just a *thought*, or *wave* of your *hand*?"

SaCee laughed, with condescension.

Angela blushed, with humiliation.

"*I* shall not *allow*, even, *SaCee*, to treat my *Queen*, with *disrespect*!" Luana shouted. She drew her sword.

SaCee stiffened. She jerked her staff above her head and balanced it on her palm. The staff began to spin. A yellow light, of a purity seldom seen by the living, spread around SaCee until it enveloped her. Her eyes returned to their familiar, serene blue state. The uncanny yellow light spread in all directions like a thick blanket being drawn over everyone and every thing inside the Citadel. The unnatural silence that had befallen the Citadel, was replaced by normal silence.

Queen Angela shook herself. Her face showed shock and understanding. Nigel's dark force had been affecting not only those whom he had possessed, but everyone within and without the walls of the Citadel to a greater or lesser degree, causing them to act out of character, or with poor judgment, or confusion.

This included SaCee. The Seer had comprehended this, and had freed herself, and everyone else, of Nigel's subtle assault.

Luana realized the peril in which she had placed herself, by challenging SaCee, and, hastily, sheathed her sword.

The horn of invasion blared from the Observation Tower. It was a metal instrument designed by Durward which emitted a horrifying sound like no other. Sentries on the high battlements and along the walls began shouting alarms.

"*Majesty*!" The wall sentry stationed closest to the Queen almost screamed his words because his fear was so intense: "The *Elves* are approaching, in *full* battle dress! It looks like they have *emptied* the Caverns! And, the *women* stand, *steadfast*, with their *men*!"

Luana took a hard swallow. The Elf women were more ferocious in battle than their men. They fought when there was no option. She moaned, softly. Nigel, of course, would provide them no option. No doubt, held their infants and children hostage. "*Guards*," Luana shouted, "into the *battlements* with you! *Provision* yourselves *well*!"

"Cease!" Angela commanded. "Remain where you are! The Elves are *immune* to our weapons," she reminded Luana. "The *most* our army can do is *repel* them as they scale our walls. *Provision* your troops for *this*. We *must* buy time, until Alaric *ends* the *threat* that *waits* beneath us."

Luana nodded. She signaled again, and her troops began rushing about. The people within the Citadel moved themselves and their stilled friends and relatives against the walls, out of harms way of possible explosions.

"What of the people *outside*?" one of Angela's personal guard asked, with despair. "My *wife* and *children* are out *there*. They were returning from visiting friends and could not *enter* before the gates were *closed*. If they cannot be allowed *in*, I beg *pardon*, to be allowed *out*, to *fight* for them!"

"*Aye*, my *Queen*," another soldier said. "As I would *yield* my life for *you*, I will *yield* it for my *wife* and *child*, if you will but *free* me of your *service*!"

"My *Queen*!" the battlement sentry shouted. "The Elves will be in *weapons* range within *five* minutes!"

Angela eyes welled with tears. She turned to the Seer. "What am I to do, SaCee? If I do not open the gates, half of our people will perish by sword. If I allow them in, and Alaric fails, they will perish by the powders. We cannot fit them *all* in at a distance from the silos that will *ensure* their *safety*!"

Aldora and her guards stopped a yard from the end of the dim passageway. She motioned to one of them. "Scout the opening. Return at the first sign of threat," she ordered.

The soldier drew his sword and crept along the left side of the passage. After his eyes adjusted to the sunlight, he sneaked a look to his left and right. He backed away, quickly, and returned to Aldora.

"My Princess," he said, "the doors to the maintenance tunnels have their pad locks engaged. Those locked inside must be depending upon conspirators to release them at the appropriate time. The buildings housing the bakeries prevent the wall sentries from seeing the tunnels, and they are an excellent place for such conspirators to conceal themselves." He changed his tone to extreme respect. "I advise *reporting* to his Majesty so that *reinforcements* can be *summoned*."

"*This* is as we have been *trained*," the other guard agreed.

The guards jerked their heads in different directions, each checking an opposite end of the tunnel. From the near end of the passageway there was the unique sound of projectiles through the air and the guards went down, on either side of Aldora. Padded arrows fell to the cool stone near them.

Aldora drew a sword from the scabbard of one of the soldiers and fled along the passage in the direction from which she and her guards had entered. She heard the muffled footsteps of two people behind her. They were approaching with unusual swiftness. A large man, whom she recognized as Bildron, a blacksmith, from Indil Town, raced passed her, and blocked her way. Before she could react, a hand cupped over her mouth, and a sinewy arm encircled her waist. From the corners of her eyes, she saw that her captor was, Vildron, the brother of the blacksmith. He was far too strong for her to break free. She raised her sword to slam the hilt against the captor's arm, but Bildron wrapped his hand around the blade and snatched the weapon away.

Bildron laid the sword on the stone floor of the passage. His palm and fingers were badly sliced, but he evidenced no signs of pain. As he inspected the wounds, they ceased bleeding, and began to heal. "Nigel cares for our well-being, just as he promised," he said, with an annoying smile. "Imagine how he will reward us for bearing his betrothed to him!"

"Don't count on gold which is not yet in your pocket," Vildron groused. "Hurry now. We have the *other* matter of Lord Nigel's, to which to attend, before we can journey to his lair."

Vildron lifted Aldora as if she were a large doll. With an unnaturally swift gait, he bore her to the end of the passage where her guards lay.

Aldora was amazed at the power with which Nigel imbued his possessed slaves.

There were five silos and five maintenance tunnels. The blacksmiths stopped before the middle portal.

"Nigel has transformed all the padlocks into solid looking illusions to fool Alaric's minions," Bildron said, with pride. He grasped the thick hoop handle and opened the heavy metal door. The padlock illusion vanished.

Vildron carried Aldora down the stone steps, followed by Bildron who shut the portal. Outside, the padlock illusion returned.

Illumination was provided by Durward's ever present lighting paint, which covered the ceiling. The walls contained no openings.

Bildron paused. "Why do you restrain our Lord Nigel's betrothed?" he said. "She is bent upon reaching her Lord Nigel. There is no need." He looked intently at Aldora. "Is this not true, my Queen?" he said.

Aldora caught her breath through her nostrils. That which Durward had explained about poor Nigel, was true. She had held doubts until this moment. Even Lords and Kings tended to shape facts to their convenience. It was vital to her now that Nigel's distorted beliefs were shared by his slaves. She tried to make answer, and Vildron uncovered her mouth.

"You have spoken wisely," she said, haughtily, to Bildron. "Lord Nigel will not look favorably on the manner in which you have manhandled me!" she said, angrily, to Vildron.

Vildron released her and dropped to one knee. "Forgive me, my Queen," he said, with obvious fear. "I sought only to bear you quickly out of harms way as Lord Nigel required of which ever of us came upon you. Please intercede with Lord Nigel on my behalf!"

Aldora felt a twinge of sympathy for the burly man. After all, he *was* possessed, and he *was* following Nigel's *insane* instructions.

"You have explained yourself *well*," Aldora said. "*Fret* no further about the matter. It is *forgotten*."

"*Bless* you my Queen!" Vildron said, as he stood up. "You *are* as *gracious* as Lord Nigel tells us."

"Where are we going?" Aldora inquired, politely. "Is my Nigel, here, in the Citadel?"

"I fear not, my Queen," Vildron replied. "As I mentioned, before, we have another matter, to which to attend, for Lord Nigel."

"May I be of assistance?" Aldora said. She was carefully scanning the tunnel for any opportunity to escape.

Vildron laughed, in an odd, disquieting, fashion. "Nigel will be delighted, if you do," he said.

Bildron frowned.

Aldora noted that Bildron was staring at a faint red mark on one wall of the tunnel.

"My Queen," Bildron whispered, "we must limit our sounds now, for your precious safety, and ours."

Aldora nodded, as though she understood.

The tunnel opened onto a high, circular room, which appeared to possess the same circumference the silo above it.

Aldora gasped at what she beheld.

Ten large urns stood in the center of the chamber. They were bright red, denoting the danger of explosive powders. Fuses ran from center holes in the tops of each urn. These lines had been woven together to form a master fuse. Set it aflame, and all ten fuses would burn, creating an almost simultaneous detonation.

There was loose powder strewn about the floor. It was so fine that it seeped from under the lids whenever the jars were moved carelessly or with haste. Aldora doubted these men were as sound of mind under Nigel's demented influence as they would be normally and were, therefore, more reckless than a blacksmith's nature, otherwise, would dictate. She realized two reasons why they wore cloths wrapped around their boots. Loud sounds had been known to detonate the powders. This is why they were stored in a special room which reduced sound. A spark from a nail on the bottom of a boot could be deadly. She glanced, nervously, at her boots.

Bildron noted this. "*May* Lord Nigel *forgive* us!" he exclaimed. He was frighteningly near panic. "We have *failed* to *wrap* our Queen's *boots* against *disaster*!"

"Our Queen walks so softly, like the refined Lady Lord Nigel tells us she is," Vildron said, "we did not note her steps. Do not fear, brother, I am prepared." He drew a bundle of cloth from a pouch in his leather apron. "If my Queen will raise her foot, I shall insure her safety."

Aldora leaned against the wall and lifted a foot. She was amazed at how swiftly the man wrapped the cloth strip around her boot. It was an artful job. The result resembled a cloth slipper. The man repeated the feat and tossed the scant remainder of the cloth onto the floor.

Aldora became depressed. It was obvious she was no match for their empowered reflexes. She fearfully doubted Alaric could match, let alone, outclass them. Hope surged in her. She spied weapons lying to the right side of the urns. Two swords and two blacksmith hammers, but no bows or arrows. She realized neither man had been armed with bows when they captured her.

"How came you to strike the guards down with arrows, but without bows?" she asked. She forced herself to sound mildly curious.

"Our concealed confederates," Vildron said. He sounded proud, and was gloating.

"Why did they use padded arrows?"

The questioning seemed to surprise and disquiet the men.

Aldora sensed their uneasiness was caused by something else.

"We had nothing *else* available," Bildron mumbled, as if distracted. "The blasphemous, false King Alaric's archers had provisioned themselves down to the last of the death arrows. Our confederates are seeking to steal death arrows from unwary guards. But, it is difficult, for the palace guards are well-disciplined."

The man sounded so frustrated and disappointed, Aldora nearly laughed, in spite of her perilous situation.

Vildron began nodding his head slowly. A moment later, Bildron joined in.

"You feel our Lord's call, to readiness," Vildron said, somberly, "as do I."

"Forgive me, brother," Bildron said, "I do not wish to commit this act, even in the service of our Lord." He turned, fearfully, to Aldora. "*Please* forgive me for my *doubts*, my Queen."

"Do not fear, my brother," Vildron assured him, "our Queen shall fulfill our Lord's wishes." He drew flint and steel from another pouch of his leather apron and held them out to Aldora. "It is Lord, no, *King* Nigel's *wish* that *yours* be the *honor*," he proclaimed.

Aldora stared at the man and attempted to conceal her horror. Her mind raced. She looked to the swords. They were so close. She sighed, with bitterness. If some miracle allowed her to reach and brandish one of the blades, would she be able to ply it with deadly result against these hapless puppets? A thought struck her and she half smiled.

The brothers appeared suspicious at their Queen's hesitation.

"How shall we *synchronize* the explosions of *all* five silos?" Aldora demanded. "Are you *certain* your fuses are *long* enough or that they shall burn *slowly* enough for us to escape. I am not as *swift* of foot as the two of you. Can either of you *carry* me to *safety* in *time*? Have either of you even *tested* and *timed* these fuses? Perhaps one of you can escort me to the entrance of the tunnel and the other can set the fuses alight and join us as we flee to Nigel."

Her rapid fire questioning appeared to confuse the men and cause them uncertainty.

"We just follow King Nigel's commands," Bildron said, with barely concealed annoyance. "Nigel *knows* all things. As his betrothed, you are closer to him than we. *Surely*, you must *trust* him, even *more* than do *we*." His eyes became dull. "Yes, Lord," he said, with deep regret, "I *beg* your, *gracious*, forgiveness. I *hear* and *shall* obey."

Aldora felt a chill. This unfortunate man was in direct contact with Nigel. How could she take advantage of this? "*Nigel*," she said, "can you *hear* me?"

"He is *gone*," Bildron said, sadly. "He is *wroth* because we *failed* to bear you to *him* the *moment* we discovered you. We must wait for *replacements* who shall have the *honor* of lighting the fuses."

"Lord Nigel cares not if the explosions are *synchronized*," Vildron said, "only that they *occur*. He agrees the burn rate is *somewhat* unpredictable. This is why my brother, I, and you, my Queen, shall be long absent from the Citadel before spark is set to fuse."

Yes, Aldora thought. Her heart pounded with hope. Delay! It will require time to sneak out of the Citadel. She knew her father well. With Angela's canny advice he will make their escape well-nigh impossible. Only an unearthly feat of magic from Nigel could foil Alaric's plans. She would do her utmost to sabotage any such evil scheme by Nigel. She reminded herself that her father was aware of the threat here. Surely, he was poised to invade the tunnels and strike down those tending the urns. Her greatest fear was that Nigel's slaves were hidden nearby, cat-watching the tunnel entrances. They might forgo their padded arrows, and resort to sword, Ax, spear. Many times, she had heard Guthrie, chillingly, remind her Arden, that a dishonorable ambush, from behind, was always deadly. This horrible fate must *not* befall her *father*!

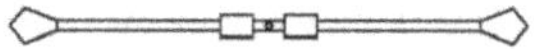

Alaric and his soldiers discovered Aldora's guards. They were groggy, and not ready to serve their King.

"Do not worry yourselves," Alaric said, "rest until you are able to be of assistance to Indwin."

The King raced to the end of the passage, but came to such a swift stop, his soldiers skidded passed him, into the sunlight. Alaric detected a sound he knew well. His reflexes enabled him to snatch the legs out from under his guards, just before the death arrows hummed through the length of the passage, and struck the earth between the silos at either side of that entrance.

"Nigel is *playing* for *keeps,*" Alaric whispered, to the soldiers, as they crawled, backwards, into the dim passage. "We *lack* that *luxury*. We must do our *utmost* to preserve *life* and *limb* of these *victims* of *possession*." To the left he heard a slight sound of a metal door settling into place.

"Sire," the younger soldier whispered, "why have they not, again, fired upon us? We are, mortally, unprotected!"

"Their initial assault was a harmless diversion, Zeirdon,"

Alaric whispered, "designed to allow one or more of their cohorts to gain entry into the center silo tunnel."

"I beg your pardon, Sire," the older soldier whispered, "but, how do you know this?"

Alaric smiled, slightly. "You must, sometimes, see with your ears, Joelib," he whispered.

The King's answer mystified the soldiers.

"You remain here until I summon you," Alaric whispered. "when you respond, keep your attention on the bakeries, directly ahead. They must make themselves momentarily visible to aim and release. You will duck and roll the moment you sight top of pate. Your King shall handle the remainder."

Alaric drew his legs up so that he was in a low crouch. "Ready?" he whispered.

"*Not*, even, *remotely*," Joelib whispered. "*But*, we shall not *fail* you, my King."

"At *least*," Zeirdon whispered, "*that* is our *fervent* intent."

Alaric was up and gone so quickly to their left, they were uncertain, for a moment, that he had moved.

Two heads popped up at an open window of the center most bakery. Bows, loaded with arrows, followed.

"*Beware*!" Joelib whispered, as he pointed them out.

"They *must* not *harm* our King!" Zeirdon avowed. He sprang to his feet and charged directly at the ambushers. As he drew his blade an arrow struck it and ricocheted with a sharp ping.

Joelib was on the younger man's back, a moment later, and they fell, heavily, behind a low wagon on the cobbled street. Two arrows embedded into the far side of the wagon.

Two men shouted: "*There away*!" They cried out, with pain. Then there was silence.

Joelib peeked around the front of the wagon.

Alaric walked across the cobbles and stopped at the door to the third maintenance tunnel. He lifted a hand as if to ask why his guards dallied.

As the soldiers joined their King they noted several wagons and empty shipping crates had provided Alaric adequate cover.

"Forget seeing with our *ears*," Joelib said, with mortification, "we need to *learn* to *see* with our *eyes* and to *follow* our *orders*."

"I fear we shall *never* hear the end of this," Zeirdon said, bitterly.

Alaric stared at the sturdy padlock on the portal. He was sure this was the door he had heard close. There was no way to unlock it from the inside, so how had someone gotten in. Perhaps one of the unconscious men in the bakery had a key? He reached for the lock, but his fingers passed through.

"Are these padlocks some sort of *trick* from Nigel?" Joelib asked.

"A *sly* one," Alaric said. He motioned for them to stand to the side. When he grasped the thick metal hoop-handle the padlock illusion vanished. Alaric, grudgingly, admired Nigel's magic spell and opened the heavy door.

Much to the relief of the soldiers, the way into the maintenance tunnel was unguarded. No opportunity to further embarrass themselves.

Several soldiers sneaked around the end silos on both sides of the King and his men.

"Captain Lartrel," Alaric said, to a guard who had silver in his brown hair, "station two men out here for each tunnel. They will use these crates and wagons for protection as they cover the backs of each team that we shall dispatch into the tunnels. Equip your archers with padded arrows. They shall enter first, to disable interlopers. Be mindful that my daughter may be a prisoner within any tunnel. You and your men *know* your *duty* to the *Princess*."

Lartrel waved a hand and his men split into five groups of equal number. Two of each squad assumed the rear sentry posts.

"Sire," Lartrel said, "these tunnels run straight. They are well lighted. There is no cover between their entrances and the chambers at their ends. We shall be heard and seen long before we can hear or sight the intruders. They can conceal themselves to the sides of the entries to the chambers and direct a lethal cross fire at us. If we dispatch shield bearers to precede my bowmen, you are condemning my bowmen to death. In close quarter combat of *this* type, a single arrow or sword blow can wound or kill several. Our archers can offer no return fire. Although their arrows be padded, the impact of one arrow against one urn of explosives, will detonate it. Our *only* option is to fall upon them with numbers greater than they can slay, before *they* are subdued or slain. If there are several intruders in each chamber repelling our advance, you will need many reinforcements to replace the perished. This, however, is not the *worst* of it. It is probable that the moment these interlopers sight us, they shall ignite their bombs, and everyone of us will die, to no avail."

Joelib and Zeirdon were amazed their King did not take Lartrel's head off for his manner of speech.

Alaric calmed himself. He realized with, self disgust, that his deep concern for Aldora had caused him to think and act rashly. The straight talk from this experienced tactician was exactly what he required, and deserved. "You have *rescued* your *grateful* King from *nearly* committing a *grave* blunder," he said. "What do *you* advise?"

Lartrel appeared to be struggling for an effective answer.

Alaric sensed the man's valiant heart was breaking with his inability to proffer a less costly plan of attack.

"Sire," Zeirdon said, with obvious hesitation, "May I speak?"

Alaric raised an eyebrow, in surprise, but nodded.

"If the Princess is, indeed, a prisoner, inside," Zeirdon said, "I deem it unlikely these men, however desperate, shall detonate their explosives. They will be forced to remove the Princess to a safer site. We can stand aside and wait until they move the Princess, and rescue her as they exit a tunnel, or enter at great cost to secure the Princess. If we venture in, we will stand a better chance of gaining control over the explosives, and the Princess. *I* shall not *hesitate* to *undertake* this *risk* if my King so *commands*."

SaCee's ethereal glow of calm enveloped everyone.

Alaric welcomed it. When he carefully closed the heavy door, the padlock illusion returned. "SaCee has been forced to act against some threat of which we are ignorant. We must discover what this is." He glanced at Joelib. "Seek an answer, and return, swiftly," he told the guard.

Joelib saluted, spun on his heel, and raced to the passage through which he, his younger companion, and the King had traveled.

"Sire," Lartrel finally said, "what *evidence* proves that Princess Aldora is, *indeed*, within one of these tunnels? Surely, these possessed men are acting from knowledge of Nigel's desire to *obtain* Aldora. I deem it *unlikely* they would *imagine* placing *her* at *risk* near these explosives. Would they not *conceal*, or place her under *disguise*, and *spirit* her away to the *gates* to be on their *swift* way to a meeting with Nigel?"

Alaric hung his head. Both men offered sound analysis. *Any* decision he made, could bring death. *Everything* hinged on Aldora's location.

"Sire," Zeirdon said, "you alerted us to someone recently entering this tunnel. If his *intent* was to *light* a fuse, he has had *more* than *sufficient* time. He and his cohorts may be *awaiting* a *signal* from Nigel or waiting for *us* to withdraw so they can *ignite* the *fuse* and *flee* the tunnel in a timely fashion *without* risk of capture or death. They may not be *possessed* enough to *throw* their lives *away* for *Nigel*. Or, Nigel may not wish to *waste* his *few* remaining mobile *minions*, even to attain *this* goal of *destruction*."

Lartrel shook a finger of approval at the younger man. "If this be so, Sire, then we can delay their plans indefinitely by doing nothing," he said. "Entering may push Nigel into forcing his minions to sacrifice themselves."

Alaric felt overburdened by what ifs.

Joelib exited the passage to their left. "The Queen has ordered the closing of the gates to prevent people from flooding into the Citadel, and harms way, if the powders are ignited," he said.

An ethereal yellow light descended on the group, clinging to man and object like water.

Alaric had experienced it a long time ago, during a period of grave peril.

The horn of invasion sounded from the observation tower.

The sentries on the walls shouted the alarm Alaric had feared to hear:

"Prepare yourselves men! The *Elves* are surrounding us! They sport *full* battle regalia, and their *women* march alongside them!"

Alaric's noble heart was rent with despair. Nigel *must* have Aldora! He would *not* assault the Citadel if she were *within* its walls!

"Two of Nigel's lackeys lie senseless within that bakery," the King said, to Lartrel. "Have them placed inside that end tunnel, then gather real padlocks and secure these doors. Those inside will either sacrifice themselves for Nigel's insanity, or wait for us to grant them freedom! Following that, you will dispatch your troops to reinforce those already atop this rear wall. Prepare to repel all attempts at scaling!"

The King motioned at Joelib and Zeirdon, and raced toward the passage through which they had first traveled.

Aldora heard the faint sound of the closing of the heavy metal door to the tunnel. She assumed the replacements for the blacksmiths were approaching.

The blacksmiths detected the echoes of two pairs of non-padded boots striking the floor. They exchanged horrified looks.

"My Queen," Bildron implored, "allow us to go forth and prevent these fools from ending our lives with their negligence!"

Aldora berated herself for not having realized how much these men trusted her and failing to take advantage of this trust in some manner.

"By all means," she agreed, "I shall not allow my Nigel's schemes, to go a rye."

The blacksmiths turned and hustled down the tunnel.

Aldora hastened to the pile of weapons and snatched up a sword. She glanced around the chamber, then at the stone ceiling. She saw a trap door three yards by three yards square. It was constructed of great beams and had many cross braces for tremendous strength. She was frustrated when she could see no release mechanism. This was just as well, for there were tons of grain in that silo. She was desperate to be of value in defending Indwin and its people. Only one possibility came to mind. She sliced through the fuses, at the top of each of the ten urns, and tossed the tangled mass at a small, lidless, empty crate which stood against a wall of the chamber. The wad of fuses caught the edge of the left side of the crate, and teetered there.

Severing the fuses was a futile gesture, at best. It would only delay the detonation until the urns were re-fused by Nigel's slaves.

She would either have to fight, here and now, or convince the blacksmiths to allow her to carry a sword so that, at an opportune time, she could attempt an escape, fending off the blacksmiths, and anyone else who interfered.

The pile of fuses toppled to the floor.

Aldora froze. It felt as though her heart was about to leap free of her. There was a square opening behind the crate! When she knelt on the cool gray stone floor, she saw an earthen tunnel. She snatched up the tangled mess of fuses and pulled the crate aside enough to crawl through with the fuses and her sword. She jammed the tip of the blade into the side of the box and tugged the box against the mouth of the tunnel, making certain she could detect no light from the chamber. Hopefully, Nigel's slaves were ignorant of the opening, and the crate would conceal it from them until she found the end of the dark passage, and freedom.

The Princess threw the fuses aside, yanked the tip of her blade from the side of the box, and sighed with frustration. She could not make a hasty escape on all fours, and it was awkward crawling with a sword in one hand with the blade pointing ahead of her to avoid banging into anything. The top of her head occasionally brushed the ceiling of the tunnel. The only sound was her breathing.

"*Halt*, you *fools*!" the two blacksmiths shouted at their replacements. They recognized them as traveling tin smiths who often visited Indil Town. One wore blue apparel, the other green.

The smiths stopped, looking perplexed and frightened.

"*Did* our *Lord* not tell you to *bind* your boots, against *noise*, and *sparks*?" Vildron demanded, with anger.

"*We* were *ordered* to *swaddle* our boots *before* we *entered* the *chamber*, and to *await* the signal to *ignite* the fuses," the tin smith, in green, said, with resentment, "*then*, to *flee*, for our lives, and to join Nigel's Elf army, in revolt."

"*We* thought it *best* to do so, *immediately*, upon *entering* the tunnel," Bildron said.

"We *demand* that you do so, *now*," Vildron said, "for, Queen *Aldora* awaits us at the chamber, and we shall not *permit* you to bear, even the *slightest* risk, unto her royal presence!"

The tin smiths exchanged perplexed looks.

"Lord Nigel said, that, for her safety, you and Queen Aldora would be *absent* from this place *before* we arrived," the tin smith, in blue, said.

"Verily," the tin smith, in green, averred. "Had we been notified, *otherwise*, we would have swaddled our boots, *before* entering the tunnel, *for* the safety of our *Queen*."

The blacksmiths shared frightened expressions.

"Brother," Vildron said, "did we *fail* to understand our King's commands?"

"*Or*, did we *fail* to *hear* all of his commands on this *vital* matter," Bildron said, with desperation. "It is sometimes *difficult* to catch all of our King's *precious* words. He is so *far* away and his voice can be so *diminished*. On occasions, it seems as though he is in the *midst* of a message, instead of *at* the beginning."

"*Aye*," Vildron agreed.

"*This*, have we *noted*, also," the tin smith, in green, said.

"Because of this, we have been *chastised* by our King for *failure* to perform *tasks* which we did *not* know we were *required* to do," the tin smith, in blue, said.

Bildron shook himself. "*If* this be *our* misfortune, *now*," he said, urgently, "we *must* return to our *Queen*, and *hasten* ourselves from this place *before* King Nigel *discovers* our *unintended* failure!"

The tin smiths drew bundled strips of cloth from the pockets of their slacks and sat on the cold stone floor. They began swaddling their boots.

"You dare not *wait* upon *us*," the tin smith, in green, advised.

The blacksmiths spun on their padded heels and raced down the tunnel with break neck speed.

Much to Aldora's relief, the tunnel expanded in height, allowing her to walk upright. The darkness was dizzying, but she kept one hand against a wall to orient and steady herself. She waved the sword side to side and up and down to check for obstacles. She slid each foot along to seek unseen holes. It was her assumption, the tunnel ran beneath the third loading dock. How long it might be, and where it might end, was anybody's guess. Surely, it could not extend beyond the wall of the Citadel. The tunnel would have to take a steep down slope to bypass the great slabs which comprised the Citadel wall. Even in this depressing darkness, such a downward path would be obvious.

Aldora took note of a glimmer of torch light in the distance. It had not occurred to her that she might not be *alone*. She had not entertained the reasons why someone had expended great effort and time to fashion the tunnel. She slowed her pace and grasped the hilt of her sword with more firmness.

The tunnel opened to a rectangular earthen chamber. A single, flaming, torch was embedded in the center of the floor. Around this, were bags of grain, skins of water, and barrels marked with the symbols of various types of dried meat.

Aldora sighed, heavily, with relief that no one was there. Then, she felt indignation and anger that some selfish individual was hoarding food and water. She dismissed this matter and concentrated on the new challenge.

"How do I escape this honor-less storehouse before those unpleasant, hirsute, iron pounders find the tunnel?" she whispered.

She speared her sword into the earth, and took up the

torch. She stepped over the supplies and inspected the walls of the chamber. To her surprise, they were of stone.

"These *are* the blocks that comprise the base of the loading docks," she whispered. "I am, *only*, a foot away from *safety*!"

She started to shout for help, but decided this would be unwise. Her voice might carry down the tunnel to receptive, but unhelpful, ears. She jammed the torch into the earth beside the left wall, took up her sword and began digging at the mortar between the stone blocks. To her surprise, the block wiggled just a little. She dropped the sword, placed her hands flat against the cold block, and began shoving on it: the right side, then the left side. The more she pushed, the more it wiggled. She could discern that it had moved outward about a quarter of an inch. She increased the speed, and force of her efforts.

"My *Queen*," Bildron implored, "where *are* you? *How* can you *not* be *here*?"

Vildron ran around the urns, as though he had lost his mind. "There *is* no way *out*," he shouted. "She did not *pass* us! She does not *hide* in an *urn*, there is not that much *displaced* powder on the floor, *nor* in this *crate*! Where *has* she gone? We *cannot* have *lost* her!"

"*Nigel*!" Bildron said, with wild hope. "Only, *Nigel,* could have *taken* her from this place! He has used his Mind Magic to achieve it!"

"Surely, Lord Nigel would have *told* us of *this*, brother," Vildron shouted, as he circled the urns.

"There was *no* such *need*, for, *we* have *seen* it, for ourselves," Bildron said.

"*But*, he has *not* issued us *new* commands, brother," Vildron shouted. "Had he our *Queen*, he would issue us *new* commands!"

The tin smiths raced into the chamber.

"Why the commotion?" the tin smith, in blue, demanded. "Are we not *ordered* to remain *quiet* around these *deadly* powders? Do you not *fear* setting them off?"

"Our Queen has *vanished*!" Vildron shouted, frantically.

"Nonsense," the tin smith, in green, chided, "no one *vanishes*."

"*Unless* our Lord Nigel *enables* it," Bildron said, doggedly.

The tinsmith in green grunted. "*This* possibility, I cannot *dispute*, for we have *witnessed* the *awesome* might of Lord Nigel, at the Hills, and the Orchards."

Vildron lost his footing on the powder and tumbled to his knees. He struck the crate with his heavy arm and sent the box skidding away from the concealed opening. He remained on his hands and knees as he stared into the dark tunnel.

"*Not* such a *magical* disappearance after all," the tin smith, in green, said, with a laugh.

Vildron used his massive arms to propel himself upright. He turned on the tin smith in green. "Do you *find* this a *matter* of *humor*?" he shouted. "If *harm* befalls our *Queen*, *wherever* she has *gone*, Lord Nigel will *slay* us *all*!"

The tinsmith in green was surprisingly untroubled. "*Calm* yourself, and be *after* her, *then*, man," he said. "An *entrance*, implies, an *exit*. Do you *wish* her to discover, *that*, before *you* discover, *her*?"

Vildron raised his huge fist to strike a rage empowered blow.

"Brother," Bildron cautioned, "*we* cannot *fit* through that *opening*. They *can*. But, *only*, if you do not *crack* their *skulls*."

Vildron grasped the tin smith in green by his shirt front and hefted him into the air. "*If* you *fail* to *find*, and *preserve*, our *Queen*," he shouted, with vehemence, "*you* will not have *time* to *concern* yourself with *how* Lord Nigel will *punish* you!" He spun around, swung his arm, and, sent the man sailing into the tunnel without him making contact with the floor and the edges of the opening. Vildron turned to reach for the other tin smith but the man in blue threw himself to the hard floor and scrambled into the tunnel.

Alaric skidded to a halt in the earth between the two loading docks beyond the end of the stone passage. He saw Angela and SaCee facing each other on the Queen's loading dock, to his right. SaCee's staff was still spinning on her upraised palm. The almost, physically thick, yellow light clung to everything. There was silence, in and outside the great Citadel. He noted Luana had heavily reinforced the battlement sentries on the front, left and right walls and the people huddled against the great blocks. He was grimly aware this was not the most fortuitous place for them to seek refuge. True, it would protect them from debris if the silos were detonated, but not from the wall penetrating psychic energy blows of the Elves. Long ago, he and Guthrie had witnessed a demonstration of this uncanny ability. Without Durward, he had no hope of warding off such an assault.

Alaric's soldiers arrived at his side. They were panting from their vain efforts to catch up with their King.

"Join the guards who protect my Queen," he ordered. "Tell her that it is my *command* that she and SaCee accompany you, with haste, to the old hall."

The soldiers scrambled up the steep steps to their right.

Alaric startled. A slight grating of stone against stone drew his attention to his right. One of the large, square, granite blocks of which the loading dock was composed was wiggling, slowly, side to side, and moving, even more inch-meal, toward him. This seemed an odd avenue of attack, but he drew his sword, nonetheless.

The tin smith, in blue, could barely see his companion lying on the floor of the narrow, low tunnel.

"Are you injured, Perlon?" he asked.

"There exists, a great ache, in my dignity, Wildred," Perlon said, shakily.

"This is preferable to a *cracked* skull and a *journey* into the *afterlife*," Wildred said.

"*I* have my *doubts*, on *that* matter," Perlon said, as he got to his knees. "We are reduced to crawling like infants," he said, resentfully. "We shall *never* overtake the Queen. We do not know how *long* she has been traveling. She may already have emerged from this fetid tunnel, into the midst of Alaric's guards. *Why* our Queen would *flee* from the *security* of the powerful *protectors* Lord Nigel assigned to her, is a *true* puzzlement."

"You have, cruelly, suffered from the rage of the largest of those brutes," Wildred said. "Perhaps our Queen lacked trust in them and preferred to seek our Lord, on her own."

"*I* surely would," Perlon avowed.

The comforting light from behind faded out just as the tunnel expanded sufficiently to allow the tin smiths to stand erect. They were able to walk side by side.

"*This* is *much* better." Perlon said.

"*Also*, much *worse*," Wildred said, "*for*, our Queen can travel, *more* swiftly, as well."

"Damn this darkness," Perlon said, "I feel as if I shall pitch off the edge of this world, and into the next!"

"Here," Wildred said, "take hold of my forearm, and keep your other hand against the wall of the tunnel. This will orient us, and lessen the dizziness."

"*This* is why I *value* our partnership," Perlon said, "*you* are *clever*, in ways, that *escape* me."

Wildred grunted. "Our *plight* may not be *all* foul," he said. "*If* Nigel discovers that our muscular comrades have lost his Queen, they may not be *breathing* when *we* return with her. *We* will be the ones *fortunate* enough to *escort* her to our Lord. *We* will receive his *gratitude*, and be *rewarded*. Not *they*."

"You have *always* known how to *cheer* me," Perlon said. "Will you *risk* running in the *danger* of this *darkness* for the *gratitude* of, and *reward* from, our Lord? I have a *sick* feeling we must make *utmost* haste *if* we are to make *full* use of *this* opportunity."

"*Aye*," Wildred agreed.

Their regret for their decision was immediate, as their heads struck the hard, low ceiling of the tunnel, causing them sharp pain.

"We shall *crouch*, then," Perlon said, with a growl, of anger, "*and* make use of haste, in *spite* of this."

They ran as swiftly as possible under their awkward circumstances.

Alaric grew impatient with the creeping progress of the would be attacker. He sheathed his sword, grasped the sides of the large stone block, pulled it straight back toward himself, and dropped it in front of his feet. His eyes flew wide, in surprise, for a moment, then he threw up his hands, as though in exasperation. "Will you *never* tire of playing *hide-and-seek*?" he said.

Aldora hissed, in mock annoyance. "A little assistance, please, father," she said, "I am being pursued by possessed blacksmiths, who are vastly stronger, and faster of reflexes, than, even, you." She held her arms through the square opening.

Alaric grasped his daughter under her arms and extricated her from her prison. For a moment, they were reminded of when she was a child and had wanted to look over the wall of the Observation Tower to see how high they were. He recalled how protective he was, and she thought of how safe she felt when he lifted her onto the top of the wall and held onto her from behind with big, strong hands.

Alaric slowly released his daughter.

Aldora looked into his eyes. "I was foolish," she said. "There is no need to have serious words with me at an appropriate, later time."

The King laughed, "Did you *gain* any intelligence, at least, scout?" he asked.

Aldora looked glum. "Probably nothing you do not already know. There are teams of, at least, two men, in the end chambers of the maintenance tunnels. There were four in this third chamber, because two came as replacements so the first pair might steal me off to Nigel. Each team is watching over ten urns of the explosive powders. They are awaiting some signal from Nigel. They imagine they shall set their fuses alight and flee to safety. Even I know their fuses are far too short and too fast burning to allow them to travel more than half the distance of the tunnels, before they die."

"How come you to know this?" Alaric said.

"Arden shares much of his training with me."

"Good," Alaric said. "Perhaps, soon, he will share some common sense, and, even, some wisdom, with you."

Aldora rolled her eyes and bumped her hip against the King's.

"How *long* can this *suffocating* tunnel *last*?" Perlon said, angrily.

Alaric snatched up the block of stone and shoved it

back into place, almost in a single movement.

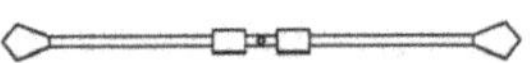

Wildred and Perlon saw the flickering, yellow, torch light and paused. Silence. They crept forward and looked, cautiously, into the earthen chamber.

"*Not* here!" Perlon said, with frustration and anger. "Our *Queen* is *not* here! *How* can this *be*? We passed *no* other openings! *None*!" He started searching behind the barrels and under the skins of water and bags of grain.

Wildred grasped his friend's elbow. "*Calm* yourself, man," he cautioned, "*or* you *will* perish of *apoplexy*." He indicated the surrounding stores. "*This* is *ours*," he said. "Our *blustering* comrades, need not be made aware of *it*. *No* one, need be made *aware* of *it*."

Perlon became irate. "Are you *insane*, Wildred?" he shouted. "*All* of this will be *blasted* into pieces. So shall we be, *if* we do not *hie* ourselves *back* to the main chamber *before* Nigel issues his command to put *flame* to *fuse*. With our Queen out of *harms* way, and with *our* failure to *wrest* her from Alaric, Lord Nigel will have no *reason* to delay his plan and no incentive to preserve *our* lives!" He raced for the tunnel. "*Leave* it, or *die*, man," he shouted over his shoulder.

Wildred's face twisted with despair. "Such a sinful waste!" he lamented. He snatched up the torch and almost hurled himself into the tunnel.

Alaric took Aldora by an elbow, guided her up the narrow stairs at the base of the silo, then escorted her, in the same, firm, fashion, across the loading dock.

Angela sighted them, ran, with delight, to Aldora, and embraced the Princess as though she would never release her.

"My Queen," King Alaric said, sharply, "did your guards fail to impart to you my instructions concerning your safety?"

"On the *contrary*," the Queen said, "they *insisted*, *almost* to the point of *insult*. SaCee *refused*, and *warned* them to back away. You know, full well, that, neither *I*, nor, *you*, would leave SaCee's side at such a time of *crisis*. She is *far* too *precious*."

Alaric glanced at the seer. "SaCee is the *only* person, in *all* of Indwin, who is *most* free, of *peril*," he said. He placed his hands on his wife's shoulders. "I have spoken to you of this yellow force shining all around us," he reminded her.

Angela drew a sharp breath, in remembrance.

A soldier raced up the narrow steps and crossed the loading dock. He knelt on one knee, then stood up. He was distraught. "Sire," he said, "the Elves have herded the people who were massed behind the Citadel and at its sides, to the front with the rest of our people. My *mother* and *father* are among them! I beseech you to release me from the honor of your service and to permit me to hie fourth to defend them!"

"Several of my guards have spoken the same request," Angela said, softly.

Alaric placed a hand on the agitated soldier's shoulder. "Do not *fear* for your *parents* or our *people*," he reassured the man and the Queen, "*fear*, for our *tragic* allies, the *Elves*."

Aldora and the guardsman shared looks of puzzlement.

"*Then*, that which you have imparted, *is* horrid truth?" Queen Angela said, to Alaric.

From beyond the front wall of the Citadel, a horn sounded. It carried an oddly musical tune that seemed out of place during a war.

"The Elves are called to *charge*," Angela said, with despair.

Alaric took a step toward the seer.

SaCee flashed, in an instant, up to her place on the Observation Tower. Her calming white light vanished, but her thick yellow emission grew more intense as her staff spun more swiftly on her palm.

The Granary Master mounted the steps of the loading dock, and fell to one knee beside his King. "Forgive me, Sire," he said, with urgency, "but, I know how we can prevent the detonation of the explosive powders!"

Alaric took the man by his elbow and made him stand up. The King stared into the Granary Master earnest eyes. "You are *certain*?" the King asked.

"*Yes*, Sire," the man said, excitedly. "There is *zero* doubt, and *zero* risk! I would not *dare* speak of *it*, if this were *not* so!"

"Then, *accomplish* this *feat*, *for* me, and I shall declare you a *Knight* of the realm!" the King said. "I have too much *heaped* upon my plate, to *supervise*. I *trust* you."

"I am most honored, Sire," the Granary Master said, with tears in his eyes. He raised his arms over his head and signaled.

There was one granary worker positioned on each loading dock at the center of the base of each silo. They stood next to a large metal hoop which was attached to a bar that pierced the wall of each silo. This long bar was fitted into a metal eyelet which was attached to the top of a trap door in the floor of each silo. Their purpose was for dumping chaff and other debris before the new harvest began.

Aldora recalled having seen one of these trapdoors when she had been held captive. She turned to her father. "*What* of Nigel's poor *men*?" she said.

The workers grasped the hoops with both hands and leaned backwards, putting all their strength and body weight into the task.

Perlon hastily crawled out of the earthen tunnel. When he stood up, he was eye, to chest, with Vildron.

Wildred nearly burned his partner with the torch as he exited the earthen tunnel.

"Where *is* our *precious* Queen?" Vildron demanded, with rage.

Wildred shoved his torch almost into Vildron's face.

Vildron backed away, quickly.

"Are you Lord Nigel's, *dog*, or a *man*?" Wildred demanded. "*Claim* your *simple* wits, and *open* your *ears*!

We searched, *everywhere*, and found, *no one*! *Unless* Lord Nigel has *granted* our *Queen* the gift of *invisibility*, she was *never* in that tunnel!"

"This, you solemnly, swear?" Bildron demanded.

"You know that *no one* can deceive Lord Nigel," Perlon said. "To lie, means to die!"

The conspirators became aware that Perlon had *fire* horribly near the powders. They fled halfway down the stone tunnel before they felt safe.

Wildred realized something. "Where *are* the *fuses*?" he said.

"What do you *mean*?" Vildron said.

"Yes," Perlon said. "I, also, *saw* no *fuses*!"

"You are *mistaken*," Bildron told them. "My brother and I spent great time, and faced wrenching risk, fusing those urns."

Perlon strode back to the gray stone chamber. He threw his hands into the air. "You are correct, partner," he shouted, "there *are* no *fuses*! They have been sliced even with the covers of the urns!" He checked all around the urns, and the crate, without success. He glanced into the earthen tunnel. "Here away!" he shouted, with celebration. He bore down on his collaborators with the tangled fuses clenched in one fist.

The men considered each other, suspiciously.

"I *swear*, by Lord Nigel's *wrath*, that *we* did *not* do this *thing*!" Wildred said.

"Aye!" Perlon concurred, vociferously.

"My *brother*, and *I*, also, *oath* this," Bildron said, earnestly.

"But, *brother*, this leaves *only* our *Queen* as the *culprit*!" Vildron said, with obvious disillusionment and shock. "Why, *brother*? Why, would our *Queen* commit this *act* against our Lord? Against her *beloved*?"

"*All* of *this* is of *no* matter," Wildred told them, with intensity. "We must *re-fuse* the urns with *due* haste, or *flee* for our lives. When Lord Nigel returns to our minds and sees that his Queen is absent and then uses his magic to find her, again, a prisoner of King Alaric and his army, and held in a place, which I am certain, will be far enough away from here to ensure her safety, he *will* order *us*, and our *comrades*, to place *fire* to fuse."

Perlon shook the mess of fuses at his cohorts. "Even *uncut*, these fuses were *too* short and *too* fast *burning* to allow *anyone* to *flee* to *safety after* they were lighted."

"You *lie*!" Vildron said, angrily.

Perlon snorted with derision. "I spent a *year* as a *guard*, and *trained* in *these* matters," he said. "I speak *reality*. If we had conducted warfare, it would have been *my* duty to *position* and *detonate* explosives charges. My *life* depended on *knowing* powders, and fuses!"

"*If* this be, *horribly*, so," Bildron said, with despair, "then, Lord Nigel intends to *sacrifice* us for his *revenge* against *Alaric* and *Arden*!"

Perlon nodded. "Now, comprehend this," he said. "We need only to leave this tunnel and wait in hiding until our allies, the Elves, breach the Citadel's walls, then join them. These urns *will* detonate when those in the silos on either side of us *do*."

"This be *treason* against Lord Nigel," Vildron said. "He will *see* it in our minds as surely as he has *seen* our *doubts*, before!"

Wildred's shoulders slumped. "This is, *tragically*, so," he admitted, unwillingly.

They considered one another, with despair.

Bildron took the tangled fuses from Perlon, and said, with forced enthusiasm, "What do you *say*, brother? Of the two of us, *I* am the *fastest* runner. After *we* reset these fuses, *I* shall *remain* and *await* Lord Nigel's *signal* to put forth the *spark*."

Perlon pounded his fist against the wall of the tunnel. "*You* do not *fully* comprehend!" he shouted. "We must *exit* the tunnel *and* be a *hundred feet* away *before* the powders *blow*, else the concussion will slay us! If you cannot *run* as *swiftly* as an *arrow* flies, you have no *hope* of survival! *Throw* down those *fuses*, man, and *flee* with me! *I* shall take my chances with our Lord Nigel's *displeasure,* rather than face *certain* death, *herein*!"

"Aye, brother," Vildron said, with decision. "Nigel cares *not* for us, or our *brethren*. No longer, shall *I* care for *him*. No longer, shall *I* do *his* bidding."

"Easily spoken, while our Lord is *absent* from your mind," Wildred said. "*Will* you *remain* so *resolute* when he is, again, *inside* your, very, head?"

Hopelessness avalanched the hapless men.

There was a loud thud of wood against stone, then a great whoosh of air. An instant later, a wall of grain buried the urns and rushed toward the blacksmiths and tinsmiths. They fled with all the enhanced speed and agility that Nigel's possession of them allowed.

Vildron shoved his muscular hands against the hatch with all of his magically enhanced strength, but it did not give. "Those *demons* have *locked* us in!" he screamed.

The men began pounding on the portal.

The thundering of the grain ceased, leaving, in its fearsome wake, a blessed silence and a cloud of choking grain dust swirling around them. When they turned away from the door they faced a wedge of grain that began at the ceiling and ended only inches from their feet.

Someone outside worked a padlock and the door was flipped open to the sunlight.

Nigel's henchmen were filled with contrasting emotions as they held their hands above their heads and surrendered to the Kings army.

"At *least* we are *alive*," Perlon whispered, as they followed the blacksmiths up the metal stairs.

"For how *long*?" Wildred whispered, bitterly. "We have *all* failed Lord Nigel, *miserably*. There is no place where they can imprison us that he cannot reach with his magic. He can *invade* our minds and drive us *insane* to the point of slaying *each other* or our *own* selves!"

Their fears were quickly stilled. The moment they stepped into the warming light of the sun and the deeper yellow of SaCee's shine, SaCee sensed them and issued her green glow to translate them into pseudo stone. They, and their comrades from the other tunnels, were now beyond harm from Nigel.

An eerie, ululating, cry, swelled up from outside the Citadel.

It grew, louder, quickly.

"Sire," one of the battlement guards called down, "the Elves are charging. Our people are brandishing weapons and farm implements. The men have formed an arc of defense at the forefront of their assemblage. They will be *devastated* by the Elf *archers*, and the rest of our people shall be *slaughtered*!"

"*Dispatch*, us, your Majesty," one of his commanders urged, "we shall not *defeat* the Elves, but we can *delay* them sufficient to allow our people to gain entry into the Citadel, and safety!"

"*Aye*!" his troops agreed, with a great shout of support.

Alaric knew that if he issued this command his soldiers would not hesitate to sacrifice their lives, but he also knew the new-found security which they might gain for the rest of his people, would be temporary, and most of his army would be slain for no true gain.

SaCee's staff increased its spin, and her thick, yellow glow began to creep up the walls of the Citadel. The force flowed over the catwalks and the soldiers like yellow water and spilled on the populace below. It continued, swiftly, toward the semicircle of advancing Elves.

A gray haired commander who strode, resolutely, at the forefront of the Elves, lifted his sword over his head. The army paused, and fell silent.

Alaric was heartened. "Assemble your troops into lines at each side of the gates," he instructed his commanders, "so that they may hasten the passage of our people into the Citadel at my command." He turned to Angela, Aldora, and

Luana. "Gather Inessa and Lara and *hie* you *all* to the Observation Tower where our SaCee can *protect* you," he commanded. "*Your* sole duty, now, *Luana*, is to the *survival* of my *family* and *friends*. Your sub commanders shall be under your Kings *direct* stewardship." He leaped from the dock and ran, with breath taking swiftness, to the front wall of the Citadel. He wended his way through the people huddled there and mounted the access way to the battlements, skipping three stair steps at a time.

"We shall do as our King has commanded," Angela said, firmly. She led everyone down the narrow steps of the loading dock, and they began the long trek to the castle at the heart of the Citadel. Along the way, they waved Inessa and Lara off their loading docks, adding them to their company.

The Royal family was surrounded by fifty guardsmen as they hastened to safety.

Alaric looked down at the scene outside the Citadel. He nodded with satisfaction. In a canny move, the women, children, infirm, and aged had been massed before the gates. They would be first inside.

SaCee's yellow magical glow had stopped three yards from the semicircle of Elves. This ethereal power was why the Elves had ceased their charge.

Alaric turned his attention to Zolazar, the gray haired, Supreme Commander of the Elf army. This was a man of great learning and vast experience in warfare. He had perfected tactics long before Alaric had been sired. Alaric's father had dispatched him to study at the feet of this Elf. Alaric was certain Zolazar had not imparted all of his knowledge to his students. This Supreme Commander, no doubt, had many surprises he could marshal against any foe. Alaric had SaCee, though he was horrified at the thought of what she might do if Zolazar drove her to the defense of Indwin's people. The King desperately hoped Zolazar's knowledge of SaCee's abilities would disrupt the control Nigel held over the Elf.

"This glow which you see before us and which has been dispatched by SaCee," Zolazar told his sub commanders, "is designed to prevent those who are engulfed within it from committing physical harm. Much to my despair, Lord Nigel's nefarious might will do battle with this force on our behalf. It will free us to complete his honor-less scheme of destruction. There will be terrifying sounds and great flashes of light, but we must persevere until we have accomplished his evil and secured the lives and freedom of our children. I *wish* this were not so!"

His sub commanders remained, grimly, silent.

"Prepare your troops with these facts," Zolazar instructed, sadly. "When Lord Nigel engages SaCee's light, this horror shall befall us, and that which we would normally eschew at all costs, will become our compelled goal."

Alaric's enhanced hearing had brought the Supreme Commander's words to his unwilling ears. His heart, physically, ached at the extreme tragedy about to ensue. He threw up a hand and sent signals to his troops on the walls. They passed those orders to the guards at the gates. The towering doors were hauled open with desperate swiftness. Women and children began scrambling into the Citadel at breakneck speed. Soldiers along the gates snatched up the old, the infirm, and the youngest and carried them into the heart of the Citadel. Soldier, after soldier took their place to repeat this life saving task.

Zolazar heard the commotion and spun on his heel. He took in the situation at the gates then looked up at Alaric and shook his head. "This *futile* act gains, *only*, brief delay," he said, sadly, knowing the King could catch his words.

"Do you *fail* to recall what we witnessed, many years ago, when the Southern Demons of Darkness threatened the existence of man and Elf," Alaric said, knowing the Supreme Commander would catch his words, "when SaCee came forth, from her Crystal Clear Mountain, and preserved us?"

Zolazar vented a cry of despair. "Surely, Great King, SaCee will *not* commit this *abhorrent* act? Surely, Great King, you shall *not* command her to commit this *abhorrent* act!"

"What of you, my old friend, and ally," Alaric said, grimly, "shall you *commit* your *abhorrent* act, to save *that*, which you would *wrest* from me?"

They stared at each other with despair.

A roaring wall of gray light sprang from the semicircle of Elves. It passed the sub commanders and the Supreme Commander without harm, but slammed into SaCee's yellow shine. The gray wall vanished as quickly as it had appeared, absorbed into silence by SaCee's force. A moment later, SaCee's yellow light of nonviolence vanished.

The Elf army cheered. Now they could fight for their children.

Alaric and Zolazar groaned.

There was an almost blinding flash and SaCee was standing outside the Citadel in front of the people of Indwin. She dropped her green staff on the grass and raised her arms straight out from her sides. "This single warning shall I issue, Supreme Commander," She said, with despair. Tears streamed down her beautiful, tragic face.

A curtain of black energy, shot through with tiny red orbs, swiftly enveloped SaCee. It flowed around the people of Indwin, then circled the great Citadel until its billowing, ebony ends met outside the center of the rear wall.

The Supreme Commander of the Elves slumped. He turned to his people, and they could sense his hopelessness. Some began to weep. "That which you see before you," Zolazar finally forced himself to say, in a loud and desperate voice, "will not only *strip* us of our *invincibility* and *immortality*, it will *obliterate* us *before* we can deliver a *single* blow for our children!"

"Perhaps the *attempt*, itself, will be *sufficient*, for Lord Nigel to *free* our children to our brethren and *release* our people from his *iron* fist!" one of the sub commanders said, wildly.

"Never, shall, we know," Zolazar said, with a shaky voice. He turned to face SaCee.

A blast of gray force roared from the line of Elves and crashed into SaCee and her curtain of Ethereal Power. Nigel's might was rebuffed backwards. It swirled, like tiny tornadoes, then vanished. Another blast, then another, and another, sprang from the line of hopeful Elves. Each assault was defeated. No further energy blasts emanated from Nigel's disheartened Elves.

Behind his back, Zolazar gestured commands to his Elves. Five hundred archers lifted their crossbows and aimed high into the air. The tips of their arrows glowed blue with intense magical force.

As the archers triggered their crossbows, SaCee flicked her fingers and her curtain of energy became a dome of protection.

The arrows rained on the magical dome, but exploded uselessly, with great peals of thunder, and bright blue lightning.

Zolazar enveloped the blade of his sword with a similar, but, more intense form of the energy his archers had tried to use. He bore down on SaCee, with tears in his eyes. A gray glow swirled around him, and he stopped in his tracks. "*Yes*, Lord!" he shouted, with extreme relief, and unrestrained glee, "I *hear*, and I *obey*! *Try* to forgive *me*, *dear* SaCee," he begged, "as *I* shall *try* to forgive *you*." He spun on his heel. "Our Lord *decrees* that we *return* to him, *posthaste*. He *tasks* us with a *more* vital goal!"

The Supreme Commander sheathed his sword and flicked hand instructions to his sub commanders. They set about forming their soldiers into ranks designed for swift march.

Zolazar was confused. When Nigel had issued his new instructions, he had inadvertently passed along his affection for the Elves. An affection that had been formed when Nigel was a child, and he, Aldora, and Arden, had spent many happy hours exploring the Elf caverns and witnessing their joy for life and their magical feats. But, Nigel had ferociously clamped down on this affection. A sense of personal failure and loathing for himself for being soft and sentimental had swirled out from Nigel's mind. Yet, Lord Nigel had relented in the destruction of the Citadel and the abduction of Princess Aldora.

Experience flooded the Supreme Commander's mind with possibilities to explain this puzzling alteration in Lord Nigel's plans. Zolazar did not find any of those suggestions to be to his liking. His mind also reminded him of that which Lord Nigel had done to their infants and children, King Avery, and Queen Elatiella. Recollection of this travesty drove the Supreme Commander to defiance.

SaCee had not moved, and her dome of energy was still in place.

Zolazar approached her with his palms up and arms outstretched before him in a sign of no threat. "I *pledge*, upon the *precious* lives of our *children*," he told her, "that we shall *not* return, *anon*, to *attempt* surprise. But, I warn you, we are *commanded* to *seek* the King's War Party and to end, *without* mercy, that *threat* to Lord Nigel!"

SaCee's beautiful face was stained with tears. "You shall *never* catch *sight* of the War Party of Indwin," she vowed.

Zolazar was shocked to silence and terror. SaCee never issued a threat unless she followed through. He regretted his defiant betrayal of Nigel's scheme. He screamed a tone that commanded his Elves to scatter in the directions of the compass.

SaCee ended her dome of protection. She drew upon the Ethereal until the Ethereal threatened to abandon her, and flashed forth her green energy. It caught the army of a thousand Elves in its inexorable grasp, before they could heed their Supreme Commanders savvy alarm. The unwilling enemy force was turned into pseudo stone, stilling their panic, fright, and despair.

SaCee's emerald energy vanished, and she collapsed, unconscious, to the trampled grass. The people of Indwin rushed forward. They lifted her, tenderly, in their collective arms, and bore her, with utmost haste, into the Citadel.

King Alaric met his people at the towering gates. He gathered SaCee, lovingly, into his arms, and bore her to the palace. Angela, Aldora, Inessa, Lara and Luana, met him at the entrance to the great receiving hall.

They appeared stricken, to the point of collapse.

"*Swear* to me, that SaCee yet *lives*!" Queen Angela demanded.

"She *clings* to life," Alaric said, with a trembling voice.

"Father, bear SaCee to Lady Lara's chambers," Aldora insisted. "She is well versed in the healing herbs which Galen keeps on hand for when he is not available. Lady Lara and I can ward over SaCee throughout the night, and tend to her needs."

One of the men who had been outside the walls of the Citadel, knelt on one knee, tugged on Alaric's sleeve, and held up SaCee's green staff. "Beg pardon, Sire," he said, nervously, "I thought it best that our Lady SaCee's staff be under my King's protection."

"You are a wise, and honorable man," Alaric said.

Inessa remembered something Durward had explained, many years past. "Place the staff in our Lady SaCee's hand," she ordered the man.

The man looked to his King.

"Do as, Lady Inessa, requests," Alaric said.

The man was trembling so much with nervousness he nearly dropped the staff, but managed to gently open SaCee's pale hand and press the mid part of the staff against her palm.

SaCee grasped the cool green stone and her white light shone forth from deep within her. Her eyes flew open and her normal serenity replaced everyone's tears with calm.

Alaric released SaCee to her feet. The King knelt, as did all those assembled. A great cheer of relief, joy, and celebration issued from the people of Indwin.

SaCee was so embarrassed by the love and gratitude that she flashed up to the Observation Tower and resumed her ever vigilant station.

Illustration 03

City: East Inner Wall Ornamentation: Landscape Orientation

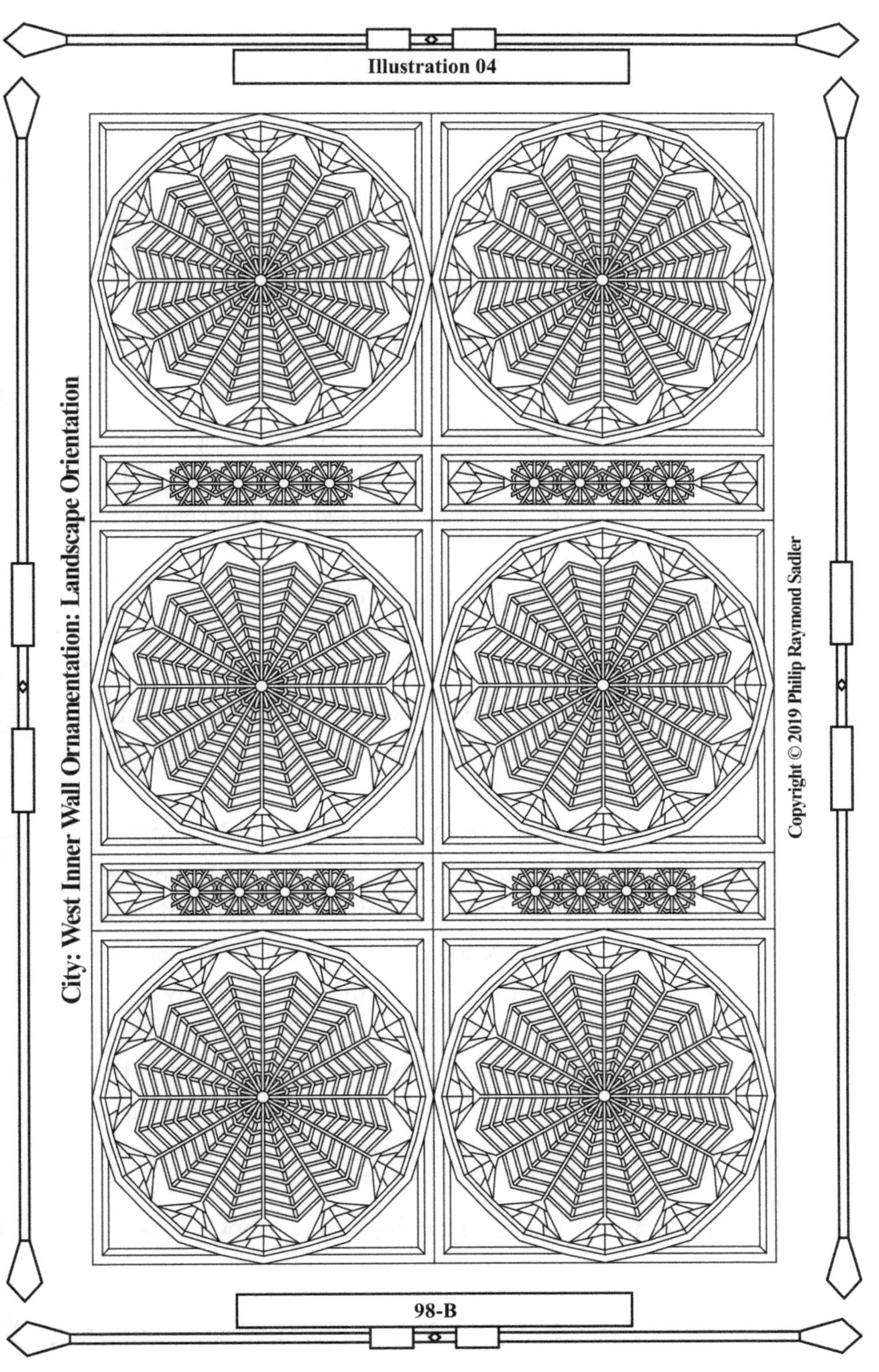
Illustration 04
City: West Inner Wall Ornamentation: Landscape Orientation
Copyright © 2019 Philip Raymond Sadler
98-B

Chapter 2
The River of Stones

Arden's War Party sighted the petrified River at noon. It glistened like blue ice under the sulfur sun. The horses became more nervous the closer the questers approached the unnatural sight.

There was an eerie tingling in the air.

An electricity.

A foreboding.

The War Party slowed their mounts and skirted the quarry where the pink marble for the Citadel and the Castle was hewn. They dismounted.

The River was only ten yards across, but it would be difficult to ford in its present unholy state. The waves had become sharp thrusts of blue granite. They were thick together, with hardly space for the hooves of the horses. The questers would have to lead their mounts carefully.

"The height of these swells is not natural for a body of water of this size, even had they been formed during the gales of the spring storms," Durward said. "Nigel must have seethed them with his Mind Magic before he translated the River to stone."

"The country folk reported that Aubrey showed them a

path across this River," Arden recalled. "Two of you, scout left for this path, two right," he ordered the guards. "How can we *end* this spell, Durward."

"We must seek a focal point," Durward said. "Destroy that, and the energy is released into the air. If there is no focal point, then, this Enchantment will end only when—when my son wills it."

"Arden!" Guthrie said.

The two left guards were returning at a gallop. They reined in, and one of them leaped from his saddle.

"Report, Ryley," Guthrie said.

"There is, indeed, a smooth path on the River," Ryley said, excitedly. "We could spy all the way across. Not even the weird shadow of a rock wave blocks the trail!"

"Lead the way," Arden said. He mounted with the War Party, and they followed the soldiers along the bank of the River. The right guards caught up with the questers and trailed along.

When they passed the quarry, Wayte and Riley halted their mounts and pointed.

"Is that not an *excellent* path," Wayte said.

"I might even *pay* for the *privilege* of *using* it," Arden said.

The War Party laughed, and dismounted.

"Tend the mounts, Hilliard," Guthrie told that guard.

Although the River was petrified, it still looked liquid.

Dubious, Arden stepped onto the stoned water. He looked left and right at the confusion caused by the varied angles and heights of the stone swells. "There could be Elves anywhere behind these waves, or in their shadows," he told Guthrie. The Crown Prince Designate motioned the three scouts onto the River path. "Be *alert* as you cross," he admonished.

The reluctant soldiers ventured onto the slick rock. They checked all the swells and shadows they could without cutting themselves on the tall, sharp, curved stone projections.

"This seems *too* fortuitous a passage," Durward said, thoughtfully.

"But, what *more* should Nigel do, *here*, with the fire wall *blocking* us from him?" Galen asked.

"Call the guards back, Guthrie," Arden said. "We are *overly* cautious and *waste* time. We shall *ride* across."

"Scouts, ho!" Guthrie shouted. "Return to party! And be—"

The Knight's message was interrupted by the unnerving sounds of stone squeaking, cracking, and crunching.

The startled guards spun on their heels and made haste toward the bank, and Arden's War Party. The unobstructed pathway turned soft and drew downward in a square, trapping the frightened soldiers inside a pit from which they could not clamber. They were unharmed, for now.

A section of the waves to the right of the pit, and in the center of the River, shook side to side, then raised into the air.

"The Enchantment protects itself with a golem of stone!" Durward said, with astonishment.

The, huge, blue humanoid was covered with razor sharp projections. It took one lumbering step toward the guards.

Swells shattered to slivers under its massive foot. "I *am* the *Enchantment*," the creature said, like two rocks clicking together. "*Calder* is *invincible*! *This* is *my* realm," it said, of the River.

"Circle it!" Arden said. "Draw it away from the pit!"

Calder laughed, like pebbles clattering over tiles. "*Calder* is no *fool*," it said.

Durward took Arden's arm and whispered, "We can not move quickly enough on the River to be effective. We *must* draw Calder *onto* the land."

"And *then*," Guthrie said, "*how* can we *fight* it?"

"There is only *utter* defeat or *total* surrender," Calder said, in response to Guthrie's question. "Calder is *unconquerable*!" It bent down, snatched up, and threw a piece of rock wave at Arden.

The Crown Prince ducked, barely in time.

Calder laughed. "Nigel shall soon be pleased with me," it said. The monster reached one hand toward the scouts.

They shrank back and drew their swords to offer as much defiance as possible.

The golem touched the edge of the pit and the stone water grew over the guards, enclosing them, except for a small air hole. "Calder *will* show you the *inside* of *your* heart, *now*," the creature said, to Arden, "*and*, I *will* give your *head* to Nigel." It took a lumbering step. More of the swells shattered. Calder kicked the shards, and they sailed at Arden and the War Party.

Durward went down with a sliver in his shoulder.

Galen ran to the Magician, smoothly withdrew the

shard, and healed the wound by laying on of hands.

Durward repaired the tear in his tunic by Psychic Welding.

Calder laughed, derisively. It kicked, sending blue waves sailing into the air.

Arden dodged a wave, and drew his blade.

The battle horses spooked, pulled their reigns free of the over matched guardsman, and raced toward the Wind Barrier Forest and the distant, unseen, Citadel.

Calder advanced onto the land.

The War Party drew their swords and loosely surrounded the golem.

Calder was moving quickly, trying to catch hold of the Crown Prince Designate.

As he retreated, Arden rang blow after blow with his keen blade. White sparks flew, but only tiny chips of Calder were severed.

The others realized Nigel had instructed the titan to slay Arden, first, and they sought ways to protect him.

Durward directed psychokinetic blows at the monster.

Calder soaked up this power that would have sent a human being flying for several feet.

Durward blasted red heat energy, from before his fingertips, at Calder's head. This wreaked no harm. He smote the beast with white, cold force.

Calder laughed, sardonically, and continued chasing Arden.

Durward was forced to resort to his blade. "It *feasts* on my *energy*!" he shouted. "We must *defeat* it with our *wits*!"

"Then, *you,* truly, are, *weapon-less*," Calder crowed.

Guthrie and his guardsman alternated in conducting savage attacks on the monster, but they failed to slow it down.

Calder swiped.

Arden's sword flew over his head.

Guthrie tossed his blade to Arden.

The ugly titan knocked the sword away.

"Free your comrades!" Arden ordered the fourth soldier. "*Break* the stone covering them!"

Calder laughed, with cruel delight. "*Only* mighty *Calder* can *liberate* those *cowering* mice," it said. "*After* you *and* your War Party are *extinct,* so they might sing *praises* to Nigel's name!" The golem increased its pace, running after Arden.

The Crown Prince Designate turned around, took in the lay of the land, then fled back toward the Wind Barrier Forest.

Calder laughed, like pebbles clattering over tiles. "The *brave* one *deserts* in *characteristic* terror!" it said. "He will not *fear* for *long*!"

Guthrie and Galen followed closely after Calder.

Galen jammed his sword between the beast's legs, but the blade snapped.

Calder slid to a stop, and swiped.

Guthrie was sent rolling across the grass, bleeding from cuts on his chest.

Galen raced to the Knight and healed the wounds.

Durward psychically tossed Arden's sword to him.

Calder slapped it out of the air.

Durward repaired Guthrie's tunic and Galen's sword with mental energy.

Calder resumed its assault on the Crown Prince Designate.

Arden was perched on a boulder in front of the quarry. There was a sheer drop behind him, and no escape to his left or right. Calder blocked the path before him.

Calder laughed, with vicious triumph. "Nigel will *enjoy* your *weak* head as a *trophy*," it said, like stones clicking together. "It will be so *easy*. Just a *twist*, and it is *his*!" It reached for the Crown Prince Designate.

Arden dodged back faster than the golem could move its heavy, flinty hands.

Calder stepped closer to the boulder and leaned toward Arden.

Galen attacked the beast with his sword.

Calder ignored the Healer.

Arden kicked at the monster's eyes, but they were unfeeling rock.

Durward tried his mental energy again. This time, he directed the psychokinesis at the earth beneath Calder's feet. Durward growled in frustration. He could not force the dirt to move. Calder still soaked up the Magician's mind power in some mysterious fashion.

Calder stretched its arms to their limits and took hold of Arden's tunic. It tugged, a little too hard.

Arden flew off the boulder and over Calder's head,

to land on his feet, unharmed.

Guthrie saw his opportunity. He concentrated, calling on his Birth Trick. His form wavered, and he transformed into a huge, red serpent. His clothes and sword became part of its thick, hard scales. Darker red triangles marked the length of its back.

The War Serpent flashed at Calder, wound itself around the massive creature's sharp legs, and began drawing the monster's feet together.

Calder tried to kick.

War Serpent would not snap like the rigid sword blade.

Calder teetered, as its balance was threatened, and brought a fist down on the Snake.

War Serpent jerked in pain, but did not loosen its grip.

Calder delivered another blow.

War Serpent lost its hold, for a moment.

Calder lifted a foot free, but this, it realized, was a grave mistake.

War Serpent tightened around Calder's other ankle and wrapped itself about a spur of rock that projected from the side of the boulder on which Arden had stood. The Snake heaved with all its might.

Calder's foot slid out from under it and the golem pitched over the boulder, and the lip of the quarry.

The Snake went limp, releasing the Enchantment's ankle, then drew itself to safety, using the stone spur.

Calder crashed into several outcroppings before it shattered to dust on the floor of the quarry, a strange blue, mar, on the pink marble.

Galen went to the War Serpent and applied healing hands to the cuts and gashes Calder had caused. When the wounds were mended, without scars, the Snake's form wavered, and became Guthrie.

"Arden!" Hilliard called. "Come, quickly! I cannot burst this stone!"

"This is terrible," Durward said. "The *crops* and the *River* should have *returned* to *normal* when Calder *died*. Calder *should* have *been* the *focal* point. Nigel *must* be able to maintain *this* Enchantment *without* one. *Only* his *defeat* or *death* will end it. *And*, we *still* are *under* the time *limit* to reach him."

"Try *striking* the *breathing* hole," Arden told the scout.

"I have," Hilliard said, with frustration. "But, it cedes only chips."

Arden drew his sword and smashed the blade into the air hole with all his strength. The sword rang, but the opening was little changed. He took his gauntlets from his belt, slipped them on, and used the sword like a hammer, slamming the hilt against the hole. The blade slid from his hands and clattered across the stone water.

The opening was little altered.

"I will have to try *my* might to free our men from this section of the magic rock," Durward said. He placed his fingers to his temples and delivered invisible force blows against the stone around the small opening. There was no effect on the blue rock, nor any sounds from the mighty energy impacts, although they should have rung throughout the area.

"This magical rock *soaks* up my battering ram force," Durward said, with frustration, "*just* as Calder *did*. I shall attempt *other* ways. We must all stand back," he said. "Can you guards hear me?"

"Yes," Wayte said, through the breathing aperture. His voice betrayed fear.

"Stay as far away from the opening as possible," Durward said. "Turn your backs to it to protect yourselves. There will be great heat. Warn me if any of you are burned, and I shall stop."

"You may depend upon it, sir!" Wayte said. "We're ready!"

Durward followed the War Party to the shore. He motioned them further back, but remained at the bank. His hands trembled as he held them toward the River. Red energy crackled from before his fingertips and speared into the breathing hole. Black smoke columned into the azure sky, obscuring the opening.

Durward paused. When the smoke cleared, the hopeful War Party was disappointed. The aperture was still too small to allow the guards to exit.

"Are you men still sound?" Durward shouted.

"Yes," the scouts chorused.

"Can you let the smoke clear out, before you try again?" Wayte added.

"Indeed," Durward assured.

Thick curls of smoke began rising from the air circle. The guards were fanning their hands inside the pit to hurry the fumes. The puffs decreased, then ceased.

"We're ready!" Wayte shouted.

"I shall heat the stone anew," Durward shouted to the scouts and War Party, "then blast it with freezing energy! The extremes should induce it to shatter!"

The Magician closed his eyes, and appeared strained. He sighted on the breathing aperture and his red energy seared from before his fingertips. The ebony smoke billowed more thickly this time. A slight breeze, emanating from Durward, prevented the choking fumes from obscuring or entering the opening.

The blue stone slowly turned red. The aperture did not grow noticeably larger, but the cherry radiance increased in girth.

Durward ceased the heat energy, and struck the sizzling rock with white cold force. Great streams of milky mist, columned into the sky. Durward's breeze kept the air circle clear. He increased the coldness, and the mist transformed into snowflakes. The energy failed, and Durward collapsed to the emerald grass.

The breathing hole was no larger.

Galen placed his hands against Durward's temples to revitalized him.

The Magician's pale and haggard face regained color and he came awake.

"I *fear* the rock will *require* grater *effort* than you can *muster*," Galen said.

"Yes," Durward agreed, as he stood up. "Thankfully, it is not *absorbing* the *hot* and *cold* power as did Calder. It will probably *succumb* with *both* of us *supplying* the energy."

"Arden!" Wayte shouted.

Arden ventured close to the breathing hole. "Are you injured?" he said.

"*No,*" Wayte said. "We're *afraid.* This Enchanted Water's too hard for Durward, isn't it?"

"He was just *tired*, and Galen *has* re-energized him. They are going to *join* forces. They *will* free you, *this* time. Do not *fret*."

"Arden?" Wayte said.

"Yes?"

"*Continue* against Nigel. The people *must* not be *harmed* because of *us*. *We* will be all *right*. This River will become *water* again when Nigel's *defeated*, won't it? We can *swim* to shore, *then*."

"It may well be *days* before we can *defeat* the Dark Wizard," Arden said. "You would *die*, for we cannot pass, either *water* or *food* through this *opening*, to sustain you until *then*."

"We have *vowed* to *surrender* our *lives* for the *preservation* of the populace and the Kingdom," a resolute voice said. "If *this* be the *appointed* time, then, so it *shall* be."

"*Aye*, well said, Zadok," Wayte and Ryley said to their companion.

"I envy your courage and selflessness," Arden said, "but, we *will* destroy this bit of Nigel's evil, soon, and free you."

"Arden!" Guthrie called.

"Durward is ready to try again," Arden said. "I *must* stand back."

"Arden?" Wayte said.

"Yes?" Arden said. He stepped closer to the opening to hear better. The tremendous heat, and the severe cold, had weakened the accursed stone more than Galen and Durward had estimated, making it brittle. It shattered under Arden's weight, and he tumbled into the pit, in an ungainly fashion.

Wayte broke Arden's fall, and they both sprawled on the floor.

Guthrie, Galen, Durward, and Hilliard, rushed to the edge of the pit, and helped their companions climb out of the hard, blue trap.

Durward telepathically calmed their hiding steeds and coaxed them to return to the War Party.

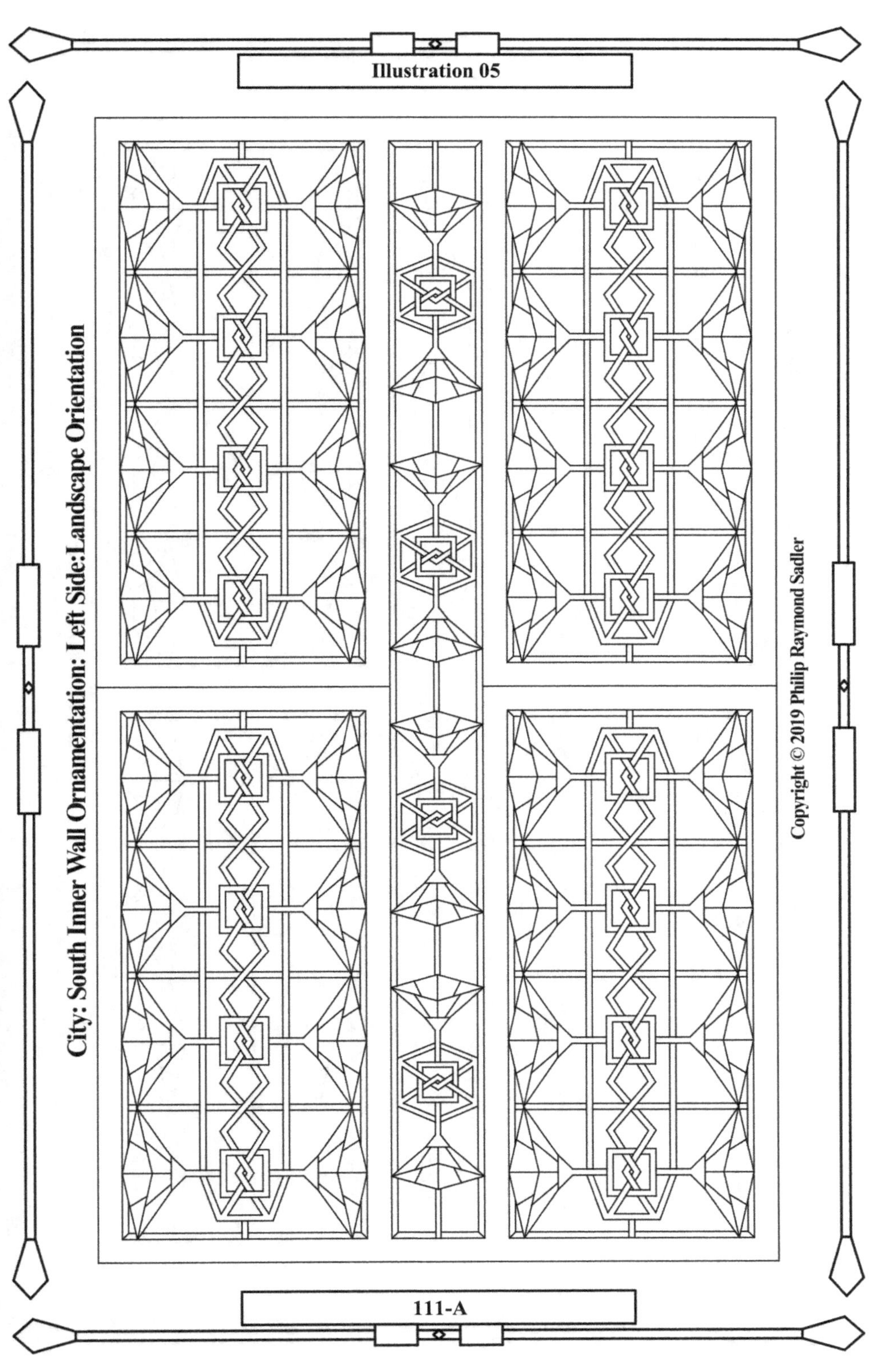
Illustration 05
City: South Inner Wall Ornamentation: Left Side:Landscape Orientation
Copyright © 2019 Philip Raymond Sadler
111-A

Illustration 06

City: South Inner Wall Ornamentation: Right Side: Landscape Orientation

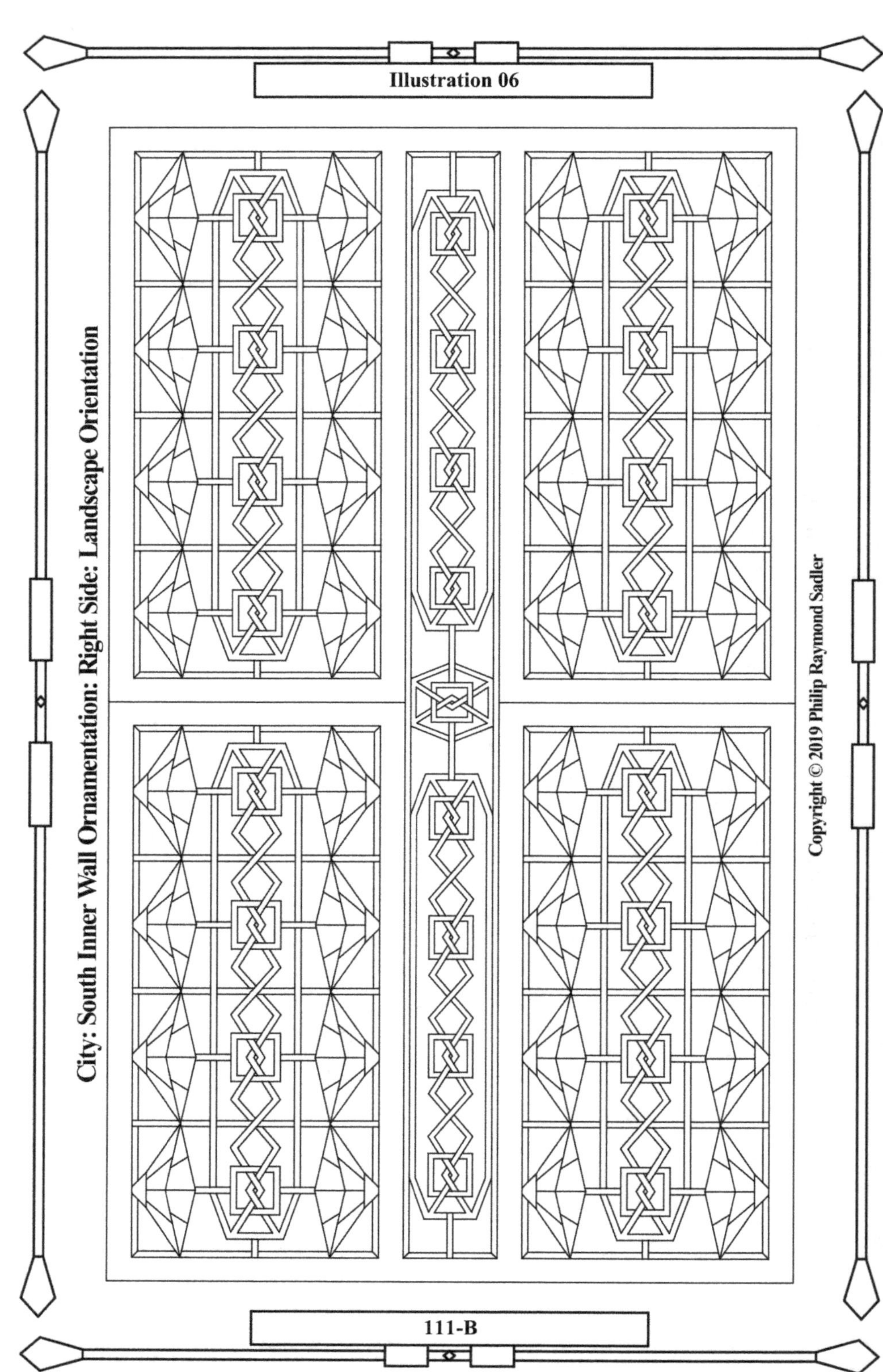

Chapter 3
A Fire in the Hills

The crimson afternoon sun paled in contrast to the fire overwhelming the Windy Hills Orchards. It burned from the West Shield to the East Shield Mountain Ranges, and the party could detect no break within it. The inferno seemed to flame almost as high as the scattered wisps of white clouds affixed in the sapphire sky. It resembled more of an upwards rolling wall of red light, than a fire. The charred trees and the ash covered earth of the Orchards looked nightmarish beneath the flickering bloody flames. Unlike a normal raging fire, which roared and crackled with burning vegetation, this magical conflagration was silent and issued no smoke or odor. Nor did the War Party feel heat until they left the last of the Farmlands and reined to a halt on a meadow that led a hundred feet to the fire wall. The warmth the flames cast was not uncomfortable. A real fire of such magnitude would have soaked them with sweat and singed their hair.

"May the *compassionate* side of the Ethereal, *preserve* us!" Arden said. "Is there no *end* to the occult Enhancer that Nigel uses? *How* can he continue directing *such* energies?"

"Once Nigel fashions the Enchantment," Durward said,

"his subconscious mind channels the power necessary to maintain the form of the curse for as long as he has need of the Enchantment. But, each Enchantment *must* be of limited scope, even *with* the Enhancer, or we could not have *broken* Calder, and *all* of Indwin would be in flames, not *just* the Hills."

"And, if it is, indeed, limited," Galen said, "it can be passed beyond, or undone. Perhaps, more swiftly, than we had hoped."

"Yes," Durward said. "We do not know whether Nigel is aware that we have defeated Calder," he added, "and SaCee has said that he has erected three other Enchantments between the Hills and the Gray fort, to impede our advance. *If* we can vanquish each of these as swiftly as we did Calder, we might have a chance of defeating Nigel quickly enough to save our people from starvation."

"What plan have you for *this* Enchantment?" Arden asked. He dismounted with the others.

A guard took the horses further back from the wall of psychic fire.

"For all of my life I have sought to discover an enhancer," Durward said. "I have failed. But, I still have my ways." He raised his hands, chest height, and cupped them. A wetness filled the warm air and a jet of water spewed from the Magician's hands. It cut into the flame barrier, but was blasted, instantly, into steam. "May the All revoke Nigel's life!" Durward said, softly. He angrily closed his eyes and held his arms out before himself, hands clenched. He trembled, and a jet of water flowed from before each fist. They flooded into the fire, but were turned to steam and ejected into the air above the War Party. He emitted two beams of cold. Their icy mist drove into the flames, then was seared to steam, as useless as the water. "Galen," Durward said, "join with me!"

Directly ahead of the Magician, the wall of fire swirled into the shape of an archway. A tunnel, the inside of which had the appearance of solid red glass, formed. No tongues of fire flickered within. The questers could see the greenness of the land beyond the charred Orchards.

"The Orchard workers and farmers spoke of Nigel opening such a pathway for them," Guthrie recalled.

"Do you suppose *Nigel* awaits us at tunnel's *end*?" Arden suggested.

"This *is* more likely a *trick* of whatever *guards* this place," Durward said.

"*Inane*, at best," Galen observed. "*Nigel* and *it* must know that we would *never* set foot inside *this* passage."

The oval tunnel filled with fire, causing a great rushing of hot air. Though nothing could live within the hell incinerating the Windy Hills, something moved inside the flames.

"The Enchantment nears to defend its domain," Durward warned. He retreated with the War Party to where the horses were being held.

The motion in the massive blaze became more distinct. A portion of the wall of fire bulged outward. It slowly assumed the shape of a man. A thick beam of flame was attached to its back, keeping it a part of the inferno, but granting it some freedom of movement.

Durward cautiously approached the Enchantment and lifted his arms toward the holocaust.

Galen placed his palms, from behind, to Durward's temples.

The cerise man of fire rushed forward and smashed a huge flaming hand against Durward's side.

The Magician flew to his left, hit the ground, and rolled across the withered grass.

Galen dodged the fire man's second swipe and retreated to balm Durward's wound.

"Distraction!" Arden shouted. He drew his sword and sliced at the flame man's wrist. The blade passed through as though it had contacted nothing.

"It was *good* to *burn* the magic *one*," the man of fire said, like twigs crackling in a fireplace, "but, to *sear* Arden will be a *great* pleasure. Brendan *will* char *you, slowly*. Your *screams* will *delight* Nigel and be a *joy* to me. Nigel will *laugh* when he hears of it!" It roared through the air at Arden, catching him in its large, blazing hands.

Arden screamed, then fell unconscious from pain.

Guthrie realized the fiery monster could make itself solid or insubstantial at will. Now, in order to hold Arden, the fire man was more solid than not. Guthrie ran and leaped, kicking the flaring arms with both feet. Arden was sent flying free to fall limply to the grass but Guthrie's feet became snared within one arm of the Enchantment. He dangled helplessly.

The golem swung its flaming arm back and forth, laughing cruelly, like hot coals snapping.

Durward's side injury mended. Galen aided him to stand up, then ran to Arden, dragged him to safety near the horses, and commenced healing the deep burns on Arden's sides.

Durward lifted his arms and flooded Guthrie with beams of icy water.

The Enchantment cried out like an animal in pain, and dropped Guthrie to the grass. The golem flared, and the water boiled away to steam as it impacted.

Durward halted his efforts.

"Brendan *is* stronger, *now*," Brendan said. "*Hotter*, too. Your *coldest* water, is *nothing* to me, *now*." It leaped forward, aiming to grasp Durward.

The four guardsmen hove their blades simultaneously against Brendan's chest with all their muscle and will power.

The unexpected strength of the blows forced Brendan off balance and the golem stumbled backwards into the obscurity of the wall of fire.

Durward and the scouts bore Guthrie to where Galen was healing Arden. Guthrie's boots were burned off and his feet were charred. He was unconscious from the agony.

"Arden is seriously damaged, also," Galen said. "I must balm them both, and, with haste. Your power is required to boost me."

Durward placed his hands to Galen's temples. "Watch Brendan," he ordered the guards. "But, remain clear of it."

Brendan emerged from the wall of red flame. The monster was straining toward the War Party but the beam of flame attaching it to the barrier proved incapable of stretching far enough beyond the Hills.

"Brendan's own magic tethers it from us," Zadok said.

"Good," Durward said. "Now, hold silence, while we concentrate."

Galen had gingerly removed Arden's burned tunic. He was alternately touching Arden's seared sides. He had also facilely pried away the remains of Guthrie's boots and was brushing the fingertips of his other hand against each of the Knight's feet.

"I fear that Guthrie is *too* injured to *mend*, Durward," Galen said. "If he could *metamorphose* to War Serpent, the burns would be relocated to his thick *scales*, and he would have a *better* chance."

"Guard," Durward said, "cup your hands beneath my forehead."

Wayte did so.

Water spewed from Durward's scalp, filling the guard's hands.

"Douse Guthrie with it," Durward instructed. "*Have* him *become* the War Serpent. *Make* him *do* it!"

Wayte complied.

Guthrie stirred.

Wayte whispered, insistently, into the Knight's ear.

Guthrie groaned, but transformed into the War Serpent. The red scales of its tail were blackened, but not as badly damaged as the flesh on his feet had been.

Galen applied both hands to Arden.

The Crown Prince's skin was renewing itself swiftly. From black, to gray, to white, to the pink of new flesh.

Then, it was as if the skin had never been injured.

"You may disconnect, now, Durward," Galen said. "I can balm War Serpent, alone."

Arden awoke with a start. He stared at his sides, then at the Snake.

The scales were regaining their bright, crimson shine.

Arden stood up and fetched a tunic from his saddlebags. After slipping it on, he picked out a tunic from Durward's saddlebags and handed it to the Magician. Arden checked on Brendan, saw that the strutting fiery foulness could not reach them, and hastened to Guthrie.

The Knight was in human form; his feet healed without scars. He was pulling on a pair of boots that Durward had psychically molded from one of Guthrie's saddlebags.

"This wall of occult fire requires vastly more energy than did the stoning of the River," Durward said. "So, unlike the River Enchantment, this Enchantment *should* vanish when Brendan *dies*. I cannot produce the cold or water long enough to contest the entire fire. So, I shall try a variation of my tricks. It *should* rid us of *both* Brendan *and* the wall of flames. Will you and the guards divert Brendan? Keep its back to what Galen and I will be doing?"

Arden and Guthrie took the soldiers a few yards to the left and began swiping at Brendan with their blades. The demon flashed around, attempting to sear them. They dodged, constantly, as in a game of tag, shouting insults at the monster.

Arden performed a canny blow, but the sword passed harmlessly through Brendan's neck. On a man, the head would have been severed, and the life ended.

Guthrie hacked at the beam of fire holding Brendan connected to the barrier of flame. The Knight was hoping a break in the beam might kill the creature but his blade shot through with no effect.

Galen reached around and put his hands to the Magician's temples. Durward raised his fists. This time, his psychic power silently ripped into the earth. The dislodged dirt was placed into a pile to the right side of the pit he formed behind Brendan. The excavation was soon twelve feet deep and six feet long and wide. When he was satisfied with his work, Durward motioned Galen away. "*Slow* and incompetent *dolt*!" Durward shouted, with disgust, causing his words to sound as though he were standing just behind the golem. "A *shadow* can defeat *you*!"

Brendan snarled like lava sputtering into water. It spun around in insulted rage, teetered on the edge of the hole, then fell in with a whoosh!

Galen dashed to Durward and placed his hands against the Magician's temples. Durward caused the piled dirt to flood into the pit like water into a basin.

Brendan screamed in terror. It wildly tried to haul itself out of the prepared grave by using the fire beam as a rope, but the earth covered it and the beam broke with an explosive sound. The wall of flame vanished more fleetly than the eye could blink, surrendering to dusk its rightful preeminence over the ravaged ashen land.

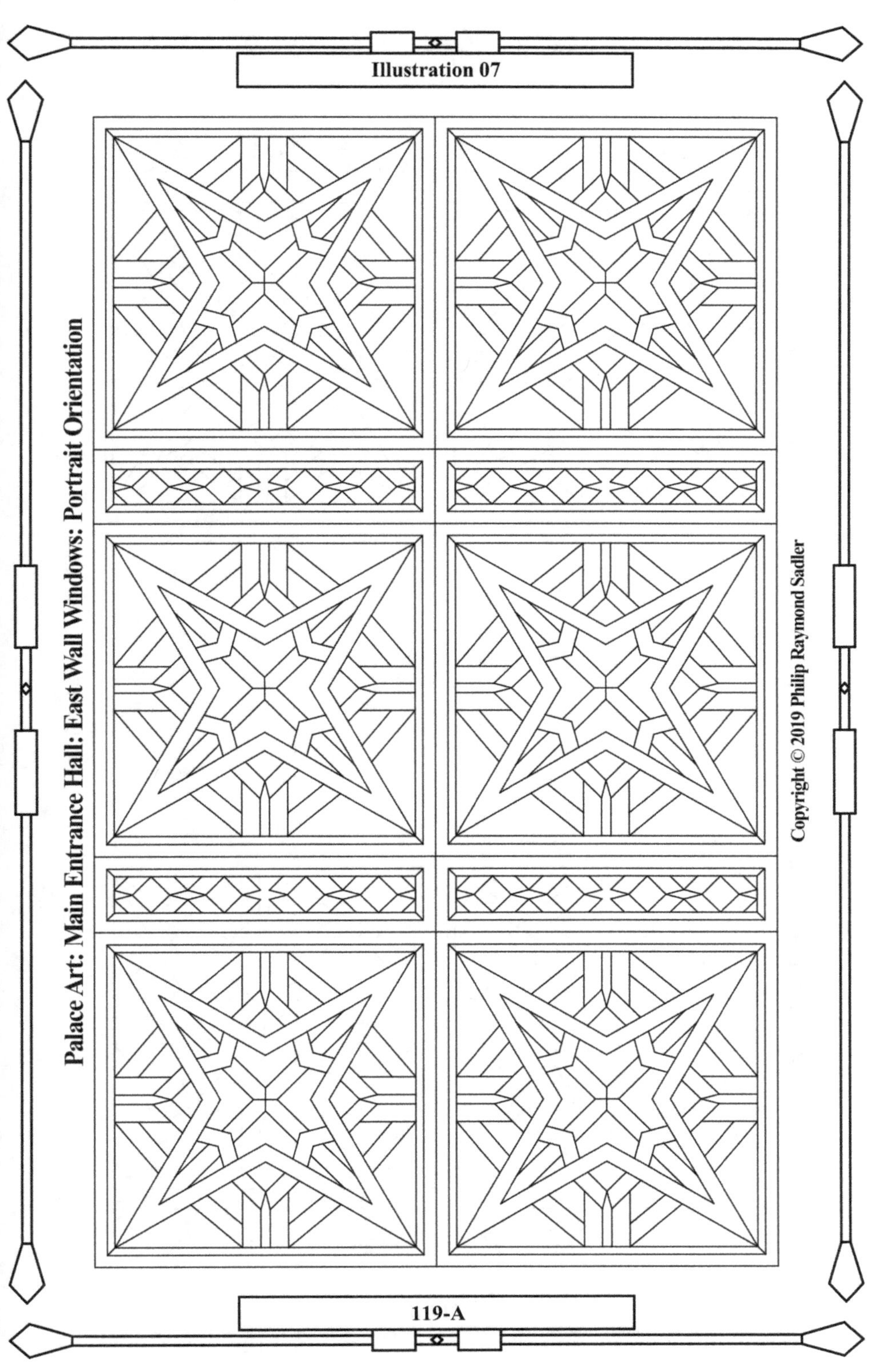
Illustration 07
Palace Art: Main Entrance Hall: East Wall Windows: Portrait Orientation
Copyright © 2019 Philip Raymond Sadler
119-A

Illustration 08

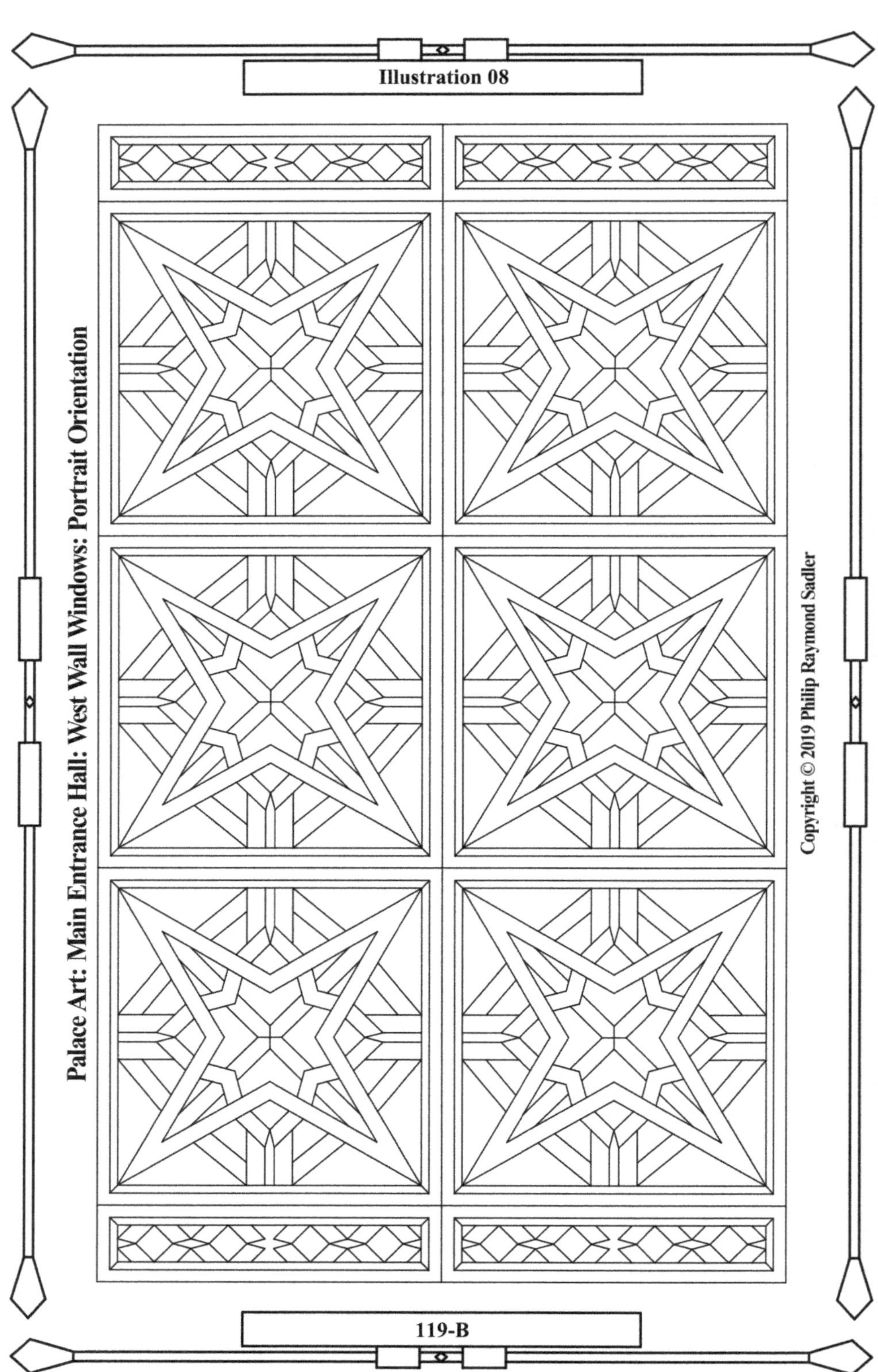

Chapter 4
The Sands of the Beach

"There is Draylon Lake," Guthrie said.

Arden nodded. He was relieved to be leaving the glum, charred Orchards behind. He had been uneasy all morning. Even decamping had not dispelled the mood. But, the gleaming Lake did. It lay from the West Shield to the East Shield Mountain Ranges. It was five miles wide and there was no fording it except by ferry. The happy noon sun danced silver reflections off the emerald waves that gently broke the surface waters.

The horses did not strain at their reins for a drink of the cold green water. They could smell the heavy metal poisons which washed down from the East Shield Mountains, keeping the great lake polluted, lifeless, and mostly useless to Man, Elf and animal for thousands of years.

Only the ferry men derived benefit from the lake. They earned their living by transporting Man and Elf back and forth to trade handmade goods and foodstuffs for the precious metals and gems the Elves mined.

The ferry boats, large and square, with tall railings and gates, were beached on the near side as usual. The loud, friendly, ferry men were nowhere in sight. Their weathered gray hut was open and deserted.

"Nigel, no doubt, terrified the ferrymen into fleeing to the Citadel," Galen observed.

"We can perform their toil," Arden said.

They dismounted at the perimeter of the wide sandy beach.

"Soldiers, free the right-hand ferry," Arden said. "We will prepare the other."

"Listen!" Durward said.

The War Party paused. A warning from Durward was never ignored. They stood on the grass at the lip of the beach and concentrated.

To Arden, there was only the breeze and the lapping of the tiny waves against the ancient stones and worn shells which lay at the edge of the water. Then, he detected Durward's, faint, strange sound.

It was a movement in the sand. No, it *was* the sand. The top layer was sliding toward the center of the beach directly in front of them.

"Back!" Durward said. "Nigel has his *third* Enchantment here!"

The sand began leaping into a heap in the middle of the beach. Soon, it sculpted itself into the shape of a humanoid.

"First stone," Arden said, "then fire. Now sand." He drew his blade and advanced on the man of sand.

"*You* challenge *Sanborn*?" it said, like rough, dried corn husks rubbing together. "Then, *suffer* his skills!"

A ball of sand the size of a horse's head flashed up from the beach and smashed into Arden's chest, knocking him flat of his back. Like a blanket, the sand began to flow over the Crown Prince Designate. Arden scrambled to his feet and retreated to the War Party.

Sanborn laughed, like corn husks ripping. A ball of sand the size of a man's fist leaped up from the beach but fell short of its target and burst into grains where the grass began.

"As with Calder and Brendan, Sanborn fights limits," Durward said. He assailed the creature of sand with water from one fist and cold from the other.

Sanborn was encased in green ice until the rime was several inches thick.

"That will imprison it until we have traversed the Lake," the Magician said. "Sanborn will perish when Nigel is defeated."

"To the ferries," Arden said, leading the War Party onto the sand.

The beach laughed. Sanborn had flowed into the sand, leaving a thin layer of its grainy substance inside the ice-trap to deceive the enemy. Orbs of sand flashed up at each man and mount. The horses spooked and fled the beach. Arden and Galen were slammed onto their backs, and the live sand flowed over them. The guards were pelted by hundreds of small, hurtful, sand balls. They were forced to retreat after the terrified steeds.

Durward dispatched his psychic beams into the sand, dragging it away from Arden and Galen.

Sanborn raised up from the beach, to its waist, clasped its huge hands together, and landed a blow to Durward's chest.

The Magician staggered, backwards, toward the grass.

Guthrie thrust his sword into Sanborn, but could not wrest it free of the monster's burly chest.

Arden and Galen sliced at the creature, but their blades grated through or bounced off. Sanborn possessed Brendan's ability to wax solid or shifting at whim. Tendrils of sand snaked up from the beach and entwined the legs of the four men.

Durward crushed the tentacles with psychic blows, and delivered, angry, invisible strikes to the chest of the sand humanoid. They wrought no injury.

Sanborn impelled more sand orbs to bruise the men.

The War Party was forced, backwards, to the grass and out of the sand monster's reach.

Sanborn rose up to its full height and approached them. "Nigel *commands* that Arden *must* be *slain*," it said, "and, *Durward* must *not* cross the old lake. Sanborn *will* obey. Sanborn, is, unlike *ignorant* Calder, and, *naive* Brendan, truly *invincible*."

Durward smote the beast with heat beams.

Sanborn flowed, unharmed, into the beach.

The Knight's sword fell free. Guthrie snatched the blade up and sheathed it.

The beach laughed. All along it, both ways, for as far as the War Party could see, balls of sand popped into the air and sand tendrils waved.

"Damn!" Durward muttered. "This beach tracts to

both mountain ranges. It would require two weeks to fuse it all. If we can not *devise* defeat for Sanborn, we *are* stopped!"

"Have you mastered levitation, yet, Durward?" Galen asked.

"Yes, but I am not yet powerful enough to lift Sanborn," Durward said.

"Sanborn would *perish* if you kept it from *contact* with the *beach*?" Arden asked.

"I think so," Durward said.

The beach fell motionless, as if its magic life had failed. Although it was merged flat, Sanborn was listening to and watching the War Party.

"Soldiers, bring your saddle blankets," Arden said, excitedly. "Durward, can you attach them, with energy, into one large blanket?"

Durward nodded.

The blankets were placed flat on the grass.

Durward melded their sides together using psychic force.

"Grasp the edges," Arden said, "but, leave the front for me. Can you stiffen that side, Durward?"

The Magician nodded, and closed his eyes. The front of the blanket drew taut, then became as hard as stone.

"On my command, scoop Sanborn up," Arden whispered to the soldiers, "and do not allow it to touch the beach again."

They indicated understanding.

Guthrie smiled. His son was operating on intelligence

rather than his usual emotionalism.

Arden drew his sword and ran onto the cursed beach, circling the center of the area where Sanborn had first grown to sham manhood. Arden dared not stand still. The sand tendrils were already coiling up to trip him and big balls of sand were hurtling at his chest and face. Arden easily leaped over the tentacles, but the orbs were hitting their mark, staggering him to and fro.

Sanborn heaved up from the beach. "You *imagine* to *trick* Sanborn?" it said, derisively. "You deceive, *only*, your *ninny* self!"

The beach fell still.

Sanborn erected a wall of sand between Arden and the War Party.

Arden started to circle this barrier. Another wall cut him off. The only free routes were to the Lake, or Sanborn. Arden designed for the Lake.

Sanborn blocked the escape route with a third sand wall.

Arden was closed off by a lean-to like structure. He charged at Sanborn, feigning a strike, then rolled side to side between the monster's legs, out of the structure, and came up to his knees.

Sanborn turned around, hardened a foot, and raised it to stamp on the Crown Prince Designate.

"Now!" Arden shouted to the War Party. He jabbed his sword into Sanborn's sole and shoved up with both arms and all the muscles in his torso.

Sanborn teetered backwards and his walls crumbled.

Just as the golem went limp to merge itself with the safety of its beach, the hardened edge of the blanket was thrust under it and Sanborn collapsed into the jury rigged bag.

Arden discarded his sword, took hold of the front end of the blanket, and held it over his head, severing Sanborn's contact with the enchanted beach.

The War Party drew the sides of the blanket together with difficulty because of Sanborn's weight. The Enchantment thrashed inside the trap, but feebly. Its magic life was seeping from it, through the blanket, into the air, and dispersing uselessly.

"Seal the blanket into a ball and harden it," Arden told Durward. "Sanborn will not have a prayer of reactivation, then."

Durward complied.

The guards rolled the orb to one of the ferries and stowed it aboard.

The War Party un-beached the watercraft, loaded the horses onto them, took up the long mossy poles, and commenced transit of the Lake.

When they were halfway across, the soldiers dumped the ball overboard and it was swallowed, with eager finality, by the cold emerald waves.

Illustration 09
Palace Art: Throne Room: East Wall Ornamentation: Landscape Orientation
Copyright © 2019 Philip Raymond Sadler
126-A

Illustration 10
Palace Art: Throne Room: West Wall Ornamentation: Landscape Orientation
Copyright © 2019 Philip Raymond Sadler
126-B

Chapter 5
Caretaker of the Cranes

"Guards, carefully survey the land between here and The Gray Fort," Guthrie ordered. "Nigel's Elves *may* be lurking in scout. If you sight any, return *post-haste*."

The soldiers saluted and reined their steeds, single file, in advance of the War Party. They were quickly out of sight.

The Crane Marsh began at Draylon Lake terminus and stretched into the horizons. Tall brown reeds and pale yellow grass lavished the shallow muddy water. The sun baked the Marsh, conjuring up a thin milky mist, making the drab land muggy.

The Marsh was the nesting grounds for thousands of Green Cranes. They glided about, jerkily, on their slender orange legs and webbed feet, honking in anger at the rude intrusion of horses and men into their ancient sanctuary.

"Is there an Enchantment skulking here, Durward?" Arden asked.

Durward reined his horse in.

The War Party halted around the Magician.

Durward meditated for a few moments.

The cranes fell silent.

Guthrie jerked his head up. There was nothing except

the War Party to frighten the birds to dumbness. Unless Durward were quietening them psychically.

"There *is*—a *presence*—here, *now*," Durward said. "It is almost as if to speak of Enchantments summons them to life." He gazed around at the birds. They were strangely motionless as well as oddly silent. Not even a breeze whispered.

"Did you muffle and still the cranes?" Guthrie asked.

"No," Durward said. "The Enchantment is preparing to strike. *It* must have immobilized them."

Galen stood up in his stirrups and scanned the area. "I can not sight the scouts," he said.

"Guards, ho!" Guthrie shouted. "Report to party! Guards, ho!" His voice echoed, then silence relived. Surprisingly, the birds had not responded to his shouts. They normally fled at loud reports.

"Listen!" Durward said, pointing ahead of them.

The reeds were rustling. The sound became more pronounced and the nearer cane began rubbing together. The reeds swayed to a standstill and the rustling ceased.

"The Enchantment?" Galen wondered, aloud.

Arden urged his horse forward.

Guthrie grasped the reins from his son. "*I* shall venture forth, Arden," Guthrie said, firmly. "*I* am the *only* expendable, now that the scouts are not responding."

Arden was angry, until he understood. He must not forget he was in line for Kingship: the Crown Prince Designate. He did this often.

Guthrie heeled his steed, slowly, toward the reeds that had first evinced motion. He drew his sword and

tightened his grip on his reins, perchance the mount became startled at what he might discover.

The cane to the right rustled, and fell silent.

Guthrie hawed his horse that way. Perhaps, he thought, a mount of one the guards has returned riderless, but is injured, unsure, or too confused and frightened to present itself to the War Party.

The reeds to the left, where they had initially swayed, rustled.

Guthrie geed his steed that direction.

The cane to the right rustled. Then the cane on the left. Then the cane ahead of him.

Guthrie realized, he was separated from the War Party by several yards. He yanked his reins, stood his horse on its hind legs, wheeled it around, and slapped the flat of his blade, to its flank. The mount bolted toward the questers.

Something darted out of the tall reeds, ripped Guthrie's pant leg, and retracted into the obscurity of the cane. The Knight glimpsed only a blur. A blur nipped his horse on a foreleg. The steed reared, whinnying in fright. Guthrie fought to remain in his saddle.

"He is *defending* against some *thing*!" Arden said, to his companions. "I will assist him!"

"*No*!" Durward said. "*That* is what the Enchantment desires; to *separate* us!" The Magician raised his hands and issued psychic energy. The reeds and the grass parted in a straight line from the War Party up to Guthrie. The Knight's horse bolted into the cleared lane and galloped to the group.

The cane, everywhere, began rustling.

"It is the *cranes*!" Galen said. "They are *stalking* us!"

All throughout the misty reeds and grass, the fowl were stepping slowly toward the War Party. Their long necks were thrust forward and their heads were low to the ground. Each movement was uncannily controlled and stealthy.

"They have *never* behaved like *this* before," Guthrie said. "Nigel's Enchantment must puppet them."

"We will form a block," Arden said, "and ride through them. *Trample* them down!"

The cranes commenced trumpeting and hissing furiously. The cacophony flowed from the right end of the Marsh to the left extremity, and back to the right. Then, it conducted from both sides of the cane, to where the War Party stood and returned repeatedly to each side, in an unnerving rhythm.

Silence descended like the end of the world. Hundreds of cranes were massing around the questers in a wide circle. Hundreds formed a second ring. Hundreds fashioned a third circle. Hundreds created a fourth ring.

"The Enchantment proffers battle tactics!" Guthrie shouted. "We can not *slay* them *all,* and we will never gallop *through* them! They are *too* numerous! Use magic, Durward! Strike! Quickly!"

The first circle of birds destroyed the quiet with wild, arrhythmic, trumpeting. Then charged the War Party, headlong.

The horses were frightened by the cries of fury. They comprehended attack and retreat but could perform neither until the questers reined them to it. They were unable to remain still.

Durward threw his psychic force out around the War Party in an increasing circle. The reeds snapped flat and the grass waved as the energy blow spread toward the cranes. The first birds tumbled rearwards into their followers, who began falling like the broken cane. They were all up just as fleetly as they tumbled, trumpeting more irately. Durward emitted another circle blow. Then a third. And fourth. The cranes bowled over. This time, they were stunned or rendered unconscious.

The second ring of fowl entered the fray, launching into flight.

Durward dispatched mind energy at them, repeatedly. He thought at their small heads, hoping to bash them senseless.

At first, there was no response, then crane after crane jerked backwards in the air, fell limp, and fluttered into the reeds and grass; splashing the muddy water. The sky was gorged with fowl raining around the questers.

The first group of cranes had reformed and were charging.

The third circle of birds took to wing in a double assault.

Durward sent a beam at the waddling cranes, then at the airborne fowl. He persisted in this until the cranes evidenced the effects of the energy. The ground birds staggered back, teetered, and flopped over. The airborne fowl spiraled down to splat into the muddy Marsh. There were thousands of cranes yet to be assigned a formation by the controlling Enchantment, and yet to be commanded into battle.

"Galen!" Durward said. "Join me! I weaken!"

The War Party was struggling, continually, with their frightened mounts. Galen suffered difficulty heeling his horse alongside Durward's

All the fowl in the Marsh that were not senseless, were trumpeting irately. The reeds and the grass, for as far as the questers could sight, were rustling from a mass advance of the cranes.

"Look!" Arden said, pointing ahead of the War Party.

A white biped was striding through the reeds and grass. It was taller than the vegetation, and the sun, even through the mist, reflected from the creature as if from burnished stone.

"The Enchantment, finally, unveils its nature," Durward said.

"It is a man of *plumes*!" Galen said, with wonder.

"No eyes, or nose, or ears," Guthrie observed.

"The cranes *are* its eyes and ears," Durward said. He hurled might at the figure but the Enchantment was too distant to be affected.

The birds abandoned their advance and fell quiescent. The only sounds were the sudden honks of cranes as they awoke from artificial sleep. They struggled to their webbed feet and stalked through the cane and weeds, toward the plumed Enchantment.

"Now," Guthrie said. "We shall *rush* this Enchantment, scattering the fowl with surprise. You *strike* the beast, Durward."

"Agreed," Durward said. "I believe I know how to decease it. I am readied."

"Form a *wedge*," Arden said. "Guthrie, you prevail *front*—"

"*No*," Durward said. "*I* must ride fore, *must* be the one *closest* to the Enchantment, at *all* moments!"

Arden and Guthrie did not like the risk. If they lost *Durward*, they *forfeited* Nigel's War. They could offer no alternatives, and they knew they could not prevent the Magician from doing as he wished.

The Enchantment, swaggered, a few paces toward the War Party. "You *connive* to defeat *me*," it shouted, taunting, like a fat, grotesque, speech-mimicking, bird, "All your forays will conquer only your dimwitted selves. Crandall does not, *skirmish*, his *slaves* obey and *massacre*. Crandall *generals*. My troops *will* eat your eyes and *bite out* your tongues."

"Let us *skirt* the fowl, instead," Galen suggested. "The birds are circling the Enchantment. I think we can gallop *around* them *before* they can contest us. I *believe* they cannot venture *beyond* the Marsh and *remain* under Crandall's control."

Arden slapped his horse on a flank to guide the War Party as wise Galen had outlined.

Crandall swept its arms up. Like drilled mercenaries the cranes fanned out, running to its left and right. There was no chance of circling them.

Arden rejoined the War Party. "Revert to first plan,"

he said.

"Durward, we will drive *at* the Enchantment. It should become muddled," Guthrie said, "Arden, Galen, diversions to each wing of their line, but retract to center *if* it recalls its birds to *us*."

Guthrie reined his mount into full gallop. Durward shadowed a yard behind the Knight. Arden and Galen split off, opposite directions.

The Enchantment did not respond.

Guthrie haltered his horse to a sudden stop. Its hooves threw up water and mud in front of them. "*Reform*!" he shouted. "*Return* to *start* point!"

He was too late.

The cranes to the laterals of Crandall fluttered into the air, in mass. Honking, stridently, they soared toward Arden and Galen. The fowl immediately around the Enchantment made flight, hissing in hatred, toward Durward and Guthrie.

"It is translating *our* strategy to its *own* benefit!" Guthrie shouted, angrily. "It *seduced* us to *foolishness*!" He reined his horse around and retreated next to Durward.

The Magician was darting his eyes from Arden to Galen.

The Healer was bearing back, but tardily. The cranes were vortexing him and his mount, assaulting them with their sharp claws, and long beaks. His horse panicked, and reared.

"Galen is *down*!" Durward shouted.

"I can not *sight* Arden!" Guthrie warned.

Durward was stung by desperation. To preserve one

might slay the other of his friends. He wheeled his steed toward Arden's last position but was intersected by frenzied birds. They dived, struck, and soared around to plunge again. He drew his sword and flailed at the fowl. He also sallied his energy toward where he had last seen Arden.

The reeds snapped and the grass parted but only the soiled water was undraped.

Durward cleaved a crane on its pate with his blade. The bird plummeted, dead. The cranes assaulting the Magician were too numerous to allow him to concentrate on more than one life. Durward issued his might at the birds in the air to save himself. His soul cried out, in despair, for his companions.

Guthrie pulled his sword, and struck, effectively, slice, after thrust, at the whirl-pooling fowl. He assumed Durward was rescuing Arden, dismounted, and sloshed toward where Galen had been unseated. Galen's horse fled blindly at the Knight. Guthrie dodged the steed and chopped at the reeds and grass. The plants seemed to confuse the airborne cranes, and few fowl were landing blows. Guthrie's arms were bleeding from numerous slashes and his face was swelling where bird claws had struck him. "*Galen*!" he shouted. "*Galen*!"

There was a feeble reply, almost overwhelmed by the trumpeting of the fowl.

Guthrie fought through the cane and weeds a few feet further and splashed to a halt, horrified.

Galen was sprawled on his stomach in the filthy water. His clothes were tatters and his back, arms and legs were rife with bloody wounds. The cranes had discarded him for dead.

Guthrie could note no respiration. He leaned over and listened for Galen's breathing.

The Healer stirred. "*Go* to Durward and Arden," Galen said, weakly. "I will be secure. I am mending, now. The cranes will not assail me, again, until I arise to join you."

Guthrie made sure Galen's breathing was deep and steady, the blood blotching Galen's arms, back, and legs had ceased flowing, and the healing was progressing. "*Durward* is helping Arden," Guthrie said. "I will check on them, and hasten return to you."

"Good," Galen said. His voice sounded stronger.

Guthrie sheathed his sword and transformed into the cerise War Serpent. It skimmed through the water, following the crazy trumpeting and hissing of the cranes. The reeds and grass were no barrier to its velocity.

A horse cantered alongside the Snake. "I have unburdened myself of cranes, for the moment, but Prince Arden remains besieged and is still fighting!" Durward shouted. "He is not far ahead!"

All the haunted fowl were wheeling and diving where Arden had been unsaddled.

Durward dispatched wave upon wave of energy at the cranes and they began hailing from the sky.

Crandall spun around and shook a feathery fist at Durward, then pointed its arms at him. Half the birds en-clouding Arden's position responded instantly, streaking through the misty air toward Durward.

Durward reined his stallion toward the Enchantment, emitted a circular fusillade of energy beams, and swept hundreds of cranes out of the azure sky.

War Serpent flashed on to reinforce Arden.

Crandall realized it was suffering its first reversal. It whirled and retreated through the grass and reeds.

The birds went insane, attacking any movement, including the cane, each other and the man of feathers.

Crandall screamed and threw its plumed arms over its downy head. Its panic at Durward's direct menace to it had broken its mastery over the cranes. It regained control as it dropped to its face to hide in the reeds and grass.

The birds began alighting around the golem. They became silent and motionless.

Durward urged his horse into the first of the entranced fowl. They did not scatter as they should have. His horse stalled, then backed stubbornly and fearfully away from the unnatural scene.

"Durward!" Galen shouted. "*Arden* requires us!"

The Healer was shoving his way through the reeds and grass. His wounds were healed and his tiredness, neutralized.

Durward magically repaired Galen's tunic and trousers as his friend approached. The Healer mounted behind the Magician and Durward reined the grateful steed away from the cranes.

Guthrie stood in the distance, urgently waving his sword. Durward directed his steed there.

The cranes remained mum and like statues.

Crandall had not reappeared.

Guthrie had Arden propped against an old, overturned, and rotting wagon. The front end of the big dray was held off the earth by a high backed seat. Arden had sought refuge beneath it when the crane assault had become too massive to respond to. He was pitted with beak wounds and his face was swollen and discolored from impacts by crane claws. He was unconscious from pain.

Galen slid off the horse and plied his healing art.

Durward dismounted and enforced him.

Guthrie watched the cane and weeds intently. There was no evidence that any life, other than the War Party, resided in the bedeviled Marsh. "It is scheming," the Knight said. "It will not *play* general *now*. Its next assault will be in *mass* and *frenzied*."

Arden's slashes and bruises began to heal and his face reduced its swelling.

Durward unlinked from Galen and motioned for Guthrie to be healed. Durward's contact with Galen had mended Durward's injuries.

"If I could ignite these reeds and keep them burning," Durward said, "I could direct the flames anywhere. But, they are too sopped." He snapped one of the thick canes, and water seeped onto his hands. He knelt and began crawling through the weeds, reeds, mud and water.

Guthrie and Galen did not apprehend Durward's departure.

Galen was facing away from Durward.

Guthrie was in front of the Healer and concentrating on his son's progress.

Arden had not awakened.

"Crandall comprehends you now!" the plume man bragged, with its mimic-bird voice. It was erect again. Sections of its billowy arms, were missing, where the cranes, had plucked it. "Crandall *divines* the Magician's *limits*. You perish *now*!"

Guthrie looked around, surprised. "Where *is* Durward?" he whispered.

Galen glanced over his shoulder. "He has *advanced* on the Enchantment!" he said. He indicated a few broken canes where Durward had crept away.

Guthrie pulled his sword. "We can supply him with a *diversion*, at least," the Knight said. "He will require only a short time to gain effective range of that *monster*."

Galen jostled Arden and whispered to him. The three men began crawling away from the feather biped, in varied directions.

Durward heard a rustle before him and projected his force to grasp its instigator. The sound ceased, and he knew the crane was hypnotized, immobilized, and excluded from Crandall's control. Durward crawled cautiously, permeating the cane and grass with entrancing power, concentrating on the vision of his green enemy. Their eyes had to be shut, then their bodies stopped. If one bird spied him, the image would be transmitted to Crandall, and Durward's life would be forfeit. Their hearing mattered little, for Crandall could not discern crane rustle from that produced by human motion. Durward edged around bird after bird that had succumbed to his subtle mesmeric influence. Their eyes were closed, their bodies rigid, and they were barely breathing, unaware of either Durward or Crandall. Inching, frustrated, the Magician drew nearer the Enchantment and, hopefully, closer to freedom and safety for his companions and himself.

Guthrie stiffened. The reeds ahead were rustling. He held his breath and parted the plants with his sword. His hope submerged. Lines of white cranes were slinking, masterfully, around the site of the wagon. He reluctantly retreated.

Arden and Galen were awaiting him under the meager protection provided by the rotting, ancient conveyance.

"The battle befalls Durward," Arden said.

Crandall laughed like a clucking hen. "*You* design to *skulk* to your advantage," it shouted, tauntingly, "but, *I* have trapped *you* under the ruined wagon, like game within a snare box!"

Arden, Guthrie and Galen felt apprehension tightening their chests.

"Rejoice, my hosts, my avengers, these four cowering worms cannot, but, capitulate and be consumed!" Crandall crowed.

Guthrie, Galen and Arden exchanged grim smiles. They had feared Crandall had located Durward, as well. It had not, or it would not have spoken as it did.

Hope remained.

Half the army of haunted cranes flapped into the air, their enraged trumpeting and hissing shattering the silence. The second phalanx raced through the reeds and grass in a collapsing circle. They followed a chaotic, zigzag course to render Durward's psychic missiles ineffectual.

Arden, Galen and Guthrie crouched, tensely, back-to-back, beneath the wagon, with their blades unsheathed.

Crandall was laughing gleefully. Its military excursion was a brilliant success.

The cranes converged on the ancient wagon from the ground and air and tore at it, wrathfully, with their deadly beaks and claws. The huge wagon rocked, creaked, and shuddered as bits of it were ripped free.

Galen, Guthrie and Arden jabbed furiously at the loud birds that probed their pecking heads under the sides of the wagon.

The wagon was subjected to wave upon wave of savage assaults, ebbing and increasing as exhausted birds were summoned back and rested fowl were dispatched to replace them. The boards of the wagon bed were cratered and the beaks of the cranes were piercing into the sanctuary. Yet, there was no retaliation via Durward.

Crandall's laughter did not slacken. In fact, it became gleeful, almost, euphoric.

The high backed bench that held the aged wagon off the earth had been weakened by repeated, relentless, pecks. It cracked in half and the wagon slammed down like a great gray trap, shoving Arden, Galen, and Guthrie tightly to the muddy ground. Above them, the wagon bed resembled a sieve. Larger openings were being beaked into it. Several thrusts struck the men, drawing blood.

"*Durward*!" Arden pleaded. "*Durward*! *Strike*! *Surmount*!"

The weakened wagon bed shattered and the throngs of trumpeting, hissing, cranes flooded, inexorably, in upon the warriors.

Despite its joy of sweet triumph, Crandall noticed an oddity. Some of its slaves were off to one side, motionless, and not responding to its brilliant telepathic commands. The cocky golem turned to investigate.

Furious, Durward stood up in the tall reeds and grass amid those inactive fowl, only four feet from the horrified golem.

"*No*!" Crandall screamed. "I *can't* lose! Nigel *promised* that *I* wouldn't *lose*!" It uttered a high-pitched squawk, then spun around to flee.

Durward's might exploded into the Enchantment, like a million tiny vengeful hands, literally plucking Crandall free of its plumage and swirling the rent feathers in all directions, far across the Marsh. Crandall resembled a pink, human-sized fledgling without down. It turned gray, fell beak first into the muddy water and crumbled to dust, adding its powerless remains to the mud.

The death of Crandall allowed the confused cranes to revert to their instincts. They fled from the broken wagon bed, trumpeting forlornly.

Illustration 11
Palace Art: King Alaric's Private Chambers: East Wall Window: Landscape Orientation
Copyright © 2019 Philip Raymond Sadler

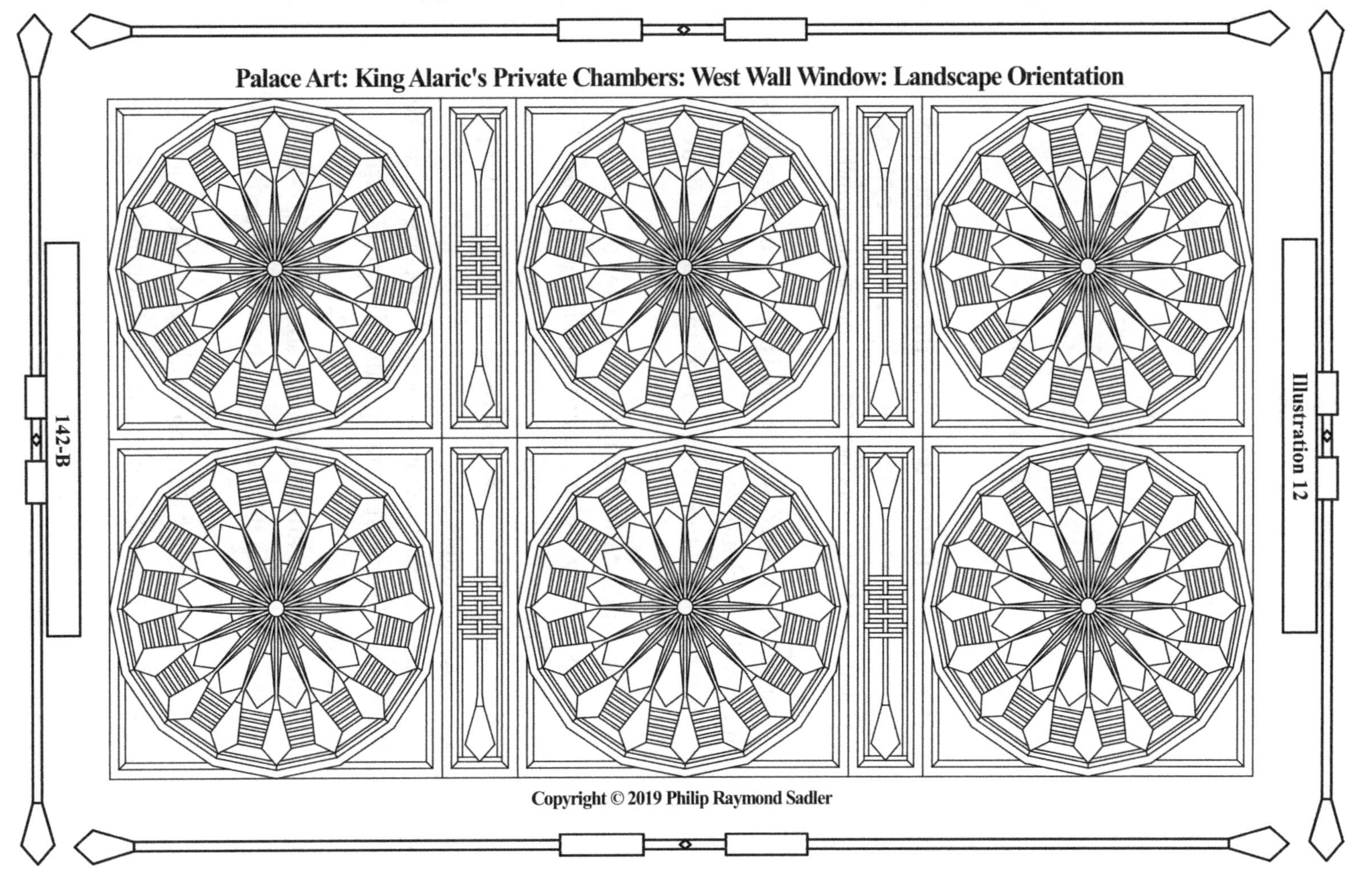
Illustration 12
Palace Art: King Alaric's Private Chambers: West Wall Window: Landscape Orientation
Copyright © 2019 Philip Raymond Sadler
142-B

Chapter 6
The Red Swamp

"We must divine the guards," Guthrie said. "They probably were downed by the cranes further across the Marsh."

Galen mended the wounds on his companions and himself.

Durward laundered and repaired their various garments using psychic techniques.

They recovered their horses near the shore of Draylon Lake.

Galen ameliorated the injuries of the steeds.

The War Party mounted and continued through the Marsh, in quest of the missing scouts

The demure cranes fled on all sides of the men, trumpeting with glum complaint.

The reeds and yellow grass swayed in a hot breeze, and the callous sun thickened the muggy mist that curled up from the soggy earth.

There were no auguries of the soldiers.

"Guards, *ho*!" Guthrie shouted, through cupped hands. "Guards, *report*!"

"Tarry a moment," Durward said. He psycho-kinetically parted the tall reeds and grass to their left, for several yards. Only mud and crane nests were revealed. He repeated the action to their right, then forward, with similar disappointing results. "Do *you* sense them, Galen?" Durward said.

Galen frowned, closed his eyes, and tilted his head back.

The zephyr intensified and the canes and grass waved more quickly. The only sounds were the rustling of the flora and the trumpeting of the birds.

"They exist, not, on the Marsh," Galen said. "I can not sense their cardiac rhythms or their respiration rates. I perceive only *ours*. Even were they dead nearby, I could still perceive their souls egressing their somas. It generally requires three days, for complete separation."

"Where *can* they be, *then*?" Arden asked. "Let us split, and search."

"No!" Guthrie said, firmly.

"Why not?" Galen asked. "There are no Enchantments, here, now. It will be, provident, to separate."

"No *Enchantments*," Guthrie said, "but, Nigel's *Elves* may have captured, or slain the guards, and packed them away on their own steeds. We *shall* stay *together*."

"All right," Arden said. "You are usually, *canny*. Let us seek."

They sloshed swiftly through the reeds and grass. The water was deepening, and the canes and grass were thinning.

"Hold!" Guthrie said. He leaped from his saddle, knelt on one knee, and ran a hand over some flattened canes. They were broken many times along their length. Trod upon. "Four horsemen passed this way," he said, "then, bore right."

He stood up. "Guards, *ho*!" he shouted. "Guards, *respond*! *Return* to party!"

Only the rustling of the reeds and grass, and the trumpeting of the cranes, answered.

"Durward," Arden said. "These birds are acting oddly. They no longer usher us on our departure. Note how they *stalk* to and fro behind us but do not *advance* even though there are a hundred feet between *us* and *them*. It is as if they are loath to venture further. It is even so with the cranes at the far left and right of the Marsh."

"*Another* Enchantment?" Galen wondered, aloud. "We *perceived* only *one*."

"Come," Guthrie said. He led his horse and the War Party through the muddy water.

The cane and grass ceded supremacy to sloppy, strangely red mud that stretched ahead, and laterally.

The cries of the cranes were no longer audible.

"*This* bespeaks of Nigel's magic," Guthrie said. "This Red Mud Swamp did not *exist* here before. There used to be a quaint, small woods. Our guards have fallen prey to a *new* Enchantment."

They continued across the Swamp. The sun raised mist off the mud as it had from the Marsh. The hooves of the steeds, and Guthrie's boots, sank into the crimson ooze.

"The guards passed this way," Guthrie said, pointing.

The trail of horse tracks led more deeply into the Red Swamp. Huge, ebony trees waited where the guards had vanished.

"Hoglan Plain and the Gray Fort lie beyond that woods," Guthrie said. "Do you *sense* an Enchantment *there*, Durward? Do you *detect* the *scouts*, Galen?"

The War Party slowly approached the forbidding Red Swamp Woods.

Both psychics concentrated.

The horse trail they followed was joined by boot tracks.

"The guards dismounted, here," Guthrie said. "You should imitate."

"Yes," Galen said, as he dismounted. "I perceive them. They live, but, faintly. They require air, soon. It seems—yes—slow respiration—hard breathing. No! Difficulty *inhaling*!"

"I sense nothing," Durward said, as he dismounted. "Galen, we must *link*."

"Can you direct *me* to *my* men?" Guthrie asked.

"Yes," Galen said.

"Bide, yet," Durward, cautioned. "Foolish, saving them now, only to lose them to an Enchantment."

Galen stood behind Durward and pressed his palms to the sides of the Magician's head.

The breeze whispered into history. Milky mist thickened. Noon sun flamed hotter. Air grew more muggy.

Arden's tunic was damp and uncomfortable, and he was nervous, as he dismounted. He felt a tingling around him, from his feet, ascending. As he had at the enchanted River before Calder had evinced itself.

"I still perceive no Enchantment," Durward said.

"Nor do I," Galen agreed. "And, I sense no Elves."

"Then, the guards befell a *careless* accident. A mud pit, perhaps," Guthrie said. "Lead us to them, Galen."

Arden shrugged at the electricity. It was stronger. "I feel—a power," he said, softly. "An harmful force."

Durward looked surprised, then nodded at Galen. "A different energy comprises *this* Enchantment," the Magician said. "The least psychically sensitive apprehends it."

"A tingling?" Guthrie asked. "As at the cursed river?"

"Yes. From the boots, upward," Arden said.

"*Then*, as, *here*, I thought it was, simply, disquiet," Guthrie said. "I should have reported it. I know better than to stone head any possible omen."

"An Enchantment surely prowls ahead," Durward said. "We can skirt this Swamp Wood, and the Mud Flat that I see at its center, to avoid it, but that *will* sacrifice our scouts."

"We will *not*!" Arden avowed.

Guthrie conducted the War Party into the woods.

The trees were rife with wide, obsidian leaves which blocked most of the sunlight, introducing the Swamp Wood to semi darkness.

Durward wove an ultramarine luminescence around each man and horse to illuminate their way, and to make it easier for them to keep sight of each other.

The massive trees seemed to lean in to hug the mist, and their shade sired a noisome coolness. The further into the woods they ventured, the clammier it became. Sickly, viridian moss embraced the trees, but shunned the crimson mud.

"Unnatural," Guthrie said. "Moss should thrive on this mud. Where are my men, Galen? We will fetch them, *quickly*. That odd tingling energy pulses more intensely!"

"Yes," Arden said. "The Enchantment, springs, *soon*."

"Left," Galen said. "To the soul of the woods."

"And the lair of the Enchantment," Arden said, solemnly.

"They lie close—close," Galen said, turning, slowly, in a circle.

The horses jerked at their reins and stamped the ooze. They yearned to flee the way they had ingressed.

"The Enchantment *approaches*," Arden warned. He was trembling. The energy from the mud coursed unpleasantly through him. Nigel's new horror was directing its malevolent might at *him*. All the Enchantments did *thus*. But, this evil conjury was even more arrowed in his direction. It was *unnerving* him and his companions.

Galen stepped aside to a tree and a large dark form.

Something struggled to inhale a deep breath. The sound encompassed the Woods, echoing through the shadowed mist.

"Here sites one soldier," Galen said, indicating the shape.

Durward coalesced a white ray. The heap of dried clay he illuminated was the distorted form of a man standing before a horse.

Guthrie drew his sword and tapped the flat of the tip of his blade against the top of the head of the shape of a man.

The scarlet mud crumbled away, revealing the slack visage of a guard. The scout was hypnotized, but gulped in a lengthy breath. The echoing inhaling noises ceased. Guthrie rapped the mud from the head of the horse, and the entranced steed gasped in desperately required air.

Another reverberating respiring commenced. Then a third. And a fourth.

"This magical foulness is *toying* with us," Arden said, angrily. "It makes us *hearken* to our friends *dying*. To *groom* us to *panic*; to *rashness*."

"Here and here," Galen said. He was a few feet to the right of the War Party and indicating two other mud encased scouts and mounts.

A wind groped through the woods, shoving the mist away before it, then perished. The harsh breathing sounds increased in volume.

Guthrie joined Galen, tugging their steeds behind him. The horses were increasingly reluctant to follow. "Come!" the Knight said to the Prince and the Magician. "*Cleave* together!"

Arden and Durward coaxed their mounts forward.

Guthrie was assisting Galen to clear the clay from the soldiers and steeds. When each man gained access to fresh air, the echoing respiring lessened in volume.

"Yet, one man endangered," Guthrie said. "Divine him, swiftly, Galen. Durward, remove all of the mud with your energy."

"Ho!" Galen said to the left of the War Party. He tapped the shapes with his blade.

The soldier and his horse rasped in breath.

The woods inundated with silence as if all life had vanished. No wind or mist, and no illumination except Durward's glow on man and mount.

"Restrain your vitality, Magician," something said, like sopping rags flapping together in a gale. "*All* you dispatch, you receive *doubled*."

The words issued from the ebony heart of the Red Mud Swamp Woods.

Durward wafted a white light there. It was reflected twice as brightly. Durward dimmed his light. The reflection diminished and the Enchantment stood before them.

"Stone, fire, sand, feather, and now, mud," Arden said, with irritated wonderment.

The, hulking, reeking, rubescent golem was motionless. It smiled with a dripping slit below a pair of void eye sockets. "Monrow *hears* the *fool* boy," it said. "Perchance he *challenges* Monrow? Monrow *gauntlets* him!"

The ooze began bubbling. Pits formed around the War Party, preventing them from retreating in any direction.

Durward sizzled heat at Monrow.

The mud Enchantment steamed, its surface layer cracked and cascaded away, then the fiery force was recoiled toward the brave War Party, twofold in intensity.

Durward deflected the sizzle, in a semicircle, to the trees, setting some of them afire.

Monrow laughed like wet cloths slapping rock. The mud in the holes percolated, and smaller clay bipeds emerged

from the bottom of each pit. They leaped out of the holes, joined their oozing hands, and circled the War Party.

Durward telepathed the horses into trance, and blasted Monrow with frigid energy.

The golem frosted over.

The icy power rebounded toward the War Party, doubled in intensity.

Durward discoursed the energy onto the flaming trees, smothering their fires and freezing their scorched trunks.

"Draw your blades!" Guthrie ordered.

Monrow flicked its slimy hands. "Advance, my children," it said. "*Cover*, *suffocate* and *crush* them! The, *sickening* boy *first*!"

Arden grasped his hilt more firmly and stepped into the center of a triangle described by his companions. Durward served as the capstone.

The little bipeds marched forward.

Durward hurled might at them; body blows.

The closeness of the minigolems rebounded the violent force, twice as strong, instantly.

Durward was unable to divert it.

The questers were butted off their feet and sent rolling, in different directions, through the ooze.

Guthrie pitched into one of the pits, and the mud began to flow over him, gluing him down.

Arden came up to his feet, smashed into one of the frozen trees, and dropped to his seat, stunned.

Durward crashed into a horse and recoiled flat of his back, striking his head against a trunk.

Galen landed on his spine in the mud and somersaulted, heels over head, to land on his knees, instantly healed of the daze wrought by the blow.

One of the small clay golems reached for the Healer's throat.

Galen blocked its slimy hand with a jab of his palm.

The creature ululated in pain and shrank back.

Monrow growled in rage, sounding like sand scrunched between stones.

Galen took stock of the plight of his friends.

Durward was unconscious and the mud was creeping over him where he was sprawled.

Arden was fazed, but struggling to his feet.

Guthrie was nearly interred in the pit.

Galen scrambled to Guthrie and plunged his healing hands into the ooze in the hole.

Monrow screamed, and the mud leaped away from the Knight, like ripples in water.

Galen hauled Guthrie from the pit.

Arden steadied his father.

Galen ran to aid Durward.

The ooze recoiled off the Magician, before Galen could touch it.

Galen helped Durward to stand up, and they joined Arden and Guthrie.

"*Retreat*, my children," Monrow ordered. "We must *adapt*. I was un-apprised of the Healer. He *negates* our might. He, *cruelly*, hurts *us*."

The little bipeds ran backwards and jumped into their

holes as if they possessed eyes in the rears of their slimy craniums.

"Disencumber the guards and their mounts, Durward," Guthrie whispered. "We will withdraw before it develops a defense against Galen."

"Disencumber the guards, oh great Durward!" Monrow taunted. "We will withdraw! *Where*?"

The pits connected laterally and became a circular trench. It widened until not even the horses could safely leap across. The War Party was stranded on an island of scarlet mud.

"I can proffer *no* defense," Durward said. "*All* my force will be returned, twice as potently, to harm us."

Galen removed his left boot and jammed his foot into the ooze.

Monrow shrieked.

The living mud irised away from Galen's foot, leaving ash colored stone behind.

Galen slipped off his other boot.

Monrow retracted all the ooze from the rock island.

"*This* is the sole granite in the Swamp Wood," Durward said. "Vibration sounding reveals this to me."

"We are secure here but, cannot tarry long," Galen said. He walked to the rim of the island and jumped into the trench.

Monrow laughed. "My children!" it shouted. "We *forfeit* our *Reflection,* but we gain the richly deserved *deaths* of our *despised* and *evil* foes!"

Galen struggled to free his feet from the mud.

Monrow held the Healer, resolutely.

Durward emitted grappling energy, and ripped the mud away Galen's feet.

Monrow chuckled, like gas bubbles escaping molten lava. "I do not hurt, *now*," it said, happily. "You can inflict me, no defeat!"

Guthrie and Arden lifted Galen up onto the rock where Galen, disgustedly, donned his boots.

Durward scathed force at Monrow.

The beast's head snapped off its shoulders and sank into the red mud behind the monster. A new cranium emerged from its torso. Ooze flowed up from the trench and onto the stone island, grasping the War Party up to their knees, and miring them from motion.

"Arise, my children!" Monrow, urged. "The *evil* ones, are *affixed*, like insects, *trapped* in amber!"

The bipeds ascended from the trench, lifted on clay pillars, to the height of the island.

The ooze covering the granite began slowly flowing in various directions, drawing the feet from under the questers, but not their steeds.

Durward scorched power at the puppets.

They sizzled, kilned-out, and shattered, almost at the same second. More bipeds sculpted up from the tops of the columns.

Durward encased them, and the pillars, in thick ice.

Monrow growled, like hard sand scrunched mercilessly between leviathan marble slabs.

Durward levitated the mud off the island, ripped it into chunks, froze them, and flung them at Monrow.

The large icy projectiles meteored into The Enchantment, cratering its slimy body. Monrow screamed. "*Nigel*!" it wailed. "I *hurt*, Nigel! I am *not* energized *enough* to *keep* from *hurting*! *Help* me, *Nigel*!"

Durward marshaled his psychic force, snapped one of the clay marionettes off its pedestal, fired it to brick hardness, and javelined it at Monrow.

The Enchantment submerged into the Mud Flat. The baked puppet plunged harmlessly into the ooze. Millions of small clay golems sprouted into blighted existence from the mud. The moat flowed to fullness with the ooze and the slimy creatures marched on the War Party.

Durward psychically cleared the mud from the guards and their mounts. He awoke the scouts. "Draw swords!" he shouted to everyone. He beamed his Arctic power to the upheld blades, imbuing them temporarily with it, causing them to glow white. He hurled frigidity at the ooze golems.

The War Party dodged the clay puppets, slapping their blades flat to them and glaciating them instantly.

Monrow, affronted, hove out of the ooze where it had first appeared and telepathed a wave of mud over everything, sweeping its profane progeny at the questers.

Durward froze, then shattered the occult ooze billow, just after its creation. When the bits sank into the mud, Monrow was absent. Its abhorrent children were inert.

Durward led the War Party to the center of the granite circle. One at a time, with great effort, he levitated their mounts there. He seared the clay golems, then set about kilning the Swamp's Mud Flat. His scarlet heat beam circled their flat stone sanctuary and slowly irised outwards.

"Have we *conquered* it?" Guthrie asked. "Sanborn pretended, *it*, was deceased. *Is* Monrow?"

"Arden?" Durward asked.

The Crown Prince Designate shrugged. "I feel no *tingling*," he said, hopefully.

With an ire-filled shriek that only an inhuman magical contrivance could utter, Monrow propelled its macabre self out of the baked layer of mud, just behind the War Party.

The guards rallied against the creature.

Monrow perked balls of ooze at them, sliming them pate to sole, and drying the mud immediately.

Durward freed the soldiers from the red clay with Mind Magic, then assaulted Monrow with Arctic force.

Monrow fractured out of its rimed outer skin before the freezing could progress and slammed its massive bulk down on the War Party, flattening them on their backs.

Durward generated magic repulsion against the monstrosity, straining until he nearly fainted.

Galen desperately struggled a hand through the suffocating, blinding muck. He found and seized Durward's wrist and translated the totality of his energy into the Magician.

Monrow erupted into the trees, shredding the branches in its path

Durward kilned, then froze, the slimy Enchantment at the apex of its flight.

Shredding more tree limbs, Monrow hurtled down, thundered into the baked Mud Flat, and shattered into

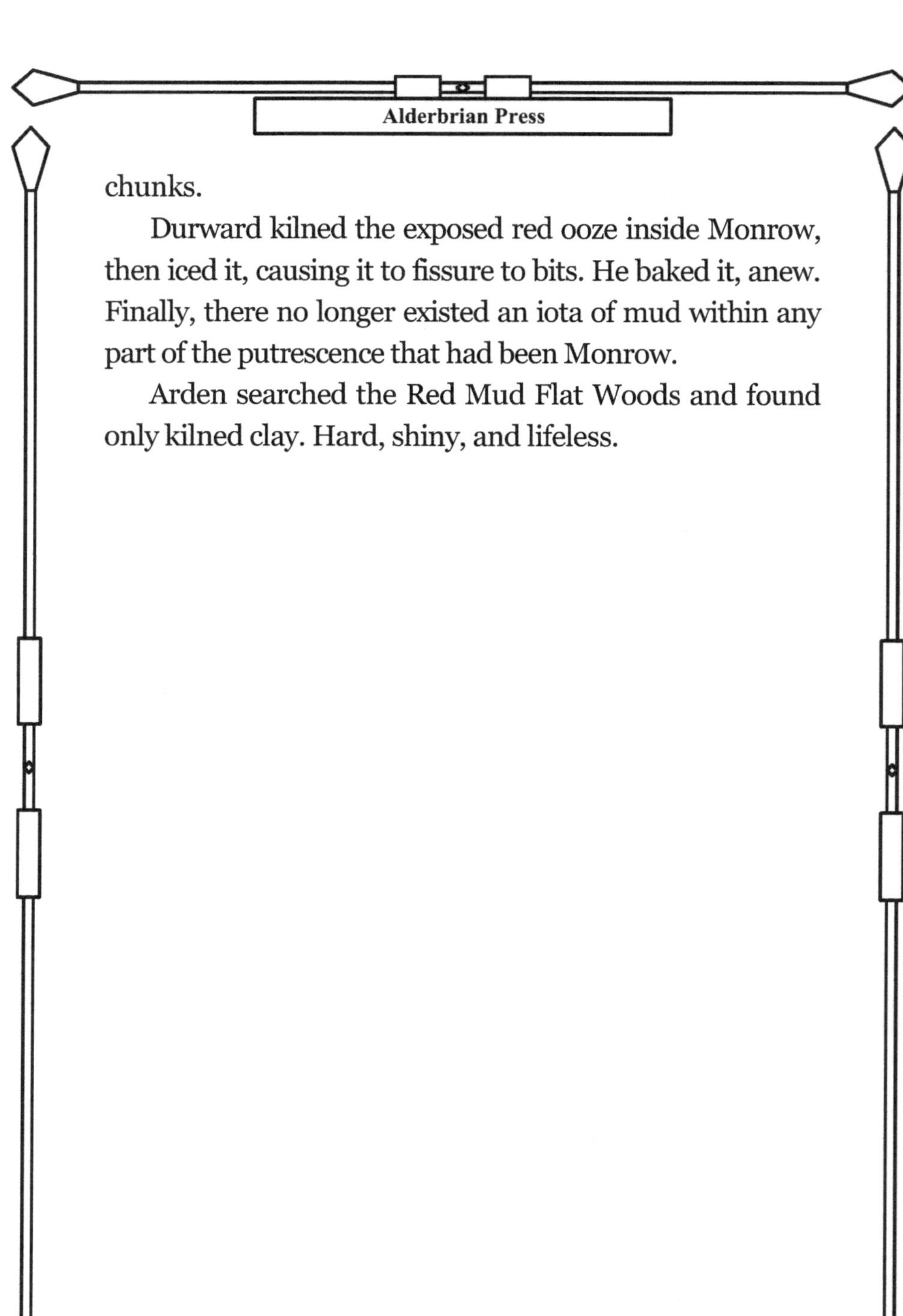

chunks.

Durward kilned the exposed red ooze inside Monrow, then iced it, causing it to fissure to bits. He baked it, anew. Finally, there no longer existed an iota of mud within any part of the putrescence that had been Monrow.

Arden searched the Red Mud Flat Woods and found only kilned clay. Hard, shiny, and lifeless.

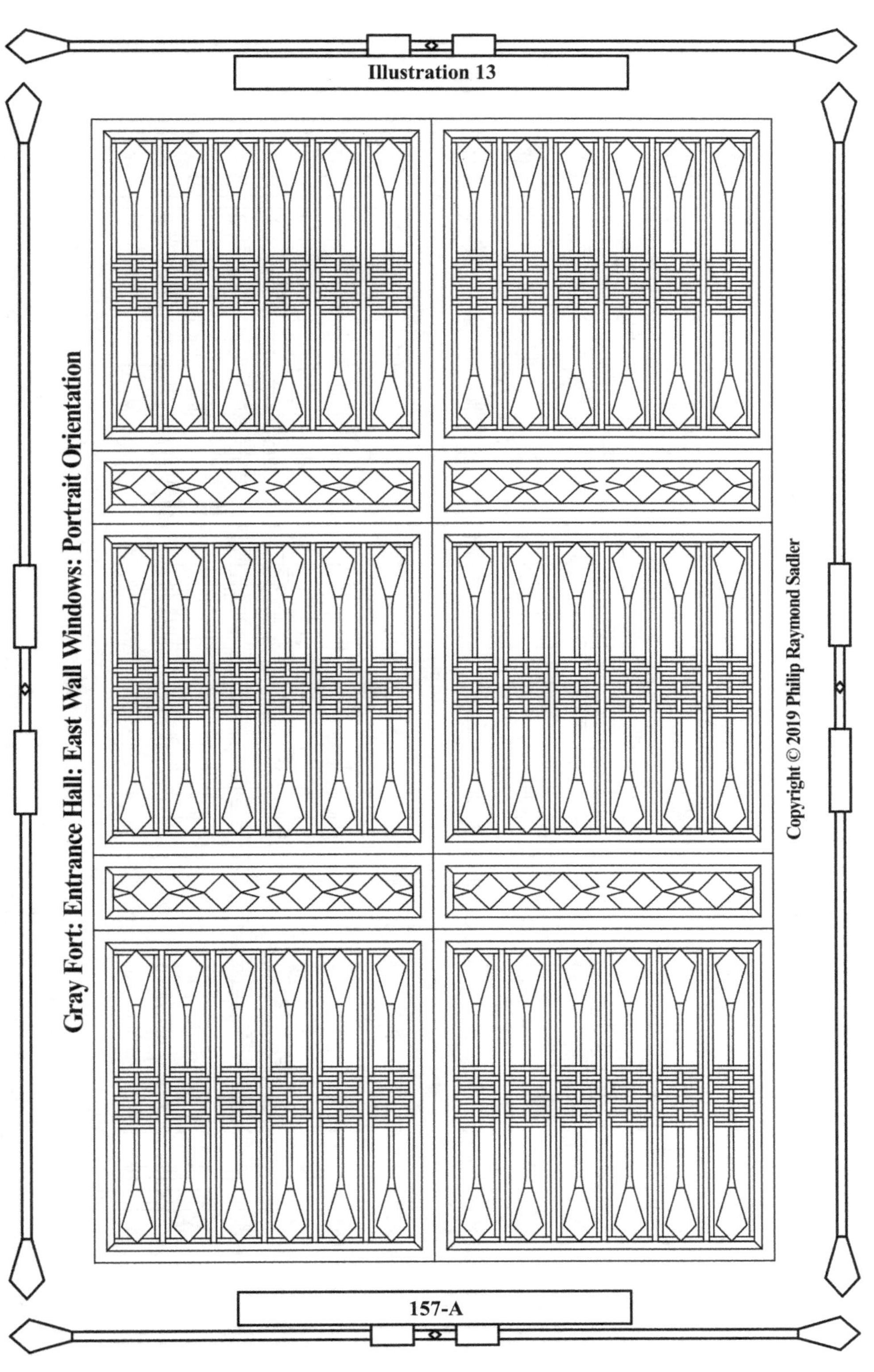
Illustration 13
Gray Fort: Entrance Hall: East Wall Windows: Portrait Orientation
Copyright © 2019 Philip Raymond Sadler

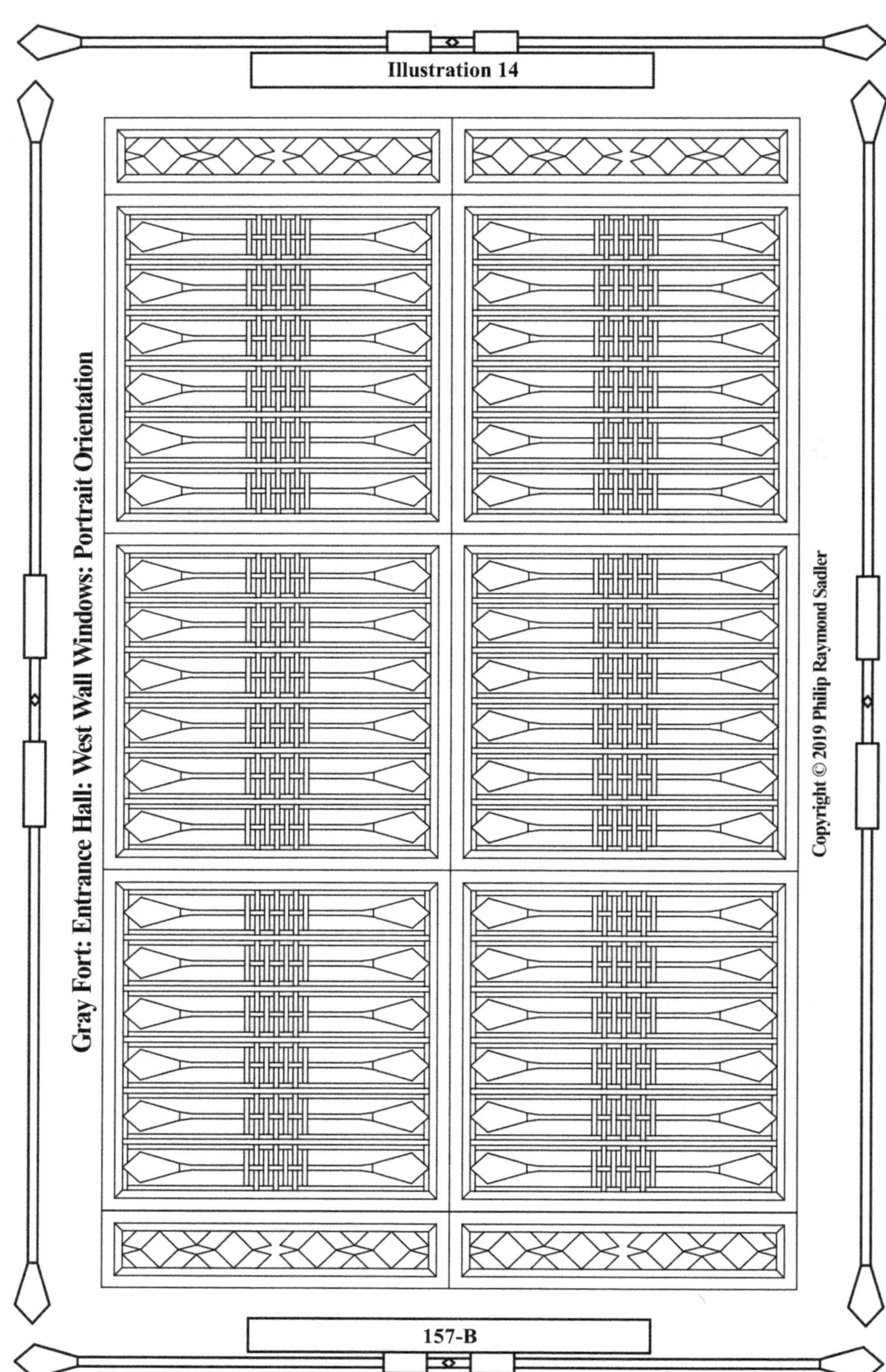
Illustration 14

Gray Fort: Entrance Hall: West Wall Windows: Portrait Orientation

Chapter 7
Only Shadows

Hoglan Plain was a tangle of tall, lavender weeds with sickle shaped leaves. Its center hosted the Gray Fort, a massive, ovoid, constructed of slabs of cinereous granite. Its battlements were deserted and silence caressed it like a jealous mistress.

Arden waved the War Party to a standstill and dismounted with them. They were at the preamble of the old Plain and camouflaged by the terminus of the Swamp Woods. The fort was several hundred yards to fore.

"Suspicion is gestating within me," Guthrie said. "*If* Nigel *haunts* this place, the parapets should be teeming with armed Elf sentries, and we should have run afoul of at least one Elf patrol before now."

Galen gazed at the somber Citadel. It had idled unoccupied for over a decade until Nigel had announced intention to inhabit it. The tares, having overgrown the ancient horse paths, offered no evidence of past traffic or present tenancy. "Ambuscade?" the Healer wondered, aloud.

"We must assume so," Arden said.

"Do you sense any quickness at the Fort?" Guthrie asked.

"No," Galen said. "It is *too* distant."

"I divine no signs of life, either," Durward said.

"How shall we assay if Nigel *is* abiding, in ambush?" Galen asked.

"A decoy *must* venture to the Fort," Arden said.

Guthrie nodded.

"Allow me, sir," Zadok said. "He will believe you are much arrear yet, assume me to be an advance scout and attempt to capture me to ascertain your position."

"Offered *well*, guard," Arden said. "We appreciate your *risk*. Be *most* wary."

"Probe slowly," Durward advised. "I will be better able to defend you."

Zadok mounted, heeled his steed onto the lavender Plain, and adopted an ambling, zigzag course toward the Citadel.

Arden twisted his reins in his clenched hands.

Zadok was halfway to the Fort and no challenge had issued forth.

Arden glanced at his companions.

Their senses were riveted to Zadok and his objective.

Arden coaxed his mount back into the Swamp Woods, assumed saddle, and reined the horse parallel to the damson Plain. When he attained the right parcel of the Swamp Woods, he exited for another woods which dappled closer to the Fort. Therein, he paused and reassessed Zadok's progress.

Zadok warily halted his nervous stallion before the towering, rust encrusted, iron gates. There still harked no reaction to his presence. "Ho, the Fort!" Zadok shouted. "Yield *courtesies* to an *official* royal *herald*! It's not my *own* fond notion, but I would converse with *Nigel*! Ho, the Fort!"

Arden transited the woods to a third and arced along a crescent of cinnabar shrubbery to the posterior of the Fort. At final glimpse, Zadok was canted from his saddle, pounding on the gates, and still unmolested via inhabitants from the Fort.

Arden dismounted at the rear wall. He scooped a scaling set out of his saddlebag and tossed the hooks up at a battlement. They caught on first try. He tested his weight against the bite of the grappling iron, and armed his way up to the parapet. When he could view through the nearest arrow niche, he enjoyed relief. There were no men or Elves concealed on the catwalks of any of the walls. He climbed into the niche and reconnoitered the complex.

Five tall circular buildings, and one squarish structure, all of ash colored granite, lay below. The circular buildings comprised quarters for servants, kitchens, barracks for guards, an armory, and a covered well, with a grain bin. The squarish structure was Nigel's private rooms. Its courtyard was paved with fine cerise gravel. No traffic distorted it. There was no motion in any of the windows in the old buildings.

The guard pounded on the unyielding gates. This garnered no interest from any enemy who might lie secreted in the inscrutable fortress.

"I dreamed *not* of speaking with Nigel, *himself*," Zadok

shouted, "but, I never expected to endure the ignominious *affront* of being ignored by his *base* underlings!"

The gray Citadel remained enigmatic.

"I did not *embrace* the *dubious* thrill of conversing with *mighty* Nigel, anyway!" Zadok shouted. He rode away, awash with gratitude that he had not been horribly rent to death by some ghastly demon of the Dark Wizard's insane devising.

Arden jumped to the catwalk and descended a stairway to the courtyard. He noted omens of recent pedestrian traffic in the ruby gravel. Human and Elf. However, these sign were no more contemporary than three days. A guise of Nigel's magic? Arden wondered if he was *actually* inside the Fort. Nigel's capacity to convene the Enchantments and the Red Swamp could slavishly serve him in erecting an illusory Citadel to deceive and slay the War Party. Arden shrugged this notion off and turned to his objective.

Nigel's grim residence resembled a squarish, lead colored, granite bottle prone on one side.

Arden shoved open the tall, weathered wood door and stepped into the main hall. Stained glass windows, at regular intervals, in the gray walls, allowed the Sun to fill the hall with colors, revealing only dust that had built up over the lonely years.

Arden strode to the end of the main hall.

Ahead, lay the corridor of bedrooms. Their doors were ajar. To the left, a passageway tracked to the kitchen and the scullery.

Arden searched these, then the sleeping chambers. All were deserted, dusty and eerily quiescent. He paused at the limit of the bedroom hall and rubbed his forehead in puzzlement. Nigel had *never* been there, except, *perhaps*, in the *courtyard*. Where, then, *was* he entrenched? Arden smiled grimly. There existed only one other harbor for Nigel.

Arden decided he had best court wisdom and open the gates for his fellows to apprise them of the irking fact that their confrontation with dark Nigel would be delayed, even though Arden's encounter with an angry Guthrie would not.

Something ducked back from the nearest chamber doorway.

Arden quietly drew his sword and warily approached that portal.

There was a motion in a doorway to the right.

It was impossible for the culprit to have traveled from the first room to the one opposite without crossing in front of Arden. Could Nigel be masking his Elves with invisibility? If so, Arden was still able to catch unclear glimpses of them from the corners of his eyes. He stared straight down the corridor. His heart convulsed. There were movements in each of the bedchamber portals. At *least* ten opponents! Arden bolted down the hallway.

Shuffling footsteps pursued.

Arden egressed into the main hall and glanced over his shoulder. He perceived nothing within the gloomy, colorful, semi darkness that could be producing those sounds. Real men or Elves would not shuffle so. They would tread stealthily and *destroy* intruders by surprise. He realized Nigel had invoked some type of evil magical warden to conserve his Fort.

The mysterious scuffling continued.

Arden reached the end of the bedchamber corridor, turned, so he could face whatever vile threat Nigel had actualized, and began backing into the great hall.

"Arden."

"Aldora?" Arden said, with a mixture of surprise, gladness, and anger. He spun around and blundered into something soft, sticky and slightly elastic. The impact repelled him flat, and he rolled side to side across the main hall. When he scrambled to his feet, he saw that Aldora was nowhere to be found, and that he was being menaced by several dozen—shadows!

They were humanoid, transparent, tarry and flat. Less than two inches thick.

Perhaps, I only *imagined* I heard Aldora, Arden thought. He backed toward the front door. It slammed shut with a sound that somehow conveyed anger. He groped behind himself and wrung the knob.

Locked!

The portals to the kitchen and pantry hallway were closed, resoundingly. There was no egress at the end of the bedroom corridor, and those aged chambers lacked windows. The only escape opportunity existed in the windows of the main hall.

Arden darted toward the first window to his right.

Several silhouettes forestalled him.

Arden veered left, only to discover this escape attempt had been anticipated.

The way was blocked by a line of shadows.

Arden had no promise of attaining the windows further along the main hall. He rammed his sword into a silhouette.

The shape bent over backwards with the blow, then snapped back erect.

Arden sliced at the shadow's head.

The figure's cranium canted down and to the side, unmarred.

Arden's blade rebounded from the shadow, the hilt nearly flying from his grasp.

"*Arden*!" Guthrie shouted from far away. "Are you *in* the Fort?"

"*Arden*! *Quickly*!" Durward shouted. "Allow us *access*! I sense Nigel's *demonic* energy *within* the Fort!"

"I am *trapped* in the *residence*!" Arden shouted.

Sundry silhouettes joined hands, like cloth strips gluing together. They described a semicircle and approached Arden, herding him toward the front door.

The remaining figures became many times thicker and darker than those threatening Arden. They began climbing the walls and pasting themselves over the windows of the main hall, and each other, forming barriers to the colorful comforting light streaming in.

"The scaling sets!" Durward shouted. "*Only* my Nigel, can batter down these walls and gates!"

"Scouts, remain with the horses," Guthrie shouted.

The shadows at the end of the semicircle reached the corners near the entrance.

This remaindered Arden dwindling space. He paced back and forth, jabbing savagely and repeatedly at as many of the silhouettes as possible, endeavoring to deter their advance. The sword depressed their abdomens or the tops of their heads, non-lethally. Arden turned and hacked at the great worn door. The wood persevered, as unyielding as brown stone. He hammered his hilt against the rusty lock with no result, then shouldered his weight against the imprisoning portal. The door refused to rattle in its stone frame. Arden heard a trio of scaling sets clang on the front battlements. "*Durward*!" he shouted. "Nigel has *invoked* gluey occult shadows! My blade fails to *lacerate* them! Can you *vanquish* them?"

"*This* Enchantment is *too* potent to *negate*!" Durward shouted. "I shall sally my beams!"

Arden heard the War Party running over the gravel. He turned toward the faceless shadows. When they deemed themselves to be prepared, they would adhere to, and suffocate him horribly swiftly. He could not leap over the phantoms. They were three heads taller than he. They paced too closely together for him to dive between their legs as he had Sanborn's.

A recurring whizzing, breaking of glass, and twanging, enticed Arden's eyes to the nearest window on his right. Durward was mentally hurling stones against the shadow cowling. The projectiles were rebounding without causing damage. There was a lapse, followed by a whistling, breaking glass, and a much louder twang.

Arden discerned the contour of a sword repel off the silhouettes.

Although the long blade had been sponsored by Durward's complete vitality, it was just as non-maiming as the rocks.

"*Futile*!" Arden shouted. "They can't be *rent*! *Cast* your *magic fire*, Durward!"

The shadows in the semicircle paused, and an eerie energy prowled the main hall. They were afraid of the Magician's thermal energy. The semicircle of silhouettes reversed away from Arden, separated from each other, scaled the walls with their gluey hands and feet, and pasted themselves against the shadows already curtaining the windows. The illumination decreased to almost the color of pitch.

"They *dread* your *flame* magic, Durward!" Arden shouted. "But, they have reinforced the barriers on the windows! Strike the *portal*! It has been *petrified*, but your Sun and Winter rays should brittle it as they did the stone at the River! At least enough for you to burst the door with your battering ram force!"

"Can you shift to safety!" Durward shouted, from just outside the door.

"Yes! No! Wait!" Arden shouted.

Silhouettes were aborning from mid-air within the center of the main hall. The moment they alighted on the floor, they shuffled toward the front entrance.

Arden dodged to the corner at his right. "It is *hopeless*!"

he shouted. "Shadows are being extruded from the ether and are re-enforcing the door! They must be able to resist your fire and ice if enough are a ply! Enlist *another* offense! *Hurry*! They will seek me, next, and I will be *suffocated*!" He scanned the main hall.

More silhouettes were aborning from the atmosphere. Some joined the shadows loricating the entrance. Others, merged with the silhouettes plastered on the windows. Each new layer thickened the gloom in the main hall.

Arden was unable to discern his hand before his eyes. He knew, with terrifying certainty, the shadows would suffer no such handicap. There came a florid, flickering at the window on his right.

Durward was sizzling a heat beam against the shadows cowling that window.

The glow enabled Arden to see.

A wall-to-wall semicircle of silhouettes was slowly converging upon the Crown Prince Designate.

Arden had no sanctuary. If he retreated to the front door, he would be glued to the shadows loricating the petrified wood. If he went to the other corner near the portal, he would be glued against the smooth gray stone, and slain. If he stayed put, the semicircle of shadows would pack themselves on him in that corner.

At the present, no new silhouettes were being created.

There *must* be sufficient shadows to deter Durward and the War Party from rescuing me, Arden thought wildly. He would be smothered within mere moments. He stepped to the window against which Durward was searing energy. The flames whirled and roared against the black silhouettes. Arden could detect no heat through them. He hacked desperately at the figures, but his sword bounced back, as uselessly as before.

"Arden!"

Arden fixed his attention to the area of the huge hall that lay just behind where the new silhouettes had been created. The fluttering pink glow of Durward's magic fire allowed Arden to see with horrified clarity. He gasped.

Aldora was there! She was being held by her arms, waist, and ankles by mystic shadows. She struggled to free herself, but was helpless. Behind her, in the far wall, Arden could see the open door of a secret passage he and Aldora, as children, had discovered years ago when seeking Nigel, who had been hiding behind it.

"*Durward*!" Arden shouted. "*Aldora* is *here*! We are *forfeit,* unless you try something *else*! There *must* be something *else*!"

"Did Arden say that *Aldora* is *with* him?" Guthrie shouted.

"Yes," Durward said. "I sense—*perhaps*, Aldora, inside."

"*Aye*," Galen said.

"Oh, Arden," Aldora said with despair. "I *thought* I could *assist* you with Dark Nigel. Could *calm* him. Could *reason* with the poor man, but I have only *slain* us."

Aldora's words tore at Arden's mind and heart.

The shadows imprisoning Aldora began circling around her, gluing themselves, to her.

"*Please*, Arden," Aldora pleaded, with terror. "*Save* me! *Help* me! Do not just *stand* there and *allow* me to *die*!"

Arden shoved, kicked, pulled, and hacked at the magic figures damming him from Aldora, and his soul raged with impotence.

The bloody flaring of Durward's emanation ceased.

Arden startled. He could no longer *see* Aldora. It was as if they were entombed in an isolated mausoleum. "*Durward*!" he shouted, desperately. "We require *light*!" Why, he thought, despondently, our death, illumined, is still death! Arden began flailing his sword. As it wrought contact more regularly, his worst fears were confirmed. The shadows were almost upon him! "Why is Durward not *assaulting*?" Arden cried out, with panic. "*Aldora*! *Answer* me! *Aldora*! *Damn* you, *Nigel*!"

A figure leaped against Arden's chest, wrapped itself around his torso, and adhered.

"I *love* you, Arden," Aldora whispered, lovingly.

The words tore Arden's heart and soul. Another vile shadow flung itself around him, the opposite way of the first, gluing his arm to his side.

"But, *only* as a *brother*," Aldora whispered, adoringly.

The unexpected words raised the hair on the back of Arden's neck. He was hemmed in more closely by the crescent of silhouettes, but his sword blows were still ineffectual.

"We can be such *dear* friends, Arden, *but* we can

never wed," Aldora whispered, lovingly.

"*You* are *not* Aldora!" Arden screamed, with cold realization, and absolute, affronted rage.

"I *venerate*, and shall *marry*, only *Nigel*," Aldora said, adoringly. "He *is*, compared to *you*, a *god* of *light*!"

"*Shut up*, you ineffectual foulness!" Arden screamed. "*You* are *not* Aldora! Do not *defile* her by imitating her *form* and *voice*, and uttering to me the *truth* she bespoke to *vile* Nigel! "

"*Brougher* is *far* from *ineffectual*," the Fortress Enchantment said, still using Aldora's soft, loving voice. "Which *fact* you *shall* experience, *swiftly* and *painfully*."

The cerise scintillation from Durward's crackling fire ghosted throughout the haunted residence.

Arden thought his terror and concern for what he had believed was his beloved Aldora, had driven him insane.

The flames were snapping and roaring against the figures curtained on all the windows on both sides of the wide main hall, and roasting the front door, tremoring it.

Durward was scorching his inferno force over the entire granite residence.

Arden could perceive the silhouettes and the false Aldora. The sticky, inky hands of the figures ringing him were up stretched toward his face, but—His heart thudded with hope. The shadows were paralyzed! Durward's assail was sapping the figures of their strength; taxing Nigel's Enchantment! Perhaps the shadows were weak enough now to allow him to flee their grasp.

Arden wiggled and twisted against the silhouettes plastered round his torso. This was to no avail. His hand was still pinioned. His respiration was impeded! Panic had obstructed previous comprehension that the shadows were squeezing him! He sawed at the silhouettes affixed on his chest. They were still immune to the keenness of his blade.

"Don't *struggle* so, *dear*, sensitive man," Brougher said, in Aldora's caring tones. "It will only *add* suffering to your *inevitable*, *miserable*, *well-deserved* end."

"*Arden*!" Guthrie shouted. "How do *you* and *Aldora* fare?"

"It is *not* Aldora! I was *duped* by a *sham*, a *vile* golem of *shadow*!" Arden shouted, with hatred. "I am glued fast, and suffering trouble breathing! Durward has immobilized the silhouettes, but they remain too elastic for me to slice my way free!" Arden attempted to wrench back away from the figure ring, but won no clue of freedom. The silhouettes around his torso were affixed to the semicircle of shapes, and *their* sticky feet were glued to the flagstones of the floor.

"*Galen*! *Enforce* me!" Durward shouted. "I am *losing* potency!"

The scarlet blaze drumming against the door and the shadows loricating the windows, began to wane.

Arden's stomach knotted, with horror. If Durward falters, even for a minute, he thought, I am dead!

The fire intensified, then vanished.

Arden was avalanched with darkness and despair.

The Stygian gloom enlivened with shuffling, everywhere.

A shadow curled around Arden, gluing his free hand against his hip, and his sword clattered to the flagstones.

"Arden, you are a *handsome, refined* man," Brougher said, with Aldora's most soothing tone, "any *other* woman in the Kingdom would be *proud* to be *your* wife. But, *I* am *twined* with *Nigel,* and you *must* accept *this* fact."

"You *waste* your breath, *monster*!" Arden shouted. "Though you *feign* her *likeness*, and her *voice*, it *harms* me *not*. It shows only the all encompassing *inadequacy* of *you* and your *deranged* master."

Arden's legs were encircled next, and slowly vised together. He strove to retain his equilibrium, but toppled to his face on the flagstones.

"Then, *suffer* my *supposed* inadequacy," Brougher said, snarling like an enraged beast.

The shadows forsook the windows for the kill, and cascaded upon the Crown Prince Designate.

Arden wagged and bobbed his head, frenziedly. If he could forestall the figures from covering his mouth and nostrils, for even seconds, Galen would revitalize Durward for further attack, re-paralyzing the shadows.

A silhouette slithered under Arden's face and coiled around his head like new flesh. "*Aldora,*" he screamed in his agonized mind.

"I am *here*, my beloved *brother*," Brougher said, speaking lovingly, as Aldora, "to witness the ignoble end to your feckless, misdirected, unwanted, unrequited love, and to finish the blight of your unnecessary life."

The Enchantment withdrew its magic vitality from the

perimeter of the residency, returning the building's materials to normalcy, and fed that evil energy to the creatures murdering Arden.

The roof exploded thunderously. Particles of shingles and beams sleeted on the shadows. Tarry smoke billowed into the main hall, then crimson rays of sun shafted through the fumes. The silhouettes squealed like scalded lizards, writhed, shriveled and fissured, decaying into unpleasant coarse, ebony, sticky sand.

The image of Aldora was gone.

"*Too* late!" Brougher screamed, with desperation. "*Nigel*! I *beseech* you! *Assure* me! *Tell* me that it is *too* late, for sweet, horrid Arden to be saved! *That* I do *not* perish, for *you*, for *naught*!"

The front door creaked with complaint, then burst open. Guthrie and Galen stumbled into the main hall. They righted their balance, raced desperately to Arden, and turned him onto his back.

Galen tore the shriveling brittle shadows free of Arden's mouth and breathed life into him.

Guthrie furiously ripped layer after layer of the silhouettes from around his son.

The shadows on the lowest laps were not yet affected by the flood of sunlight and were still compressing Arden's rib cage. When the sun finally accessed them, they screeched, and withered.

Guthrie rent them to shreds, hurling fistfuls of their dying substance aside.

Durward staggered into the main hall, and propped

himself against the ruined portal. He was rice paper pale, and shaking. He had strained in the production of psychic force as never before, to breach the roof and had nearly burst his valiant heart. "Does Arden *survive*?" he gasped.

Galen stared in shock, then hastened to Durward and clasped the Magician's head in his medicating hands. "Yes," the Mind Healer softly assured the Magician. "Arden *will* arise restored after a night's slumber. So shall *you*."

Brougher shrieked, like a thousand panicked animals perishing in pain.

Silence.

The coarse, tarry, particles faded away from Arden, the windows, and the gray flagstones of the floor. Soon, there was no evidence in The Gray Fort that any unnatural life had infested its sad, ancient and stately hallways.

Illustration 15

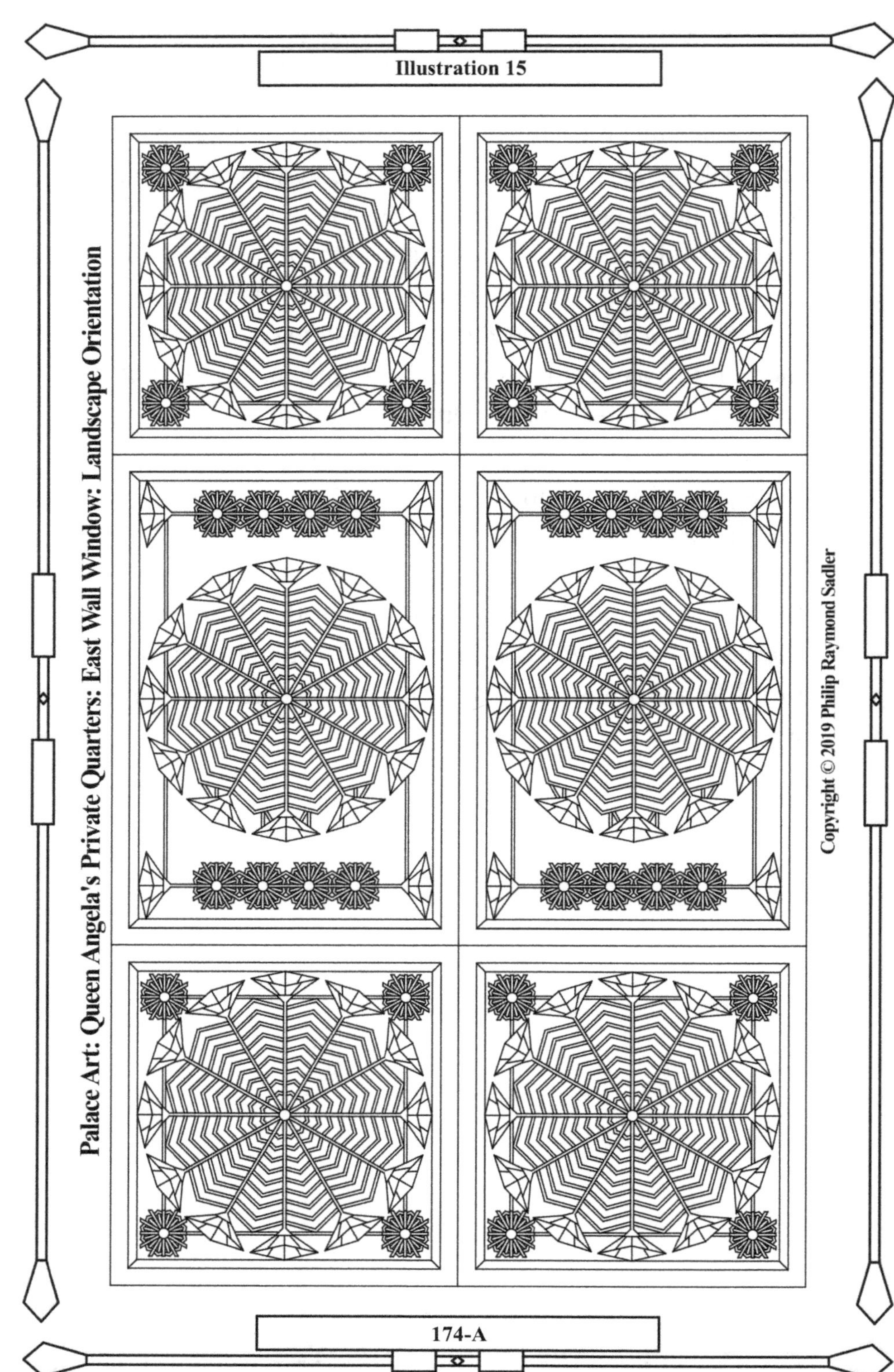

Palace Art: Queen Angela's Private Quarters: East Wall Window: Landscape Orientation

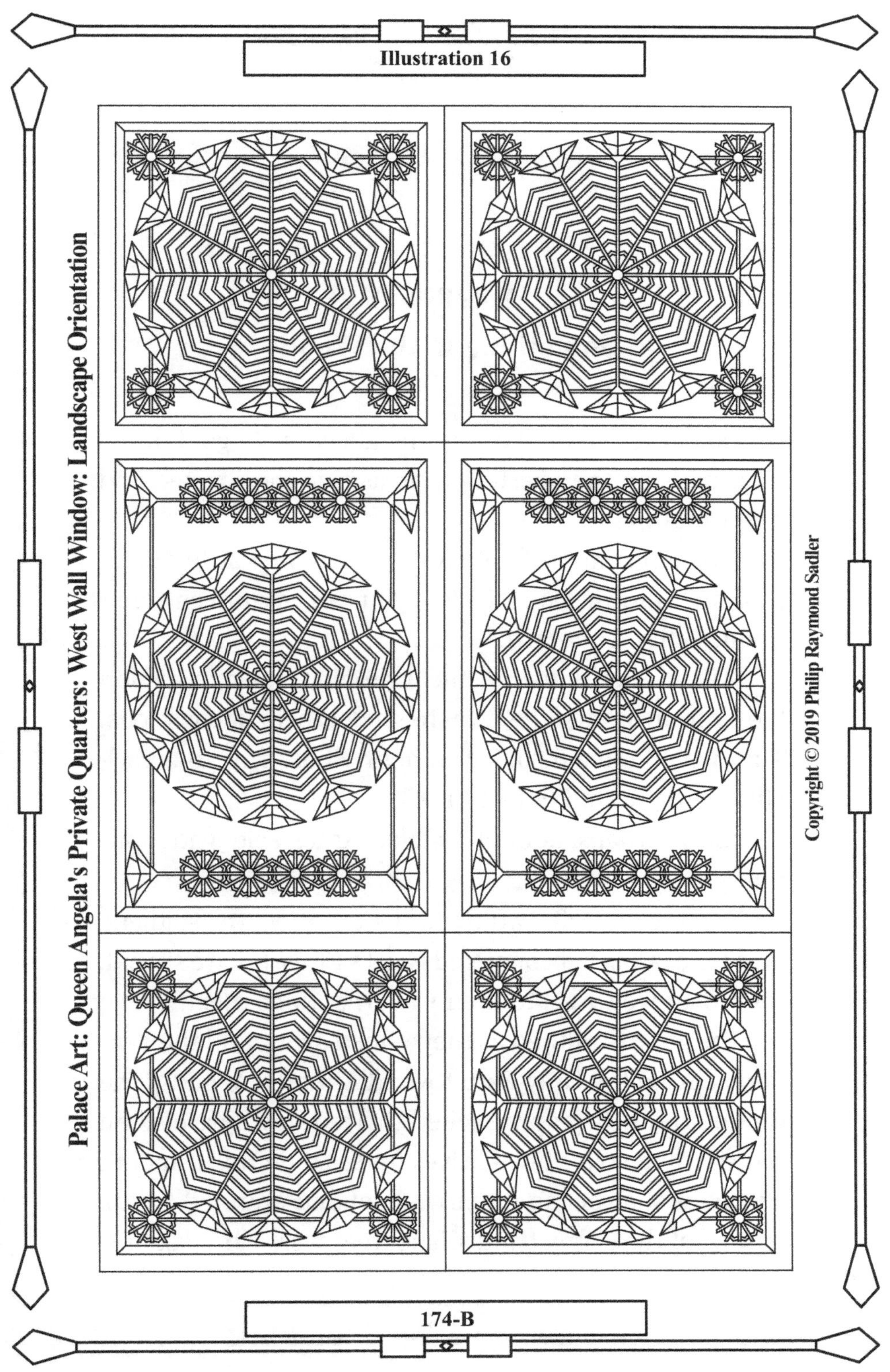
Illustration 16
Palace Art: Queen Angela's Private Quarters: West Wall Window: Landscape Orientation
Copyright © 2019 Philip Raymond Sadler
174-B

Chapter 8
Something in the Woods

Outside the Gray Fort, in the affectionate gold of the morning sun, the questers were astride their rested and eager mounts.

"Nigel triumphs if Fate decrees that we battle the Elf Nation," Guthrie said. "Unless you can circumvent their invincibility, Durward."

"With Galen enforcing me, I should be able to suction the air from around the Elves to render them unconscious. They would remain so, for an hour. Short time to breach Nigel's might and defeat him."

"But, perhaps, not impossible," Arden said, with optimism.

"Two scouts left, two right," Guthrie told the soldiers. "We have not *yet* encountered Nigel's Elves, but we should, the closer we travel to their Caverns. *Keep alert*!"

The guards saluted as they reined away, and the War Party circled the Gray Fort, toward Anomaly Woods. The unique trees they approached thrived nowhere else on Indwin. Wide olive hued leaves fluttered on thick smooth branches that began at earth level and spiraled to the crowns of the ebony trunks. The trees were close-set, impelling the War Party to proceed single file.

An unexpected clearing gaped grimly in the heart of the somber woods. Several of the giant noble trees had been burst asunder and fired recently, and a deep crater had been gouged in the emerald moss and fertile raven earth.

"Durward," Galen said, "do you recall the large, peculiar meteor which day-lighted midnight a month past? Here, rings its impact signature, but where lies the stone?"

The questers paused at the edge of the double crater.

Galen held his hands over it as one would above a welcomed campfire on a snowy night. "The sad earth yet complains of the violence wrought here," he said. "And—curious—"

"Yes," Durward agreed. "There oscillate *two* forces here. The one of collision, the other, an energy which scans similar to Nigel's psychic vibrations."

Galen looked knowingly at the Magician. "This, then, un-riddles the enigma of Nigel's increased potency," the Healer said. "The meteor is a *reservoir* and *radiator* of psychic energy which sensitives can detect and utilize via aura absorption, if close to the stone, or through ingestion, which is the best of the two methods. The meteor *is* Nigel's *Enhancer*."

"Nigel *has* claimed the sky stone," Durward said. "He has probably pestled it, mixed the powder with water, and is *imbibing* the pure solution."

"What does *this* portend for *us*?" Arden said. "Can we sift the dirt for crumbles of this uncanny alien rock, that you might port them with you and draw upon their energy while inside the Elf Caverns?"

"*If* there remained worthwhile powder or stone here, Nigel would be protecting it with Elves or an Enchantment," Guthrie said. "What do you sense, Galen? Durward?"

"I divine nothing that bespeaks Nigel," Galen said.

"Nor I," Durward said. "Just the dregs of the force of the impact of the out world rock. What do *you* feel?"

Arden and Guthrie sought any strange sensations which might be omens of disaster or aid.

"No electricity," Arden said.

"No apprehensions, or trembling," Guthrie said.

"Then, there is no substantial part of the meteor buried here," Durward said, with disappointment. "We practice wisdom, to press forward."

They skirted the right side of the crater.

Durward felt a twinge in his stomach. There were no birds singing or animals stirring in the aged woods, now. The hooves of their horses sired no sounds against the mossy ground or the occasional bedrock they traversed.

Guthrie perceived these omens, and reined in his steed. "Guards, *ho*!" he shouted. "*Guards*! Return to *party*!"

Galen and Durward muttered with dismay. As in the Crane Marsh, the Knight's words had not flown six feet. The scouts could be twenty yards distant and not hear Guthrie even if he screamed.

"We are again isolated by Nigel's conjury," Durward said. "He has slyly permeated the woods with his energy."

Wind whispered and swirled around the War Party. It was a gentle breeze, and it broadcast some warmth, then it began whirling more briskly.

"Comes an Enchantment," Arden said, nervously.

They strained to discern any menacing shape in the fluttering leaves of the funereal trees, but this was impossible. The low guttural laughter of something insane, scrabbled throughout the Wood. The cachinnation continued sans halt. Whatever laughed, required no breath. A cachinnation erupted behind. Then, on each flank. Then, all around. There seemed to be hundreds of unseen fiends laughing without hint of respiration.

"It sounds like every tree in this Wood is chortling in victory, before the battle has commenced," Arden said, nervously.

Durward flicked his hands up, with his fingers spread wide, and clear energy flowed forth, evolving into a transparent dome around the questers. "This will *bar* the wiles of a Monrow, or a Sanborn," the Magician said. "But, if this Enchantment attacks with Nigel's full vitality, I fear that it will still penetrate to us."

Galen stared at Durward, with disbelief. "Do you fathom what you are doing?" the Healer said.

Durward startled. The shield began to flicker. He calmed himself. The magical umbrella regained its firmness. "I did *not*," he said. "I have *never* been a *carver* of shields. I have never *mastered* sufficient power, before."

"I still spy no Enchantment," Guthrie said.

The humming wind whirl-pooled around the safeguard as though frustrated at its inability to buffet the men.

"The crater!" Durward said. "The energy that lingers there *must* enable me to en-shield us! Into the crater so that I may better draw upon its radiance and preserve us against this invisible Enchantment!"

The gale died as though the Enchantment were expressing its dismay at Durward's idea, but the laughing survived, encompassing the War Party.

"Woodruff's opening gambit."

Arden brushed at his ears. Was *that* the *wind*, or is that how this Enchantment *speaks*, he wondered? As a *whispering* subtly born upon the wind?

Guthrie, although he was close beside Arden, seemed not to have heard the words.

A tree arrear the War Party cracked in half at the middle of its length and thudded into the moss with such violence that it was half interred. Many of its long branches snapped off in all directions as though the ebony trunk had been smitten by the massive fist of an irate giant.

The horses spooked. The questers fought them under control.

A tree broke in half and slammed into the moss in front of the War Party. A tree thundered to earth beside them, shattering along its length and raining branches. One more tree drop, and they would not only be banned from the crater, but penned into a prison with ready-made bars.

"Here!" Arden shouted, ushering the War Party toward the open end of the tree fall.

Mossy earth was hoisted, by no visible source, into a towering green wall, damming them from the crater.

"Checkmate," Woodruff's wind voice sighed in Arden's ears.

"*Durward,*" Galen said, "the *radiation* in the crater may enable you to *levitate* us!"

Instead of lifting the War Party, Durward flipped one of the trees up and out of their way, wedging it between two other trees still rooted. The questers galloped into the shallow crater under the protection of Durward's clear shield, and paused at the heart of the pit to make their stand against the cordoning malevolence. Durward domed the shield over the crater, rim to rim.

"Countered with *surprising* cunning," Woodruff's wind voice whispered in Arden's ears. "I move. You lose."

The branches of the ancient trees bordering the crater began resoundingly exploding free of their trunks. They slammed into the shield, shattered, then bounced away.

The War Party fought with their mounts again.

Galen was bucked to the earth.

"Durward!" Arden shouted. "Entrance our steeds *before* they trample us!"

There was a slight crackling of energy from Durward. The horses ceased moving.

Arden leaped from his saddle and helped Galen up. They remounted their motionless steeds.

The many branches hailing and thumping into the shield from all directions prevented the War Party from seeing beyond their sanctuary.

Durward transmitted motive force at one side of the dome. The long branches smashing into the shield, were swept away. Incredible darkness was revealed. More branches re-coated the crystal wall.

"Nigel has *won*!" Arden shouted, in terror. His words were barely audible over the banging din of the raining tree limbs. "He has *injected* us into some inky *abyss*!"

"An *illusion*," Durward said, firmly, "to *frighten* us to *folly*. The Woods *still*, exists around us. We will have to *bide* this attack out. I can, *if* the energy in the crater *lasts* long enough. My shield should *prevent* the branches from harming us." He added a colorless floor to the dome.

"Heed *not* the prevaricating Magician," Woodruff's wind voice said in Arden's ears. It's words were difficult for Arden to discern above the drumming of the attacking branches, and it sounded like the evil Enchantment was *inside* the safeguard. "You *are*, in fact, entombed *forever* within the *inescapable* Abyss of Nightmares of yore. For, it is a *fact*, not a *fancy*, as liars have told you since childhood. It is a never ending reality of suffering that Nigel has convened, and my Dark Lord has *dispatched* you all *here*. I *am* it's perpetual *guardian* and *your* everlasting *tormentor*."

"Durward would not *lie*!" Arden shouted, angrily. He stared around the dome, expecting to find the Enchantment hulking near him.

"What ails you, Arden?" Guthrie said, soothingly.

"Your *pitiful* mind is *riddled* with *misunderstandings*, *distortions*, *exaggerations*, and tragic *blank spots*," Woodruff said, closer to Arden's ears. "A *defect* of your aborning."

"*Woodruff*!" Arden said, "The *Enchantment*! It is in here with *us*! It is *taunting* me, *insulting* me, telling me we are *sealed* in the *Abyss* of *Nightmares*!"

"We hear nothing," Galen said, moving his hands in a circle above him. "I sense only ourselves."

"They do not *believe* you," Woodruff's hissed, in Arden's ears. "They think you *mad, ill, unfit*."

"I am not—" Arden realized what Woodruff's stratagem was. He shrugged his shoulders. "I will not *play* living *prey* to your verbal *hound*," he said, firmly. "You may direct at me what was uttered to Nigel of his ailment, but it will be *here*, just as it *was* in the Gray Fort, *wasted* effort."

"Not so," Woodruff's whispered, in Arden's ears. "See your fine *friends*, how they stare at you with pity and sad concern. They think you, *mad*, for you are speaking to *yourself*. They *will* turn upon you, soon. *Lie* to you. *Placate*, you. *Deceive*, you. *Betray* you with words of love while plotting your demise. My effort *is* well-used."

Galen leaned from his saddle to place hands to Arden's temples.

Arden drew back, insulted. "It *speaks*," he said, angrily. "No amount of *healing* will *erase* that *reality*."

"Of this, I have no doubt," Galen said.

"Did I not *charitably* impart to you the sad truth," Woodruff's sighed, with tragic dismay, in Arden's ears. "*Already*, they *placate*, while they *plot*. Trust in *me*, Galen *will* sap your *life force* until you *die*. *Better* you be dead, than they face the *shame* of an *insane* Crown Prince Designate."

Guthrie and Durward took hold of Arden's shoulders and arms.

Arden fought to pull free of his friends. "I am *not* insane!" he told them, angrily. "The Enchantment *is* speaking to me! I *oath* this upon my *soul*!"

"We *understand*," Galen said. He reached to place his gentle palms to Arden's temples. "If I connect with you, I can *hear* what you *hear*. *Feel* what you *feel*."

"*Trust* them, *fool*, and you *perish*!" Woodruff whispered urgently and fearfully, in Arden's ears. "Hear *my* voice of *pure* wisdom, and *stinging* experience! *Fight*! *Flee*!"

Arden moved his head back and forth, avoiding contact with Galen's hands. The Healer still managed to latch onto Arden's temples.

"*Simple*. So *simple*. Now, your dear loved ones shall *end* your *sick pitiful life*. Then, *I* shall *vanquish* theirs," Woodruff's eerie wind voice exulted, sounding in the dome like the hissing of a giant serpent.

Arden relaxed, with relief.

"Not so," Woodruff sighed, with dismay. "They can not hear, *unless* Woodruff *wills* that it shall be *so*! How *be* this *abomination*, Nigel? For, I am half impaired if they can hear my attack upon the smiling Prince. The handsome *monster* who *rends* you in your *nightmares*."

Durward pressed his palms to Galen's hands.

Red energy briefly crackled in the air between Durward and Arden.

Durward laughed, with satisfaction. "Now, Woodruff's insipid words can be heard by all of us no matter how it and Nigel ineptly connive to prevent this," he said.

Galen and Durward released Arden's head.

"*Lies*, Arden, from warm faced *deceivers*," Woodruff's weird gale words whispered under the dome. "*No one* supersedes *my* Master's *black magic*."

"I heard you, construct of vileness," Guthrie said. "*You* are the *sole* self-deceiver *here*, and now you are *unmasked,* and *laughable*."

"Though this horribly be so," Woodruff screamed, with its wind voice, "yet, shall I *slay* you and *rend* your flesh until none shall recognize that it once was of mortal origin."

A tree on their left was uprooted and slammed lengthwise, with an ear drum stinging thud, against the shield.

The War Party was preserved by the dome.

However, Durward was shaking with the intense effort of maintaining the integrity of the safeguard.

The questers dismounted and huddled in the center of the umbrella.

"Endure *this*, oh, *wondrous* Magus of *might*!" Woodruff's scorn filled voice, breezed around them.

A second tree crashed into the clear shield, with a tremendous boom, vibrating the seekers. Then another. And a fourth. The dome flickered, and a trunk pierced its top, scattering the War Party, barely missing the entranced horses, and spearing into the ebony earth.

Durward gasped in deep breaths.

The shield ceased faltering, but it was not as solid as before.

"How the *exalted* old one *trembles* and *wanes* in his *piteous* fright of Woodruff's *undeniable* and *majestic* might!" Woodruff's delight hissed in their ears. The words were almost inaudible over the drumming of the sharp branches against the safeguard.

The War Party regrouped around the limb stripped trunk that had punctured the apex and floor of the magical dome. The boughs were still raining down, preventing outer visibility.

"No *brave* rejoinders, no *fiery* retorts?" Woodruff's glee voice gusted about them. "Great Nigel, *stop* and *look*, these puny *pawns* be *mated* soon!"

A tree speared into the shield, penetrating the side wall by a few inches. Another bounced off of the sanctuary. Then a third. And a fourth. Three denuded trunks impacted at once. Each pierced part way into the top of the dome.

"*Galen*!" Durward cried, painfully. "*Now*, help to *maintain* our fort!"

"Takes these tiny *two* to respond to *one*! What *boring* fun! I thought you promised great *delight,* within this *fight,* to *tax* my *might*! Nigel, my *sacred* master and dark *delight*!"

The Healer placed his hands to Durward's temples, enforcing him.

The shield waxed more concrete.

There were fewer branches sleeting into the dome, but the shreds into which they had been impacted were raining and banging down.

A trunk sheared through the side of the shield.

Guthrie was butted, rolling, across the shielded earth. He lay limp and pale, as though unconscious or perished.

"One *cowering* Knight's been *handily* taken, if Woodruff's *eyes* are not mistaken!" Woodruff's delighted voice whistled in their ears.

Arden fearfully monitored Guthrie's heart and respiration. "Father *is* alive!" Arden shouted, over the drumming. "But, I do not know if he *requires* healing, to awaken!"

"I dare not decouple from Durward!" Galen shouted. The Healer was frustrated because he could not transmit his healing across so short a distance.

"I know!" Arden shouted. Memory of his harrowing encounter with the Shadows in The Gray Fort flashed, grimly, at him. He felt frozen. There was as little hope here as there had been then.

"A *fearful* pair!" Woodruff's voice whirled around Durward and Galen. "You *should* despair!" it said to Arden. "Now, *resort* to *prayer*!" it said to all.

A tree sliced into a side of the shield for about three feet, just short of the hypnotized horses. The dome waned fainter. The bits of branches were thudding upon it like boulders against a crystal bowl. Another trunk smashed flat on those already penetrating the clear roof, nailing them in further. The War Party was squeezed into a six-foot space.

"I can withstand *only* two or three more such tree assaults!" Durward shouted, desperately. "Then, the shield shall surely collapse!"

"To *me* his *sage* advice he bespeaks *aloud*, a *stupid* vice of which he's *simpletonly* proud!" Woodruff's breeze words taunted, in Durward's ears.

"*Durward*!" Galen shouted, with hope. "If we contact the meteor shards *directly*, we can utilize their force more *swiftly* and *completely*!"

Durward and the Healer knelt on the clear floor.

The Magician absorbed its energy, adding it to the dome.

Galen whispered into the Magician's ear.

"Aye," Durward said. He drew the rim of their safeguard down the sides of the crater and extended the shield several feet into the soft earth. He formed a thin floor, catching the dirt of the secondary impact crater which contained flakes of the meteor, between themselves and the base of the safeguard.

"Now, they *counter,* before I *move*," Woodruff's breeze words said, with annoyance and grudging wonder, "of which I heartily *disapprove*."

The earth which pressed against the sides of the dome, formed rock hard spurs, and began alternately and repeatedly ramming the safeguard, weirdly producing no sound.

"It appears unable to spare much force to enliven the earth," Galen said.

"If not for your *timely* advice, Woodruff probably would have hardened the soil beyond our use," Durward said. He dug into the secondary crater and cupped some of its dirt in his hands.

Arden twinned the effort. "What identifies the sky stone?" he shouted.

"It flamed *orange*," Galen shouted, careful to keep his vital palms to Durward's forehead as the Magician continued digging, "and the remnants should claim identical hue!"

"Even *if* there *exist* some corrosive *bits*, that, *if* you *eat*, will cause you agonizing *fits*," Woodruff's gale sounds said, disapprovingly, "it will be too *late* to prevent your *fate*!"

Several trees plummeted toward the shield, but collided with each other and caromed harmlessly away.

"Though my *face* be *red*, don't *lose* your *dread*, you'll *soon* be *dead*!" Woodruff's wind voice chortled.

Durward became frustrated with excavating. He psychically flowed the ebony dirt away from the sparkling orange grains they urgently sought, until one of his palms was graced by a small pile of the Enhancer. He repeated the process with the dirt and meteor dust in Arden's hands.

"No *might* to *waste*! I *must* make *haste*!" Woodruff's harsh breeze words resounded in the dome, sounding concerned.

"Swallow this!" Durward shouted over the pounding of the shards. "It *energizes* Nigel, it *will* en-power us!"

Galen opened his mouth. Durward placed half his portion of the Enhancer onto the Healer's tongue. Durward ingested the remainder of his hard to swallow powder.

A tree speared through the top of the shield and into the earth, separating Arden from Galen and Durward.

"Nigel, a *dry* and *empty* plate! I *struck* too *late*, my dark *prelate*! My *endeavor* has *failed* to *sever* the only *two* who threaten *you*!"

Arden struggled, in vain, to reach them his store of the Enhancer.

"I *sense* the growing *counter* force! I have been lax! Now, to butler the final course! Before his power has time to wax!" Woodruff's gale words sounded urgent, pressed for time.

There was a terrible rending of wood. The trees half embedded in the dome began wagging back and forth or up and down, prying at the shield. The safeguard began cracking, ever so slowly.

Durward drew away from Galen, pressed his back against the trees piercing the safeguard, closed his eyes, and placed his palms flat against the top of the dome.

Arden felt a sunny warmth in the hand in which he clutched his bits of the meteor. He saw blue energy coursing from the back of his fist, to the nape of Durward's neck.

Galen did not note the glow because he was concentrating on Durward's pale face. The Healer was searching for the slightest sign that he should offer reinforcement.

The Magician seemed unaware of the occurrence, or did Durward slightly turn his head in recognition of receipt of the unexpected added might.

The blue ray ceased.

Arden opened his hand. The orange grains of the sky rock had turned black, their energy store depleted. Arden allowed the bits to fall at his feet, praying that the added might would enable Durward to surmount the invisible monstrosity Nigel had dispatched to slay them.

Durward whooped in victory. "I have manhandled the vitality this Enchantment is bludgeoning against us!" the Magician shouted. "I am recycling it! I am—"

Incredible frightening thunder shook the dome. Every tree was ripped free of it. The shield repaired instantly, but was still weak.

Galen leaped to his feet and set his hands to Durward's temples. "Your counter ploy was *excellent*!" he shouted.

"It was not *me*!" Durward wailed, with frustration and fear. "It was not *me*!"

"You have *slimily* dared to *invade* my *sanctity*! My very *being*, Magus of *Malevolence*!" Woodruff's wind words railed, with affront, in the dome. Its scorning, playful and pitiful rhyming was abandoned in its sudden battle for its life. "It is *time* for *me* to *check* and *mate*!"

A swarm of denuded trees, some flying level with the shred littered ground, others whistling from overhead like gigantic spears flung by enraged gods, pierced the shield, one by one, by several inches, fissuring it like lightning bolts cracking glass.

Woodruff's wind voice screamed for some time with an eerie heartfelt emotion the questers could not identify. Perhaps, it was the shriek of ultimate effort.

The earth spurs ceased ramming into the sides of the crystal psychical safeguard. The skin tingling ululations mercifully faded away. A profound silence amazed the War Party, shivering their achy spines and contracting their stomachs.

Durward and Galen collapsed to the soil, exhausted.

Guthrie moaned and slowly sat up.

"Is it finished?" Arden whispered.

Only the trunks of trees and the shreds of branches could be seen.

Durward weakly waved a hand. The shards flowed away from a portion of the shield, revealing bark-less trunks. He stood up and shakily pressed his palms against the wall. The log before him creaked, rotated side to side, then flipped up and back to the litter with a normal sounding thud, clearing a slim viewing port.

Arden caught his breath. The devastation scattered before them was as terrible as the charcoal ruination at the Orchards. Shattered trunks in crazy piles, and heaps of shredded branches, lay for as far as they could see.

The shield started flickering. The weight of the trees embedded in it, widened the cracks.

"With *haste*!" Durward shouted. "*Egress*! The meteor power of the crater is *depleted*! I can no longer *sustain* this shield!" He aimed a finger at the horses.

The steeds came fearfully awake.

Durward held a fist toward the cleared area of the

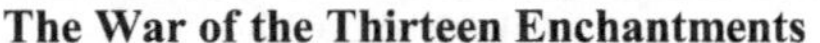

weak dome. He formed an opening by absorbing part of the energy of the shield.

Arden led Durward and Galen through the escape breach. The horses were nervous and balky at the ruination awaiting them. Guthrie slapped the lead mount on a flank. The horse bolted through the opening, with its herd mates faithfully trailing it. Guthrie somersaulted out of the exit, rolling up to his feet.

The trees defeated the dome with their mass, shattering it into a million glistening pieces.

Durward returned the shards to force; assimilating it.

The trunks settled into final position on the fertile ebon earth of the scarred crater floor.

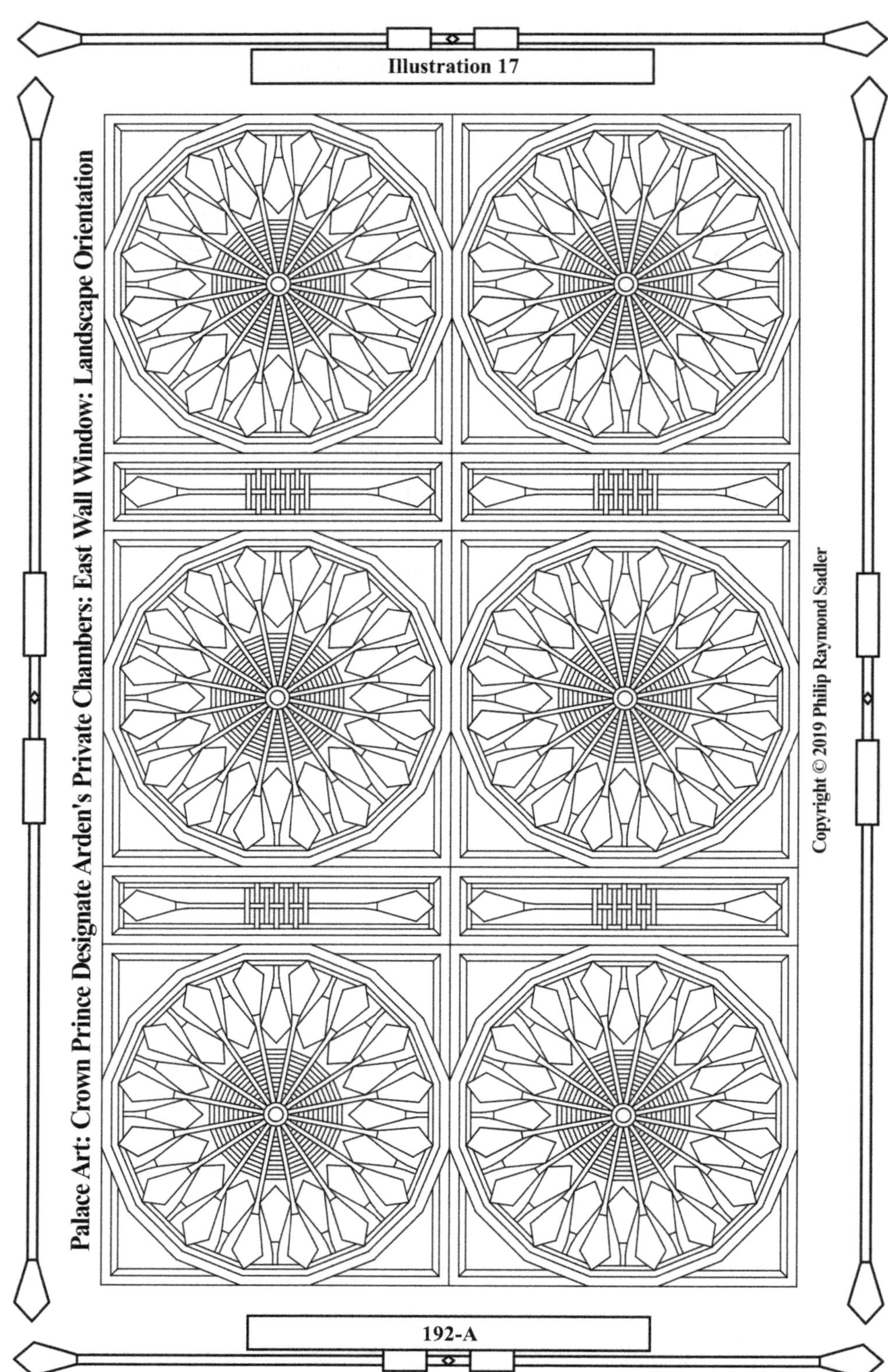
Illustration 17
Palace Art: Crown Prince Designate Arden's Private Chambers: East Wall Window: Landscape Orientation
Copyright © 2019 Philip Raymond Sadler
192-A

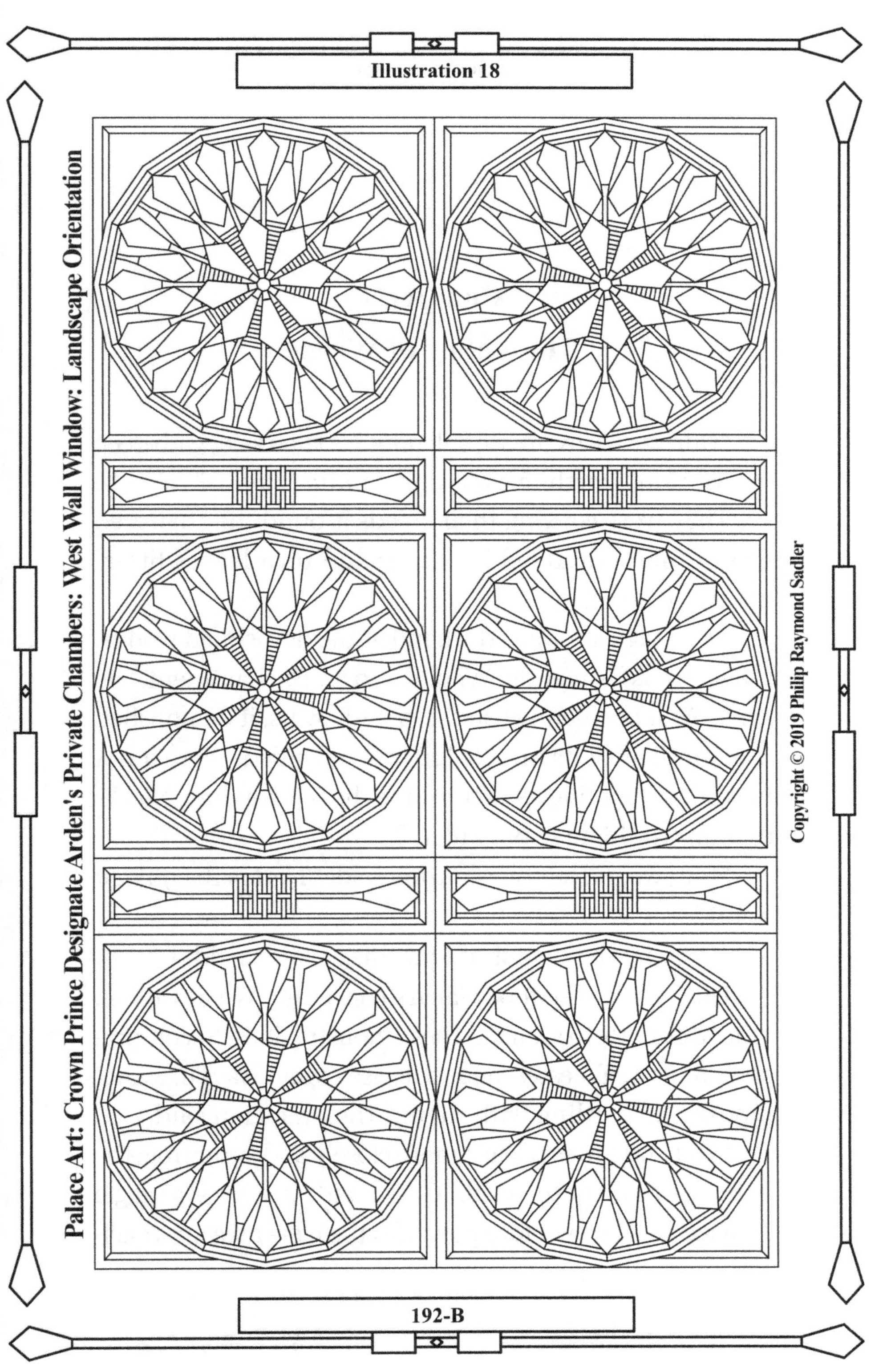
Illustration 18
Palace Art: Crown Prince Designate Arden's Private Chambers: West Wall Window: Landscape Orientation
Copyright © 2019 Philip Raymond Sadler
192-B

Chapter 9
The Valley of Weeds

"Durward, why are we still *alive*?" Galen said, with deep frustration, startling everyone. "I *must* know."

They were coaxing their steeds around the shattered tree trunks, shredded branches and torn leaves littering the ground.

The Magician waived a hand at the devastated woods. "Nigel transformed the Woods into an Enchantment," he said. "As it obediently sought to destroy us, it demolished itself until all of its unholy life was expended. Were it not for your prompting us to consume the meteor dust, Nigel's demon would have prevailed."

"But, we *did* survive," Arden said. "*That* is the *golden* point."

"Only by the barest of margins," Galen said.

Durward understood Galen's concerns. "We must seek more diligently to scan out these monstrosities, to comprehend their weaknesses, and to devise cogent ways to avoid, if possible, battling with them," the Magician said.

"You and I must cleave more closely and surely together from this point forward," Galen said, "for Nigel's magic menace shall grow more powerful the closer we approach to him."

"Nigel will seek to preclude our contact," Durward agreed, "almost as determinedly as he strives to slay Arden."

"Galen!" Guthrie said, urgently.

Afar ahead, at the perimeter of the devastated woods, the scouts and their proud mounts stood rigidly unresponsive to the hasty approach of the worried questers.

Galen dismounted first and raised his palms toward the guards. "Fear not," he said. "Our friends and their steeds have been magically hypnotized by the rude Woods Enchantment and are unharmed. I shall awaken them." The Healer touched each man and mount.

"*Arden*," Wayte said, "you're *alive*! Thank the *Fate* that puppets us!"

"We heard that *devilish* cackling and reversed to assist the War Party," Zadok said, "but we were *paralyzed* by Nigel's evil."

"We *feared* the *worst* for you," Ryley said, "then *eerie* unconsciousness claimed us."

"As usual," Hilliard said, with a chuckle, "our *fretting* was a *model* waste of time. It only worsened our *own* travails while you sat out the magic attack, no doubt, in *comfort*."

"On the contrary," Arden said, "you lucked the best. You *enjoyed*, a restful slumber, while we, *dodged*, impolite tree trunks."

"And, some complain there exist *no* rewards for *serving* as a guard," the soldiers chorused.

The War Party laughed.

Guthrie growled, imitating irritation. "Mirth *later*," he said, "duty *now*."

The Knight led the War Party into the tall grass of the rolling Hillocks of Jeddro, toward the Hunson Mountains which were a part of the North Shield Range that stood at the far end of Indwin Valley.

The little Valley looked peaceful in the bright canary sunlight. The War Party paused at its entrance.

"This Dale is *different*," Guthrie said. "There is *water* where *none* should be. And I have never *seen* the likes of *these* weeds."

Galen nodded. "There *is* a strange aura here," he said. "Nigel has patterned his conjury in the place."

Durward gazed across the glen at the long, thick, vine-like purple weeds, and the patches of sunlight reflecting from a thin presence of moisture along the hilly basin. "The water emerges from the center of the Dale," the Magician said, "as if an artesian spring succors the vegetation. This could be a *natural* phenomenon, a subterranean offshoot which has worked its way up from the Great River."

"Just a month past, our border scouts reported only sparse Kale Grass here," Arden said. "Such tares as those cannot mature in less time, except through magic."

"This is a *trap* we *shall* avoid," Guthrie said. "We can pass around this Dale, with little moment lost. I see no weeds on either side."

"Let us act *before* Nigel's guardian *discovers* our presence," Galen said, with a shiver.

"Guards," Arden said, "you scout left and right of the Dale, and report omens."

The sentries heeled their nervous mounts around and split, two to each direction, disappearing around the ends of the Dale.

"*We* had best *retreat*," Guthrie said. "There is no telling what Nigel may have concealed here."

Arden heeled his horse about and directed it to press forward.

A great line of weeds, spanning the mouth of the valley, speared up out of the earth, creating a wall that blocked the War Party's path.

"*This* Enchantment is *clever*," Galen said. "While we *connived* to outwit it, it sent its weeds around to take *us* by surprise."

Guthrie reigned his stallion into a rear. The odd weeds looked brittle, but the horse's hooves struck them with a metallic sound. The tares bent back slightly, like fine leather, then snapped straight. Guthrie's horse backed away.

"We are *joined* in battle," Durward said, morosely. "And, the *weeds* are our enemies."

Guthrie drew his sword and dismounted. "Chop them!" he said, "*before* the Enchantment *arrives* and has that sea of tares behind us to abet it! At least *now* we have a *chance* to break out of the Dale!" He began hacking at the glistening purple weeds.

Arden and Galen handed their reins to Durward, left their saddles, and joined the effort. Their swords rang against the weeds like a smith's hammer striking an anvil, but the keen blades wrought not a scratch.

"Durward," Guthrie said, angrily, "it will *require* your skills to part *this* barrier. Nigel has transformed them into pliable steel!"

There was a rustling from the Dale.

Arden looked, and his skin crawled.

The weeds were leaning forward like enraged snakes, straining to reach them. They began waving side to side, and the rustling increased.

Durward raised his right hand as he concentrated. He nodded, indicating his companions should draw back. Flame licked at the weeds, bringing great heat. The tares bowed toward Durward and the War Party, but did not ignite. Durward released all the reins and directed fire from both fists.

Arden backed further away. "*Beware*, Durward!" He shouted over the crackling of the fire. "The weeds have *doubled* their *height*! They seem *strengthened* by your *flames*!"

Durward ceased the fire.

The tares shot forward, snaked around Durward's arms, legs, chest and throat, snatched him from his saddle, and dangled him in the air.

Galen grasped desperately at the Magician's leg.

Guthrie and Arden hacked at the tares imprisoning Durward.

Galen began leaping, struggling to catch hold of the Magician's hands to supply him with added force.

The weeds were swinging the Magician to and fro, and raising and lowering him like irate waves. They were squeezing him, slowing his breathing, pinning his arms to his sides, and doubling his legs behind him.

Arden and Guthrie were panting in rage and frustration. The ugly weeds would not yield, nor even pay heed to their blades, however mightily they struck, or sawed.

Galen managed to catch one of Durward's arms, and held on for dear life.

The weeds lifted both into the air, and shook them like rag dolls.

The tares constricting Durward's throat would not slacken. He was nearly unconscious from depletion of oxygen. Even so, he was able to sense the energy Galen was transmitting, clung to its warm, reassuring, tingling, drew upon it, and forced it out of his body as psychokinesis. The squeezing of the weeds stopped.

The tares ceased waving the men, and concentrated on tightening their coils around the Magician's neck and chest.

Durward coalesced his energy and applied it against the weeds around his throat and torso. Slowly, they were loosened, but the tares on his arms and legs squeezed more painfully. He managed to breathe deeply three times, and it invigorated him with power. He applied his force to the weeds in a sudden irate burst, and the tares were forced away from him.

Durward and Galen tumbled to the ground.

The weeds resumed their places in the wall.

Arden and Guthrie pulled their friends to their feet, and the War Party retreated to the frightened horses on

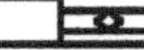

the small patch of dry dirt where no weeds grew.

The tares conforming the tall wall had been coiled under the earth at the mouth of the Dale and had been unnoticeable. The rest of the Valley, including the sides, was rife with the lethal weeds.

"We have *safety* only *here*," Guthrie said. "And, I *doubt* the Enchantment will *allow* us *this* for *long*. How can we fight?"

Durward had recovered his breath and energy with the help of Galen and was deep in thought. "Neither fire nor blade harmed them," he said. "I can only try all of my tricks, as I did against our prior obstacles. But, we must not *leave* this *sanctuary*."

Arden was staring into the heart of the evil Dale. He shaded his eyes against the sun. "There *is* a *path*," he said. "The weeds are not *bent* to the *sides* to *deceive* us. I can see *earth*."

"No *water*?" Galen said.

"None," Arden said. "See."

"Yes," Durward said. "But, there is no space for us to pass without the tares attacking." He turned to the weed wall and raised both hands. "Galen, enforce me."

Galen stood behind Durward and placed his hands on the Magician's forehead.

Cold frosted from Durward's fists and struck the plants, audibly.

The weeds writhed and bent forward but did not wither nor freeze. Ice formed on them, and frost coated the earth, but the tares twitched their tips like cats wagging their tails, awaiting the optimum time to pounce on an unwary bird.

"No use," Durward said. He ended the cold and began hammering invisible force against the weeds. The ice shattered to the earth but the tares only swayed with the blows. "I shall part the weeds," Durward whispered to the War Party. "Arden and Guthrie, mount and be ready to ride through the breach. The weeds are gaining strength from my efforts, or some other source, and I will be able to hold them open only briefly."

"*We* will not *flee* and *sacrifice* you two to the tares!" Arden avowed.

"Better *two* of us perish, than *all*!" Galen said, gruffly.

Durward pressed laterally at the wall with all his force.

The great weeds parted as if there were no occult life in them.

Guthrie held Arden from testing the tares.

"A *sly* ploy," Guthrie said, to Galen and Durward, "but, one, by which, we shall not be *fooled*."

The weeds snapped upright, sounding like wooden blocks banging together. They lashed forward, straining at the War Party.

Durward hurled his might down, pinning the tares to the earth. "*Now*!" he shouted. "Arden! Guthrie! *Through* the pass with *you* and the *mounts*! We *will* follow!"

Arden swung himself onto his mount, in sync with Guthrie, and snatched the reins of the other horses.

Something laughed like taut ropes straining and creaking under remorseless weight. "You are *more* clever, than

Nigel has begrudged," it said, arrear them. "But, this will avail you *only* suffering and death!"

Guthrie and Arden were jerked from their stallions, by weeds.

The Enchantment was a humanoid of tares with red, burning-coal eyes. It had no nose, but a round opening served as a mouth. Its arms and legs were unusually muscular. Weeds, waving like tentacles, grew around its waist. It coiled Guthrie and Arden in those and began squeezing the helpless men.

Durward and Galen faced the beast.

Durward rallied his force at the weeds imprisoning Arden.

"Fiend!" the Enchantment screamed. "Stop!" It rushed from the tares and lashed at Galen and Durward with the weeds on its back.

Durward deflected them with force, then riveted his energy on the weeds crushing Arden. He uncoiled them from the Prince's throat and hauled on the place where the tares were rooted to the golem's waist.

The Enchantment screamed in pain and retreated to the extent of its waist weeds. With its muscular hands, it grasped the tares Durward was yanking and tugged on them to ease its suffering.

Guthrie metamorphosed into the War Serpent, slithered from the waist weeds binding it, then along them, coiled itself around the beast's neck, and struck repeatedly at the creature's eyes.

The purple golem was astonished. It released Arden

from its waist tares, grasped War Serpent with its huge weed hands, yanked the viper from around its neck, and ensnared the Snake with its waist weeds.

Galen bore Arden to safety and applied healing to the Prince's bruises and cracked ribs.

Durward pounded force against the beast's temples.

The Enchantment's head rocked back and forth, but it did not suffer harm.

War Serpent continued striking the monster's beady eyes.

Durward directed his energy blows there.

The golem squealed like ropes on the verge of snapping. It dropped the Viper and fled into the obscurity of the weeds.

Guthrie reformed to man. He and Durward scanned the Valley for signs of further attack from the vine man.

"We must seek escape in some manner *other* than me *levering* the weed wall down," Durward said, angrily, to his friends. "This monster gains vitality from my psychic assaults. See how much *taller* its vile tares are. Though I *am* increased in output *and* ability since the Enchantment in the Woods, I still cannot levitate us and our steeds that high, for even the few seconds required."

The creaking, squeaking laughter came at the edge of the weed field.

Arden checked behind to be certain they were still beyond the reach of the slowly growing tares of the wall there.

"Marsden *outwits* the old *fool*, though, I was not warned of a few of the *poor* trickster's *puny* abilities. I *shall* still *triumph*, where *others* have *failed*. Do you see how I have improved in this short period? I *drink* your energy. No *form* of it can *harm* me or my extenders. Come forth, magician, man of *might,* and *joust* with Marsden! I will even *turn* my *back* for *you*! I will use *only* my *arms*, not my *waist* tares! What do you say, oh *master* of the *arcane*?"

Guthrie glanced to the sun. "We are lost if night finds us in this den of stranglers," he said. "Surely, Durward, you possess *some* arcane *device* that can *destroy* this Enchantment."

"I have fire and ice, force and light," Durward said. "These have failed, so far." He stepped forward. "Ho, Marsden," he said. "I *accept* your *bogus* challenge. Come forth and place *honor* behind your *cowardly* braggadocio!"

"What do you plan?" Galen asked. "If it can touch you with a *single* waist tare, it will *hurl* you into its *army* of weeds, and not all the force in both of us will save you."

Durward stared at the tares. "You *must* do as I *instruct*," he said. "When I have engaged the beast, convinced it I shall direct my energy toward it, I will, instead, force down the weed wall. In the Enchantment's surprise, will be time for you to guide our mounts into the clear. I *believe* I *can* levitate *myself* to *safety*."

"Is this *self-sacrifice*?" Guthrie demanded.

"*Can* he *lift* himself, Galen?" Arden asked.

Galen looked at Durward with admiration, then shook his head.

"Then, *we* can not abandon *you*," Arden vowed.

"*We* have little *choice*," Guthrie said, gruffly. "*We* must press the fight against Nigel, or our people will *die*."

"What *hope* do we have against *other* Enchantments if Durward cannot master *this* one?" Galen asked, angrily. "We will *die*, for sure, *then*, without *him*."

"You *must* find an escape for *all* of us," Arden said, firmly, trying, unsuccessfully, to stare his father down, "or, *I* shall divert the ugly beast, while you three make advantage of the breech of the wall. Better *you* are alive and free to battle *further* Enchantments and Nigel, with some *hope* of success, than for *all* of us to die *here,* while *arguing*." He darted forward.

Guthrie held Durward and Galen back.

Marsden laughed. "Nigel, who thinks with clouding emotion, would fall for this ploy and slay the slow minded boy," it said. "But, Marsden was born no *imbecile*, and is not *cursed* with emotions. The lad may play among my army all day and be only tired when night descends. I can bide until then. Until I have you *all* at my *beck* and *call*." The golem whispered. A wave of tares in the Dale fanned into Arden, sending him reeling backward toward his friends.

Arden fought with the tares, vainly trying to shove himself through the weeds and toward the pathway in the Dale. The tares cupped and hurled Arden into Guthrie's waiting arms.

"So much for *nobility* and *self-sacrifice*," Marsden chided. "Give *eager* thought to *suicide*. For, if you *force* me to *toil* to *kill* you, your *demise* will not be *swift* or *easy*."

"This Enchantment," Galen said, "is more vile than its predecessors."

"And, just as *frail* in *some* facet," Durward said. "We have forgotten *that*. They *all* have suffered from a *fatal*, though not tragic, *flaw*. Study our opponent with your seasoned tactical mind, Guthrie, and root out its vulnerabilities."

"The root of the matter," Guthrie said, softly. He hoped the homely tare beast could not hear with its magical weeds as Crandall had with its haunted cranes. "You have spoken, perhaps, what you seek. Did not Marsden seem wounded when you plucked at its waist weeds? Did it not surrender Arden in fear of the pain, as if the weeds could be uprooted; pulled free of its foul body?"

"And, it directed our attention away from that fact," Durward said.

"It seemed to me as if the monster aimed us *to* that fact," Galen said.

"There is one way to factor it out," Arden said.

Durward turned to the weed wall and spun his force around one of the tares.

Galen enforced the magician's strength.

Durward hauled against the weed, pulling it flat to the earth. The tare began trembling.

"Is it true," Marsden said, "that, one should let sleeping dogs lie?" The Enchantment was standing outside the field of weeds.

Guthrie and Arden faced it, with swords drawn.

"It is *scheming*," Guthrie said. "You must be *threatening* it, Durward. It is attempting to divert us from the wall."

"But, I am gaining *nothing,* for our *effort*, and the tare is *lengthening* by *absorbing* my *power*," Durward said.

"My soldiers *like* the earth," Marsden said. "It is their *provider* and *defender*. Come *die*. No *resistance,* equals no *agony*. I *can* be *merciful* and *swift*. The *peace* will you *gain*, without a *moment* of *pain*."

"It is giving us *clues*," Guthrie said.

"But, *what*? *Why*?" Arden said.

"It is *toying* with us," Galen said. "It *slyly* warns us of a threat that we will understand from its words only after it acts."

"Galen," Durward whispered, "I shall shift my aim on the count of two. Be ready to swing around."

"*Aye*," Galen said. "*One. Two*."

Durward spun, singled out one of Marsden's waist weeds, and pulled on it with all his concentration and might.

Marsden screamed and tried to run backwards into the weed field. It struggled against Durward's draw, but could not budge. The tare skin at its waist bulged.

"The earth is too hardened by Nigel's magic to uproot the weeds, but Marsden is not so toughened," Durward said, through clenched teeth. "Perhaps a breach in its skin will deprive it of some liquid that is vital to its odious life."

Marsden ceased struggling and allowed itself to be yanked toward the War Party.

Durward ceased his force.

Marsden's waist tares snatched up Arden and Guthrie, then, Galen from behind Durward.

The Magician struck force at the weeds around Arden's, Guthrie's, and Galen's throats.

Marsden found itself unable to choke off their breath. It coiled other tentacles around the men, and began squeezing. "My *foul* enemy *nurtures* me," Marsden said. "My *odious* foe is my most *beneficial* friend! Beware, behind you, Magician of *foiled* might!"

Durward ignored the taunting mock warning, placed his fists to his forehead, and strained to put force against the long tares wound around his vulnerable allies.

There was a slithering from the weed wall. Tares snatched Durward into the air with his arms and legs held away from his body. Other weeds encircled his neck, chest and abdomen, in agonizing grips.

Galen, Guthrie and Arden watched in helpless horror. As Durward's occult energy faltered, they felt the weeds around their necks begin to slowly tighten.

"Save *yourself*!" Galen screamed. "*Durward*, use *all* your power for *yourself*!"

Durward was doing his utmost to that end, but dared not withdraw all his force from the tares on his allies' throats. Otherwise, if he did liberate himself, his fellows would die too swiftly to be saved.

Marsden was laughing with its eerie, irritating, creaking voice. The golem was stepping backwards, teasingly slowly, one pace at a time, toward its field of demoniac weeds. The tares were leaning eagerly at the beast, to receive its captive prey for the kill.

Guthrie engaged his birth trick, wriggled free of the weeds

holding him and slithered toward Durward. Before War Serpent could reform to its man self, the tares of the wall had it bound, head to tail, against the earth. They squeezed so tightly, not even the mighty War Serpent could convulse itself free.

"*Durward*!" Galen screamed. "The *Woods*! The *shield*! Remember how—"

Marsden's laughter halted as if its power of speech had failed. It covered Galen's face with a coiled waist weed, cutting off Galen's wise warning words. Arden had been similarly silenced. Neither man could catch more than the smallest of breaths through their nostrils.

Durward was losing consciousness. The fight to save his friends, and the lack of air, were robbing him of power. Still, the Magician understood the intent of Galen's choked words. Durward covered himself in a clear shield like the one he had used to save them in Anomaly Woods. He enlarged the safeguard, forcing the weeds to relax their hold on him. He sucked in air, with desperate renewed hope. This brought more power. He dispersed that energy to War Serpent, enclosing the Snake in a slowly expanding shield.

Guthrie found himself free enough to resume his man shape, and draw breath.

Durward sent shield energy to Arden and Galen and forced Marsden's fat waist tares to widen their coils.

Galen sucked the deepest breath possible and managed to grasp hold of Arden's pale fingers. Their shields merged at their hands. Galen coursed healing energy into his friend.

Arden was shocked to consciousness by the invigorating force.

Marsden had rooted to the spot. "I am *betrayed*!" it screamed. "Lord Nigel *betrays* me through keeping me *ignorant* of your *traitorous* capacities! Why? How can I *perform* as he *commands*, without *knowledge*?" The dispirited man of weeds uncoiled its waist tentacles and threw Galen and Arden at the tare wall.

The cruel weeds caught the men.

Marsden fled into the obscurity and comfort of its tare field.

Durward used mind power to pull on the weeds holding Galen, until he was able to grasp Galen's firm hand. With the enforcement of the Healer, Durward clawed them all free of the coiled tares and rolled the members of the War Party onto the dry patch of dirt. Durward absorbed the energy of all the shields.

Arden scrambled to his feet and hugged the weary Magician. "We now have the route of passage!" he said, jubilantly. "You can en-shield us and the horses, and we can pass through even the heart of the Valley!"

"We had best do so, *quickly*," Guthrie warned. "This Enchantment is showing a *nasty* tendency toward adapting to each new defense you present. It is cowering and no doubt, doing just that right now."

"Yes," Durward said. "Mount. We pass through the wall."

Marsden laughed.

"Too late," Galen said, dourly.

Hundreds of weeds speared out of the dry brown earth and began whipping the questers and their horses without mercy.

The steeds neighed in terror and began bucking and rearing.

"Durward!" Guthrie shouted. "*Quieten* them, or we will be *trampled*!"

Durward sent forth comforting energy and placed the steeds into a deep protective trance. Around the War Party, he emanated a clear umbrella shield which pressed the weeds under its shiny hard floor.

The tares lashed at and beat on the force field with fury.

Marsden screamed, with rage.

"Can you *move* the shield," Galen asked, "and, take us *through* the weeds of the wall?"

"It *will* travel as we *do*, but, only an *inch* at a time," Durward said. "I have not the power for both the shield and *true* levitation to send us forward except very slowly."

Galen and Arden watched the tare wall.

"*Ten* feet to *freedom*!" Arden said, with frustration. "*Surely*, you have power for *that*?"

Durward did not answer. He stared at the weedy earth, thinking of forward movement. After a moment, the umbrella began to creep toward the tare wall.

Guthrie and Arden felt hope.

"Look!" Galen shouted.

Even Durward glanced to where the Healer point-

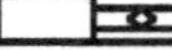

ed, such was the urgency and dismay in Galen's voice.

On the edge of the accursed Dale, high above the questers, stood the four guardsmen. They had made a full circuit of the Glen, found no sign of the War Party, and returned to the narrow mouth of the Valley, to discover the way in blocked. Now, they had managed the tortuous, slow climb to the summit of one side of the Dale, and were poised precariously, watching their comrades trapped inside the glistening domed shield.

"If they venture into the Valley, they will be *slain* in *seconds*!" Durward said. "I can not save *them* without *weakening* the shield."

Galen and Guthrie waved their arms, and began shouting for the guards to retreat and wait.

The soldiers waved back, but gave no indication of understanding the warning gestures, or hearing the shouts of alarm.

Marsden laughed. It strutted out of its tare field and pressed its ugly purple face against one side of the umbrella. It said nothing for a while, then flicked its waist weeds in an unmistakable sign of attack. The tares surrounding the shield began spearing into it like nails hammered into ice.

"*Forget* the guards!" Guthrie ordered. "*If* you can move us *out* of the Valley, they will *see*, and will *not* enter!"

"Help me, Galen!" Durward urged. "They are sapping my might with each opening they manage. I do not understand how they can."

Galen did as bid.

Durward concentrated on inching them through the wall of weeds.

The tares paused their attack.

Marsden laughed, pounded a fist against the side of the umbrella, then pointed at the wall of weeds.

They split wide apart, then fell to either side of the shield as though life had failed them. This revealed a barricade of huge blocks of black earth. Tares were intertwined through it, reinforcing it and endowing it with incredible resistance. The weeds in front of the earthen barrier began spearing themselves into the wicker-like work for added strength.

Marsden pounded on the shield. "My army *loves* the *earth*," it said, tauntingly. "It *protects, feeds,* and, *abets,* them! You *die* now! No *mercy*, even if you collapse your *cowardly* shield and offer me your *swords*!" Marsden ran backwards into its tares.

Purple weeds resumed piercing the umbrella, leaving holes wherever they struck. The tares that were flattened beneath the shield, withdrew into the earth, then speared up through the floor, striking at the men, and separating Galen and Durward. The shield shimmered, and faded, for a moment. Durward drew the clear protector from around the stilled mounts, so it domed only the imperiled men, and the holes in the shield vanished.

The weeds whacked their sharp tips into the umbrella without damaging its crystal surface.

Galen stood behind Durward, and wrapped his arms around the Magician's waist. Arden and Guthrie did the same. The Magician decreased the area the shield had to cover and this thickened its transparent skin.

Marsden raced from its weeds and roared furiously at Durward. "My every *victory* is *denied* by the clever folds in your *devious* brain!" it screamed. "*Yet*, I shall *prevail*! I will not *fail* my master, for his *punishment* is too *terrible* to *face*!" Marsden slammed its weedy fists into the umbrella.

The force field cracked.

"*Ethereal* be *merciful*!" Durward said, with a desperate groan. "This *horrid* creature's might is *doubled* each time I use my force! What must I *do* to *protect* us? Yield up the power of the atoms of my body?"

Marsden raised its fists in ire and hammered them into the top of the shield, breaking in just inches from Durward's bowed head.

Durward grabbed the golem's hands with a weak energy beam.

The beast tore free, shattering the top of the umbrella. A large oval section of the energy dome flew over Marsden's head. The Enchantment shrank back inadvertently.

With wild hope, Durward sucked in a deep breath, and his heart pounded with inspired understanding. Before the Enchantment could make another assault, and with no time to apprise the War Party of his risky strategy, Durward absorbed the shield. He projected his total psychic energy into the form of a round, flat disk that had long saw-teeth, and sent it spinning at the glowering golem.

Marsden screamed. It stuck up its waist tares to block

the circular saw from striking its head, and began fleeing backwards into its weed field.

The energy weapon flipped sideways in the air and sheared through the golem's waist weeds as if they were cobwebs.

Marsden ululated in agony, and dove backwards into the tares. Weeds matted over the monster in the form of a wall, and other tares swiftly pulled the Enchantment further into the safe heart of the Valley.

The weeds behind the War Party encircled Durward and lifted him into the air.

Durward recalled his weapon. It sheared through the tares binding him, and he fell to the earth. The saw mowed down the remaining weeds in front of the high earth barricade, then chopped those tares into mulch.

Galen and Arden helped the Magician to stand up.

Durward directed his clear saw to mince the weeds in the area of the once dry, safe, dirt. "To your horses!" He shouted. "I will *clear* this barrier and *free* us!" He removed the protective trances on the horses.

The War Party mounted.

Marsden was shrieking from somewhere in the bowels of the weed field. It was not expressing further pain or terror. It was insane, with affront and rage.

"*Can* we escape *while* this Enchantment yet *lives*?" Guthrie said. "*This* has not been so *before*."

"We have not *had* this opportunity *before*," Arden said. "This may *be* our *lucky* time."

Durward projected the whirring crystal weapon, on the

vertical, at the barricade. The saw screamed against the barrier, but the teeth did not cut into the earthen blocks.

Marsden bellowed with insulting satisfaction.

"*It* has *hardened* the earth, *magically*," Durward said. "We can not *rip* through it *now*, but we *can* climb over."

"Abandon everything!" Arden ordered.

They dismounted and ran to the towering wall.

Durward kept guard with his whizzing weapon in the likely case Marsden would approach.

"These weeds make good climb joists!" Guthrie said. "Up with you!" he shouted at Galen and Arden.

"*All* of you go *now*!" Durward ordered desperately. "*It* has *devised* another *offense*!"

Arden and Galen glanced over their shoulders as they climbed up the barricade.

On the tops of the Valley walls, the weeds had sliced up their first layer of earth. They had formed other barriers spanning the length of the Dale. As these barricades were settled into place by the tares like a mason sets bricks, Marsden hardened them. The Valley would be domed over with the impenetrable earth-and-weed wicker-works in less than an hour. The tares were increasing their length to reach the roof to transport up the sections of black earth they sliced out for the construction.

Arden tumbled from the front barricade.

Weeds on the far side of the barrier had begun the same sealing up process as their comrades, and a dome was rapidly forming over the War Party to meet with the main cupola.

"Can nothing *stop* this weedy *Gorgon*?" Guthrie shouted, lividly. "What *monstrosities* Nigel *harbors* in his *twisted* mind!"

"The *best* defense is an *offense*," Arden said. He shook Guthrie. "*You* have *taught* me this, *remember*? What *is* our *most* potent *offense*?" he demanded.

Guthrie controlled his anger and nodded at his son. "Yes, yes," he said. "The *saw*. Durward, your *saw*! *Reap* our *victory* with your *messenger* of our *wrath*! *Mince* Marsden and its *weeds*. Once they are dead, this earth will soften, and we are free! I doubt it can defend itself, *now*!"

"*Yes* it *can*," Galen said. His words were hushed by the frightening vision he culled from his analyzing mind. "It can *seal* us *in* and itself *out*, and we will suffocate though we mow down *all* of its accursed tares!"

"*Then*, I shall *destroy* it *before* its damned *dome* is *completed*!" Durward vowed. "Mount and follow *me*!" He pulled himself onto his saddle, and heeled his shy horse toward the weeded heart of the enlivened Valley.

The cupola was more than half-way finished. The sun was being blocked from the Dale and pure darkness was slowly approaching.

Durward sent the circle scything forward, down the center line of the tare field.

Marsden hardened the weeds.

The saw met strong resistance.

Durward created a second scythe, then enlarged both, making them wide enough to cut a path that would be wider than the remaining weeds could reach across in an endeavor to block the War Party's advance.

The circles swept down the divide, one above the other, cutting the tares into thirds.

Galen rode close to Durward, to keep contact with him, to enforce his energy.

Arden and Guthrie followed, in single file.

Marsden had ceased ranting, and had been silent as if it did not exist. It began laughing. The skin crawling sound echoed around the Valley, bouncing off the hardened dome.

"*Has* this *fiend* adapted *again*?" Galen said.

"It's *not* laughing *just* to hear *itself*," Arden said. "What *can* it do *now*? Can you scythe *faster*, Durward?"

There was a strangled cry behind them.

Arden heeled his horse around and drew his sword.

Guthrie had been swept off his stallion by weeds.

The deadly tares had grown up behind the questers almost as swiftly as the weeds had been mown down by the Magician.

"Durward!" Arden shouted. "Guthrie's *entangled*!"

Galen and the Magician reined their mounts around.

Durward directed the top saw to slice Guthrie free.

The tares sprouted up again.

Guthrie did not have time to catch his breath or mount his frightened stallion.

Durward split the saw into two. They backed each other up, mowing.

Guthrie was able to mount and rejoin the group.

Durward split the front saw into two and made them orbit the War Party as they slowly advanced.

Marsden was still laughing, almost as gleefully as Crandall had before the Caretaker of the Cranes had unleashed a surprise with its controlled fowl.

Guthrie heeled his mount up beside Durward and Galen. "Why does it *not* grow the weeds *under* us as we *pass*?" the knight asked. "You would be *unable* to use your saws to *free* us."

"It is leading us to what it believes is a trap," Arden said. "And, we had better be doubly alert for it."

"We shall unmask it, then," Durward said. He split the four saws into a hundred smaller ones and sent them, on the horizontal, across the wide tare field, in a line which spanned the width of the Valley. Durward kept one large saw to protect their backs.

Wave upon wave of weeds fell before the saws. There was nothing unusual revealed until the War Party reached the second third of the Dale.

When the saws scythed through the next growth of tares, the clippings fell into a crevasse three hundred feet wide and ten feet deep, running the width of the Valley. It had been dug by the weeds and was clear of them except for the shards that had just been mowed.

Faintly, Marsden could be heard at the far end of the Dale, laughing its squeaky, infernally annoying glee.

"*Cast* your saws *forth*," Guthrie shouted. "*Show* us that *devil*! *Scythe* it to, *silence*!"

Durward encircled the War Party with half the saws.

The weeds had regrown behind and around the War Party more thickly than before. Durward sent the remaining saws across the chasm. They swiftly reached the mid point.

Marsden strutted out of its tares and stood defiantly at the edge of the crevasse. "You've not only *taught* me *slyer* ways," the Enchantment shouted, "but, *supplied* me with *suggestions* for your *defeat*. My weeds have *hearkened* to your *words*, Healer! And, *now*, you *die*!" It raised its arms in an extravagant gesture of command.

A rumbling filled the chasm.

Arden and his War Party stared at the far wall of the great gap.

Like a valley-wide, straight edged fan, row after row of weed-and-earth blocks, which had been bound together in layers in the crevice, were lifted by the embedded weeds, toward the enclosing dome, making the wide chasm even deeper.

Evil Marsden was doing as Galen had feared. It was erecting an impenetrable barrier between itself and the questers. The Enchantment could lounge safely behind the earth wall as its tares completed the cupola over the War Party, literally sealing their fate more quickly and surely.

Durward reacted faster than words could be spoken, quicker than despair could course through him. He dispatched the middle saw of his line, with his entire psychic force behind its velocity, over the rising barrier, straight at Marsden and his gloating purple face.

Marsden screamed. Weeds shot up before and around

the Enchantment, but too late.

The glistening saw cleaved into the creature's weedy body and halved the golem. Marsden's top half landed on its armpits and tried vainly to use its arms to reach its lower half.

With desperate rage Durward, directed all his saws, except for the ones in a protective orbit around the War Party, into the beast.

Marsden screamed, then was reduced to a million pieces.

The fan wall collapsed with an intense earthshaking thud.

Durward swept the blades throughout the Valley, clearing it of all tares.

The weeds did not grow back, this time.

Marsden did not respond from its bits.

Guthrie was about to cheer when logic spoke to his mind. He snapped his head up, and stared at the nearly completed earthen-and-tare dome. "To the *rear*!" he commanded. "*To* the *rear* and *to* our *right*!"

"*Why*?" Arden asked. "Marsden is *dead*!"

"So may we be, *if* we can not ride *fast* enough!" Guthrie shouted. He reined his horse into motion. "With the Enchantment *dead*, its magic is *dissipated* and the weeds are no longer *strengthened* by *it*! They cannot support the *weight* of the *dome*! They will *snap*, and we *will* be buried *unless* we can gain the *safety* of the *open* part of the Valley!"

Arden and Galen were fast on Guthrie's trail.

Durward delayed, to recall his saws and absorb their energy. He heeled his mount into a gallop. Above, there was rumbling like a landslide, then snapping sounds like taught ropes overtaxed by weight. The great cupola was giving way, crumbling toward the sides of the bedeviled Valley.

The War Party reined their horses in different patterns of evasion as they dodged the falling hunks of earth. Though the slabs were no longer hardened by Marsden, they were still cumbersome, and heavy with moisture. Just one block could crush man and horse.

Guthrie reached the clear area, followed by Arden.

Galen and Durward were delayed by the increasing number of fallen blocks.

A slab smashed into the ground beside Galen. The Healer's horse spooked, almost throwing him.

Durward applied gentle force to the Healer's back and righted him in the saddle. They galloped aside one another to safety.

A moment later, the main portion of the dome gave way, and the great blocks of weedy soil avalanched into the floor of the Valley, shaking the earth for a mile in all directions.

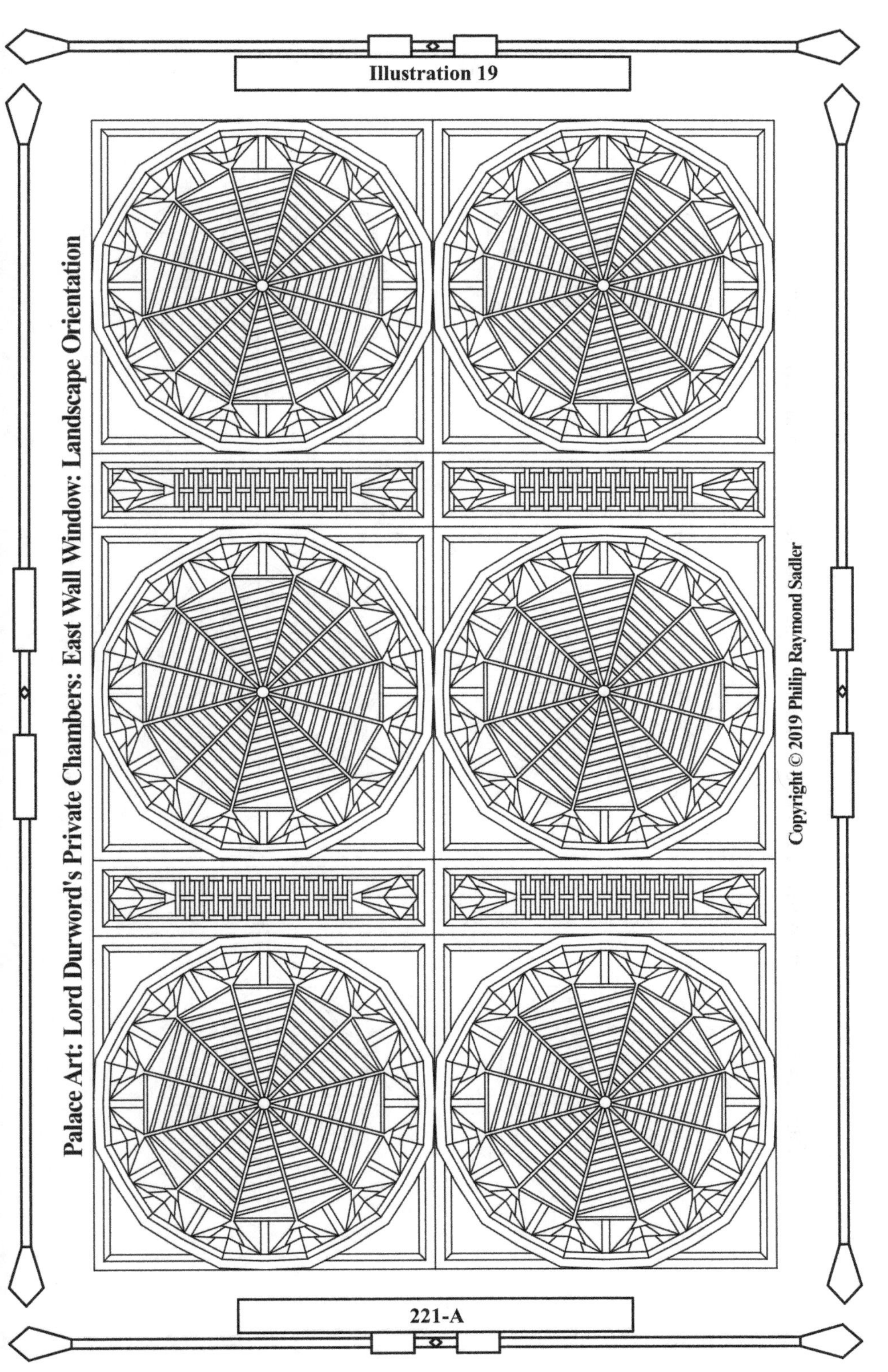
Illustration 19
Palace Art: Lord Durword's Private Chambers: East Wall Window: Landscape Orientation

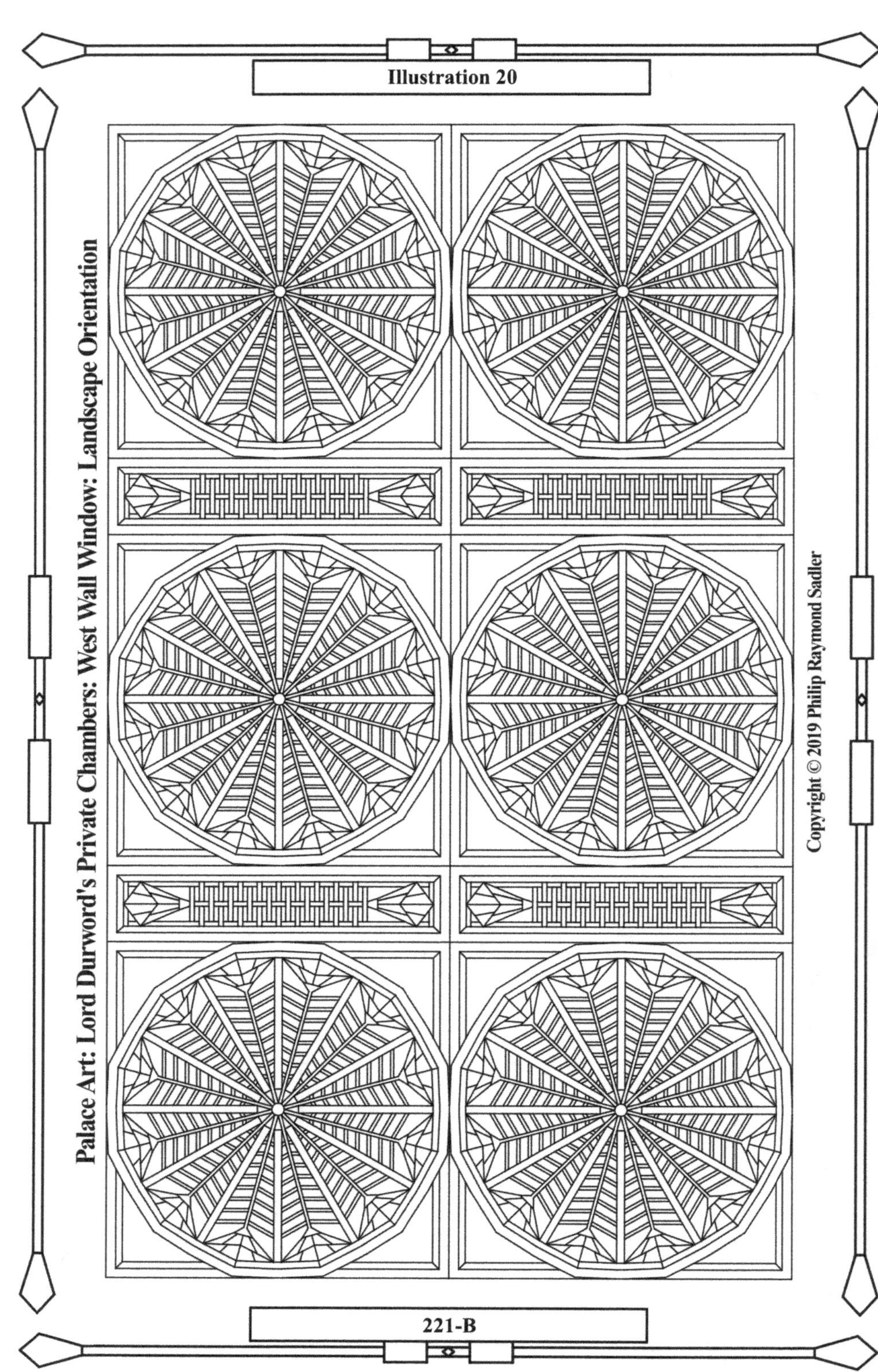
Illustration 20
Palace Art: Lord Durword's Private Chambers: West Wall Window: Landscape Orientation
Copyright © 2019 Philip Raymond Sadler
221-B

Chapter 10
Cloudy Thinking

"It is obvious we cannot pass over the trench Marsden and his weeds dug," Arden said.

"Yes, we will have to exit the way we entered," Guthrie said. "The earthen blocks have tumbled from the mouth of the Valley."

"Where *are* our guardsmen?" Galen said. "I hope the tares did not slay them after the dome blocked them from view."

"We will *know* soon," Durward said. "If they are unharmed, they will be waiting at the Dale mouth."

Arden motioned to the black earth as they traveled. "These weeds are rotting away," he said. "The Valley will soon be like it was before Nigel altered it with his evil might. Dry and dusty."

"No pity there," Guthrie said. He heeled his stallion into a trot.

When they reached the Mouth of the valley, they leaped their stallions over the crumbled remains of the earth-weed wall.

"Guards, *ho*!" Guthrie shouted. "Guards, *report*!"

Arden and Galen reined toward the left side of the Valley. Durward and Guthrie rode to the right. The four men gazed into the distance toward the far end of the Dale.

"There is no one in sight, Guthrie," Arden shouted. "It is like they do not exist. I sight no tracks, even."

Guthrie and Durward joined the other two.

"Aye," Guthrie said. "Some *untoward* fate has befallen them. They are too well schooled not to report, *if* able. What do you sense, Galen?"

The Healer held his hands out with his fingers toward the azure sky. The air was still. Not even the songs of distant birds despoiled the lonely silence. "Their trail is distinct," Galen said. "Two went along this side of the Valley, and returned. Two came from around the other side of the Valley, and all four traveled along this side. Their vibrations should lead us to the spot on this side of the valley where we saw them, and to wherever they are now, *whether* they are *alive* or *dead*."

"Can you not discern whether they have *left* their bodies?" Durward asked.

"The energy is strong enough here, to be either," Galen said. "But, this could change in a few yards."

Arden motioned the War Party along the side of the Valley.

They kept careful vigil of the towering grassy Dale, for any signs of the guards.

Durward made it his responsibility to scan to their rear.

"This *is* puzzling," Guthrie said. "I descry no tracks on the grass or earth. No signs, whatsoever, that anyone has passed this way, yet Galen detects their life energy, and we saw them on the lip of the Valley. How can *both*, be?"

Durward mulled the matter. "Perhaps, Nigel ensconces another of his Enchantments, here," he said. "Magic *can* erase the physical traces, but finds it difficult to *diffuse* the psychical." He glanced at Galen and raised an eyebrow. "What do you sense, now?" he said. "And, you, Arden? Anything similar to what you discerned when we faced Monrow in the Red Swamp?"

Arden directed his attention to his abdomen, hands and feet. He shook his head. "Nothing, Durward," he said. "I have noticed energy only with Monrow, though we do not understand why."

Galen rubbed his hands together as if he were clearing them of some invisible dirt. He cupped his palms, thumb to thumb, and held them out at arm's reach.

The War Party paused midway along the Valley.

Guthrie dismounted and inspected the ground around them, close to the grassy slope of the Dale, then far into the small hills to their left. He discovered nothing.

"As I sensed before," Galen said, "the guards came to this spot and climbed up the Valley side. They remained at the rim for the duration of our final battle with Marsden, and one, I think, stepped out onto the dome to see if it would support him, but the weeds grew up and out and chased him back. The soldiers waited on the rim until the dome began to fall—" He leaned forward, concentrating. "I *seem* to *lose* them," he said, angrily.

"What does that *mean*?" Arden asked, apprehensively.

"I am *uncertain*," Galen said. "It is *not* as if they have *died*. And, it is *not* as if they are *alive*."

"Perhaps, a psychic buffer?" Durward suggested.

Galen nodded and opened his eyes. "Yes, *very* sly, *wonderfully* disguised, but still there," he said. "I now determine they *are* alive, held *inactive* as Monrow did within his Swamp."

"That proves another Enchantment is ahead of us," Arden said, irritably. "We will *never* reach Nigel in time to help our people. He is packing his hell sites closer and thicker together, the nearer, to him, we draw."

"*That* is to be expected," Durward said. "His might *is* stronger, the closer we approach. His Enchantments shall *wax* more terrible, *yet*."

"I cannot *imagine* anything more *horrible* than Marsden," Arden said.

"Do not try," Guthrie said, "Nigel, will probably divine it and enact it against us." He remounted. "I still uncover no omens of my men. Lead us to them, Galen, and we *will* rescue them *if* it can be accomplished *without* engaging the *next* Enchantment."

"*Surely*, you will not *abandon* them to the Enchantment?" Durward said.

"*Hard* times decree *hard* measures," Guthrie said, sadly. "It is *not* an easy *task*, war. But, we must remember, we *are* at war. *Desperate* war."

Arden heeled his horse along the side of the Valley. The members of his War Party followed, ever alert.

"Is it not strange," Galen said, "how the blocking energy, in trying to *bar* us from what we seek, *warns* us of *itself,* and what we *seek*?"

"It is *impossible* to *divine* whether the Enchantment *allows* us that *sensing* of its might to make us *overconfident,*" Durward said, "or, simply, that no source can *disguise* itself, *completely*."

"Note the *moisture* in the air," Guthrie said. "We have passed beyond the artesian spring that watered the Valley earth for Nigel's infernal ugly weeds, so there is no *natural* source to account for it, *here*."

"The newest Enchantment is very close to the Valley. Just beyond it, perhaps," Galen said. "The signs of our scouts are increasing in potency, as is the masking might."

Arden wiggled his shoulders as though he was trying to shrug off an ill-fitting cape.

Guthrie and Durward noted this and exchanged glances.

"Hold," Guthrie said. "Arden, why did you shrug so?"

"I—*What*?" Arden said. He had been unaware of his motions. He thought about it. "There *seemed* to be a *weight* on them; an *uncomfortableness. Hard* to explain."

"Like, the tingling you sensed at Monrow's Swamp?" Durward said.

"Yes," Arden agreed. "But, what does it *foretell,* other than a way of *feeling* the *presence* of a new Enchantment?"

"What did your tingling *mean* in the Swamp?" Galen asked.

"That Monrow was of the *earth*. Could this, on my shoulders, mean—" Arden craned his neck and stared up.

A huge white Cloud drifted over the questers. Its unusually black shadow befell them, blocking out the warm sunlight. The Cloud was unnaturally low, almost within reach of an arrow fired from a half-drawn bow.

"*This*, then, is our *Enchantment*?" Guthrie said. "What *harm* can it *inflict*? Where did it *hide* before we saw it? It was *not* aloft before."

They had rounded the end of the Valley. Before them, lay a flat section of hard, dry earth. To their left and right, the Cloud curved downward until it appeared to be pressing its sides against the dusty, gray ground.

"Nigel plays us more *cannily* than, previously," Galen said. "While we were alert to the next danger, we missed it, and it has us caught within its initial gambit." He pointed to their rear, then forward.

The Cloud had met the earth, just beyond the end of the Valley, and was on the hard ground, far ahead.

"*Sealed* in, as Marsden *attempted*!" Arden shouted, angrily. "*Break* through, Durward, *behind* us, *before* this Enchantment can *harden* its foul self, and *suffocate* us!"

"A *noteworthy* suggestion," a voice said, sounding like sleet against shale. "One that I shall *reserve* for *after* I have *exhausted* your *fumbling* Magician's *tepid* defenses. We have all the time *I* wish. You *shall* regret *every* moment."

Durward reined his steed into a trot and approached the part of the Cloud arrear them.

That end of the Cloud receded, without lifting from the earth.

Durward returned to his friends.

"We can ride out *anything* this Enchantment offers," Galen whispered, to Durward. "You need only place a shield over each man and horse when this monster strikes."

"I suspect, *even* the safeguards will be of *little* succor against the *possibilities* of harm this weather conjury can offer," Durward said, morosely.

The sunlight struggling through the Cloud was dim, but a comfort.

Guthrie gazed up. It was late afternoon. Darkness would come in four hours. "We can not remain under this *abomination*, until nightfall," the Knight cautioned. "Take your best *device* against it. Be on the *offensive*. Do not allow *it* any *time* to set *its* traps or to *adapt* as Marsden did."

Durward nodded at his advice.

"Why not ride *toward* the Caverns while we can?" Arden asked. "Every *inch* of ground we *cover*, brings us that *nearer*, Nigel. Besides, this Enchantment may have a set site *beyond* which it cannot *stretch* itself. We may be able to ride out from under it in spite of how it appeared when Durward tried toward the Valley."

Durward smiled. "I was thinking in *elaboration*," he said. "A *simple* attack may work, though, I doubt it if—"

The curved Cloud began to darken, becoming in appearance, like a rain nebula.

Arden dismissed all further discussion, and began riding hard in the general direction of the Caverns. The rest of the War Party kept close to the Crown Prince Designate.

The Cloud laughed, like sleet upon slate. It waxed

more ebon. The sunlight was dwindling, swiftly. Soon, it was at dusk dullness. Winds began blowing from the direction of the War Party's flight. They grew stronger, buffeting the men and their horses.

"*Heel in*!" Durward warned. "The Cloud no longer *expands* before us!"

Arden heard, but ignored, the warning. He reined his mount into a gallop. As he approached the Cloud wall, he saw that it swirled and eddied insubstantially. He smiled. *Perhaps* one *ability* had been *denied* this Enchantment.

"*Restrain* him, Durward!" Guthrie pleaded, as they rode after The Crown Prince Designate. "He will *kill* himself *if* the Cloud *hardens*!"

"*Or,* he will be *separated* from us *if* the Cloud *vitrifies after* he passes *through*!" Galen warned. "He will be at the *mercy* of whatever *horror* Nigel may have waiting beyond it!"

Durward was emitting his psycho-kinetic energy. He wrapped Arden in a shield and tried to deflect the horse with a psychic shove.

The steed reared in surprise, then bucked.

Arden sailed over his horse's head, tumbling through the air. His back slammed into the Cloud wall as if he had struck a stone mountain, and he rebounded roughly to the hard, dusty earth.

The Enchantment chortled, like hail striking a hollow, dried gourd. "You *have* learned from the *failures* of my *fellows*," it said, with the same sound, "but, they did not *possess* my *inestimable* abilities. Try, if you will, to escape your *Fate*. I have no *flaws*, no *flukes*, no *weak* points. I *am* the *perfect* avenger. Does the Magician *dispute* this?"

Durward absorbed the energy of Arden's safeguard.

"An *insufferable* egoist," Galen said, as he checked Arden for harm. "As *offensive*, in its way, as Marsden was with *its* vile talk."

Durward and Guthrie were inspecting the Cloud. It remained insubstantial in appearance, as if, at any moment, a breeze might dispel it into the sky, but to the touch, it was at least as hard as the occult weeds upon which Marsden had depended.

Durward considered this likely. He motioned for his companions to lead the horses several yards back from the Cloud, and pounded against it with battering ram force.

The Nebula rang, sounding like an iron gong smitten by stones. "You *amuse* Kelsey, *mightily*," the Enchantment said. "Is *that* what *you* consider your *proudest* defense? It does not even *tickle*."

Durward backed up several paces and smote the wall with fire from both fists.

The Cloud shuddered, and the heated section appeared less solid. "Better," Kelsey admitted, a bit less haughtily. "It *is* a *trifle* uncomfortable, but, not damaging. I can *bask* in it for all *eternity*. Try again."

Durward was confirming, he hoped, his assessment of the magic Cloud's capacities. He ceased the flame, and struck with bitter numbing cold.

The Cloud became more substantial. "*Wonderful*!"

Kelsey shouted, from every inch of its peppery colored being. "*Continue*! I find *this* attack most *enjoyable*! Most *refreshing*! How *reasonable* of you to aid me in your *demise*!"

Durward switched to fire on the frozen spot.

Kelsey cried out with its grating hail against gourd voice, and loud thunder rumbled from its outermost regions.

Durward hearkened, and commenced freezing and firing the same spot, again and again, straining more with the production of the flames, upon each salvo.

The warning thunder grew louder, and closer. In a moment, the angry rumbling was directly overhead.

Durward warily watched the part of the Cloud above him as he kept up his Summer and Winter assault.

The spot on the wall was less thick, as if the inner part was burning away from the Magician's repeated flame strikes.

"*You* are beginning to play *rough*," Kelsey said, at the site over them, where the thunder was continuing to reverberate. "*Like* for *like* is only *equitable*. I shall treat *you* with the *same* deference with which you attend *me*. Behold, and *beg* for *mercy*. I *may* be moved."

The volume of the thunder increased until the earth began to shake. The peals blurred their vision and deafened their ears.

The horses became terrified, and tried to escape the hold that Guthrie and Arden had on their reins.

Durward en-slept the wild steeds without pausing

his assault on the weakening section of Kelsey's wall.

Greater peals of thunder waved over the War Party until the vibrating earth toppled them from their feet and kept them from standing.

Durward continued his fire and ice from where he lay on his back. He could see the light of the sun through the wall. Barely any of the Cloud remained between them and freedom.

"Cease!" Kelsey ordered.

Another peal slapped at the War Party. It was so loud, the vibrations felt like pins pricking their skin.

Guthrie and Arden covered their ears and rolled onto their stomachs.

Galen drew himself to Durward to enforce the Magician's power.

"We are *through*!" Durward shouted, triumphantly. The Magician placed a clear, thick ring of energy in the breach within the Cloud wall. This prevented the Nebula from closing the opening. The Cloud seemed unable to build more substance to fill the great wound in its occult skin."*Up* with you! *Mount*! I shall hold our escape way open until we are free!"

The thunder ceased.

Durward tried to awaken the horses, but failed. He noticed Arden and Guthrie had not roused themselves. "What *ails* them?" he shouted.

Galen stepped over and inspected the Knight and Prince. "They are *asleep*! No, *entranced*, just as you placed our mounts!"

"*Kelsey*!" Durward said.

"Like for like, indeed," Galen agreed. "But, that means the Cloud monster has *ice*, yet, to *inflict* upon *us*."

Durward sent a wake up charge at his friends. It struck resistance. He determined this because the energy was reflected back to him. He sent a pinpoint of power at Arden. "A *shield*!" the Magician said. "But, if *it* can *make* safe-guards, why did it not *prevent* this opening?" He slammed force into the shields around Arden and Guthrie.

The force fields cracked like ice, then dissipated.

Arden and Guthrie stirred and sat up, groggily. Galen boosted their energy. They became alert, and aware of what had happened.

Guthrie noted the silence. "The unholy creature prepares an attack," he said. "Waken the horses, Durward. That exit of yours will not be left unplugged, for long."

"The shield around each horse is too thick for me to destroy, without removing my ring from the Cloud," Durward said.

Galen linked with the Magician.

"I still cannot break the steeds free without releasing the circle," Durward said. "We are best advised to abandon the mounts and provisions."

Arden approached the opening and put his hand in. It met no resistance, so he lifted a leg to step through.

Kelsey giggled like a mischievous child with an unpleasant surprise.

With his mind, Durward jerked Arden back from the breach, and flung a psychic blow at its center. Blue-white lightning crackled from top to bottom of the orifice.

"No wonder *why* it did not use the shield," Guthrie said, "with *that* energy within itself to stop us."

Durward turned back to the breach and lifted his arms.

A tiny bolt of lightning discharged from the top of the hole, causing a miniature clap of thunder.

Durward was struck in his chest, receiving a strong electrical shock. His control over his magic was momentarily shaken, and he retreated.

The opening within the wall of the Cloud, freed of Durward's energy ring, irised shut with a metallic click. Kelsey laughed from all directions. It threw a few thunder claps around the questers. "If you *came* with *strings*, I couldn't have *moved* you to my *drama* more *capably*," it said, cheerfully. "Will *you* write the *next* scene, or shall I *dazzle* you with my *refinement* and obvious *superiority*?"

Durward actualized one of his circular saw energy forms and hurled it toward the wall.

Lightning blasted toward the Magician, barely missing his head.

Durward tumbled backwards.

The scythe energy dissipated before it could strike its target.

Durward shot out a saw from flat of his back.

A bolt of lightning responded.

Durward rolled aside.

The energy discharge melted the hard earth where the Magician's head had rested.

Durward scrambled to his feet, recalled the saw, and

absorbed the energy.

"*Like* for *like*," Kelsey vowed, with its hailstone striking a dry gourd voice. "*Hit* for *hit*. This *is* more *fun* than I *hoped*. Perhaps, Nigel will let me keep you for *pets*. I could *play* with you *all* the *time,* then. *Forever*. Would you like to be my *toys*?"

"This like for like requires thought," Durward said. "Any ideas on how I can avoid *gifting* this Enchantment new *weapons* each time I avail myself of my energies?"

"Kelsey seems frightened that you will inflict your psychic saws on it. Obviously, your shield is demanded," Arden said. "*Block* the bolts from you."

"Aye," Guthrie said. "You said the Cloud is at least as hard as the tares that Marsden used, so it must be vulnerable to your scythes."

"I doubt that I can en-shield us, and project a saw, as well," Durward said. "It will strike at you three, even if I *am* the threat."

"We will hide among the horses," Guthrie said, "using the safeguards *it* has on them to block its lightning from us."

"Galen, perhaps, with *your* vitality, I can manage *both* acts," Durward said, as he watched the Cloud where his breach had been.

Lightning crackled from the wall, toward Galen.

The Healer threw himself aside, and to the ground.

The bolt described an arc in the air and surged toward Galen.

Durward projected a shield over Galen.

The buzzing lightning exploded into the safeguard, with a brilliant blue glare.

Galen was undamaged, but reluctant to leave the security of the shield.

Durward faded the safeguard away, and Galen stood up.

The response from Kelsey had been as the Magician had expected. But, also faster than he had thought, and quicker than he had been able to react against it, even though he had been watchful for the possible strike. Galen was fortunate that his healing abilities provided him with such swift reflexes.

"You are a *frightened* child, Kelsey," Durward admonished, trying a different track. "You do not *truly* want to *play*. And, why must *we* proceed by *your* rules, only? *If* you *dread* my *merger* with Galen, what *else* do you *fear*?"

Galen inched nearer Durward. Arden and Guthrie did likewise, to attempt confusion of Kelsey, and to draw its fire.

Kelsey did not speak.

The War Party heard wind, thunder and, splattering to their right, and peered through the gloom.

A fast approaching, drenching rain, was drumming on the earth.

Guthrie knelt, and ran his fingers over the dirt. "This earth has been baked hard, probably by Kelsey's lightning, in preparation to our arriving, as you kilned the earth to kill Monrow," he said.

"This rain Kelsey produces, will gather as in the Royal Reservoir and *inundate* us," Arden said. "There is *no* place of *safety.*"

A circular breach appeared in the end section of the gray Cloud, and sunlight flooded toward the questers.

"What *ploy* is *this*?" Guthrie said.

The horses awakened. They neighed in fear of the thunder and the cold rain stinging them, then fled through the opening.

The Cloud closed the escape way, like the eye of a huge evil lizard.

"This is just as well," Durward said. "They could aid us not, and I would have been forced to spread my abilities thin to protect them *and* us." He blossomed a domed safeguard around the questers.

The precipitation progressed to their position, then beyond, until the storm was in full force. Winds began buffeting the shield, shaking it side to side, nearly tipping it over. They swirled around it, spun it crazily through the air, and dropped it onto its side under the center of the dark Cloud cover.

Durward reformed the bell in an instant. The War Party stood up, back-to-back, holding hands to offer the Magician whatever enforcing they could.

The rain lashed at the shield with more violence. The winds drew back, then slammed into it, tumbling it and its precious cargo end to end.

Durward reformed the shield into a wide box, so that the force required to overturn it was greater than the winds could muster.

The gusts slid the box back and forth with their buffets,

as if it were a paper toy. The rain was collecting into a minor lake around them. Soon, they were floating on top of the water. The gales were slamming into them from above, dunking them beneath the water, again and again.

"Do *something*, Durward!" Arden said. "We can not bob about like this until your power and Galen's fails! Get us *out* of this Enchantment!"

Durward frowned, but continued concentrating. He and Galen sat on the floor of the box, across from each other. Guthrie and Arden sat at their sides. Durward drew the shield to a bare clearance of the War Party.

The magic winds ceased for a moment as if Kelsey were checking on the questers, then slammed viciously into the box, whirling it, end for end, under the water. The waves took over and kept the box submerged. Currents in the water continued to spin and shake it.

Arden was so dizzy he had to press his hands against the floor of the shield to keep from falling onto his face.

Galen and Durward were bracing each other with their palms together to pass energy.

Guthrie was hunched over, slightly cramped by the close quarters.

Lightning flashed blue and white within inches of the surface of the newly formed lake, followed by horrendous thunder that sounded strange through the raging water. Kelsey was showing off, with obvious relish.

Durward whispered as if he were issuing himself a command, and the box sank against the earth.

The water rushed frantically against the shield from all

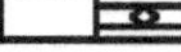

directions in wild rhythms, but its attempts to budge the safeguard were in vain.

Durward created a tiny wheel and pressed it by hand to the side of the force field beside Arden's head.

The scythe passed through the box without harming it.

Durward increased the saw's size and thickness.

The water tore at the scythe with invisible hands but could not deflect the wheel from its course. It soared out of the wind ravaged lake toward the wall of the Cloud to the right of Durward. The teeth of the spinning wheel screamed eerily in the frenzy of the wind and rain of Kelsey's malevolent storm.

A gigantic bolt of lightning, blinding bright and ushering thunder that vibrated the water around their shield, exploded from the center of the ceiling of the Cloud and sizzled into the heart of the saw.

The saw flipped wildly end for end into the water, but rebounded to its course.

Durward could not see through the seething water how his weapon fared, but he felt the impact of the lightning and the regaining of the saw's course.

Kelsey hurled more lightning into the magic disk, deflecting it left and right and tumbling it end to end, trying to force it into the water toward the hardened earth.

Durward drew on Galen's might, stabilized the saw, and it hewed through the wall of the Cloud, into the sunlight.

The wall healed immediately.

Durward brought the saw back through the Cloud and made it attack that area without cease. The keen teeth sliced faster than the wall could seal. The wound grew larger and the sun's light filtered through the water, feebly reaching Durward.

Kelsey screamed with rage. It ceased the rain and its Cloud-self grew whiter. It pelted the water with sleet, snow and frigid cold, emanating the chill from every inch of itself. The lake began to freeze from the top down, progressing incredibly swiftly.

Durward tore his saw through the ice and directed it to the far end wall of the Cloud. He ripped at the barrier until he had an opening more than large enough for their shield box to pass through.

The saw frantically maintained the breach.

Durward slowly inched the box toward freedom.

Though the saw was passing in and out of the wound in the Cloud without encountering any of Kelsey's magical shielding, the water did not flow through.

Durward did not understand why.

Kelsey abandoned its winds and sleet and intensified its lightning and cold.

The lake was half-way frozen.

The War Party was yards from the escape breach.

Kelsey spoke to them through the water with a gurgling voice that was high-pitched and irritating. "*Cede* the *effort* and *admit* my *supremacy,* as is only *proper*," it said, smugly. "Though you *rip* down my *entire* wall, my *waters* will *contain* you. My *cold* will *freeze* you into *pitiable* statues, *draining* you of your last, warm, *life* energy. Lord Nigel has decreed *my* success and *his* triumph. Open your shield,

Magician, and *end* your *sad miserable existence* now. You shall falter soon, anyway, and die *painfully*. But, not *I*. *I* shall *endure* though the sun, itself, sputters out!"

"*That* will be when *I* succumb!" Durward raged, despite his despair at his inability to force them to and through the opening he had hewn. He was weakening, even with Galen to enforce him. The box was thinner and bulging inward on all sides. Durward's saw was spinning less swiftly; fighting the waves with less vigor. The opening in the Cloud wall was slowly healing itself.

Arden and Guthrie were enraged at their inability to aid in their defense and escape. They despaired as they watched Durward and Galen losing strength and color, and the shield's sides sagging under the weight and pressure of the ever pounding tides.

Durward dispatched his saw toward the heart of the Cloud, from where the strongest lightning and Kelsey's voice issued.

Kelsey gathered its energy and discharged several hundred bolts of lightning. They merged, and sizzled into the saw.

The saw was flipped to the horizontal. It skidded in the air for several feet, on a downward track, then burst through the ice. Its speed was not lessened as it bored its way, spinning horizontally, into the baked gray earth.

Durward saw the impact, and held the saw in the ground. He thinned the shield, realizing the danger, and channeled more power to the saw. He rotated it horizontally as it spun, and it hurled earth out of the round hole that it drilled.

Kelsey began firing lightning into its water like a Needle Boar protecting its young. Thousands of bolts sizzled into the rimy lake, sending great puffs of steam into the air between the ice and the Cloud.

The bolts failed to reach the saw.

Kelsey bunched its lightnings until they were a single, magnificent bolt as thick as a tree trunk. It seared through the icy water, and exploded the saw into shards. This created a waterspout around the War Party.

Durward's contact with Galen was severed, and Durward's control over his energy faltered.

The safeguard shattered.

Water and ice inundated the men. The waterspout roiled them up out of the frigid water, hurled them onto the surface ice, in different directions, and subsided.

Kelsey laughed with delight and relief. It commenced pelting the men with hail the size of a human fist.

Durward gasped for air and en-shielded himself.

Lightning melted a hole in the ice where Galen lay. He clawed desperately at the ice but slid into the frigid water.

Kelsey began to freeze the water over the Healer.

Durward struggled to his knees and psychically pulled the Healer out of the drink before the water crystallized. Durward en-shielded Arden, Galen and Guthrie, latched onto them with his energy, and drew the four force fields together.

Kelsey slammed angry tongues of lightning into the

safeguard. The bolts sparked small holes through the clear shield, then dissipated, trailing thunder and its echoes.

Durward and Galen connected and the tiny openings in the force field closed.

Kelsey slammed lightning into the box as a continuous salvo.

Filled with the ear drum stinging peals of thunder, and the explosions of the blue bolts crackling against its sides, the shield shuddered but did not give way.

"How long?" Galen asked, through gritted teeth. The effort of generating energy to enforce Durward was showing on the Healer's whitened face.

"One *hour*, maybe," Durward said, his lips taut with extreme effort and exhaustion. "*Then*, I can control, no longer. Can channel our powers, no more, without *rest* and *food*!"

"*Then*, we are *lost*!" Arden despaired. "*Aldora* is *forfeit* to *Nigel* and Indwin is *enslaved* by that monster! Not even *death* will ease the *agony* of *that*!" He stared wildly into the haggard Magician's tormented eyes. "Durward!" he pleaded. "There *must* be a *way*! *Something* you have not *tried*! *Something*, that, tried *longer*, might, yet, *save* us! There *cannot* be *failure*! The *price* of *that* is too *high* for *all* of us!"

There were no words Durward or Galen could offer. Indeed, there was little energy to spare, for either to speak.

Guthrie hugged his son and bade him to silence.

Kelsey ceased the hail and increased its cold. The frigidity began leaking through the shield. At the same time,

Kelsey nailed every inch of the box with lightening bolts, without cease.

The questers bounced around inside their sanctuary and prison, helpless to save themselves.

Kelsey gathered its bolts into larger ones. They speared into the safeguard with more violence than the tree trunks in the Woods. Some bolts dented the box, others burned tiny holes, through which Kelsey poured rain. The water slowly began filling the box.

Durward conformed the shield to fit the four men. The openings vanished, but the water stayed with the questers.

Kelsey increased the size and strength of its lightning. Holes were seared into the box. Kelsey pelted the surface of the lake with warmth, by spreading its blue lightning into miniature bolts, and crackling them constantly, melting the ice.

The box inched down into the softened ice. When the lake thawed, water swirled over the shield and it subsided to the hard ground.

Kelsey began refreezing the water. The leaks in the shield did not seal, and water seeped in faster.

Arden hammered his fists against the safeguard. "Let us *free*, Durward!" he screamed, in fury and despair. "*One*, alone, might *survive* and *escape*! *You*, with a *shield*, and all your *magic* helping you, *can* blast through the Cloud! The war *can* still be *won*, by *you*! You do *not* need *us*! *Let* us *out*!"

"*Aye*!" Guthrie agreed. "*Do* it! At least *try*! It *is* worth a *try*!"

"Yes!" Galen said, firmly. "*You* could *manage* it! *Just* enough energy for *one*! *Do* it!"

"No!" Durward raged. "There *is* something! I *know* there *is* a *way*! I saw it! But, I can not *recall*! So much has assaulted *us*, my poor senses *reel* as though I am *intoxicated*! Think! I caused *something* that drove Kelsey *wild*! That made the fiend *break* our—My *saw*! Kelsey used all its lightning on my *saw* as it *excavated* the earth!"

"Yes!" Galen said, with hope.

"Every one lie down, side by side," Durward ordered. He magically forced the water out through the leaks in the safeguard, and reduced its size. This sealed the openings but left little room for the questers to move. He stared at the ground. A saw formed on the underside of the box. He enlarged the saw and the sides of the shield weakened. The water pressed eagerly toward them, sagging the sides and the top of the box so the men were forced tighter together.

Durward's saw began to whirl, creating a muddy eddy beneath them. He directed the saw into the earth, then turned the saw on end, and set it rotating laterally, as well as spinning. He segmented the saw into a hundred tiny saws, and spread them in a line, from wall-to-wall of the submerged part of the Cloud layer.

Durward sent the saws forward, tearing grooves into the hard earth. When the saws reached the wall at the end of the Cloud cover, Durward called them back, and set them to grooving the earth to the opposite end of the Cloud cover.

Kelsey's power and control faltered.

Durward and Galen grasped each other's shaky hands, and strained to their utmost. More tiny saws spun off the sides of the shield and tore into the earth, moving in the opposite direction of the first saws, furrowing the ground into tiny squares, then digging it up, so that dry earth that had not been hardened by Kelsey's magical lightning, was revealed.

The questers heard Kelsey scream through the water. Its voice was fraught with horror and despair. "Nigel! You *swore* I could not *die*! You *lied*! You *used* me! *Damn* you! *Damn* your *black* soul, *Nigel*!"

Bubbles of air began perking out of the earth. Kelsey's energized waters were being absorbed by the thirsty ground. The Enchantment fought to pull the shards of its hardened earth into place to seal off its waning life force, but to no avail.

The saws, never ceasing, sliced at Kelsey's earth, chopping it into finer particles of nonabsorbent, chaff.

"*Hope*!" Kelsey shouted, through the water. "I *shall* defeat you *yet*!" It struck at its water with frigidness from its Cloud-self. The lake began freezing more swiftly than before. The normal earth absorbed the water, but not quickly enough to deplete it before Kelsey could freeze and retain it and its unnatural life.

Durward drew air out of the water and into the shield, increasing the internal pressure.

The safeguard became buoyant, and floated up toward the downward growth of the ice.

Durward directed some of his saws up into the ice,

and hewed it into slush.

The slush floated atop the water, blocking what little light the evil Cloud had not already filtered out.

Kelsey wildly tugged at the chaff of water sealant earth to reaffirm its floor, and simultaneously pumped more cold into its slushy water.

Durward directed half of his saws to the ground and half to the surface of the lake, to prevent the slush from refreezing.

Kelsey drew its Cloud-self down upon the slush. The cold it emanated struck the shield like a vacuum, sucking at the heat in the four desperate men. The slush began icing over.

Kelsey's frantic efforts failed to re-harden the floor of the lake, but this did not matter, if Kelsey succeeded in freezing its water.

Durward and Galen noted a shine

The magic saws below were glowing with a ghostly blue light.

The Healer and Magician looked up.

The saws above were, likewise, irradiating.

Durward tried to push his weary abilities to an even greater limit. He caused the shield to radiate heat from all sides. This warmed the War Party and began melting the ice and slush around them.

Kelsey sizzled lightning into the slush and struck the thin force field.

Durward turned his bottom saws into energy, thickened the walls of the safeguard, and increased the heat it emanated.

The surface of the shield began to glow like a coal.

Durward directed the heat away from the safeguard, preventing harm to himself and his hopeful companions.

"Can *nothing* I *devise* destroy *you*, Magician?" Kelsey railed, in horror. "Can not *even* Nigel's *might* quash your *sickening* life? *Spare* me, *Nigel*! *Hear* me! *Enforce* me! *How* can I *serve* your *needs,* if, you will not *provide* for me?"

The earth had absorbed all the water it could.

Durward directed a dozen saws from the surface, through the slush, toward the ground. He began excavating, hurling the dry dirt up above the water and slush, and draining the water and slush into the pit.

Kelsey hurled ire fueled frigidness. The lake surface began to refreeze.

Durward's red-hot emanation caused the slush to bubble and steam. He felt the box's form waning. The cerise radiance was decreasing, and the ice was descending toward the demise of the questers, and to the sustenance of Kelsey's life.

Durward pulled the surface saws through the slush and into the ground.

They opened dozens of huge pits, submitting the waters to more of the thirsty earth that had not been hardened by Kelsey.

Soon, the water was gone, leaving thick ice covering the shield.

The Cloud Enchantment was flat and taught against the

icy lake. Kelsey could afford neither movement nor easing of its cold force. It could not invest in dispatching a bolt of lightning through the nearly depleted safeguard to dispatch the hated men without opening itself to Durward's killing heat.

Durward sucked deep breaths and increased his heat. This melted the ice around the shield, freeing more air. Durward drew the air into the box. With the oxygen, came energy. Each breath Durward and Galen gasped increased the heat around the safeguard. Slowly, inevitably, all the ice melted.

Kelsey, too overtaxed to whisper, strove, in utter silence and total despair, to increase its Arctic force. The loss of more than half of its precious self had caused too grievous an injury. The Enchantment was dying with each drop of its water absorbed by the soft earth being thrown up by the saws still excavating around the shield.

The only question; who would die first. Kelsey, or Durward?

This battle had drained Durward so completely he was functioning only on the energy he and Galen painfully drew from the air. Galen had always been able to do so for his healing work. This ability was new to Durward, and it was the sole thing keeping him alive and conscious. The available energy was small and decreasing as Kelsey seeped away.

"Perhaps," Durward gasped, to his friends, "this, is a *stand-off* to *mutual* death. Only time will tell, for I can not blast even myself free now. *Pray* for us."

Kelsey drew itself tighter around its melting, dwindling waters, decreasing the area it must protect. It derived no aid from this, for its overall energy dwindled.

Durward's red heat melted the last of the ice.

Only warm water remained.

Kelsey's Cloudy skin was white, and it was so thin the red sun shone through it.

Evening was falling, casting symbolic crimson across the battle field.

Durward drew his saws out of the pits of mud and merged them with the shield. The box strengthened. Durward increased the size of the safeguard, sat up straight, and gazed at the taught skin of the odd white Cloud. Fissures appeared in it. Gaps opened. The scarlet sun shafted comfortingly into the box.

Finally, all the water was absorbed. Kelsey turned into a brief, morose rain, leaving the men barely alive it as it perished.

Durward assimilated his shield energy. He baked the surrounding earth with a gentle heat. After an hour of rest, he struggled to his feet and began kilning the remaining black mud to brick resilience, forever destroying the twisted unnatural thing that had been Kelsey.

Durward gazed to where the end wall of the Cloud Enchantment had been, and where their alarmed mounts had fled to safety. There, stood the guards and horses. They had been placed under hypnotic trance by Kelsey.

They were awakening.

Kelsey had failed to destroy a single member of their War Party.

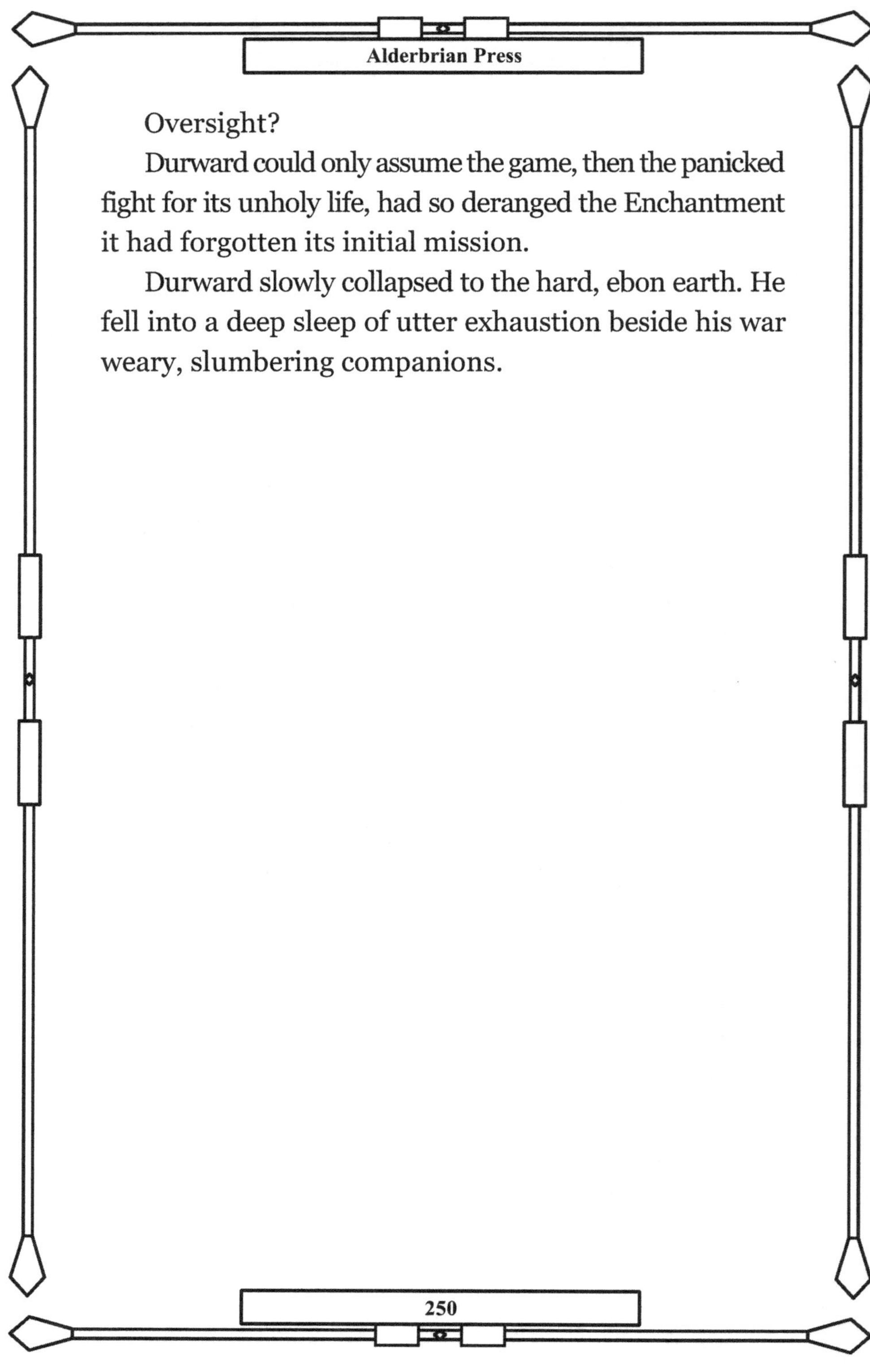

Oversight?

Durward could only assume the game, then the panicked fight for its unholy life, had so deranged the Enchantment it had forgotten its initial mission.

Durward slowly collapsed to the hard, ebon earth. He fell into a deep sleep of utter exhaustion beside his war weary, slumbering companions.

Illustration 21
Palace Art: Lady Inessa's Private Chambers: East Wall Window: Landscape Orientation
Copyright © 2019 Philip Raymond Sadler
251-A

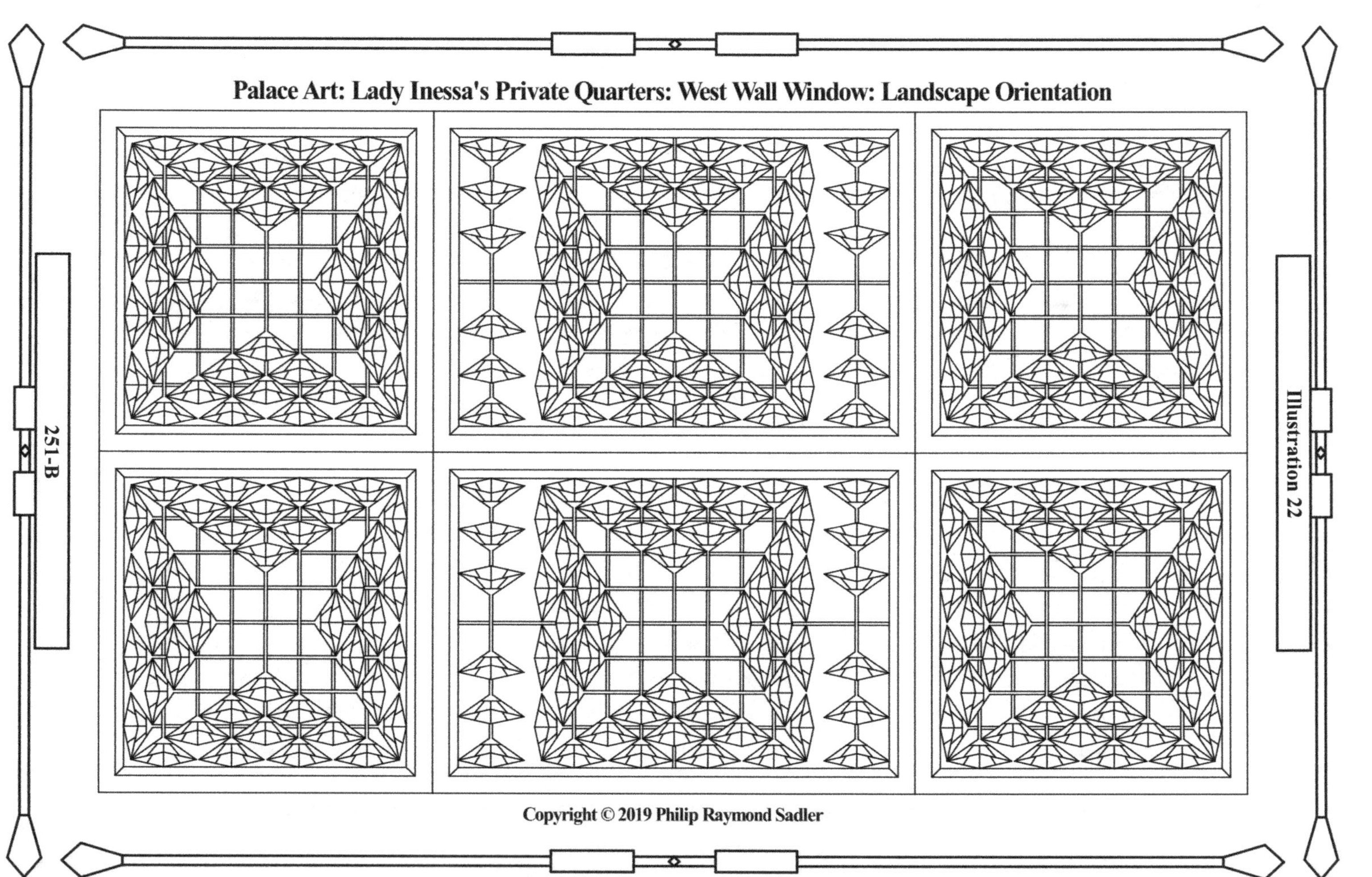
Palace Art: Lady Inessa's Private Quarters: West Wall Window: Landscape Orientation
Illustration 22
251-B
Copyright © 2019 Philip Raymond Sadler

Chapter 11
Sounds Familiar

"Sleep and food create amazing results," Durward said.

"Aye," Guthrie agreed. He signaled and the guards forged ahead of the War Party.

Arden shook his head in wonder and heeled his horse into motion. "Last night," he said, "you and Galen looked like the Twins of Death. Today, you are almost robust."

"At least, hale," Galen said, with a laugh.

They were bound toward the crags and tors of Jeddro Gulches. An offshoot of the West Shield Mountains where the Elf Caverns lay.

The soldiers entered the Gulches, each man following a different branch of the deep, wide main gouge that wended its way through the ebony bedrock.

Galen held his hands into the air. "If there are further Enchantments, they are not close together as before," he said, cheerfully. "I sense nothing but natural earth essence, and the vibrations of the scouts."

"No *heavy* shoulders, today, Arden," Guthrie asked.

"No *tingling* in the feet, *either*," Arden retorted, playfully. "Maybe Nigel has abandoned his war."

"I will *not* complain," Galen said. "It is *fine* with *me* if he does not create any *worse* magical *threats*. If *that* is within the *faintest* realm of *possibility*, considering what he has *already* brought to life."

"Ho, Guthrie!" a voice called from their right.

"*That* is Hilliard," Galen said. "I recognize his dulcet tones."

The War Party heeled their steeds to the right. The ravine they took was sided by black masses of shining stone. Little dirt lay under the hooves of their mounts, and no vegetation grew.

"Guard!" Guthrie called. "What *game* is this? If you have intelligence, *report* it!"

"It is embarrassing," Hilliard said, with chagrin. "I have mislaid my horse and gotten myself lodged between a rock and a hard place."

The War Party laughed.

"Shout us to you, then," Galen said, "and I will check you out for damage."

"You are headed correctly," Hilliard said. "I am in plain sight, more so the pity for my ego."

"You will have much greater reason for self-pity *if* this is a *prank*," Guthrie warned, good-naturedly.

"You *know* your guardsmen *better* than *that*," Hilliard said. "*Or*, you *should*."

Durward reined his horse in, then caught the reins of Galen and Arden's mounts on each side of him, stopping them.

Guthrie pulled up in surprise.

"What ails you, Durward?" Arden asked.

"That last comment by the scout," Durward said. "Did you not *detect* a *note* of *challenge*? Perhaps, *smugness*?"

"I did not," Guthrie said, with a smile. "You are *too* cautions. Galen has *cleared* the way, and even Arden has given us the *stamp* of *safe* passage. Let us get *on* with it."

"Guthrie!" Hilliard shouted, sounding nearby, and to their left. "The sense has returned to my legs, and my ankles are killing me! Not to forget, my bottom!"

Arden and Guthrie shook their heads at Durward.

"Is there *anything* but *exaggerated* self sorrow in that voice?" Guthrie said.

"Let us see who can discover him first," Arden challenged. "I need a little play, and not the type Kelsey so unkindly offered." He reined his horse ahead of the War Party and took a fork on their left.

"It's *about* time!" Hilliard called. "I thought, sure, you were going to punish me for my carelessness by leaving me to the hairy rock spiders."

"We may *yet*," Arden shouted. "Where *are* you? For one who is in *plain* sight, you are *very* hard to see!"

Durward and the others came around the bend of the fork and stopped behind Arden.

The voice did not respond.

Guthrie dismounted. He handed his reigns to Arden and began checking behind the old rocks and boulders scattered rifely about. "Your *scarlet* face *should* be a *beacon* to *me*!" he said. "But, your *voice* will *fare* a better *director*! *Speak* up, soldier! Or, has this self professed *embarrassment* sealed your previously *large* mouth?"

Galen tested the air with his palms and frowned. Guthrie was there, in sight and vibrations, but no other life touched his senses. "Durward," he said, almost below hearing, "I now agree with you. There *is* no one *here* save *us* four."

"Not *even* the *energy* of an Enchantment?" Durward whispered.

"Nor, the *unique* power of any *disguise* for an Enchantment," Galen whispered.

Guthrie started climbing up the left side if the rocky fork.

"You are *warming*," Hilliard said.

"So, this *is* buffoonery," Guthrie said. "We will teach you not to *wax* so miscreant."

"*Guthrie*!" Durward shouted. "Come here! *Immediately*!"

The War Serpent glanced over his shoulder. "Why?" he said. "I am about to educate my soldier further than he has ever imagined."

Durward latched onto Guthrie with an energy beam.

"You *are* a *spoiler*," the sham Hilliard voice said, with annoyance. It vented a powerful high-pitched resounding shout.

Several boulders, precariously perched on the left side of the rocky fork, broke loose and swiftly rumbled down.

Durward encased Guthrie in a shield and pressed force against his back to brace him.

The boulders slammed into the Knight with more impact than Durward had expected, overcoming the restraining energy.

Guthrie was shoved down the side of the fork, with the great rocks grating against his safeguard. He crashed into the base of one of the stone columns and the boulders covered him.

"*Not* such a *spoiler* after all!" the voice said, like distant thunder. "Will Durward, *vapidly*, contend, with Sumner?"

Durward ignored the jibe and dismounted. He handed his reigns to Galen, quickly neared the pile of boulders, grasped one with his force, and slowly rolled the huge stone away.

Guthrie peered out from the opening. He appeared safe inside his shield.

The drain on Durward's power told him the safeguard was weakening under the weight of the massive ebon rocks. He tugged a second black boulder off the pile, then a third, and fourth.

Guthrie was half free, with his legs caught beneath the huge stones.

"I've *nearly* fooled for Kelsey's *fatal* error!" Sumner reverberated around the War Party. "I *almost* forgot to *divide* to *destroy*!" Several shrieks tore the air. Their vibrations and echoes clawed at larger boulders hulking on the sides of the fork. The great rocks trembled and began a fast rumbling descent.

Arden and Galen dismounted and lead the four stallions to where Durward stood beside Guthrie.

Durward threw up a shield around the War Party and mounts. The boulders smashed into it, sounding like thunder from Kelsey. The force field shook, and cracked with tiny fissures, but held.

The horses began swaying their heads, and stamp their hooves, in growing fear.

Durward placed the steeds into trance to prevent them from injuring themselves and the questers.

Durward opened the shield on one side and continued prying at the huge stones imprisoning Guthrie.

The Knight chided himself and became the War Serpent. This caused the personal safeguard to reform itself and the boulders settled more tightly against one another. War Serpent wriggled through a gap and entered the main shield.

Durward added the energy of the small safeguard to the large one, then sealed the opening.

Guthrie resumed his man shape. "This is *not* the *lesson* I had in *mind*," he said, wryly. "*Nor*, is it *aimed* at the *deserving* victim I had *intended*."

"This *is*, also, not a *comfortable* position," Arden said.

Durward agreed, but remained silent. He took Galen's hand and began psycho kinetically shoving at the boulders ringing the safeguard.

"*Exercise* your *faith*!" Sumner shouted, sounding as though it were atop the force field. "*That* is all *your* many *parlor* tricks will *avail* you!" More of its echoing shrieks scrabbled around the fork. Boulders began rolling down upon the War Party.

Durward struck at them with invisible fists of energy. He succeeded in deflecting the smaller ones but several boulders larger than both man and horse piled into those already ringing the safeguard. They blocked the path Durward had been clearing, and strained the protective shield with their added mass.

Durward took more thoughtful stock of their position. Sumner did not seem able to lift the rocks and boulders, so it could not pile them on top of the safeguard. They were safe from attack from above. He feared they might have to shoulder their supplies, abandon their horses, and climb over the boulders.

Durward tested the resistance of the ring of boulders. They moved with as much difficulty as he had dreaded. He scanned the sides of the old fork for boulders Sumner could call down on them. There were none.

Durward knew their escape would not be easy, and that he had not seen Sumner's only ability.

"Can you *lever* us *out* of *this*, Durward?" Guthrie asked, softly.

"Can you *lever* us *out* of *this*, Durward?" his voice echoed, vastly magnified in volume, throughout the fork.

Thunder sounded as the great shelves of stone on either side of them began to crack and snap into loose shale.

Sumner's second capacity, Durward thought, is not a weak one. He continued slowly shoving at the boulders and rocks. One tumbled down behind the others.

The crunch of the rock against the coarse dirt on the stone floor of the fork was picked up by Sumner and eagerly intensified. It became thousands of grinding sounds everywhere. Thunder rumbled throughout the fork, and the first layer of broken black shale cascaded upon the War Party, piling up around their shield higher than the boulders, bringing darkness.

Durward shot force at one side of the pile and the shale flew away from the safeguard, bringing daylight. He realized his mistake and attempted to gather the shale into a shield. His momentary anger cost the questers much. The bits of shale that he missed, a considerable amount, clattered into the side of the fork.

Sumner pounced on the thousands of sounds and increased them into ear stinging explosions. The slick sides of the fork shattered, as if from underlying volcanic activity, and the shards showered the War Party, covering the force field, bringing darkness.

Durward filled the safeguard with his blue light.

"Every sound of escape we make will be used to hold us," Galen whispered.

"Every sound of escape we make, will be used to hold us," his voice echoed throughout the fork. Shale exploded from the stone walls and thudded into the shield. The sounds were caught by Sumner and intensified, producing cracks in the walls of the fork and fountains of shale. This became a self-powering cycle.

Durward and Galen fused their power more intently.

Durward used it to maintain the integrity of the safeguard. The weight of the broken rock was sagging its top, and pressing in its sides, as had Kelsey's water. The War Party held as still and silent as possible as they endured the millions of impacts.

Arden started to say something.

Guthrie shook his head and covered his son's mouth

with a firm hand.

Durward closed his eyes and listened intently. He nodded, with a smile, and began pressing force against the shale on the side of the safeguard that faced the area from which they had entered the fork. The bits of rock began cascaded away, creating a small landslide, and clearing the dome of the shield.

Durward ended his blue light.

The scraping and clattering of the shale was picked up by Sumner, in hurtfully loud echoes, but there were no resulting explosions of shards from the fork.

When Durward had the side of the bell cleared of the shale, he pried at the boulders and rocks pressed against it.

Every sound was picked up by sly Sumner and hammered around them with enough volume and violence to shake the force field, but no further shards hampered Durward's escape activities.

"Sumner is out of his stone arrows," Durward whispered, knowing the Enchantment would snatch up his words and hurl the vibrations back at them, as it did. "We can speak, softly, for now."

The Magician worked at the boulders until he created a path through them. When he cleared the remaining shale from the shield, the War Party saw why Sumner could no longer strike them with rock shards.

"It has *destroyed* this *entire* fork of the gulches!" Arden exclaimed, to his immediate regret.

Sumner greedily echoed the loud retort, driving the sound vastly louder against the bell.

The shield shook as though storm gales were pounding on it, but no one was injured.

"Sorry," Arden said.

"Sorry," Sumner slammed back at them, but with less force, so that it was more of an annoyance, than an attack.

Durward absorbed the force field and awakened the horses. They began shuffling and neighing, in uneasiness.

Sumner seized on the sounds and stung the animals and men with weird, sharp noises that did not resemble the neighing and shuffling.

Durward entranced the steeds.

Sumner fell silent.

"We are clear, for now, of true menace from Sumner," Durward told the War Party. "But, there are many more stone forks to traverse."

"*Must* we *leave* the mounts?" Arden said, softly. His words, like Durward's, curiously did not echo.

"Sumner is planning," Galen said, with a normal tone. His experiment proved his words.

Echoes did not scratch their skin, as they should have.

Durward awakened the steeds. The War Party quietly mounted. They heeled the horses slowly out of the circle of ebony boulders, and paused.

Arden shrugged. "Any way we travel will bring us into Sumner's reach," he said. "And, we cannot *bypass* the gulches without losing a week, or more."

"We *all* know we have no *week* to *waste*," Galen said.

Guthrie looked to both ends of the fork. "Where *are* my guards?" he said. "Has Sumner crushed them beneath its shale in some other fork? Or, have they passed through? If so, it will not be long before they miss us and venture back into harm's vicious arms."

"We *must* do, *likewise*, as *risky* as that *is*," Durward said. "I *shall* endeavor to protect us."

Arden decided to commence their hazardous trek in the direction they had originally taken. He reined his mount into motion, and as quickly heeled it to a stop. "What has *transpired* with our *sounds*?" he asked. His horse shuffled nervously, but its hooves made no noise on the shale littered stone floor of the fork.

"I have muffled it," Durward said, "absorbing it, as I do the shield energy. But, it supplies me vastly less power than it avails Sumner."

"Which hearkens a question," Galen said, as they were proceeding toward the far end of the ruined fork. "*Has* the destruction of this fork *vanquished* Nigel's latest nightmare? Or, is it busily setting up some vile trap?"

"Ho!" Durward shouted as forcefully as he could. "What say you of the Healer's query?"

"*Little*," Sumner whispered from around them. "My *exploits* shall *speak* for me, *eloquently*. Probably, their words shall be *beyond* your *tiny* intellectual abilities to *comprehend*. As, is *justly* fitting, since they flow from one so *superior*, as *I*."

Guthrie halted his horse at the end of the fork. Beyond, were many forks, some leading left, some leading right, and one running in the general direction of the War Party's destination.

"This multi crossroads is an excellent spot for our foe," Galen said, softly.

"Are you *reading* minds *now*?" Guthrie asked. "That was *my,* exact, thought."

"We *must* proceed," Arden said, impatiently. "Sumner can no longer use our *sounds* to strike us, and even when it devises an attack, we must still endeavor toward the Caverns, and Nigel."

"Yes," Durward said. "Time *is* graining *short*. More brief, than I had hoped. Rein your mounts close to me at all times."

Durward billowed a shield and held it over them like an umbrella, a hair's breadth from the stone floor. The bottom rim thudded against the larger stones in their path.

Sumner remained disturbingly inactive.

The War Party passed the large intersection and entered the main area of the gulches.

Guthrie and Durward spotted their blunder immediately, but this was still too lax a reaction.

Sumner knew its domain intimately. Its first shriek shattered the surface of the walls at the mouth of this fork. Great boulders toppled resoundingly onto the floor behind the War Party, like giants planting their feet firmly against intruders. The way back was blocked, and the massive rocks were beyond Durward's energy to budge.

The War Party faced the widest fork of the bewitched gulches. Throughout, stood gnarled rock columns, towering as high as the rock-and-crag-cluttered walls. Boulders the size of the Royal Reservoir lay between the ebony columns. Gaps in the stone floor yawned in scattered patterns beside these rough leviathan rocks, and around the columns. To travel here, even without Sumner's magical menace, would have been dangerous. Now, it was insane to press on.

Even if Sumner gifted them the option, they could not, for the sake of their people, yield to reason and skirt the threat.

"*May* the *Ethereal* prepare its *place* for *us* in their *Kingdom*," Durward said.

Galen stared at him, aghast. If the old Magician believed *all* was *lost*, how could *he* or the *others* have the *tiniest* glimmer of *hope*?

"*Guard* your *tongue*, good *Durward*!" Guthrie hissed. "*See* that you do *not* allow the *savage* wonder of the *danger* of Nigel's *insanity* to *defeat* you *for* Sumner! We have *faced* more *hell* than *any* men before us, and you *have* preserved our *lives*! *Remember* only *that*!"

Durward shook his head, sadly. His frightened face brought chills to them.

Even Guthrie's gruff and practiced hardness, melted.

"If—" Durward silenced himself. Desperately, he shook a fist at the enchanted hazard. "You speak *wisely*," he said, not quite hiding his uncertainty. "We *have* survived *wonders* never before *faced*. We *shall* surpass this *ugly* miracle!" He ended the bell safeguard and placed individual, contoured, flexible barriers around each man and his mount. "Perhaps," he said, "at least *one* of us *will* live to *fight*

Nigel."

Guthrie understood his intent.

Galen and Arden slowly glimpsed it.

They lined up their mounts; their clear force fields glistening in the golden sun.

Without a word, the War Party heeled and reined their shy steeds into a gallop along the fork. They spread as wide apart as the walls of the fork allowed, and they did not permit their horses to slacken pace.

Durward muffled the sounds of horse and rider.

Sumner was not tied to the necessity of these. It emitted a low rumbling eerie unbroken cry. The ululation snaked around the black columns and dipped into the gashes in the stone floor, resonating therein like hundreds of irate leviathan bees in their nests. First, one sickening crack of stone, then another, joined the rumbling cry. Boulders began crunching their way down the walls, bringing with them slides of shale and greater noise. Sumner collected every rumble, every scratch and clink of the shale, and threw it back at the ebony walls. This brought more boulders and shale. The thunder of the approaching boulders reverberated like the mumbling of angry giants. Some boulders crashed like massive hammers into rock columns. One stone tower snapped in half and collapsed, shattering from bottom up like thin ice.

Durward reined his mount to a stop and slid it, with his mind force, away from the hurtling tower fragments. The stallion neighed in terror and obtained a gallop to the right of the thundering, dusty mass of loose stone.

Galen leaped his horse over one of the small ravines and glanced behind.

A boulder the size of a loaded dray plummeted into the fissure and struck bottom thunderously.

Sumner enforced the sound.

The boulder exploded into millions of pieces, pelting the fleeing Healer with sharp pebbles, and sending up a cloud of stone dust.

Galen swerved his mount from a second crevice. An onrushing bolder struck his horse on one flank. Man and beast crashed to the pebble strewn stone floor.

Guthrie's stallion screamed in fear and leaped into the air with an arched back. Its hooves barely cleared the boulder that thundered under it. The steed landed unsteadily, slipped on a shard of shale, and tumbled on top of the Knight.

Arden galloped his stallion toward the second fourth of the fork. Several smaller boulders were in an intersecting course with him. If he continued straight, they would slam into him. He could not veer left to out run them because a fissure too wide for his mount to jump, yawned beside him. Behind him, a rock tower, toppled in one piece by the largest boulder dislodged by Sumner, was falling toward the Crown Prince Designate.

Durward noted the imminent threat to Arden and reined his stallion in that direction. The Magician removed his shield and added its energy to the force fields around Arden and his horse. Durward checked on Guthrie and Galen. They were struggling to right their mounts, and un-

harmed. Durward stripped them of their clear safeguards and enforced the force fields on Arden and his steed. The Magician struck both horse and rider with as much psycho kinetic energy as he could, while still maintaining the shield power.

Arden and his stallion tumbled onto their sides, skidding wildly across the rock-littered, slick ebony stone floor.

The massive column exploded onto the rolling boulders and the floor, shattering with a roar that drowned out even Sumner's constant low cry. Sharp slivers of stone shot in all directions with the force of black arrows dispatched from fully drawn bows.

Arden's horse managed to stand. It reared in terror, spun around, and fled toward the side of the fork. Slivers of stone pelted it, but the shield held it from harm.

Arden was covered with rocks, shale and dust, but was not struggling to come out from under it.

Sumner laughed like a thousand Kelsey thunder bolts. The top layers of the sides of the fork shattered into the air. The shale fell short of the men, but caught Arden's horse and buried it.

Guthrie and Galen managed to mount their steeds and bore down on the place were Arden lay motionless.

Durward directed his psycho kinetic energy at that rubble, clearing it from the Crown Prince Designate.

Arden waved a hand to show that his magic shield had endured, then struggled to his feet.

Durward pushed force into the pile of shale on Arden's horse, sending the debris flying in all directions. The steed bolted from the last bits and fled toward the center of the fork.

"*Revert* to *plan*!" Arden shouted through cupped hands, trying to be heard above Sumner's laugh, and its low ululating. "*Separate*! As we *know* we *must*!"

Guthrie did not catch his words, but guessed what he must be shouting. He would have done likewise. He heeled his stallion on course for the far end of the fork.

Galen continued toward Arden.

Durward latched onto Arden's horse with his force and led the steed back to Arden.

The Magician spun safeguards around the men and their mounts, then followed Guthrie's lead, but to the Knight's far left, and made for the fork terminus.

"*Divide* and *conquer*!" Sumner crowed. Each of its words brought down rock columns or showers of shale from the walls. "*This* is *what* I *advised* myself! And, look, they use *it* to contest *me*! Sly *fiends* that Nigel has sent for *me* to *slay*! A *better* joust than I had *hoped*! *Come*!" It thundered, with vibrations that shook the gulch. "*Fly* into my *killing* hands! You have nowhere *else* to *flee*!"

Durward started to direct his mount to leap a chasm, caught a movement from his left, and reined back. A jagged column was plummeting toward him, but he had detected it too late. His horse pumped its legs mightily, trying to obey his commands, and skidded toward the edge of the crevice. Durward directed his force against the chest of the horse and himself, but it did no good. Man and mount hurtled over the sharp rim of the chasm.

Half the column slammed across the fissure and hurled a third of its deadly mass after the plummeting Magician.

Durward placed the stallion into a trance to spare it from further terror, wished regretfully that he could do the same for himself, and tried to reinforce their shields without drawing from those around his companions and their steeds.

Arden and Galen raced side by side toward the crevasse.

Guthrie, who noted the event when he was checking positions over his shoulder, wanted to turn back with all his soul, but realized, if hope was left, Durward would free himself. If it was lost, Guthrie's was the best chance to reach, and pass beyond the far end of the fork. If Sumner gloated over the Magician's circumstances, it might not note Guthrie's position until it was too late for the Enchantment to intervene.

Galen and Arden dismounted and knelt at the edge of the fissure. Below them was a jumble of rocks, shale and thick piles of stone dust. Nowhere could they detect Durward or his mount.

Sumner fell silent.

The echoes from the falling boulders and showers of rock shards caused by the toppled tower, faded.

Galen and Arden heard the distant clattering of the hooves of a horse striking stone. They glanced toward the sound. It was Guthrie.

The Kings Knight was making swift progress toward the end of the fork despite the towering piles of shattered rock columns, and the gatherings of displaced boulders.

"*Durward* is no longer *muffling* Guthrie's sounds!" Arden shouted. "Our *shields* are *gone*!"

Galen watched in horror.

Guthrie galloped his stallion toward a pair of columns, between which, lay a narrow crevice.

Surely, Guthrie *knows* he is no longer *protected*, Galen thought. *Surely*, he will pull *back* from that *hopeless* path!

"*Durward* is *dead*!" Arden shouted, fearfully. "*We* are all *lost* to *Sumner*! *Vulnerable*, like *never* before!"

Sumner emitted a high-pitched squeal that stung the skin of both man and horse. Their mounts startled, and fled in opposite directions.

Guthrie's steed reared, refused to leap the fissure, and tried to run away from the yawning pit.

Sumner's second screech felt like pins striking into their flesh.

Both towering columns of rock cracked at the base, then at the centers, then shattered, and dropped out of the sky like stricken fowl, upon Guthrie and the crevice.

"No!" Galen screamed, with ultimate frustration and rage at Sumner. He started running, pell-mell, toward the churning cloud of ebon, stone dust. The cinereous nebula was billowing above the remaining towers of ebony rock, and over the walls of the lethal fork.

Arden watched Galen for a moment, then collapsed in despair, staring into the confusion of rubble in the crevice that had claimed Durward and his mount.

Sumner was laughing like a happy child. Its soft giggling wafted around the columns, and chased itself in and out of the fissures, leaping over the piles of rubble, and the heaps of boulders. "Calder, Brendan, Sanborn, Crandall, Monrow, Brougher, Woodruff, Marsden, Kelsey! *Blundered*! *Floundered*! *Failed*! But, *Sumner* succeeds! *Triumphs*, as Nigel *foresaw*!"

Galen reached the great mountain of rubble where Guthrie had vanished. The Healer began digging at the spot where he had last seen the Knight. He dug furiously. There was no physical damage, other than Nigel's insane mind, that he could not reshape and repair. *If* he reached Guthrie *in* time, he could *save* the Knight!

"Mourn *not* your slain *friend*!" Sumner whispered, beside Galen. "Mourn *yourself*! No *force* can *aid* you, *now*! *No one* can *save* a man, once *Sumner* has *called* his *end*!"

Galen clawed at the black rubble more wildly, hurling rocks and handfuls of dust past his sides.

Sumner giggled like a child with a secret new toy, and carried its depraved voice to Arden. "*See* how the *poor*, *foolish*, Healer *fights* his *fate*?" Sumner whispered, sympathetically, to Arden, from both sides. "*See* how, *maturely* you *accept* what is *decreed* by *Sumner*! I have *pride* for *you*! It is *almost* a *shame* to remove *your* life! But, Nigel is *firm* on *this* matter! You know, *now*, that Nigel *cannot* be *disobeyed*!"

"Shut up!" Arden screamed, shaking with fury and grief. "There *must* be some *shred* of *decency* within Nigel that *you share*! *Spare* us your *glee*, and your *mock* concern, and put an *end* to our *misery*! *Damn* you, and *damn*

Nigel's *twisted* soul, *for all time*!"

Sumner made a sound of reproval. Then returned to chide Galen.

Galen responded to Sumner before it could utter a word beyond the Healer's name. "*Why* have you *held* your *hand* from *us*?" Galen screamed, with rage. "*Are* you *reduced* below it, *with* the *effort* it *took* to *murder* our *friends*? *Or* do you *simply* enjoy *tormenting* us? Not even *dark* Nigel is *that* ill!"

Sumner emitted an expanding circle of high and low-pitched sound.

The fork shook with incredible violence.

Galen and Arden were thrown flat on their stomachs.

Sumner issued just the low-pitched sound, then only the higher pitched noise.

The men's skin was stung by these vibrations.

The mounts began galloping in circles of fear.

"*Slay* us!" Arden screamed. "*Slay* us! *We* shall *never* cease *clawing* after Nigel *if* we *live*! When we are *dead*, we will *haunt* him with *hatred* in *every* iota of our souls! *Slay* us and be *damned* and *horrified* when our souls *return* to *rend* you to *whining* bits! *Slay* us!"

Sumner ceased its sounds. "*Very well*," it thundered, with an evil voice as cold as ice, and filled with vehemence and disgust. "*Perish*, and be *welcome* to *it*!"

Sumner emitted sound beam after sound beam at the ten old rock towers still standing within the fork. They shattered with the frightening squealing of twisting and rending stone, and plummeted to the earth. Clouds of stone dust

billowed into the air, and trillions of slivers of rock flew in all directions like arrows, nicking both man and horse.

Sumner waited for the last eerie echoes of the impacts of its assault of sound to fade, and for the black stone dust to settle. The proud Enchantment looked around its domain with its magic sight.

Galen and Arden lay unharmed, except for tiny cuts and bruises where slivers had managed to strike them. The horses were lying exhausted, in a similar condition.

"This *is* strange!" Sumner whispered resoundingly to itself, with confusion and wonder. "They *are* at my *divine* mercy, *yet*, I *harmed* them *not*! Such was *not* my *intent*! Nigel knows *this*, only, *too* well! *Perhaps*, I was *goaded* into acting *unwisely*. Little is left of me to *complete* Nigel's *unalterable* will."

Arden rolled onto his side, and groaned. There was meager emotion, or the energy to express it, left in him. He glanced at the place where his father had perished, then stared into the bleak fissure where Durward had met disaster. He began to silently weep, paying no heed to Sumner's puzzled self conversation.

Galen clenched his fists and rolled up to his feet. He looked hopelessly at the heaps of rubble. There was twice as much shale and stone dust on the place where Guthrie and his stallion lay buried. There was no hope of digging them free in time to offer aid. He glanced toward Arden, saw slight movement, and his heart surged with hope.

Sumner seemed spent.

Perhaps, *I* and *Arden* will *escape* to *fight* Nigel, Galen thought. We *have* to *try*, even *without* the necessity of Durward's *vital* magical talents. It *is* our *duty* to *try*. He raced to the Crown Prince Designate. "*Arden*!" he said, urgently. "Sumner *appears* unable to *harm* us! We *must* escape and *continue* the *war*! We *must* try! At least, *one* more *effort*! We *owe* it to *Alaric*, and our *people*! We *owe* it to *Aldora*! We *owe Guthrie* and *Durward that* much!"

Arden gazed up with red rimmed eyes, and grim determination entered his expression and voice. "*For* my *father*!" he said, shakily. "*And* my *Aldora*!"

Galen helped him to his feet and proceeded to heal their cuts and bruises.

Arden wiped his face of tears. "Our poor horses," he said. "We *must* assist them, and be gone from this *monstrous* graveyard. *Soon*, or I cannot *bear* to leave my *father* and *Durward* behind."

"Now," Galen agreed. "We leave, now." He led the way to their horses.

After five minutes of balming the cuts and bruises of the mounts, and calming them down with his special touch, he energized them, Arden, and himself.

"*Still*, they *endeavor* to *defy* us, Nigel!" Sumner said, with wonder. "These *are* truly *determined* men! *If* we were not *mortal* enemies, I could *begrudge* respect for them! *But*, I *must* slay them for the *pleasure* of my dark, *noble* master!"

Galen and Arden mounted and reined their horses into a cautions trot. They skirted the ravine where Durward had fallen, and neared the tragic site where Guthrie lay interred with his valiant horse.

A low-pitched rumbling arose from the floor of the fork. Sumner caught it, amplified it, sent it around the walls, boulders, and crevices, and shot it, in a thousand sound fingers, at the sides of the ebony fork. They cracked with loud snapping sounds. Sumner increased all resulting noises a hundred fold, and the floor of the fork crackled, buckled and shattered gently beneath the horses.

Arden fought to remain in his saddle.

Galen lost his grip on his pummel and hove backwards off his mount.

Arden caught the reins of the Healer's horse and heeled his own steed into compliance of his directions.

Galen pulled himself up by the stirrup of his steed, and started to mount.

Sumner sucked in its sounds, and spat them out, twice as loud. There was a resulting earthquake.

The mounts fell to their knees.

Both men tumbled onto the piles of rubble.

"*Too,* determined, to think *straightly*," Sumner chided, beside the men. It inhaled its noises, and their echoes, pausing for its strike. "*Too* determined!" it whispered, with fake pity.

"*Not* as *determined* as *I*," someone said. The voice resounded throughout the fork as loud as Sumner's last earthshaking exhalation of noise, yet, without tremoring the floor of the damaged fork. "*Not* as *angry*, nor as *affronted*, as *I*!"

"Durward?" Galen and Arden exclaimed. Chills raised

the hair on the napes of their necks and ran down their spines. They stared toward the crevice where the Magician had fallen prey to Sumner's seemingly fatal attack.

Sumner, astonished, held its sounds, and directed its nebulous vision to that place of tragedy. "How *so*?" it whispered, to itself.

Galen and Arden could barely hear the Enchantment.

"It is as if that *heartless vile* conjurer is *now* a *part* of *myself*!" Sumner said. "Of *Nigel*!"

A plume of stone dust, rubble, pebbles, and small rocks shot up from the deep fissure, far into the air. It petered out, leaving dust swirling over its place of origin.

A horse neighed.

Galen and Arden realized, in wonder, that it was not their mounts, or Guthrie's.

Stones rattled, as if scattering down a hill of rock, followed by hooves clopping on stone.

"*Not so*!" Sumner bellowed, in fear. "*No one* comes to *live* again! *Not* once *Sumner* has *plied* his *might* and *done* his master's *will*! *Not so*! *Eyes*, do not *betray* me with this *grisly* sight! *Not so*!"

Durward and his steed, under glistening safeguards, appeared above the rim of the crevice as they ascended a long ramp of stones and dust. They trotted onto the cracked floor of the fork. "It *is* so, *Sumner*!" he said, projecting his voice everywhere. "I am not *resurrected*, I am *preserved* and *enlarged* of *capacity*! Again, I challenge *you* and my *son*! We are *ready* to war, *monster*!" He heeled his horse over to Arden and Galen, and looked around in surprise.

"Where is Guthrie?" he asked.

Galen somberly pointed to the great mount of rubble cruelly concealing the Knight from the world.

Durward frowned, his face drawn with worry. "After I struck bottom, I sent a shield to him," he said. "I know it is there. I feel it still projected. I dispatched safeguards at the two you, as well. Yet, you do not have them!"

"No," Arden said, his voice crowded with grief. "Sumner *failed* to kill *us*, but *prevented* us from digging to my father."

Durward looked stricken with self-hatred. "How could I have so *misread* my abilities?" he said. "I am *sure*—" He sucked in a breath. "Galen, cast about. Do you feel my shield energy below that rubble?" He absorbed the force fields coating himself and his horse.

Galen dismounted. He ran his hands over the pile of debris smothering Guthrie. "I sense *nothing*," he said, with deep regret. "Not *even* the *energy* of his *soul*."

"My safeguard would block *that* almost entirely," Durward said. "It would be difficult to feel the shield through all of this stone. It is not like the mud of Monrow or the earth of Kelsey." Durward shoveled his force into the mound of black rubble, sending it spewing to one side, building a hill of stones and dust as he excavated.

The accursed Magician was frighteningly strong after his ordeal in the crevice. Sumner rumbled, in renewed preparation to fight. It could not wait to strike. It began asserting its control over every inch of the fork walls, and ravaged floor. It crackled and clattered together all the shale and column shards at its disposal. The noise level soared steadily. The ground started trembling. Both ebony walls of the gulch fissured, and shale began sliding toward the floor, adding to Sumner's sound might.

Durward sighted a glimmer of shield energy and dug faster with his power.

Arden and Galen ran forward and began clawing at the rubble in desperate hope. Soon, Guthrie and horse were freed of the heartless debris.

Durward removed the safeguards from Guthrie and his stallion.

Galen examined the Knight for injuries. "He is almost *dead* from *suffocation*!" he said, as he warmed Guthrie with his restorative might.

Arden cradled his father in his arms.

Guthrie gasped a deep breath. Then several more. He sat up, fighting against his son's hold until he recognized Arden. He stared at Galen and Durward. "Faith rewarded!" He said. "I *knew* you *would* pull *all of* us from the *flames*! Aye, Durward?"

"*Barely*," Durward said. "We are still too *close* to the *inferno* for *safety*. Hear, *now*, Sumner *rallies* its *might* and *positions* for a *final* tug of war. *Prepare*!"

With a frown from Galen, Guthrie struggled to his feet and helped his horse to stand. It was weak from oxygen starvation.

Galen began healing both steed, and Knight.

Guthrie hugged his son's shoulders, whispered something, and they wiped away tears.

Sumner's sound was growing in volume, greater than anything it had produced. The ground increased its shaking. It was a battle for both man and horse to remain standing.

Durward entranced the frightened steeds, dismounted, and stood close to his companions. He covered the War Party with a stronger shield than before, formed it into a wedge, and began sliding the War Party toward the other end of the fork.

Sumner expelled all the sounds and echoes of damage it had inhaled. They slammed into the walls and floor of the fork like millions of tiny invisible meteors.

The shield fissured as though it had not been doubled in strength.

The walls of the fork exploded into the air in a single huge assault. The first layer of the floor erupted as though it were responding to the pressure of a massive artesian well coursing inexorably from beneath.

Durward, Arden, Guthrie and Galen fell to their knees and hid beneath the bellies of their horses.

Durward decreased the size of the shield. The walls thickened, and the fissures vanished.

Sumner's fork collapsed upon and shoved up volcanically at the War Party, simultaneously. Tons of roaring, sparking heated stone and dust overwhelmed the small block of protective energy.

Faintly, as if from a thousand miles away, the War Party heard Sumner's triumphant voice:

"*Grant* me the *eternal* life you *promised*, Lord Nigel! They are *slain*, *vanquished*, beyond even *your* power to pull them *back* from the world of death! Bestow the *gift* that I have *earned* and I shall *worship* you for *beyond* eternity!"

Utter silence.

Darkness smothered the wedge of force. It was a blackness familiar to Durward. It made them dizzy. Though they knelt on all fours, it felt as if they were constantly on the verge of tumbling over a high sharp cliff into a bottomless chasm of endless nightmares.

Durward did not give them time to voice fear or despair. He filled the shield with his blue light. He applied force to the rubble above, compacting it into a dome. In the dome he created a cone shaped force field and began swirling its pointed top, like an upside down tornado, against the dome.

Durward spun the cone more quickly, illuminating the debris with blue and white sparks. He increased the diameter of the bottom of the cone until it was the size of the wedge, plus three feet, and hove it harder against the tons of stone and dust.

At first, only the white and blue sparks appeared as the result of his monumental effort, then a dull red glow in the debris around the tip of the force cone, cast a brighter light into the wedge. Heat filtered through the walls of the shield, but was not uncomfortable. The bubbling cerise rubble darkened in hue. It turned white, then became a blue that Durward expected. The heat reflecting back on the wedge became stifling. Slowly, the cone of force melted up through the barrier of debris.

As the psychic drill created space between itself and the wedge, the molten stone was channeled by Durward around and underneath the shield, causing the safeguard to follow after the energy drill.

The glow was overwhelming. All they saw was this incredibly pure blue, even when they looked at each other.

Durward tinted the wedge, and filtered out half the brilliance, but the light still stung their eyes. He created coolness inside the wedge, but the searing heat of the molten rock fought it to tepidness.

"*This* will *require* your *life*!" Galen said, with desperation. He took Durward's hands.

The Magician pulled free. "Save *yourself* for the *second* half of the *excavation*," Durward said, through teeth gritted with effort, "when I will be *exhausted* and *nearly* unconscious, from the effort. *Then,* you link. *Even* if I *cry out* for *aid*, do *not* offer it *until* I *faint* from *exertion*! *Promise* this!"

"*Yes,*" Galen said, though he doubted he could force himself to sit by for that long without helping. This would tug against his born instinct to heal. Yet, what could he do? Durward *must* know, from his prior experience in the crevasse, what will be *required*.

"Can you two *truly* endure long enough to liquefy us free of this *mountain* of debris?" Arden asked. His eyes were half shut due to the blue luminosity and the increasing heat conducting through the walls of the shield. His heart was racing in fear that this was more than Durward, who had championed them before, could force from himself *and* Galen, though the Magician seemed to have twice the power he had before his ordeal in the rock crevice.

Guthrie realized a similar but less arduous effort had freed the Magician and his mount from the rubble in the fissure, so he dared not distract Durward from his awesome task.

With a slight increase in its volume, Sumner's voice could be discerned:

"Lord Nigel! My focal fork is *obliterated*! My power rock lies shattered *upon* your *enemies*! Why do you *not* come to *claim* your *triumph* and *reward* your *devout* servant? Have I not *prevailed* when *all* the *others* who *pretended* to *proclaim* you *master*, have *failed*? I *hear* you *not*! I *sense* you *not*! Our *contact* is *broken* except for a *mere* vibration of *high* sound!" It rumbled the fork with inner turmoil and sudden agonized realization. Its life would last as long as its power rock, so shattered, and nearly all dust, held the charge of magic energy which it had been infused by Nigel had. Perhaps a month. A week. Surely only a brief day if it had been forced to fight the accursed Magician for *one* additional hour. "*Busy*!" Sumner shouted to the emotionless sun as it transited toward noon. "*He* is *busy* with *vital* matters, and will *reward* me *soon*! It can be no *else*! He *is* me! I *am* him! We are a *part* of *each other*! If I pass, *surely* he *loses* some of his *might*! *Busy*! He is *simply* busy! How can *I* know who *else* might be *fighting* him from this wide earth? He is just *occupied* and *will* come! He *will* arrive!"

Durward groaned and leaned against Guthrie and Arden. Galen reached to reinforce him, but bit his lip and held back.

Durward was still conscious and generating his cone Energy.

Galen must wait. *If* his soul would allow it.

"Are we near half-way?" Arden whispered to Guthrie.

"How can we possibly judge?" Guthrie whispered.

Galen placed his palms against the top of the wedge and listened to the sounds caused by the drilling of the cone. He received an answer to their query via the aegis of Durward's magic, plus a fact he had not sought. He shook Durward, gently.

The Magician raised his head, barely lifted his eyelids, and looked at Galen.

"You are *wasting* energy by *muffling* the *vibrations* of your *drill*," Galen said, firmly. "*Cease* the *muzzling* and *add* the power to the *boring*."

"Sumner—Sumner will detect," Durward, said with great effort, "Will strike into the rubble, breaking the cone."

"If you cannot *risk* this, then *allow* me to *merge* with you *now*," Galen insisted. "We are *more* than *two-thirds* to the *top*, and you are so *close* to *unconsciousness* there can be no *argument* for my *delaying* your *aid*."

Guthrie jostled the Magician. "*Aye*," he said, as concurring as possible. "*Let* him *merge*! We can not have you *die* at the *breach* of the mound."

"Do it *now*, Galen," Arden said. "He does not even *hear* you. *Or*, if he *does*, he cannot *understand*."

Durward snapped his head around to Arden and stared

at him. A smile played at the Magician's lips, then dropped away from exertion. "The *boy* is *correct*," he managed to say. "*Meld*, Galen."

Galen almost leaped to the task. He grasped Durward's pale hands and coursed his healing energy into the trembling older man.

The cone increased its rotation with a whine that Durward could not muffle.

Durward withdrew the weak, wasteful, muzzle energy and added it to the drilling effort. "Sumner will know now, any way," he barely whispered.

"From the sound of it," Galen said, "the Enchantment will gain no advantage from the foreknowledge."

The single sound was the high-pitched whine of the drill cone.

Galen and Durward stared at one another, in hope.

Arden and Guthrie watched the great cone penetrating ever upward.

"What *is* it?" Sumner said, sounding frightened. "Is *it* my *master*? *Yes*! *No*!" it screamed, with wild hatred. "It *is* the *damned* Magician! He, *yet,* lives! *I* am *all* but *dead*, for Nigel *spurns* me! *I* have *killed* myself for *him*, and he *cares* not! *Damn* you, Nigel! *If* I have life *beyond* this one, which you have so *cruelly* created, I *shall* return upon you with the *vengeance* of all my *comrades* which you have so *vilely* used! *Hear* me, son of *foulness*! *Feel* my *razor* sound in your *heartless* mind! *Suffer* from it, as I *agonize*!"

Durward stirred.

Galen, Guthrie and Arden glanced upwards.

The cone had melted the stones and dust. Durward ceased its spin and absorbed its energy. The wedge slowly hove up out of the red magma until it floated atop it like a cork on a still pond. Deprived of the heat caused by Durward's magic, the molten stone began cooling. Durward hastened this process with his Winter energy until the stone was cold.

Galen and Durward renewed themselves.

The sun warmed the War Party through the shield.

"*If* Sumner *attacks*," Guthrie warned, "it *will* be the *moment* you *reform* this *safeguard* for *individual* shields."

"We shall supply it no such opportunity, then," Durward said. He awakened the steeds, and altered the safeguard into an umbrella beneath which Sumner could not vibrate one pebble.

The War Party mounted and reined their horses into a trot.

There was silence from Sumner.

The questers passed along the spine of the mountain of rubble. There were no walls left to this fork, and this was the main one; the heart of the gulches. Beyond the ridge of debris there was hilly earth, and little distance to the Elf Caverns.

"*Nigel*!" Sumner screamed.

To Durward's dismay, it was not a cry of despair or hatred, it was a cry of recognition, hope and excitement.

"*Nigel*! You *have* answered my *prayer*! Discerned my *need*! Power *returns*! Sound *reverberates* throughout my *being*! *Magician*!" it rumbled, with great vigor. "You *must* perish *swiftly*, now. My *might* is *greater* than that which came *before*! Lord Nigel expects *much* for this *grant* of new *life*! Thus, *shall* he receive *it*!"

The mountain of rubble began moving and shifting. The stones and dust started vibrating. It felt and looked like an ebon leviathan serpent preparing to coil both ends upon its center to crush everything on its broad back.

Sumner's magical sound circled out repeatedly, roaring over the gulches. It was as if thunder storms and volcanoes were building toward a catastrophic climax of their natural destructive might.

"*Durward*!" Arden shouted, in terror.

The Magician closed his eyes. Galen leaned over to couple with the Magician. Durward trembled.

Silence fell within the umbrella, and the horses became less agitated.

Durward shook more.

The rumbling, snapping and explosions of sounds fell back from them.

"*Nigel*!" Sumner shrieked, hysterically. "He *nulls* me, Nigel! *Advance* and *strike*, for *yourself*! It *must* be of your *own* hand! I cannot *draw* the *might* required to *slay* them! *Nigel*!" The scream climbed to such a high pitch, even the horses could not hear it.

Silence.

Durward felt compassion toward the non-human creation, but the comment he offered for Sumner's death was a sad smile which spoke of inevitability.

Illustration 23

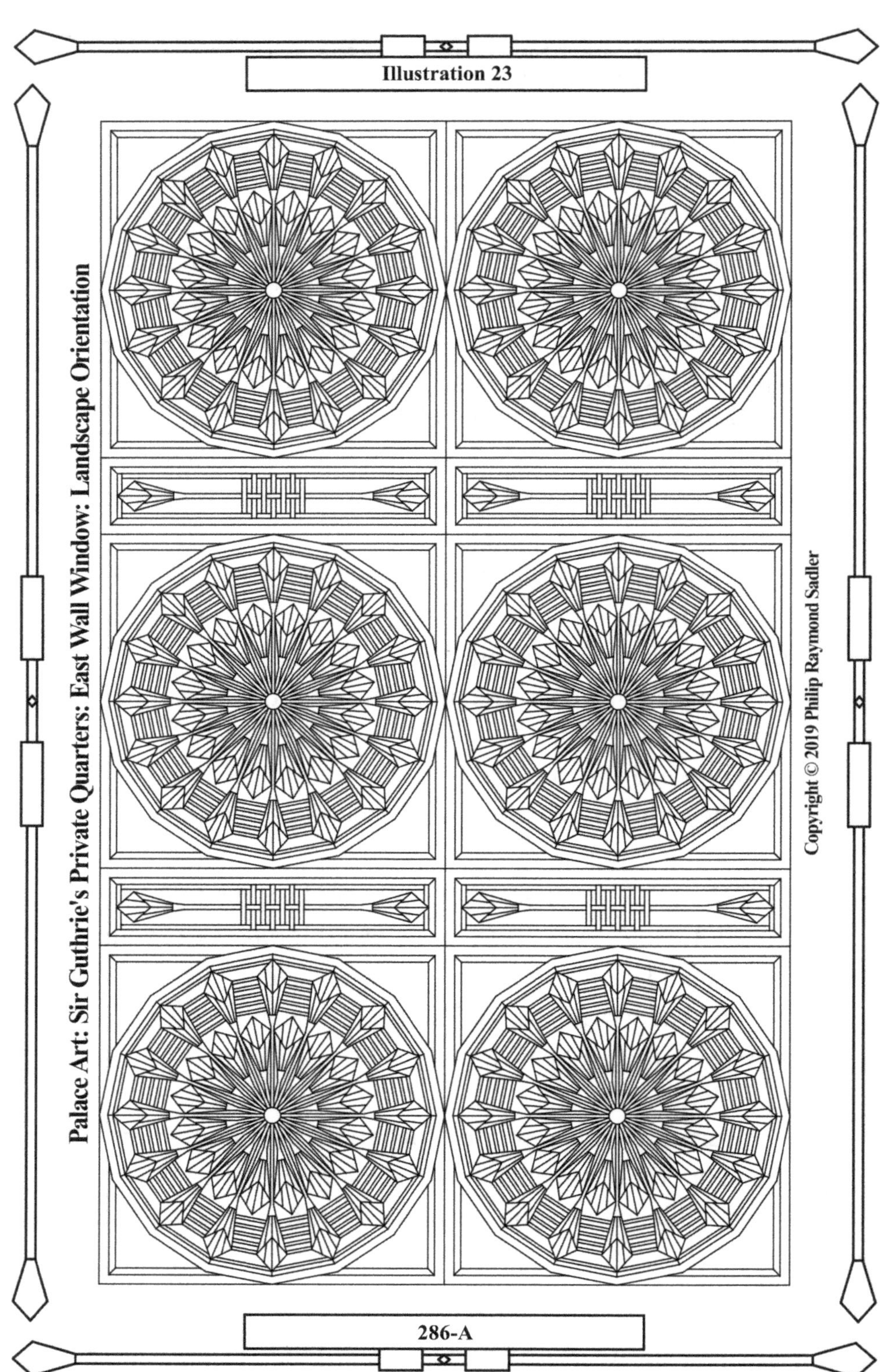

Palace Art: Sir Guthrie's Private Quarters: East Wall Window: Landscape Orientation

Palace Art: Sir Guthrie's Private Chambers: West Wall Window: Landscape Orientation

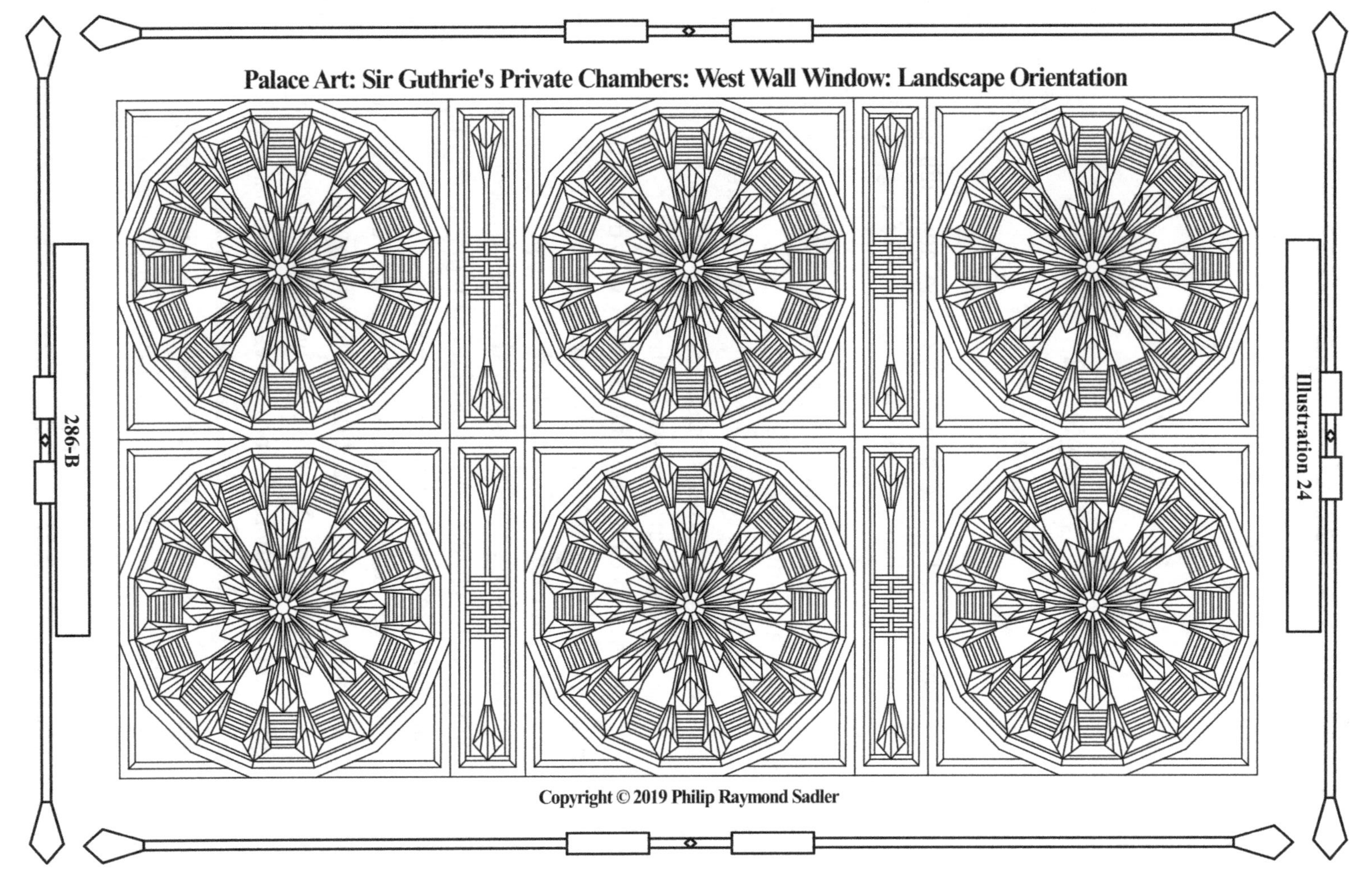

Illustration 24

Chapter 12
Thorns and Water

Guthrie reined his steed to a halt on the grassy hillocks. "*Ho*, the *camp*!" he shouted, with a mixture of anger and relief.

The scouts were squatting before a campfire. They leaped up and spun around.

"Do my *eyes* behold *apparitions*?" Wayte shouted. "Or, are these *truly* the King's Questers, *alive* and *well*?"

The War Party arrived beside the scouts.

"Your eyes *speak* truth," Guthrie said. "Why do you *cower* here, rather than *fight* alongside *us* as *honor* demands?"

"*Hold* your *wrath*," Zadok said. He surprised everyone with his anger. "You have drilled us *not* to *vocalize* in *ignorance*. Perchance you, sir Knight, can *grant* even *us*, your lowly *pawns*, the same *courtesy*?"

Arden reached to hold his father, if necessary, from flying out of his saddle and drubbing the guard.

Guthrie nodded. "*You* have always been one to set the high and the mighty back onto the earth when justified," he said, begrudgingly. "This had *best* be such a *time*."

The three scouts looked to their irate companion.

Zadok stepped unflinchingly forward and stared into

Guthrie's eyes. "As we left the Gulches we heard an unholy wailing behind us, then horrendous explosions and thunder like none before," he said. "We hied our mounts back to the main gulch fork to investigate and render timely aid, if necessary. As we have been well-trained, and freely choose to do.

"We galloped headlong into an invisible barrier of deafening sound that flung both mount and man backwards to the black earth. No matter how forcefully we hurled ourselves into this obstruction, it flung us back. We raced to all the minor forks we could find, but similar barriers awaited us. We could only return to the main gulch fork and watch in horror as all of you were buried beneath an immovable mountain of rubble."

"His words are *true*, Guthrie," Ryley said. "When we saw you were lost, we fell into despair. After much angry discussion, we decided to camp, make plans, and continue against Nigel on our own."

"We knew we didn't stand, a snowball's chance in a forge, of success," Hilliard said. "We would rather die in the attempt than return home as failures. Perhaps, even branded as deserters and cowards."

"We were about to press on when you hailed us," Zadok said. "*If* we have *failed* in *any* way to *perform* with *competence* and *honor,* it was *without* our *knowledge* or *intent*."

"Well said," Durward commended them.

"I guess *you* told *me*," Guthrie said. "I *knew* that *you* would," he said, to angry Zadok.

"You have the apologies of the realm," Arden said. "Plus, our admiration for your determination to proceed with the war, though you were so grossly out matched."

The War Party laughed, easing tensions. The guards stamped out their campfire and mounted.

There was grass and bushes around the questers as they proceeded. The Hunson Mountains rose from the horizon, like swarthy, glowering, giant sorcerers wearing long conical hats. They turned parallel to the cones and strove for the West Shield Range on the right side of Indwin Valley. This was where the Elf Caverns lay, and Nigel hid.

"To point," Guthrie told the soldiers. "*Surely,* we shall engage *Elf* patrols *now*. There is nowhere else Nigel can headquarter and attack with accuracy."

The scouts saluted and galloped away.

Durward frowned. "The size of the impact crater explains the size of the sky stone," he said. "With a reasonable liquefier, Nigel could expect as much as five hundred gallons of Psychic Enhancer! He could place it in a psychically prepared crevice in the Caverns. Little of the Enhancer would be required to supplement his power for long periods."

"Perhaps we should *locate* and *commandeer* his reservoir," Guthrie advised. "*Then* attack him. When his might fails, and he realizes that you draw upon his Enhancer, his only recourse will be surrender."

The guards returned to the War Party.

"Arden!" Wayte said. "Nigel has ringed the Elf Caverns with a fence of thorn hedges. They have no breaks, and stand ten feet high. We tried to hack into them, but the branches would not be cut. We couldn't see through, and our horses were terrified of them."

"Did you sight any patrols?" Guthrie asked.

"No, sir," Wayte said.

"*This* is *another* of Nigel's Enchantments," Durward said. "I suppose he feels no need for patrols when he has such psychic barriers to hinder and delay us."

They directed their horses to the top of the last of the Hillocks, and paused, looking down at a gigantic spur of rock which was a part of the West Shield Mountain Range. The spur ran all the way back toward the Castle. There was moist, black earth heaped around the spur, and the front of the great projection of rock was, indeed, bounded by a growth of huge hedges.

The Yarron Stream broke through the West Shield Mountain Range, parallel to the Gray Fort, and coursed along the top of the spur. The War Party could hear the water falling into the pool below the front of the spur, but could not see it through the hedges.

About a thousand feet to the left of the questers, the hedges crossed the stream as it flowed toward, then parallel to, the North Shield Range, at the end of Indwin Valley.

Guthrie pointed to the hedge crossing. "We might pass beyond the thorns by swimming under them," he said.

"Scouts, see if there is free passage there," Arden ordered. "Be *most* careful. Those are *Razor Thorns* I see before us. *One* brush against them, and you have *lost* an arm!"

The guards saluted and reigned away.

Arden and the War Party descended the Hillocks to a meadow in front of the hedges. They dismounted, leaving the horses about two hundred feet away from the thorns. The questers approached the hedges with historical wariness.

Durward stepped close to inspect the thorns and the intricately intertwined branches which bore them. "I hope Nigel has not managed to imitate the invincibility of the Elves and imbued it into these deadly plants," he said. "Before I attempt to breach these shrubs, let us await the report from our soldiers."

"They are returning," Galen said. "I sense that one is injured."

The dripping scouts dismounted and joined the War Party.

Ryley held out his hand. The palm was bleeding freely.

Galen placed his hand flat on the wound. The pain ended and the bleeding ceased. Galen smiled and lifted his hand.

The grateful scout's palm was healed without scarring. "I was careless," Ryley told Arden. "But, we made a thorough search under the Stream."

Durward dried the soldiers with a gentle heat beam.

"There is no way beyond the hedges there," Hilliard said. "They are rooted deep in the bed of the stream. The water flows through, but the thorns are as unbreakable there, as they are here."

"Is there an opening anywhere in them?" Guthrie asked. "One large enough for a snake to pass through?"

"No, sir," Ryley said.

"Stand back while I attempt to breach the hedgerow," Durward said.

The questers joined the horses.

Durward backed up ten feet. He lifted his hands and his psychic energy leaped forth with its blue glow. A circular area in the center of the hedges became red-hot, then blue-hot, then white-hot, but did not burn or melt.

Five minutes later, there was no damage to the thorns.

"Galen," Durward shouted, "enforce me."

The Healer did so.

The blueness of the beam deepened, but did not burst through the hedges, and caused no sign of leaf shrivel.

Durward stopped his heat beam and sent out cold energy. The mist struck the hot spot and turned to steam. When the circle on the hedges was coated with ice, Durward switched to the heat beam, bringing the thorns to white-hot. He repeated the process four more times, ending on white-hot. "I will use psycho kinetic energy to test their brittleness, now," Durward said. "Continue to enforce me, Galen."

Guthrie took the reins of the horses, knowing they would become frightened as Durward and Galen delivered the magic blows to the hedges.

"Now," Durward said to Galen.

The Magician pounded on the white-hot circle. The thorn hedges rattled metallic-ally as though struck by a gigantic club, but stretched backwards only slightly. Durward pounded the hedges again, but harder. The branches did not break, nor did one of the razor sharp thorns chip free. The hedges rattled again, and again, and again as the invisible force smashed into them.

The horses tried to pull away from Guthrie, but he leaned back to put his full weight against the reins, speaking soothingly at the same time.

Durward grasped the occult hedges with his psychic force. He attempted to rip them from the ground or tear a hole through them at the white-hot circle. The dark green hedges swung in and out, stretching only so far, before bouncing back. He stopped the power and shook his head. "They are *more* tough than *Marsden's* weeds," he said. "They will not *brittle* like the River stone. We shall try something else. Let us rest first, Galen."

"We will try now, Galen," Durward said. "I am going to tear up the earth and pile it in front of and over the hedges, to construct a ramp for us," he explained. "Assuming that you and I can muster enough power long enough to pull up that much earth."

Galen placed his palms, from behind, to Durward's temples.

Durward pointed his hands at the earth, thirty feet from the hedges. The grassy dirt began to fly up, heaping at the foot of the hedges as he burrowed with his energy fingers.

Durward frowned. The earth was failing to come loose from the bottom and sides of the pit. He concentrated harder, then dropped his hands.

"What is it?" Arden shouted.

"*Nigel*, or his *Enchantment*, has *counter moved*," Galen shouted.

Durward angrily turned around, walked to Arden and Guthrie, and pointed his hands at the earth in front of them. His force came forth, trembling the ground slightly, but failed to tear up any dirt. He stalked further away from the hedges, and tried his power against the ground. Nothing happened. He walked further.

The War Party could barely see him.

Durward lifted his hands.

The War Party saw no earth flying into the air.

Durward stalked back. "Nigel, or his Enchantment, has turned the ground, probably for miles around, into material that is as hard as the thorns and hedges," he said, with rage. "I *cannot* construct a ramp for us!" He returned to the hedges and hurled a saw at the center of the heated spot.

The cutter's teeth screamed against the thorns and branches, showering white sparks in all directions.

Galen enforced the Magician.

The saw spun with greater velocity. Its whining increasing an octave. Its sparks flew further in every direction.

Durward absorbed the saw and inspected the hot spot. "Not *even* a *scratch*," he said, with frustration. He formed a cone and slammed it into the hot spot. The magical drill whined with a frequency so high the questers almost could not hear it. Heat wafted back at the Magician and Healer. Sparks showered further toward the rest of the War Party.

Durward abandoned his effort, reabsorbed the cone energy, and checked the obdurate hot spot. "Yet, no hint of damage," he said to Galen. "Nigel has done himself proud, with this conjuration."

Arden went to his stallion and took his scaling set out of his leather saddlebags. He uncoiled the rope as he walked back to the War Party. "Durward," he said, "fashion a shield around me, so I can climb. These hedges *should* hold the hooks and *support* our weight."

Durward wove a form fitting shield around the Crown Prince.

Arden took aim, whirled the hooks around, and threw. Just before the keen tips of the grappling iron reached the top of the shrubs, they split in half. The hooks fell to earth with a thud and the hedges repaired their split.

"Damn!" Arden said. "*Nigel* is up to *Marsden's* tricks, *here*!" He coiled the rope around the grappling iron and returned it to his saddlebags.

Durward reabsorbed Arden's shield.

"Arden," Guthrie said, "do you remember those ferry poles?"

Arden smiled. "Scouts," he said. "Did you sight any trees nearby?"

"Aye," Zadok said. "But, they are, perhaps, thirty minutes away."

"Lead me to them," Durward said to the scouts, "We *shall* have our *poles*."

The Magician and guards rode away at a fast trot.

The rest of the questers moved further back from the enchanted hedges for additional safety and waited.

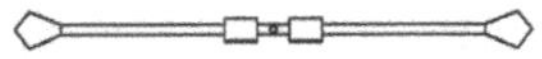

Durward and the scouts appeared over the grassy horizon. The guards held their reins between their teeth and awkwardly carried a twelve-foot-long pole in each hand. When they reined in, four poles fell to the ground and one scout lost his saddle, falling in a heap, unhurt.

"There is *nothing* between us and the Caverns, *now*," Arden said.

There was a sound like metal striking metal. The shrubs were shaking; thorns hitting thorns. The hedgerow seemed to be preparing to advance upon the War Party. Instead, a section of the shrubs split and a pathway was opened; large enough for one man at a time to squeeze through.

"It *is* a *trap*," Guthrie said.

"Yes," Durward agreed. "If we step into the opening, the walls will snap shut. Even with our shields, the razor thorns will chop us to death because the hedges will use all of this Enchantment's might. Thank you, Enchantment, *but* we shall *vault*, instead."

The hedges rattled harder and the opening grew larger. The sections of the shrubs that were turned inwards to form the portal, separated from the main hedgerow and fell to the emerald grass inside the enclosure. These detached segments shriveled, turned black, and crumbled to dust.

"It is *still* a *snare*," Guthrie said. He took up one of the long poles and stepped slowly toward the ominous opening.

Durward covered the Knight with the thickest shield the Magician could muster without restraining Guthrie's freedom of movement.

The rattling of the thorns ceased as the hedgerow fell still.

"Just like a cat before it springs," Guthrie said over his shoulder. He poked at the ends of the hedges with the tip of the pole to goad them into any planned attack.

There was no response from the animated shrubbery.

Guthrie jumped through the opening, safely.

Galen, Arden and Durward took up poles. The Magician shielded himself and the others. They tested the ends of the opening as Guthrie had. Each time the hedgerow showed no signs of hostility, one of the men stepped through the thorn lined portal.

Durward spun safeguards around the scouts.

Zadok passed into the enclosure without testing the shrubs with his pole; a tribute to his nerves.

Wayte, Hilliard and Ryley followed so quickly at Zadok's heels, they almost tripped over their poles.

The hedges snapped resoundingly shut faster than

the eyes could note, sounding like massive steel dungeon doors closing for the last time. The thorns along the hedgerow rattled wildly, as if celebrating a victory.

Arden swallowed his uneasiness. "*Since* we were *allowed* through," he said, "that means there is *another* Enchantment, *inside*, with us."

"The little *odd* one speaks with *surprising* intelligence and wisdom," a voice said, like a wooden pole slapping against the pickets of a fence. It came from somewhere within the hedges. There was an increased clattering of the hedge thorns. A man of thorns stepped away from the shrubs. It was not attached to the hedges as Brendan had been connected to its wall of fire. It could prowl more freely and dangerously than Brendan.

"To the *water* and the *Caverns*," Arden ordered.

"*Yes*," the man of thorns agreed, "*Thornton* will be *pleased* to see you in the *drink*." It reached toward Arden with a massive, thorny hand.

Arden discarded his pole, drew his sword, and smote the beast square on the palm.

The blade careened off, causing no damage to even the sharp thorns.

Arden retreated toward the water, with the rest of the questers.

Thornton laughed; pole slapping pickets. "Lynn *is* waiting. *Lynn* will *abet* to *destroy* you," it said.

There was a gurgling from the waterfall.

The men turned warily around.

A glistening, crystal clear golem of water stepped from

the bubbling waterfall. It was attached to the little fall by a ribbon of water, so it could not move far. The water Enchantment's limitations mattered little. There was now a smaller area in which the questers could maneuver to avoid contact with one or the other of the Wizard's murderous Enchantments.

Durward raised his hands and a mist billowed forth.

Thornton was covered head to toe with the cold vapor and the monster stopped moving. After several moments, a frost whited the surrounding grass, and a light snow fell.

Durward ended the freezing beam.

The thick fog cleared.

The thorn man was encased by a dense layer of ice which distorted its ugly features.

Durward turned toward Lynn to attack it with cold.

Thornton laughed. "This *infantile* rime does not *harm* Thornton," it boasted, with its unnerving voice. "*Nothing* harms *Thornton.*" It took one step, and the block of ice shattered to the grass.

Durward shot his mist at Lynn.

The golem of water snapped back into the waterfall, untouched by the energy. "*Bring* them *to* me," Lynn gurgled from the old fall. "He will *hurt* me with his *cold* if I *leave* my domain."

Thornton rushed at Durward.

The rest of the War Party attacked the Enchantment with their long swords, diverting the beast's attention. Thornton struck out at the defenders.

Durward directed his heat beam toward the waterfall.

Lynn laughed; a trickling sound. "It needs the sun itself to dry up Lynn," it said. "I am as endless as the Stream flows."

Durward flung power at the fall, parting it in half.

Lynn cried out, in pain.

Durward tossed another blow and parted the section of the fall to the left.

Lynn wailed again.

Durward struck a third time, parting the fall into a fourth and fifth segment.

"*Thornton*!" Lynn screamed, in terror. "This *criminal* tears me apart! *Help*!"

Thornton roared like lumber rolling down a wooden chute and threw itself bodily at the guards.

They fended it off with their swords as they scattered. Two scouts landed on the ground. Another guard was slashed across the cheek by one of Thornton's hand thorns.

Galen healed the man's cheek.

Durward readied more psychic force and prepared to fling it.

Thornton swung its arms forward, driving the War Party back from Durward.

"The evil doer dies, *now*, Lynn," Thornton rumbled. It grabbed Durward in its huge thorny hands.

The thorns pierced Durward's shield as if it did not exist, and drove into the Magician's torso. Durward cried out in pain, and struck force at Thornton.

The golem's head snapped back flat against the crea-

ture's thorny spine, but the neck did not break. Thornton laughed.

Durward applied his energy against Thornton's arms.

The monster's head snapped back into place, but the massive hands were loosened.

Durward thickened his shield, forcing the thorns out of his body.

The unbreakable thorns began to grow toward the Magician, through the improved safeguard.

"The poles!" Arden shouted.

The questers ran to the long shafts, grabbed them up, and began jabbing them savagely against Thornton.

Arden repeatedly struck at the head and the eyes.

Guthrie and Galen poled at the creature's huge forearms from opposite directions, trying to force the hands away from Durward.

The guards slammed their poles into Thornton's legs.

The man of thorns began to twist this way and that with the blows.

When this strategy did not free Durward, the soldiers concentrated their strikes on the same leg.

Thornton teetered, dropped Durward into the pond, and pitched in after him.

The Magician lay limply on his back, half on the pond bank, and half submerged.

The man of water emerged from the fall and sloshed toward Durward.

Guthrie struck his pole repeatedly at Lynn, trying to delay the golem.

Arden ran to drag Durward to safety.

Thornton reared out of the water and swung at Arden.

Arden retreated.

The guards and Galen attacked Thornton with poles.

Guthrie's pole was passing uselessly through Lynn.

The waterman continued its advance on Durward.

The scouts managed to keep Thornton at bay long enough for Arden to drag Durward from the pond.

Galen joined the Crown Prince and began healing the deep gashes around Durward's torso.

"If he were not a *natural* power source," Galen said, grimly, "he would be *beyond* healing."

Guthrie joined his guards.

Thornton was stalking back and forth along the pond bank, trying to get past the poles.

Lynn was standing ineffectually near the waterfall. The watery beast was hawk-eyeing Galen's movements.

"We are at impasse," Arden told Galen. "Thornton cannot circumvent Guthrie and the guards, and we cannot pass beyond it and Lynn, through the waterfall, to the entrance of the Caverns."

Durward gasped and his eyes flew open. He took a long deep breath. "*You* have *summoned* me *back* from *Afterlife*, Galen," he said, weakly. "You have greater restorative ability than you have said."

"Then, I have *just* increased it," Galen told him. He stepped back and helped Durward to stand up.

Lynn saw this and leaped back into the waterfall. "The

vile Magus *lives*!" it gurgled to Thornton. "You *failed* to *slay* the *traitorous* Magic One!"

Thornton was standing still in the pond. It was raptly watching the guards and Guthrie. It did not respond to Lynn's babbling. It chuckled, for no apparent reason.

Lynn snaked a tendril of water from the edge of the pond, just in front of Thornton. The tentacle glued around one of Wayte's legs, jerked the hapless fellow into the pond, pole and all, and dragged him over the surface of the water, to Lynn.

"*Good ploy*!" Thornton complimented.

"We *need* only be *patient*," Lynn said. "We will *serve* Nigel *well*."

Wayte was floundering in the pool.

Lynn grabbed the guard out of the water with its huge clear hands and pushed him inside of itself.

Wayte floated there, holding his breath, unharmed, for the moment.

Durward used his force and split the fall into ten sections.

Lynn screamed in agony and spurted Wayte out of its chest with so much force, the soldier landed at the shore.

Wayte lay gasping. His stay inside Lynn nearly suffocated him in spite of the magic shield Durward maintained around him.

Guthrie and the other guards began assaulting Thornton, to busy it, so Galen could tend to the downed man.

Durward latched onto Wayte, with his mind force, drew the scout to safety, and removed the guard's shield.

Galen applied healing to the half suffocated man.

The moment the healing was completed, Durward re-shielded Wayte.

Guthrie and his scouts backed away from Thornton and the magical pond, hopefully beyond the reach of Lynn's tendrils, and stood sentinel against both monstrosities.

Lynn stepped a few inches from the fall and snaked a tendril toward Guthrie's throat.

Durward pointed, and rimed the Water golem with icy mist.

Lynn screamed and fell back into the fall. The Enchantment's frozen facade subsided into the pool.

Guthrie and his soldiers retreated further from the pond. "The farther Lynn forces us to retreat," the Knight said to his guards "the harder it is for us to police Thornton's movements. We may as well rejoin the main party."

They backed away.

Thornton charged directly at the nearest soldier, moving with more speed than something with such bulk should have been able to achieve.

Hilliard spun to flee.

Thornton reached around Hilliard, slapped the scout across his pole and chest, and sent him flying into the center of the haunted pond.

"*Well struck*!" Lynn chortled. It leaped from the fall to engulf Hilliard in its bubbling chest.

Durward split the fall into ten sections.

Lynn wailed and dumped Hilliard into the churning water.

With frightening swiftness, Thornton continued its charge, reached out, and yanked Guthrie's pole from him. It swung the shaft, causing it to hum through the air.

The guards and Guthrie scattered.

Thornton changed direction and slammed the pole into Galen's chest.

The Healer stumbled backwards toward the pool.

Thornton javelined the long shaft at Durward.

Durward diverted his energy from the fall to the pole, reversing the shaft's course.

The pole thudded against Thornton's thorny green chest and shattered into wood dust. Thornton stumbled back a few paces, surprised.

Lynn leaped from the waterfall and returned its murderous attention to Hilliard.

Hilliard was desperately clambering up the slippery bank.

Lynn slapped tendrils of water onto Hilliard's spine and dragged him under the torrent of the fall.

Durward hit the fall, segmenting it again.

This time, Lynn forced itself against the rocks behind the fall and stood proudly defiant and unharmed by the splitting.

Poor Hilliard was thrashing inside the monster's transparent chest. He was valiantly trying to hold his breath, but time was about out for him.

Despite his protective shield, Galen had received a couple of broken ribs and deep bruises from Thornton's blow. He cured himself and stepped into the pond hoping Lynn would attack him and free the guard.

"The *waterfall*!" Arden shouted, excitedly. "Lynn said it, *itself*! Do you not see, Durward? The Stream *bestows* Lynn its *life*. If you damn it up, even for *seconds*, Lynn will splash *apart* as the pond drains *dry*!"

Durward directed some of his energy to the top of the fall and created a translucent dam which channeled the Stream over the right side of the spur, through the thorn hedges, toward where the War Party's horses waited. The downward flow of water at the end of the spur ceased, and the waterfall stopped, bringing silence. The pond began to drain down stream, toward the far hedges.

Lynn screamed with despair, flowed into the mud on the bottom of the pond, and was soaked up.

Hilliard was left motionless, face down, in the ooze.

Galen hastened to him.

Thornton began running toward the pond.

Guthrie and the guards attacked with their poles.

Thornton swung its huge thorny arms wide, knocked the assailants aside, and continued toward Galen.

Durward groaned. If he attacked *Thornton*, the fall would resume, *Lynn* would be *reactivated*, and *Hilliard* would *die*. If he did not, *Galen* would be *killed* and there would be no healing of future *injuries*, no *reinforcing* of his *abilities* for *final* confrontation with *Nigel*. No *chance* of *victory* for the *people* of Indwin.

Guthrie turned into the War Serpent and flashed toward Thornton. The Snake wound itself around the thorn man's sharp legs and drew them together, just as it had

Calder's.

Thornton roared in surprise and pitched face down on the grass.

War Serpent released Thornton's legs and reformed to Guthrie. He and the scouts swarmed the golem and began wildly hacking at it with their blades, hoping to keep it prone.

Galen dragged Hilliard from the mud to the grassy bank and began breathing life into the snow-white soldier.

Durward released the fall by absorbing the energy of the dam. "*Guthrie, guards, away*!" he commanded.

Thornton awkwardly started to scramble to its thorny feet.

Durward placed a box shaped shield over the vicious monster, then closed his eyes. The force field receptacle began to turn black.

"*No*!" Thornton screamed. "*Need sun*!" It thrashed inside the box, the way the guard had fought inside Lynn, and with as little chance of escape. The receptacle became pitch black. Thornton's movements and sounds ceased.

Durward added a sixth shield to the box, sliding it under the man of thorns. He used his might to push the case up on end. He tested the earth with his energy fingers. As he had hoped, the ground inside the hedgerow had not been hardened by Nigel, or the Enchantments. He excavated with his power until he had a pit large enough to contain the energy box. "The sun's rays imbue Thornton with life," Durward said, "so it must be kept in darkness until we can defeat Nigel. We shall bury Thornton, as we did Brendan."

Lynn gurgled. Its watery voice sounded amplified. It shot out a long tendril of water and snatched Arden off the grass and into the fall.

Durward cursed. If he helped Arden, he released Thornton.

Galen placed his hands to the Magician's temples and said, "You can *freeze* Lynn *and* keep Thornton, now,"

Durward doubted it. He was maintaining shields on eight people and Thornton. Safeguards were the hardest of psychic constructs to maintain.

Lynn was softening itself up to place Arden into its chest, to drown him. It was caught unaware by the cold beam. The top layer of the front half of the water monster froze. Lynn drew back into the protection of the fall. The icy layer of its substance crashed into the water, releasing the Crown Prince.

Arden hastily swam to shore and staggered to the War Party.

Lynn remained motionless inside the fall. The man of water was chuckling to itself as though it had discovered a secret, or had thought of something clever.

Durward psychically pulled the shield that imprisoned Thornton, into the prepared trench. It was six feet deeper than the box was tall. He used his energy to shove the dirt over the black case. He packed the earth down tight and absorbed the power that had comprised the box.

Lynn stepped from the fall and waved its hands. A giant hardened ball of water shot from the pond.

The orb passed through the valiant Magician's shield like lightning through mist, and caught Durward flush in the face, bursting upon impact. Durward sailed backwards. He landed brutally hard on his shoulders with his neck at an odd angle.

Galen raced to the Magician and ran his expert hands over Durward's neck. He cried out with despair, "It is *broken*! Durward is *dead*!" He flung himself head long at the beast of water.

Lynn stepped out of the pond to meet Galen, a thing the water man previously could not do.

Guthrie attempted to trip Galen with one of the poles, to keep him from Lynn, but missed.

Lynn swung one of its clear hardened hands but froze, transformed into ice.

Galen skidded to a stop, drew his long sword and severed the ribbon of icing water which attached Lynn to the fall.

Durward arose.

Arden hugged the Magician, in joy and relief, saying, "You *are* a *pair* of *sly* old *foxes*. *When* did you cook this up?"

"It was spontaneous," Galen said. "He was just stunned, so I gave him the cue, and he played along."

"What do we do with our friend?" Guthrie asked.

"An excellent question," Durward said. "The sun will melt it, so we have to keep it from draining into the pond and becoming reactivated."

"Can we bury it next to vile Thornton?" Wayte asked, hopefully.

There was an unnerving clawing and digging. Thornton leaped out of its grave, sending dirt flying in all directions. With a roar of rage, it turned and charged toward Lynn, intending to drag the water man back into the pond, to revivify it.

Durward struck an invisible blow to Thornton's chest.

The monster staggered back.

Durward directed strike after strike at the thorn man, preventing it from moving in any direction.

Arden was thrilled by sudden realization. "I wondered why the earth inside this enclosure is not hardened as it is outside the hedgerow," he whispered to Durward. "Mayhap our thorny enemy gains its vile life force through its foot thorns. Keep it at bay, Durward. Guthrie, guards, take up your poles!"

Arden led the men toward Thornton. He issued firm orders, then returned to Durward and Galen.

"When I give the command," Arden told Durward, "stop striking Thornton. Guthrie and his soldiers will prepare it for your shields."

Durward nodded.

Guthrie decided he and his guards had the magical monster evenly surrounded. He signaled with a wave of his pole.

"Now!" Arden shouted.

Durward's blows ceased thudding into the confused thorn golem.

Thornton shook its head to clear its thoughts, then started to reaffirm its course toward Lynn.

Guthrie and his guards jammed their long poles into the thorny man's arm pits, chest and spine. Straining against its great weight, they lifted Thornton into the air.

Durward built a block of energy under the creature's feet.

The poles were jerked away.

Durward encased Thornton in a black shield box.

Thornton screamed with desperation and fear. It pounded and kicked against the occult safeguard, its blows growing less loud as its strength began to fail.

"Enforce me, Galen," Durward said.

Galen gladly did so.

Durward directed Galen's power at the spur above the hedges beside the waterfall. A cascade of stones and large rocks flowed over the edge, thumping into the grass in front of the shrubs. Durward shoved the rock pile flat with his energy. He struck it with his heat force until it was white-hot, burning the grass around it for several inches. He used his force to push the shield case into the center of the glowing magma, then formed the magma into a box around the safeguard, elongating the top into a bottleneck. Durward drew his darkened shield energy from around Thornton, back into himself, then used his power to seal the top of the coffin. There was a muffled scream, and faint sounds of movement inside the smoking stone case, then silence, as Thornton died of malnutrition.

Durward caused another pile of rocks and stones from

the back of the fall to slam into the earth near Thornton's casket. Durward pushed the rocks flat, spreading them out and began melting them with his heat energy.

Guthrie stepped to Thornton's coffin and inspected it for leaks. There were none. As Guthrie turned back to the questers, he became aware of a slow movement to his right.

A thick tendril of water, from the bottom of the frozen water man, was flowing toward the pond. It would make contact in moments.

Guthrie drew his sword and began chipping dirt onto the tendril.

The tentacle drew back, then angled a few inches parallel to the pond, and began stretching toward the water.

Guthrie started chopping at the tendril, hoping it was solid enough to sever.

The tentacle just flowed around the tip of the blade each time.

"*Durward*!" Guthrie shouted. "*Freeze* this water *tentacle* or Lynn is *alive*, again!"

Durward frowned. He cut off the heat beam and sent a mist at the tendril.

The tentacle solidified itself and jumped out of the way.

Durward chased it back and forth with cold beams until he hit his mark and froze it, coating it with extra ice. He returned his attention to the hot pliable stone.

Durward formed the slab into a box. He hit the case with cold power, then pulled it over onto its side. Durward drew Lynn, including the errant tendril, across the

grass. He tipped Lynn on its side and shoved the ice man, head first, into the stone box. Straining, he lifted the coffin upright. He heated the top of the case to red, then blue, then white-hot and started squeezing it shut.

A tentacle of water projected out of the coffin and down toward the pond, but it was too short to reach the water it desperately sought.

Durward used his energy to reel in the tendril, stuffed it into the casket, and fused the top closed.

The heat from the sealed top thawed Lynn. The water horror gurgled and splashed inside the coffin for a few moments, then was stilled, as its magical life failed.

"Durward," Arden said, as though he was preoccupied. "Do these regions produce sky *illusions*, this season of the year?"

"Such phenomena occur in the northern most lands of Indwin," Durward said, distracted by the odd question. "Do you *perceive* something *unusual*?"

Arden pointed past the left of the pool, to an area beyond the far side of the stream. The War Party gave this their undivided attention.

"Who, but Nigel, himself, could fashion such a sign?" Guthrie said.

Against the backdrop of the far hedge wall, about six feet above the stream, and made even more visible by the contrasting low afternoon light, floated, in white letters, the word, Futility!

"But, why?" Galen asked. "It *really* is *not* frightening."

"How can we be *harmed* by a shining *word*?" Guthrie

agreed.

There was a subtle change in the atmosphere of the hedged in compound. The air around the white, glowing word became oddly unclear, like the surface of a pond rippled by a constant wind. The distortion became a dark humanoid twelve feet in height; massive and threatening.

"Is this, then, *yet,* another *damned* Enchantment?" Durward whispered, to himself, disheartened.

Arden picked up a chunk of the fused rock that Durward had left behind after preparing the coffins for Thornton and Lynn, and hurled it at the heart of the blurry apparition.

The chunk struck the Enchantment with weird silence, slowed down as though passing through molasses, then exploded with a brilliant red glare, but did not father any sound.

"Your test answered few questions," Durward said. "I shall attack before its trap, which it has no doubt been setting as we disposed of Thornton and Lynn, can be sprung."

"Durward!" the figure flashed, changing its chest words. "Though all your past actions were *futile* and *puerile,* I salute you for your *insane* perseverance!" The Enchantment floated forward until it stood inches from the edge of the waterfall pond. "Nigel knew the *lowest* of his creations would, at best, only *annoy* you, thus, he *endowed* Doyle with *greater* magic than the *other* Enchantments *combined*. I am the *ultimate* foe you shall, *briefly*, face, before *extinction*! None other, save *Nigel*, can approximate *me* in destructive *might*! Yet, Lord Nigel is *firm* on this *matter*! If you *return* to your *so called* King, I must *deign* to *permit* you to *live*! If not? *Unspeakable* horror!"

Winds began rushing from behind the War Party. They became stronger than Kelsey's buffets, slowly pushing the War Party toward the pond.

Durward planted rectangular shields behind each man.

The winds hammered at the barriers with no success, then roared around the safeguards and spun into Doyle, like raging waters gurgling into a bottomless sinkhole.

"Met and checked," Doyle flashed on its blurry chest. "Test for test."

Durward stared at the words and was stung by growing uncertainty. If Doyle was what he suspected, its utterances might not prove to be egocentric boasts as had those of the other Enchantments.

The winds fell away and Doyle's chest ceased glowing its last words. The Enchantment was a huge, man-shaped blot of unfocused darkness, blacker than any substance the men had experienced, even in their worst nightmares.

Durward merged the shields behind them into one. "Stay with your backs to this buffer," he instructed, sternly. He caused the shield to glow blue, so they could discern its borders.

"If I were *hampered* with *humor*, as was Kelsey and his flawed friends, I would laugh at your unthinking reactions to my threat!" Doyle flashed. "The promised challenge appears not to be forthcoming. Nigel instructed that

I not play with you as did the others. Come to *death*, Magician! You have *yearned* for its *final* comforts ever since Nigel *rebuffed* your *smothering* imagined superiority!"

The winds slammed into the shield.

The War Party whirled around.

The protective wall had shattered like thin ice.

Durward's instinctual response had grasped the bits of it with psychokinesis and kept it solid against the gales, preserving the War Party.

The winds came in rapid, thundering, bursts, bending the buffer almost double toward the men, then roaring around and into Doyle's vortical center.

"It is unable to *direct* the winds as did vile Kelsey," Arden said. "It seems only able to *pull* upon them."

"Aye," Guthrie said. "To suck at them, like a fire draws air."

"Perhaps, somehow, you can plug Doyle beyond sucking at the winds?" Galen suggested.

Durward was furiously thinking on all possibilities for fighting the Enchantment.

Doyle leaned forward a little. Its dark surface twinkled with bright white lights.

Invisible hands dragged Arden toward the pond.

Durward grabbed the Crown Prince Designate, with his force.

There was a momentary stalemate.

Durward was forced to absorb the safeguard to save Arden.

A great wind blasted into the questers.

Arden flew from Durward's energy grip and slid into the pond.

The rest of the War Party tumbled head over heels, landed on the grass on their stomachs, and fought against the drag of the gale by digging their fingers, and the toes of their boots, into the soft earth.

Durward set up a shield behind them, diverting the wind.

Durward and Galen linked.

Guthrie came up to his knees and stared at the rippled surface of the pool where his son had vanished.

Doyle ran its invisible force hands over the three men. It broke Galen's contact with Durward and tugged the three men toward itself.

Durward applied a backwards energy pull.

Stalemate ensued.

Splashing desperately, Arden bobbed to the surface of the pond. The fall forced him under, twice, before he flailed away from it and swam to the bank.

Doyle released Guthrie and grasped Arden, shoving him to the bottom of the pool.

Guthrie changed into the War Serpent, flashed across the grass, into the pond, found Arden, and coiled its tail around his waist.

The Snake fought against Doyle's push, but could garner no head way. Although it was nearly impossible to force itself to do so, War Serpent released Arden, slithered out of the water, and wound itself around Doyle's black, unfocused legs. The Snake found itself in a tight coil, squeezing nothing.

Doyle had made its legs as insubstantial as a wisp of ebony, blurred fog.

Durward snatched War Serpent across the pond to the shelter of the safeguard, then plunged his might into the water and hauled Arden to the surface.

Doyle locked onto Arden with force.

Deadlock.

Arden's head was barely clear of the rippling pool. He was gasping for air as if he were in a sealed room.

The winds ceased battering the shield. Not because Doyle had abandoned them as a weapon, rather, it was absorbing the air into its vortex more swiftly than it could be replaced by natural processes.

Durward assimilated his shield, unlinked from Galen, directed all his force to Arden, and snatched him from Doyle as though the Enchantment had expired.

"Air!" Arden gasped. "How can you bring air?"

Guthrie cradled his son in his arms and fought for breath.

Galen connected with Durward.

The Magician created a thick rectangular shield large enough to cover Doyle, and flung it at the Enchantment.

The blocker thudded into Doyle, creating thunder. The Enchantment's vortical inhaling ceased.

Air rushed in around the War Party. Almost as quickly as it took them to draw a desperate breath, the glowing shield buckled in the center and began slipping into black Doyle's vortex waist.

Durward pulled the blocker back into shape, then absorbed it.

Doyle sucked in the air.

Durward placed a shield around himself and his companions and filled it so thickly with atmosphere that a mist formed around them.

Doyle melded its might onto the front of the safeguard and dragged the questers toward the pond.

Durward tried to latch onto the earth behind them for an opposing tug, but could not manage it against Doyle's greater drag.

Durward formed a saw on the top of the shield and hurled it, spinning with a whine, at Doyle's neck.

With its force, the Enchantment tilted the saw to the vertical and inhaled it through its black waist. The saw exploded with a brilliant purple flash. Doyle staggered backwards and its grip on the safeguard failed.

Durward drew their protective box back against the hedgerow. He realized any upset to the Enchantment must be taken to full advantage. He absorbed his barrier and struck at the Stream with his force, constantly directing a current of water into Doyle's vortex.

The in-flooding water exploded with a scintillating blueness that danced and flashed around the Enchantment. Doyle started swaying side to side as if it was struggling to maintain a standing position.

Durward approached the Enchantment and struck at its ebon head with mighty energy fists. The head went misty, and Durward's blows passed through, to smite the hedges behind the monster, causing their thorns to rattle.

The beast had the capacity to suffer the water of the Stream, and be insubstantial.

Durward hurled several saws into the monster's head, arms and legs. The saws whined through without harm. Durward recalled the saws into himself and struck the misty figure with searing heat. The crimson fire vanished into the Enchantment's head; inhaled like the water. Durward switched to stunning frigidity. This was absorbed by the intractable golem.

Doyle hardened itself again.

Durward tried both ice and fire. They were taken into the monster as if they did not exist.

Doyle slapped at the water Durward was force-feeding its vortex as if it were trying to deflect the current away from itself. The ebony golem failed and returned its attention to the men.

Durward ran backwards as quickly as he could. Doyle adhered its pull to the Magician and drew him toward itself.

The rest of the War Party charged forward, wrapped their arms around the Magician's chest, waist and legs and wrestled against the force binding him. Their efforts did not slow the pull toward the Enchantment.

The air whistled around the questers as Doyle started sucked it into its vortex.

Durward smote the stream of water with cold energy, freezing it just before it entered the vortex. The blue lights of continual detonation doubled in brightness and explosive sounds echoed around the hedgerow.

Doyle staggered back until it bumped against the hedge wall behind it. Its grasp on the Magician failed and it flailed at the stream of ice rushing into its waist.

Durward blocked the wind from their backs with a safe-guard. He grabbed onto Doyle with his might and dragged the monster closer to the fall.

Doyle continued fighting to deflect the flow of ice from its vortex.

Durward created a thin front shield with a black tint, to filter out the scintillating blue flashes of explosions inside the Enchantment, so that he could better see what he was doing.

Doyle sucked faster at the wind, as if just inhaling atmosphere would strengthen it, and fought against Durward's pull.

Galen placed his palms to Durward's forehead and concentrated strenuously on supplying the Magician with energy.

Doyle tottered toward the waterfall.

The stream of ice grew thicker the closer Durward drew the beast to the source of the water.

Doyle lashed out with its force and hauled Arden and Galen over the front buffer and up against the flow of ice.

Durward released his hold on Doyle to place counter power to his friends. Durward frowned. It was as if Arden and Galen had become part of the ice. Durward could not budge them free without using more power. This meant releasing the ice stream from its course into the Enchantment. Durward understood this was Doyle's intent, to give itself the upper hand. Durward smiled grimly and absorbed half of the magical shield behind himself, Guthrie and the soldiers. Durward threw out force saws and hewed them through the ice stream, just to the left of Galen, and to the right of Arden. He snatched the men and the ice chunk out of the path of the vortex, then shoved the ice flow together across the gap, without allowing Doyle a moment's surcease from the blue explosions caused by the ice spearing into its murky form.

Doyle shook itself.

The questers sensed anger creeping around the hedgerow. It felt like tiny fingers painfully prying at their pores. In the wink of an eyelid, all the heat in the area was withdrawn into the vortex.

Frost formed on the War Party.

Durward created a safeguard around them, barely in time. He warmed the shield box to counter the cold, and studied the Enchantment.

Doyle was coated with the blue of the explosions but appeared no longer hampered by them. The sounds from the detonations, like millions of small thunder claps, were slowly increasing in volume.

Durward was not sure what this meant. He was sorely challenged in bringing forth new defenses against the creature.

Doyle dropped to its knees. The ice stream snapped in half and struck the Enchantment's ebony head without resultant explosions. Doyle spun away and ran to the high hedge wall, then aside, to the far stand of thorns on Durward's left.

Durward made the wide flow of ice follow the Enchantment like a long, deadly frozen finger.

Doyle began zigzagging, ducking, and turning itself from side to side, in a confusing pattern of evasion.

Durward attempted to follow it with the ice stream, but had little success.

Doyle was less inconvenienced with its motions than Durward. Doyle latched onto the Magician with force, ripped Durward out of the box shield, and flipped him up, somersaulting, toward Doyle. Doyle lifted its dark arms to enfold the Magician.

Durward en-shielded himself, drawing half the energy from the small protective box around his companions, then diverted water from the fall and coated himself with frost until he was a hominid of ice larger than Doyle.

Doyle flashed with twinkling gray lights. The Enchantment's deep fear crawled around the hedge enclosure, poking painfully at the rest of the War Party in spite of their shield. Doyle threw itself to the waterfall side of the clearing.

Durward smashed into the hedges. The ice shattered from his safeguard, and he tumbled unhurt to the grass.

Doyle leaped across the enclosure, landed in front of the Magician, and swept him against its vortex.

Durward widened his safeguard so it caught against the monster's hips, then lengthened the safeguard to cover Doyle.

Doyle ceased its gripping force.

Durward fell to the grass.

Doyle jumped backwards against the hedgerow and hurled energy. The blow shattered the thin protective box around the War Party. The seven men were sucked toward the golem's vortex.

Durward blocked the monster's intent with a shield, covering most of Doyle's ebony form.

Doyle held the questers against the safeguard. Doyle vacuumed in the warmth in the clearing, then the air, then ceased its grip on the safeguard.

The War Party fell to the grass, undamaged.

Durward absorbed his force fields, hurled crackling red heat at the vortex, added creaking frigidity, then struck with rolling, thundering sounds, both higher and lower than the human ear could perceive. He augmented this magic onslaught with pure psycho kinetic blows, raining them without cease into the vortex.

The questers struggled to their feet, gasping for air and shivering from the intense cold Doyle was creating.

Galen raced to Durward and enforced the Magician.

Durward raised the Stream out of its bed, iced it and directed it into the vortex, adding it to the other forces of his desperate assault.

Doyle raised its huge back fists and hammered on the ice column invading its vortex waist, hoping to break it, and to divert it to one side, but failed. Doyle began stumbling backwards toward the hedgerow. The incoming ice was exploding with blue searing light and loud waves of thunder.

Durward seized the light and peals with his mind and hurled these into the vortex, along with his other forms of force.

The Enchantment pressed its back against the thorn wall. Doyle was slowly bending double from the incredible energies pouring into its center. Doyle pulled desperately on the warmth in the enclosure and the air. Its winds were not as strong as before, and they did not threaten the War Party. Its cold, however, was effective.

"*Into* the *Caverns* with *you*!" Durward commanded Arden, Guthrie and the scouts. He was screaming to be heard over the cacophony of the noises of the might inundating Doyle's vortex. "So this unholiness cannot weaken my assault with threat to you!"

Arden, Guthrie and the guards realized there was no deed they could perform that could aid Galen and Durward. They reluctantly ran toward the Caverns which lay behind the splashing waterfall.

Doyle tugged desperately at the men, using its gripping power. The pull was weak, but it still prevented them from advancing on the Caverns. The monster gained an insight and drew on the warmth of the men. It began tugging on Durward and Galen with its gripping force.

Durward groaned with frustration and despair. "This evil chimera is the endless *abyss* it claimed!" he shouted, between teeth clenched with effort. "More energy! Galen! You must bring forth, more might!"

The Healer was pale from exertion and the growing cold. "Can you warm us?" he shouted, fearfully.

It was almost impossible for the Magician to hear the Healer over the roaring and thundering of the energy assault.

"This cold is draining even me of vital heat faster than I can heal from the loss!" Galen warned. He shook his head with fury and drew on every iota of transmittable energy in his body.

Durward became heart-achingly aware of his heat loss, and the taxing of his psychic abilities. He slowly sank to his knees on the grass and braced himself with his hands so that he did not fall on his face.

Doyle straightened a bit, still more than half-way doubled over, and drew harder on the War Party with its pulling might. They began to inch across the frosted grass. Doyle reached out its huge ebony hands, wiggling its long fingers with desperate hope because its victory was almost within its grasp, and with wild affront that it stood so closely to powerlessness and death.

Durward and Galen skidded to the tips of the monster's grasping occult fingers. Durward leaned backwards, to protect his face from the sharp, pointed fingernails. He tried to muster a thin shield in order to block both the frosting cold Doyle was creating with its warmth absorption, and the iciness Durward was hurling into the vortex.

Arden and Guthrie slid to the edge of the waterfall pond. They managed to twist their backs away from Doyle and fought against its grasping power. Their feet slipped from under them, and they splashed into the pool. Doyle drew them across the buoying water with relative ease, but hit drag when it tugged them face down onto the earth at the bank.

Durward wrenched a thin safeguard out of the energy fists he pounded into the vortex. This lessened the cold gnawing on him and Galen, but would only delay the inevitable if Durward could not rend, from his fatigued, and pain fogged mind, an equally useful idea to defeat the Enchantment. Durward's and Galen's faces were frostbitten.

Doyle finally pulled Arden and Guthrie up against Galen's hunched back. The scouts were not long in joining them.

Doyle seemed to gain strength now that they were grouped against one another.

Almost chaotically, Durward searched his mind for a wisp of inspiration to, at the least, stalemate Doyle. To allow them to recover, somewhat, from the destructive ravages of this insane battle. There were only foggy and muddy thoughts oozing relentlessly toward the blackness of Doyle, and frozen death.

"*Durward*," Galen whispered into Durward's ear, "I feel the *break point* upon *me*! I have *nothing* else to *give*! Please! *Save* us! Nigel must not *win*!"

Durward barely understood the words because his mind was dimmed by his exhaustion and pain. Similar needs had washed over him moments before, then receded into a muddy patch of ooze and blackness. He returned to the darkness. It was being altered by some section of his mind yet able to contend against Doyle's insatiable vortex of absorption ability. "*Oh, Ethereal*!" Durward gasped, through frostbitten lips.

A note of dissociated hope entered his voice. "*Yes*! *Galen*! *Yes*!"

The Healer caught the tinge of hope, felt it well up in his mind and heart to a trickle of added energy. He knew only moments separated him from failure of his ability to heal. Only seconds remained for the attempt to use whatever hopeful new weapon Durward's mind had presented to the Magician. He dropped his head onto Durward's shoulder and prayed.

Durward twisted his head toward the pond.

Doyle noted this but was so certain of victory it did not wonder why the Magician directed valuable attention to the waters. They were already being used as an ice weapon. What more harm could come from them?

Durward had heard the splashing of the waterfall and this had spoken to some deep, creative sector of his beleaguered mind. Perhaps this would bring the tiny extra even vile Doyle could not withstand. Durward absorbed the thin shield before himself and his friends and directed it at the pool. He scooped, then channeled in a steady current, the oozy mud on the bottom of the pond, up through the bubbling water, and into Doyle's vortex. The mud created continuous purple explosions within the Enchantment.

Doyle staggered backwards against the hedgerow with resounding force, rattling the thorns like a million shields under a hail storm. The Enchantment wrapped its arms around its torso, from the agony caused by the added weapon.

Durward froze the ooze and hurled it faster and harder

into the black vortex. The iced mud detonated with twice as much sound, adding to the thundering of the exploding ice stream, and the purple flashing intensified, mingling with the blinding blue scintillation.

Doyle began fading out of existence. Its darkness became gray. It swirled like a wind whipped mist, then vanished with incredible swiftness.

Durward blinked back tears of triumph and relief. He ceased his energy emanations and collapsed, unconscious on the grass, with Galen, Guthrie, Arden, and the scouts, around him.

Galen's healing ability grasped the freed might of both Healer and Magician and began balming the eight men.

The yellow sun shared its warmth with the warriors, and wondered at their capacity to overcome such an implacable enemy, and retain the frailest shred of life.

Durward startled awake, sat up, and looked around wildly.

Galen and Guthrie sat up nearby.

Arden scrambled to a kneeling position.

The soldiers struggled to their feet.

"There are limits to all things," Durward whispered. "I must rest *overnight* before I can perform more magic feats." He peered through the dusky gloom at the Healer. "Galen, too, is still exhausted."

"*We* can not *delay*!" Arden protested.

"*Aye*!" Guthrie agreed. "The time *limit* on *food* for our *people* is *almost* elapsed. Nigel *must* know we have *defeated* his *last* three Enchantments. He *will* move to *attack* us *with* the *Elves*."

Zadok drew his sword and strode to the hedges blocking them from their mounts. He held the hilt with both hands and hacked at the hedges. The thorns rattled like steel, showing no signs of damage. He sheathed his blade and dejectedly rejoined the others.

"We *still* can not pass *beyond* the hedges to a *safe* camp," Guthrie continued. "We are *vulnerable* here. *Unless* you can muster a psychic shield for our protection, *all* night?"

Durward groaned. He sadly shook his head.

"Shouldn't those hedges have returned to *normal* when Doyle *died*?" Arden said angrily.

"It may take days for the energy in them to dissipate," Durward whispered.

Galen placed his hands to his temples. He closed his eyes and looked surprised. "You are *correct* about me," he told Durward. "I *do* have *stronger* healing ability than previously. I *have* developed during this frenzied war. *I* will be refreshed in a few more minutes." He pressed his palms to Durward's temples and frowned. "But, you, old friend, will take *long* to regenerate. I did not *imagine* you were *this* horribly *drained*." He shook his head at Arden and Guthrie. "We *shall* camp *here*, with the guards taking turns at watch, because it will be *several* hours before Durward can *ply* his *might* again."

"This *is* best," Arden reluctantly admitted. "It would be *foolhardy* to venture into the Caverns *without* Durward's *magic.*"

"It is *foolish*, even *with* my *abilities*," Durward chided. "When I enter, there will be a face to face confrontation between myself and Nigel. I *am* stronger than before, but not *that* potent. I fear Nigel will attempt to slay me without a twinge of feeling. *If* he *is* aware that we have destroyed these Enchantments, he will be laying in wait somewhere in the Caverns. He will strike as he has not struck before."

As Guthrie and the nobles slept, Zadok and his fellow guardsmen agreed upon a plan of action.

Hilliard passed behind the waterfall to stand guard at the entrance of the Elf Caverns.

Zadok, Wayte and Ryley examined the poles and selected the two with the least amount of damage from the battle with Thornton.

Wayte hurled one pole, like it was a javelin, over the hedgerow that blocked them from their steeds.

Zadok took the other pole, held it out in front of him with both hands, sprinted forward, jammed the far end of the pole at the base of the hedgerow, and vaulted over the deadly wall of thorns.

"*Stay alert*," Zadok ordered, "I will return, *anon*."

Wayte and Ryley, worried, paced back and forth at the hedgerow.

"*Incoming*!" Zadok warned.

Parcels of food and leather bags of water started sailing

over the hedgerow.

Wayte and Ryley were hard-pressed to catch the goods and set them aside before they hit the ground.

"*Stand back*!" Zadok warned. He sailed over the hedgerow and landed on his feet like an acrobat.

"What took so long?" Ryley asked.

"Our intrepid horses figured out how to untie their reigns from the tree branches to which they were bound," Zadok said. "They were far down the stream munching sweet herbs. *Long* way there, *long* way back."

"I'm surprised they didn't eat *our* food right off each others backs," Wayte said, with a laugh.

"*Whatever*," Zadok said. "We have *insured* that Prince Arden, Lord Durward, Lord Galen and Guthrie will *not* venture into battle *without* sustenance."

"As well as *us* dependable expendables," Ryley said.

"*Never* war on an *empty* stomach," Wayte said, quoting a renowned general.

Illustration 25

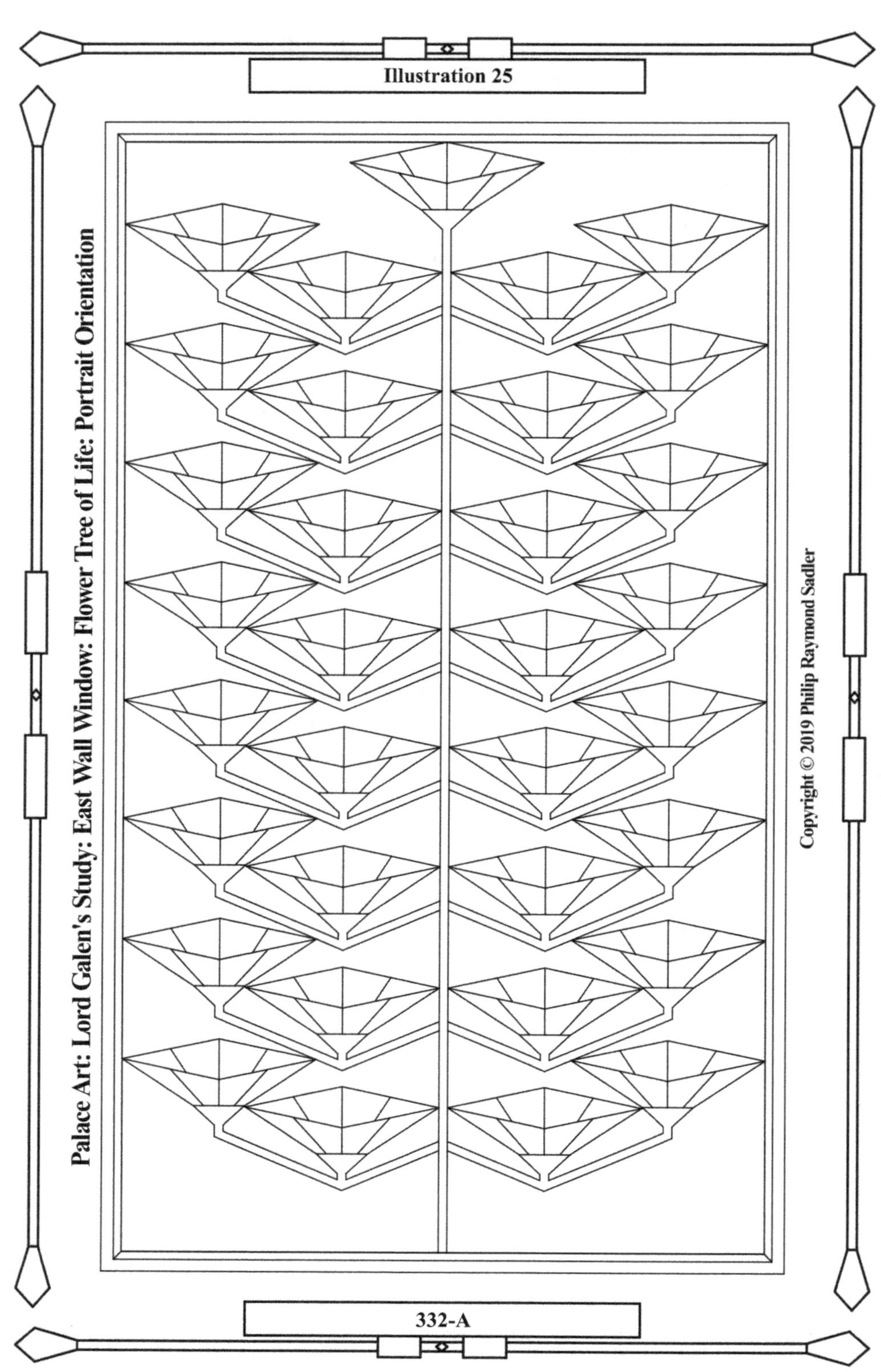

Illustration 26

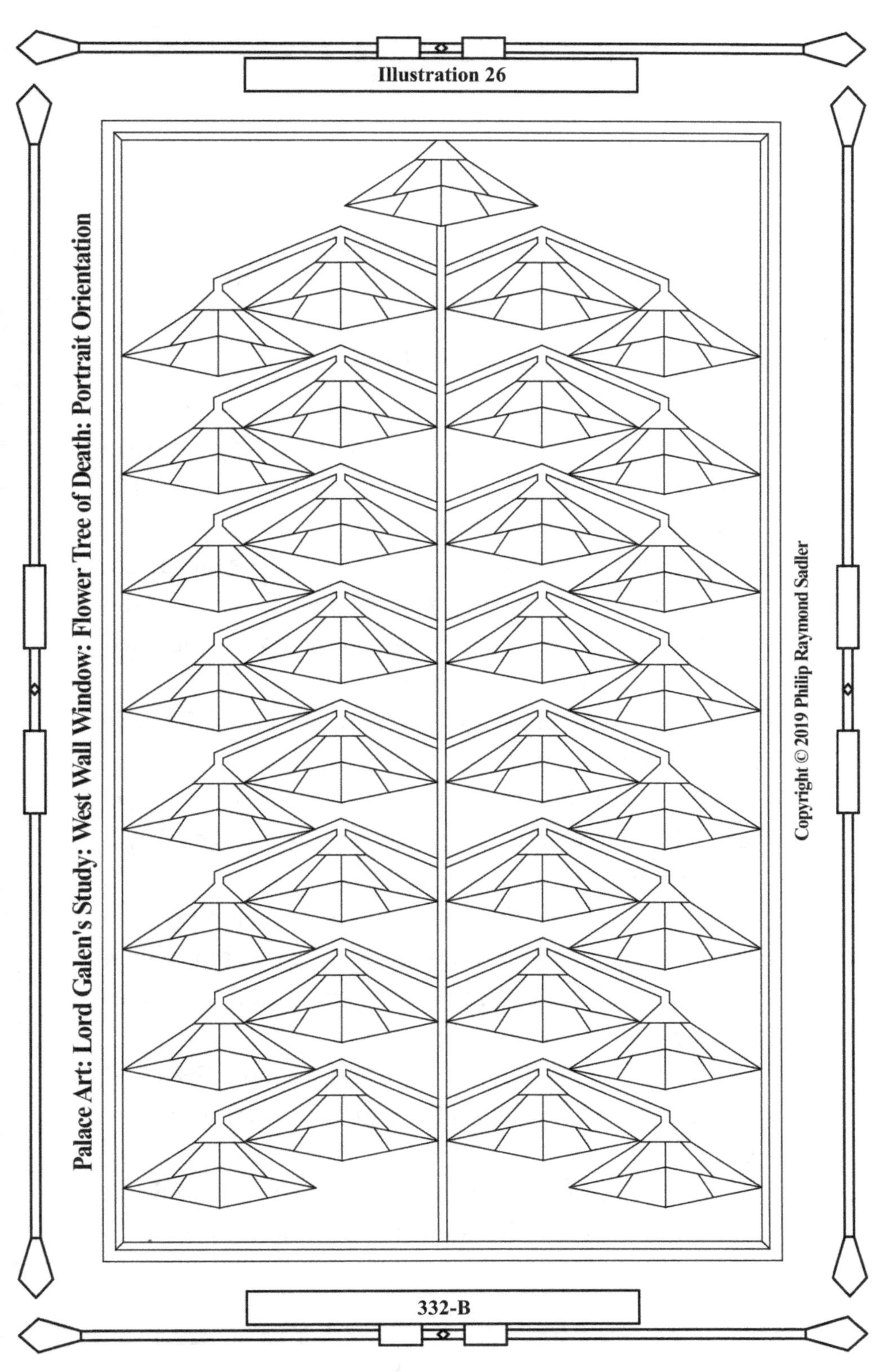

Palace Art: Lord Galen's Study: West Wall Window: Flower Tree of Death: Portrait Orientation

Chapter 13

The ruler of the Elves

The rays of the swollen red sun danced off the waterfall and the bubbling pond, casting shadows around the green thorn hedge enclosure.

The War Party stood at the near side of the fall. There was a space of three feet between the falling water and the end of the rock spur. A towering rectangular opening led into the spur and to the distant Elf Caverns.

"Leave the remainder of our supplies here," Guthrie told the guardsmen.

"Elves see as keenly in the dark as in the light," Durward said. "They do not illuminate their Caverns. I will reveal our way with a psychic glow."

Durward entered the darkness first, enveloping himself and each member of the War Party with a blue shine. Their glows reflected from the gray stone, and their footsteps echoed sharply.

Guthrie frowned. "Can you mask our sounds?" he asked Durward. "We will be heard for a quarter of a mile, otherwise."

Durward waved in affirmation. Their echoes ceased and their hushed speech did not carry beyond four feet.

They rounded a gentle curve and Durward stropped. He pointed to the left wall and the War Party stepped over to see.

"A painting of King Avery!" Arden said. "It looks *almost* three-dimensional!"

The image of the Ruler of the Elves stood three feet high; life-sized. A thin, silver ring on his black hair served as a crown. His smooth, oval face was vacant of emotion, but his green eyes blazed rage. He wore purple tunic, slacks, and brown boots.

Galen passed his hands above the painting. He sucked in a breath. "This is *not* a *portrait*!" he said. "It *is* King Avery! *Nigel* has *placed* him *onto* the stone!"

Durward bent close and examined the image more carefully. "You are correct," he agreed with dismay. "*This* is why the Pretender, Aubrey, is *able* to command the Elves."

"Can you *free* him?" Arden asked. "He would, surely, *join* our quest and the Elves could do no less than *rally* around him."

Durward used his index fingers to trace the outline of Avery. He ran both palms over the vibrant image. "Yes," he said. "*Perhaps*, I *can* free him." He motioned to the guards and said, "Hold your swords so their blades form a rectangle around Avery."

Durward dispatched heat energy at the long swords, fusing tips to blades, near the finger guards.

The soldiers were forced to release the swords because of the heat, but the weapons clung to the wall as though the stone and blades had become magnetized.

Durward bent the four handles up from the wall. "Cold steel cuts magic," he said. "Psychic energy is shorted out when properly grounded, or channeled into a receptive vessel, or into one who absorbs or utilizes the energy completely."

"As, in a body who heals," Galen said, sourly.

"Be at ease, Galen," Durward said, "I shall disperse *this* energy throughout *this* metallic stone until it *releases* its *noble* prisoner."

The Magician held his hands several inches from the blades. A gray square of light flashed forth. It struck the blades resoundingly, forcing them half their height into the cavern wall.

There was a beautiful trilling. The image stirred and became three-dimensional. The Ruler of the Elves used the bottom blade as a rung and leaped down from the stone, leaving an impression of his form within the cavern wall.

"Aye, *Durward*," Avery said, with his deep hearty voice, which always seemed incongruous from such a short slight being. "*None* other could have *freed* me!" He looked at the War Party. "Guthrie! The War Serpent coils to strike, I see. And Arden, the impetuous one. Good Galen, your visit to our aged ones is overdue. But, this is understandable." He saluted the guards.

They wasted no time in returning the honor.

With his energy, Durward straightened the hilts of the swords and separated the blades. One at a time, he yanked the swords free of the cavern wall, and returned them to their rightful owners.

"Has Aubrey *complete* control of your Elves?" Arden

asked.

Avery's face colored with rage. "Yes! The Pretender has handed his *own* people to a *non* Elf! There is no *forgiveness* for such a *traitor*! But, good friend Durward, I mean not to *hurt* you. It is not with *malice* that I be Nigel's enemy, but through *undesired* necessity."

"No apologies *necessary*," Durward said. "We must quickly move to *reassert* your ruler-ship over the Caverns, Avery. Nigel has worsened in his madness. He has almost destroyed all of Indwin."

"So it *shall* be done," Avery vowed. "*I* shall guide you."

Durward enveloped Avery in a blue glow.

The Elf King started to lead them into the ancient Caverns, but paused; suspicious. "What *omen* speaks, *now*?" he said. "Our *echoes* are *dead*."

Durward laughed. "Fear not, this augury is of my design," he said. "I quashed our sounds to prevent our detection. I should have apprised you of the matter."

"No import," Avery said. "I would have pestered you into it, anyway."

"Avery," Guthrie said, "are you aware of where Nigel secrets his power Enhancer?"

"Aye," Avery said. He was frustrated. "It is ever at his side. Where he goes, it follows on wheels, drawn by psychic force."

"Then, only *trickery* will *separate* the two," Arden said. "I know of *two*, no, *four* old foxes who may be crafty enough to *achieve* that *feat*."

Avery, Galen, Durward and Guthrie laughed.

Avery directed them through the twisting Caverns. They passed branch after branch where other sections of the Caverns led into obscure darkness.

Arden nudged Guthrie, and said, "Fate was generous. Without Avery, Galen and Durward would have taken days of psychic searching to find Nigel."

Guthrie nodded. He expected an assault from Nigel or the Elves. He could not understand why this fate had not already befallen them. His restless eyes roved the gray pocked stone. There were so many places for attackers to hide. Holes. Outcroppings. Side tunnels. No one man could check them all. He glanced back at the guards and was pleased; they were searching the Caverns with their trained eyes and ears. He had selected wisely.

"You say Nigel has become worse," Avery said, to Durward, as they walked side by side. "How so?"

"Aldora weds Arden," Durward said.

"Ah, yes," King Avery said. "*I* would go *insane* if *I* could be *denied* the one I *loved*. Has the Enhancer contributed to the harm?"

"It is probably the cause of this latest relapse," Durward said. "You would not believe the might my son sends forth. He fired the Windy Hills, from Range to Range. They burned even *after* the Orchards were charcoal. He *rotted* the grains and vegetables on the farmlands and turned the Zelam River into *stone*. At every step along our way here he constructed Enchantments, some of which were psychic *golems* we almost *failed* to defeat. The last one of the three guarding the Caverns, was the most formidable."

Avery's face was wrinkled with amazement and worry. "Yet, you have advanced *this* far in *spite* of Nigel's *horrors*, so he *can* be *fought*," he said.

"And *defeated*," Arden said, from behind them.

Avery chuckled. "The impetuous one, as always," he said. "*First*, you *determine* your enemy's *might* and *position*, then *compare* it to your own, *before* you *decide* whether he can be *fought*, let alone, *vanquished*."

"*Only* when there is ample *time*, and a *choice*," Arden said. "*We* have the *luxury* of *neither*. We *fight*, or *die*, and even the *Caverns* may be *destroyed* by *Nigel*."

Avery looked at Durward. "True enough," he said. "Your *poor* Nigel may yet phase so insane he will *slay* his chosen *allies* to *win* and, *perhaps*, even if he *loses*."

The branching tunnels ended, leaving only the main passage they traveled. There were still no signs of life.

Avery halted. "There in much knowledge being emanated from this place," he said. "The sounds of my people should have crowded around us, by now. We should have seen many of them. Even the guards usually posted in the side tunnels back aways, were absent. Has Nigel *left* the Caverns *with* my people?"

"There is *only* the route we entered," Durward reminded the Elf King. "Nigel would need to *pass* us. Only invisibility and masking could slip them by. I am sure he could not resist striking us, if this were so. You know, all too well, your Elves would flock to you, no matter what control my son is using on them. No, Nigel, is *still* inside these Caverns."

"*Or*, he has *bored* an *exit*," Avery said.

"We *must* determine whether this is *true*," Durward said.

They moved quickly after the Ruler of the Elves. The gray stone changed to multi-colors. It reflected the glows from the travelers, with sparkling beauty. No one paid attention to this Elfin glory. They strained their senses to catch sounds of life.

A small boulder slid aside on the left side of the tunnel. Four Elves charged out of the revealed doorway. Their longbows were set to strike. The Elves froze in astonishment.

Avery beckoned.

The Elves dropped their weapons and ran to hug their King. They babbled in Elf Tongue, sounding like a brook over a rocky bed.

Avery hushed them. "Where *is* Nigel?" he said, so the questers could understand.

One of the Elves scratched his head. "Good question, sire," he said. "We see *only* low Aubrey. *He* brings the *orders*, and *punishes* us when we *disobey*. *Only* he sees Nigel. Yet, we *hear* Nigel's might *rumbling* within the *deepest* parts of our Caverns."

"He is *excavating*?" Durward asked, with surprise.

"Yes," the Elf said, "since he arrived, five *long* days ago, to *aid* the *Pretender*. He stopped only once to throw up his Enchantments."

"Which *way* does he *dig*?" Arden asked, fearing the answer he assumed.

"We guess, back along the spur, toward Alaric's Castle," the Elf said. "*Many* of us have *tried* to find *where* he *digs*, but he has placed stone between himself and our tunnels. He and Aubrey pass through the rock for short distances like ghosts through fog."

Guthrie was swearing under his breath.

"What is it, War Serpent?" Avery asked.

"*Diversions*," Guthrie said. "The *Enchantments* were *diversions*. They were his *toys* for *us* while *he* forged toward the Castle. He will *surface* there and *destroy* everyone as he *abducts* Aldora. *We* have *played* into his hands; *given* him the *time* he needed. How *strong* are the vibrations, *now*?" he demanded of the lead Bow Elf.

"Almost *undetectable* from the tunnel ends," the Elf said. "You have to place your ear to an upturned mug to catch them. We *estimate*, Nigel *must* be *under* the Castle by now."

"Come," Avery, said. "Guide us to tunnel ends. We can judge somewhat better, with our magic, how far Nigel is."

The Elves snatched up their longbows and arrows and darted into the side passage.

Avery called them back by clearing his throat. "Your manners are in need of refinement," he scolded. "We have honored guests who cannot travel our scout tunnels."

The lead Bow Elf looked unhappy. "The *only* way to the tunnel *ends* is *through* the scout tunnels," he said.

"How did Nigel *pass* to the terminus, before he *ghost-*

ed through the rock?" Avery said.

"He miniaturized himself and that strange tank on wheels which he draws behind him," the Elf said.

Avery cast a questioning glance at Durward.

"*No*, my friend," Durward said. "I *have* gained more *strength*, and *developed* new *abilities*, but I am *not* mighty enough to *shrink* and *regrow*."

"Where *are* the *rest* of my Elves?" Avery asked.

The bow Elves turned red with rage.

"Dark Nigel has *imbued* our *infants* and *children* into the walls of the great Hall of Judgment," the Lead Bow Elf said, through clenched teeth.

Avery tuned pale, swayed, then steadied himself with a hand against the wall of the tunnel. "Continue," he said, shaking.

"Five days ago, Nigel issued orders to Zolazar and your Majesty's army, and they exited the Caverns. We know not where away they went, nor the purpose of their mission."

Guthrie did not like what his mind presented. "Nigel has allowed your army to pass overland through the Enchantments, probably along the West Shield Range, where we could not sight them," he said. "They will be encamped within the Wind Barrier Forest, awaiting orders from Nigel. Zolazar will strike the Citadel from without, while Nigel and the remainder of your Elves attack from within."

"There appears to be no end to the number of reasons why we must stop my son, here and now," Durward said, with great sadness.

"Continue your report," Avery bade the Lead Bow Elf.

"Some of us guard the tunnel ends," the Elf said. "We are *forbidden* to *leave* the Caverns, and are *ordered* to *kill* all *intruders*. The *rest* of your people are *slaves* to the *whims* of Nigel and Aubrey."

"What punishment do Aubrey and Nigel threaten for disobedience?" Avery asked.

"The *least*, is *pain* and *old age*," the Lead Bow Elf said, "the *worst*, is the *destruction* of the Great Hall of Judgment!"

Avery swayed, with horror.

"Even though *insane*, my son will *not* commit such an act," Durward assured the Elf King. "It is a *threat*, only, to *guarantee* the *cooperation* of your people."

Guthrie felt the Magician was attempting to reassure himself, rather than the King of the Elves.

Avery nodded, but appeared unconvinced. He gazed at the War Party. "Even *if* I *reassert* my *dominance* over my *Elves*," he told them, "*Nigel* will be *free* to *destroy* the Great Hall of Judgment. *This* is a *tragedy* that is *too* monumental for *me* to *risk*."

Durward looked stricken. He backed away from the King of the Elves and said, "You would *ally* with Nigel *because* of this? You would *battle* with *us*?"

Guthrie placed his hand on the hilt of his sword.

Arden followed suit.

Galen glowered at the Knight and the Crown Prince Designate because they thought of striking Avery.

"You *misunderstand* me, old friend," Avery said. "I *beseech* you to journey *with* me to the Great Hall of Judgment, and *assist* me and my Elves in freeing our progeny from the Mother Stone, as you freed me, and while your Nigel yet excavates."

Durward relaxed. "*Forgive* my *misunderstanding*, Great King," he said. "How *many* must be *freed*?"

Avery looked to his Elves.

"I have counted, seven hundred and six," the Lead Bow Elf said.

Durward gasped and slumped against the wall of the tunnel. He was a picture of defeat.

Avery rushed to the Magician and demanded, "What *is* it? *What* do you *know*?"

Durward waved his hands. "What you demand of me would require hours, or days, depending upon the number of swords we have available to form the cutting squares," he said.

"But, *Sire*," the Lead Bow Elf said, with exasperation, "Nigel required *only* five *minutes* to *imbue* the Mother Stone with our progeny!"

"To imbue is far simpler than to release," Durward lamented.

"Can we not *reverse* the *imbuing* process?" Galen said.

"I know of no way," Durward said, dejectedly.

"Can we not *speed* up the *release*, if *I* lay hands on the stone and *siphon* off Nigel's power?" Galen said.

"Have you *performed* a *similar* feat before?" Durward said.

"You *have*," Guthrie said. "*You* have *pulled* power from Galen throughout our war against the Enchantments. *Sure-*

ly, you can, *likewise*, draw upon the *energy* which Nigel has *instilled* in the stone."

Durward appeared hopeful.

"Perhaps we *both* can achieve this feat," Galen said, "for *faster* results. Avery and his bowmen, as well. They naturally channel mystical power."

Durward stood away from the wall. "What say you all," he asked, "shall we offer our best attempt at this noble task?"

"*Before* we *attempt* this," Arden said, with impatience, "we *must* know how *close* Nigel is to the *completion* of his *tunnel*, to *determine* if we have a *realistic* hope of *beginning* this task, let alone *finishing* it, *before* he *assaults* the Castle."

"With *this*, I reluctantly *agree*," Avery said. "If you will wait here, I will travel to the terminus of the scout tunnel and gauge Nigel's closeness to the Castle."

"How *far* is it to the Great Hall of Judgment?" Arden asked. "It is long since I have been here and cannot recall."

"Thirty yards," Avery said.

"If *we* press on to the Hall, while *you* seek the extent of Nigel's *progress*," Arden said, "*we* can be at work *before* you return. A *double* use of *time*."

"Well said," Guthrie approved.

"You two, with our friends, to the Hall," Avery told his Elves, "you two, with your King." He and his chosen companions vanished down the side tunnel.

The Lead Bow Elf looked to Durward.

"*I* am in *command*," Arden said, impatiently, "Lead us to the Hall, at a *run*!"

The War Party was hard-pressed to keep up with the Elves.

The Great Hall of Judgment was a glory to behold. At Avery's request, Durward had applied his glowing paint to its ceiling. This light was reflected from the multi colored stone, and entering the Hall was like walking into a rainbow. There were ornate stone chairs lined up in rows to accommodate vast numbers of Elves. Their backs faced the great doorway. A judgment dais stood at the far wall.

Durward entered the Hall and collapsed to his knees.

Arden knelt beside him, with concern.

Durward waved his hand at the walls.

When Arden looked carefully, he understood why the Magician had lost hope.

"*No, no, no*!" Galen said, with despair.

Guthrie and his guardsmen, like their Elf guides, stared in stunned silence.

The Elf progeny *were* embedded in the Mother Stone, but they were arranged in rows that ran from the floor to the distant ceiling. Unless ladders or scaffolds were constructed, or one were capable of levitation, there was no hope of releasing ninety percent of the infants and children.

Arden stood up and turned to the Lead Bow Elf. "*Why* did you not *impart* this *fact* to us?" he demanded, irately. "*You* have *wasted* our *time*! Time that might have *seen* us *defeat* Nigel!" He turned to Guthrie. "We shall *resume* the *search* for Nigel!" he commanded. "There will be no *other* side actions!" He tugged on Durward's elbow. "Stand up *man*! Have you *lost* your *will*?"

"You may be in *command*," Guthrie said, sternly. "You may be *Crown Prince Designate*, but *you* shall not *address* Lord *Durward* with such *disrespect*. *You* shall *apologize* or I shall *drub* you, *soundly*!"

Shocked, Arden stared at his father, then at Durward. He knelt and gazed into Durward's distraught eyes. He realized the Hall had made Nigel's crimes even more of an undeniable and stunning horror to Durward.

"*Gentle* Durward," Arden said, with heartfelt sympathy, "I *meant* no *disrespect*. I *beg* you to *forgive* my *words*, and my *attitude*."

Durward did not move. He darted his eyes from infant, to child, to infant, seeing the *sadness* in *their* eyes.

Avery and his Elves entered the hall.

The King of the Elves looked at the walls and fell to his knees.

Galen shook himself free of despair. He ran to the nearest of the imprisoned Progeny, knelt on one knee, and passed his hands over the infant.

Galen could feel the life force of the suspended infant, but no indication of Nigel's dark power. Galen gasped with understanding.

Nigel had utilized the infant's life force to imbue the infant into the stone.

Galen managed a slight smile and flowed his energy into the image.

The infant stirred.

Galen was elated.

The infant was be-stilled.

Galen groaned in a manner that caused everyone, including Avery and Durward, to look his way.

"Only cold steel will cut each of these children and infants free of this abominable spell," Galen said, dejectedly.

A chilling, high-pitched clanging began echoing throughout the Caverns. It was a warning.

The bow Elves looked frightened.

"Nigel, *himself*, is summoning us," the Lead Bow Elf said. "If we *fail* to *answer*, he will hurl *pain* into us. He will *detect* you, *Sire*!"

Durward stood up and drew on the inner resources which had sustained him while battling the Enchantments. He nodded his head, sadly, and looked at Avery.

"This *must* mean Nigel has reached a *strategic* area beneath the Castle and is marshaling your Elves for the *attack* on the Citadel," he said. "Our *only* chance to *free* your Elf Progeny, and to *save* Indwin and its people, is to *confront* Nigel while he is *awaiting* your brethren to *rally* to him; *before* he *vacates* your Caverns." He drew himself to his full height. "Please take me to my son, by the *fastest* route *possible*, Great King."

Avery leaped to his feet and motioned to his bow Elves. They raced from the Great Hall, to the location of one of their scout tunnels. The Lead Bow Elf placed a hand against an outcropping. The door slid to his left.

Arden shoved the Elves aside, bent low, entered the side passage, and ran.

Avery motioned his Elves after Arden.

Guthrie followed, then Galen, Durward, Avery and the scouts. The tunnel roof brushed at the heads and shoulders of the War Party. They ran as best they could in that awkward position. Durward was masking their sounds.

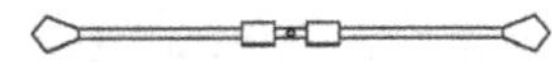

Arden's glow vanished.

The Elves returned to Avery.

"Prince Arden is like a *madman*," the Lead Bow Elf said. "He *runs* as if *magic* propels him."

Durward motioned to Guthrie. "Can the War Serpent move faster than the man?" he asked.

"Twice as swiftly," Guthrie said, anxious to pursue his son.

"*Catch* Arden and *keep* him in *tow*," Durward said. "He fears for *Aldora* and our *people*. He thinks *poorly*. Do not *allow* him to blunder into Nigel's hands."

Guthrie shimmered into the War Serpent. A moment later, the Snake was gone. Its blue psychic light vanished several seconds after that, far down the multicolored passage.

"Do your best to catch up with and protect War Serpent and the Crown Prince Designate," Avery ordered his Elves. "Obey Guthrie's commands."

Durward placed a glow around the bowmen.

The Elves vanished from sight almost as quickly as War Serpent.

Durward stopped and sank to the floor of the small passage. He leaned back, trying to lessen the sharp pain in his fatigued back muscles.

Galen had no such trouble. "Stand up," he said to Durward. "As we continue, I shall keep my hands on your back. We will be able to travel longer and faster."

They resumed their trek behind Avery, gathering speed. There was no sight or sound of Arden, War Serpent, or the Bow Elves.

The soldiers were following slowly trying to bear the aches in their backs.

Durward halted the group. "See to the guards," he said, shamefully, to Galen. "If *I* am *eased*, they shall be."

The glowing bow Elves appeared from the darkness. They were agitated. The Lead Bow Elf babbled to Avery in Elf Tongue.

Avery gasped. "War Serpent and Arden have *vanished*!" he reported. "My men had their lights in sight. There was a frightening trembling of the Caverns and Arden's and War Serpent's glows were gone. There are no side tunnels or crevices there. *Nigel* or *Aubrey* has them!"

Durward sent a blinding light along the tunnel, revealing nothing within the reflected rainbow colors.

Avery dispatched his Elves ahead.

The War Party raced after them. The pace seemed a snail's, although the walls flew by.

Durward continued search-lighting every crack and

boulder along the small passage. There were no shadows before or behind the questers. He dispatched psychic feelers for Arden and War Serpent. He could detect Avery's bowmen, but not Arden or War Serpent.

Galen experienced the same.

Durward paused.

Galen started to speak.

Durward waved for silence. He placed his palms against the right side of the passage, then cupped his hands and pressed his ear to them.

Avery and Galen did likewise.

The guards settled to the floor, massaging their back muscles.

Durward nodded with self affirmation. "They were *transported* through *here* by *vast* energy," he said.

"There is a scout tunnel six feet beyond," Avery said. "It turns away from us, then meets another, which leads to tunnel ends."

Galen hissed. "There is *movement* in that passage," he said, "and *voices*."

Durward ceased his searchlight and the glows of the War Party. He formed a large, luminous, blue cone of energy and pressed its round base against the right side of the tunnel. The cone began to resonate and words could be heard.

"*Watch* that serpent *closely*!" said a husky Elf voice. "Now that you have it *coiled* up, hold it *tight*! If it gets *loose*, it could *squeeze* ten of you at *once* until you *suf-*

focate!"

"It is *Aubrey*!" Avery said, vehemently. "Nigel *shares* his *power* with the *Pretender*!"

Durward made the cone larger. The voices increased in volume.

"*Nigel* is *awaiting*, master," an Elf with a high-pitched voice said. "*Please*, let us *go* to him. He will *pain* us."

"*Not* while you assist *me*," Aubrey said, harshly. "We *must* compel these two to *betray* their *co-conspirators*. Let the boy's mouth free."

Arden cried out.

Aubrey, or one of his Elves, had applied injury or hurt to the Crown Prince Designate.

"*Where* is the *rest* of your *vile* War Party?" Aubrey demanded. "*In* the *other* tunnel?"

Arden did not reply. He cried out twice more.

Galen growled with rage and frustration.

Durward stepped back from the cone and rotated it so the tip touched the wall and the round base faced him.

The voices came through with less volume.

Durward increased the circumference of the cone until its round base matched the height of the tunnel.

"He's too *proud* to speak, *master*," the Elf with the high-pitched voice, said. "The *viper* can't be *harmed* without *conjury*."

"All *right*," Aubrey said. "A *little* magic *heat* will *loosen* its forked *tongue*. I'll *sear* out one of its *ugly* eyes."

There was slithering.

A loud painful sounding thump occurred.

Aubrey cried out in rage.

Footsteps receded both ways down the other tunnel as Elves fled the great Snake's slapping attack.

"*Return* to your *task* or you'll have more *pain* than Nigel's *ever* given you!" Aubrey screamed. "*These* men weren't *afraid* to *stay*! They've got the viper *stretched out* and *still*, now!"

The footsteps returned slowly.

"*If* you flee *again*, I'll *turn* you *older* than your great grandfathers and *hang* you in the *sun* to *die* of *hunger*!" Aubrey threatened. "*Now*, wind that viper up again! We'll take these two to Nigel. He'll *tear* the Snake *apart* for us. It will *chatter* then. *So* will the boy. We'll *get* a *reward* for them, *although* the *information* would *garner* more."

Galen was staring hopefully at Durward.

The magical cone began to spin, and the friction of its tip against the tunnel wall caused the stone to glow in rainbow colors. The faster the cone rotated, the deeper into the wall it struck, and the brighter the stone glowed.

Galen placed his hands to Durward's temples.

The cone gained speed. Soon, it was whistling, and red sparks began to fly.

Avery and the guards stepped back several feet.

The sounds from the other tunnel became louder, amplified by the whirling of the cone.

"*Wait*!" Aubrey shouted. "There's *something*—"

Silence fell in both passages, except for the whining of the cone drill.

Despite his best efforts, Durward was unable to mask

all the noise.

The cone was half-way though the wall.

"*Somehow*, they're *breaking* into *this* tunnel!" Aubrey said. "*Hie* these two to *Nigel*! Now, we can tell our *Wizard* where to *rain* his *terror*! Move!"

Footsteps echoed through the cone. The Elves were bearing War Serpent and Arden away from the questers.

"*Watch* that *viper*!" Aubrey screamed. "It's *strong*, I *warned* you! *All* of you *hold* it, and *don't* drop your *guard*! I'll *take* the *boy*!"

There was a loud grunt from Aubrey and the sound of a body striking a wall. There were wild frightened shouts from the other Elves as someone attacked them.

"*Trip* him!" Aubrey shouted. "*He* can't hurt *you* with his *kicks*, you *fools*!"

The tunnel and the War Party were alight with the stinging red sparks from the drill, and the glow of the heated stone. The magic cone's wide flat base was almost flush with the multicolored wall.

"*Delay* him," Avery said softly, although Arden could not hear him. "*Just keep kicking*! *Just* a *little* more *delay*!"

"*Avery*!" Galen said. "*Join* with us. I *know* it is a *risk* to *you*, but we *believe* we can *prevent* harm to you." He and Durward knelt on the floor.

Avery felt a chill down his spine. To meld improperly with a human could tear away his invincibility, his age retardation, and his psychic control over the Elf Nation. He hesitantly pressed his palms to Galen's temples because he knew they could not blast through the six-foot thick wall in time without him.

The whine of Durward's drill doubled. The sparks turned a deeper shade of red and the cone cut into the wall as though it were soft wood. Sounds from the other passage were thundering around the War Party, amplified by the increased spin of the drill.

Every blow of Arden's boots sounded like hammer strikes.

Each Elf grunt of lost air was a drum beat.

War Serpent's wriggling was a constant unnerving scraping sound.

Aubrey's enraged commands were explosions.

Durward, Galen and Avery were sweating.

Durward's hair was being singed by the heat from the melting stone and the sparks from the cone.

There was a crunching, and the drill shot through the wall.

Durward ceased the spinning of the cone and cooled the red-hot opening with his Winter force.

In the other tunnel, the cone of energy glanced off the wall to the right of the War Serpent.

The startled Elves freed the snake and scattered.

The hot drill dropped, on its flat base, to the floor and lay motionless.

War Serpent flashed at Aubrey.

The Pretender ghosted through the tunnel wall, drawing Arden with him.

Durward threw himself at the wall, but was unable to follow in the wake of Aubrey's energy.

The stone had regained its cruel hardness.

Durward angrily absorbed the energy of his cone.

Galen helped Avery disconnect himself, and they stepped into the other corridor, with the guards close behind.

Guthrie reformed to man. "I *tried* my *best*," he said, with frustrated rage. "*But,* your *Elves* are *invincible*, Avery, and *Aubrey* has *great* magic!"

The Elves abandoned by Aubrey sighted their rightful King and froze with astonishment.

Avery motioned to them. "Go to Nigel's call and do not allow our brethren to harm Prince Arden," he instructed. "Nigel can no longer threaten you with pain or premature aging, for, I am fully powered, thanks to Galen's healing."

The Elves gleefully scuttled down the tunnel, taking the left turn, straight toward tunnels end.

"*We* must *hurry*, also," Guthrie urged Durward.

Durward smiled at Avery and said, "We *shall* defeat Nigel, *now.* Between you, Galen and myself, we will wear Nigel down until he is too weak to raise a hand!"

Durward threw blue glows around everyone and began running down the tunnel, bent over as before.

Galen, Avery, and the guards, followed.

Guthrie, as War Serpent, vanished ahead.

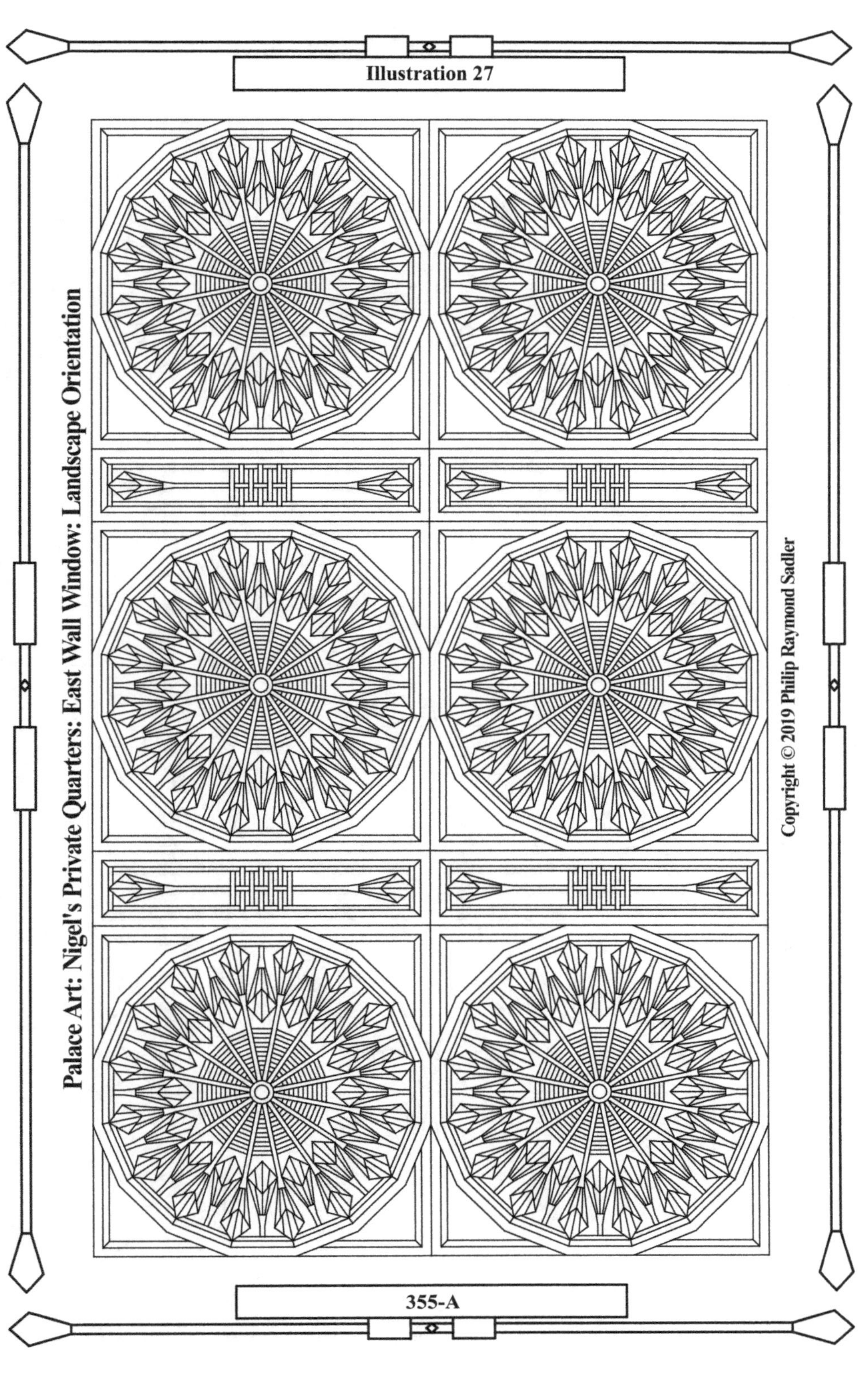

Illustration 27
Palace Art: Nigel's Private Quarters: East Wall Window: Landscape Orientation
Copyright © 2019 Philip Raymond Sadler
355-A

Illustration 28

Palace Art: Nigel's Private Quarters: West Wall Window: Landscape Orientation

Chapter 14
Nigel

A white light ghosted into view, growing brighter as the questers approached, until it was a small oval on the floor of the passage.

"That is tunnels terminus," Avery said.

Durward ended their blue glows. "We shall not send a warning to the enemy," he said.

They crept toward the end of the tunnel.

Guthrie stood up from behind one of the numerous outcroppings along the walls. "You are just in time," he whispered. He held up a cautionary hand and edged to the rim of the pool of light. He craned his neck, then motioned the others to him.

The tunnel ended at a stairway hewn into the side of a huge cavern. The left and right walls glowed magically, illuminating every crevice and crack. Male and female Elves were crowded around the foot of the wide stairway. The attention of the Elves was directed to the far wall.

"Even the *women* have been given *blades*!" Avery said. "He makes *callous* use of our remaining might! *We* would not *request* their *aid* in *battle* except under *dire* circumstances!"

Aubrey stood with his back to the right side of the far wall. Arden stood to the right of Aubrey; hands bound in front of him with rope. To the right of Arden was Nigel.

Durward gasped in dismay and despair.

Nigel was a gaunt shell of himself. Raven hair was tousled. Handsome, dark features were garish and pale. Ebony eyes were large and wild. Black stubble covered his face. Raven tunic and slacks were dirt smeared. In his madness, he had forgotten of personal hygiene.

Next to Nigel was a large metal tank affixed, with iron bands, to a wooden cart that had two iron axles and four wooden wheels. One end of a magically created flexible tube was attached to the underside of the tank, the other end was leather-thong-strapped against Nigel's forearm, its magically produced needle piercing his pale flesh.

"He *conveys* the Enhancer *directly* into his *blood*," Galen said. "No *wonder* he does not grow *weak*. He leaves off his attacks on us because he *achieves* desired *delay* each time for his *diggings*. He *torments*; like *cat* with *mouse*."

"But, he *loses*," Guthrie said.

Galen whispered into Durward's ear and the Magician nodded.

"My people are ready," Avery said. "I have protected them from the pain and old age energies of Nigel. When they see me, and I signal to them, they will attack him with fury."

"No," Durward and Galen said together.

Guthrie almost shouted angrily, "*Why*? The *fastest* way is *best*! To give him *even* a *moment* to return *strikes* is *fa-*

tal error!"

Nigel took one step forward. The long tank came easily with him, drawn by his psychic force. "The *noble* time is *now*," he said, with a feverish, cracked voice. "We *conquer* the Castle, and the *wealth* goes to *you*. I want *only* Aldora. *Only* Aldora." He seemed to get lost in his thoughts of Aldora. Perhaps his insanity led him astray. His mind drifted back to the moment. "*I* open the *way* for us, *now*."

"*Why* can *they* not *strike*?" Guthrie asked. "They are *ready*!" He took hold of Durward's shoulders.

The Magician shook free.

"We think we can heal Nigel," Galen said.

"You *think*!" Guthrie hissed. "We can not *risk* the *ruination* of our *people* just because you *think* you can *heal* him!" He grasped a bow and arrow from one of the Elves and sighted on Nigel's heart.

Nigel's concentration melted. He regained it and turned to face the far wall of the cavern.

Guthrie sighted on the Wizard's spine and drew the string taut.

"Would you be so *eager* to *abandon* hope and *slay*, if it were *your* son?" Durward asked. "*Please*, allow me to try *my* way. I will approach him. If he *strikes* me, kill him. If he *hesitates*, Galen, Avery and I will be *powerful* enough to *heal* him of his *madness*."

"What of his *love* for *Aldora*?" Guthrie snapped. "Can you *balm* him of *that*? Can you *guarantee* the *madness* will not *return* if he does not have *Aldora's* love?"

A pleading look of desperate hope for his demented son paled the Magician's war lined face.

It melted Guthrie's heart. A father's heart. He lowered the bow.

Nigel raised his hands. A square of red light appeared against the wall, expanded until it was twelve feet by twelve feet, and heated the stone to red, then blue, then white-hot, almost instantly.

"Whatever we *do*, it *must* be *before* he *opens* the *way* to the Castle," Avery said. "Though I will *prevent* my Elves from *following* him, I am sure Nigel will *swiftly* continue to the Castle and *wreak* terrible damage."

Aubrey was watching the magic of his master. He was so absorbed, he paid no heed to Arden.

"Look," Durward said hopefully to Guthrie. He pointed.

Arden lifted his bound and trembling hands toward the thick tube connecting Nigel to the tank of Enhancer.

Nigel caught the movement in the corner of his eye and sent energy at Arden without interrupting the heat beam.

Arden cried out and was flung to his side on the stone, rolling until he came up against the feet of the Elves standing below the questers' vantage point. He lay limp, but breathing.

"We go *forth*," Durward told Guthrie, firmly. "*If* I *fail*, if we *cannot* heal Nigel, use the arrow. *Only* as a *last* resort."

Guthrie nodded grimly. He shoved aside his concern for his son, for his duty to Indwin. He nocked the arrow.

The Magician, the Healer and the King stepped out of the tunnel onto the short landing and began descending the wide stone steps.

The Elves sighted Avery. They began cheering joyfully and waving their blades in celebration.

Nigel ceased his heat force, whirled about-face, and glanced around, with his head darting like a snake's. He saw Durward.

Aubrey shrieked in terror. He fell to his knees and covered his face with his hands. There was no escape for him, even with Nigel's vast magic. Aubrey's invincibility and age protection could be stripped from him by Avery in an instant.

Nigel remained motionless. He seemed to be seeing things no one else saw, hearing things no one else heard. He said something only he could hear.

Durward reached the varicolored floor of the cavern. "Nigel," he said, soothingly. "I have come to take you home, to Inessa, your loving mother."

Nigel said nothing. He resembled a grotesque statue.

Galen was sweating. At any moment, Nigel could hurl more force at them than previously known by Mankind, and Durward had not placed a shield around them.

Durward stepped carefully and slowly closer to Nigel. "*Will* you come *home*, son, for your *mother's* sake?" he asked.

"*No*!" Nigel screamed hoarsely. He emitted a black power beam.

Durward was struck in the center of the forehead. He

was slammed into Galen and Avery, and they all crashed to the unyielding floor.

Nigel turned to face the white-hot square he had formed on the wall. Guthrie's arrow struck the Wizard in the middle of his spine. The metal arrowhead and the wooden shaft, shattered to bits against an invisible shield. Nigel was not aware that he had been attacked.

Guthrie roared with rage. He discarded the bow, pulled his sword, and charged down the stairs.

The King's Guardsmen followed suit.

The Knight's affronted cry startled Aubrey, and he lowered his trembling hands from his pale, frightened face. When he saw Avery lying motionless on the stone, Aubrey leaped to his feet, drew his sword, and ran to press the flat of the blade to Avery's throat, to strangle the King of the Elves.

The other Elves fell upon the Pretender, disarmed him and pinned him on his back against the cool stone floor.

Nigel dispatched his magic energy. The stone within the red glowing power square shimmered, misted and vanished, revealing a huge new tunnel. He levitated himself and his tank through the portal, to the floor of the new tunnel, and turned toward the opening.

Arden came to and groggily took in the action. Hatred for Nigel galvanized his mind. He scrambled to his feet and raced across the cavern. Leaping through the portal, he hurled his full weight against the tank, staggering backwards from the impact.

The conveyance rocked back, then forward, and fell

onto its side, the liquid inside sloshing.

Nigel psychically tossed Arden against the other wall of the great tunnel.

Arden rebounded and crumpled to the floor.

Nigel applied his occult power. The opening in the wall misted, shimmered and filled with stone. Nigel's glimmering red magical square faded from existence. Except for the white glow of the cooling square, the wall appeared as though it had never been breached.

Guthrie reached the wall an agonizing moment too late.

"Sir *Guthrie*!" Avery shouted. "I *think* Durward and Galen are *dead*! Our *cause* is *lost*!"

Guthrie twisted awkwardly around and raced to where Avery was examining Durward and Galen.

There was a large round wound on Durward's forehead and no sign that he was breathing.

Galen was just as still.

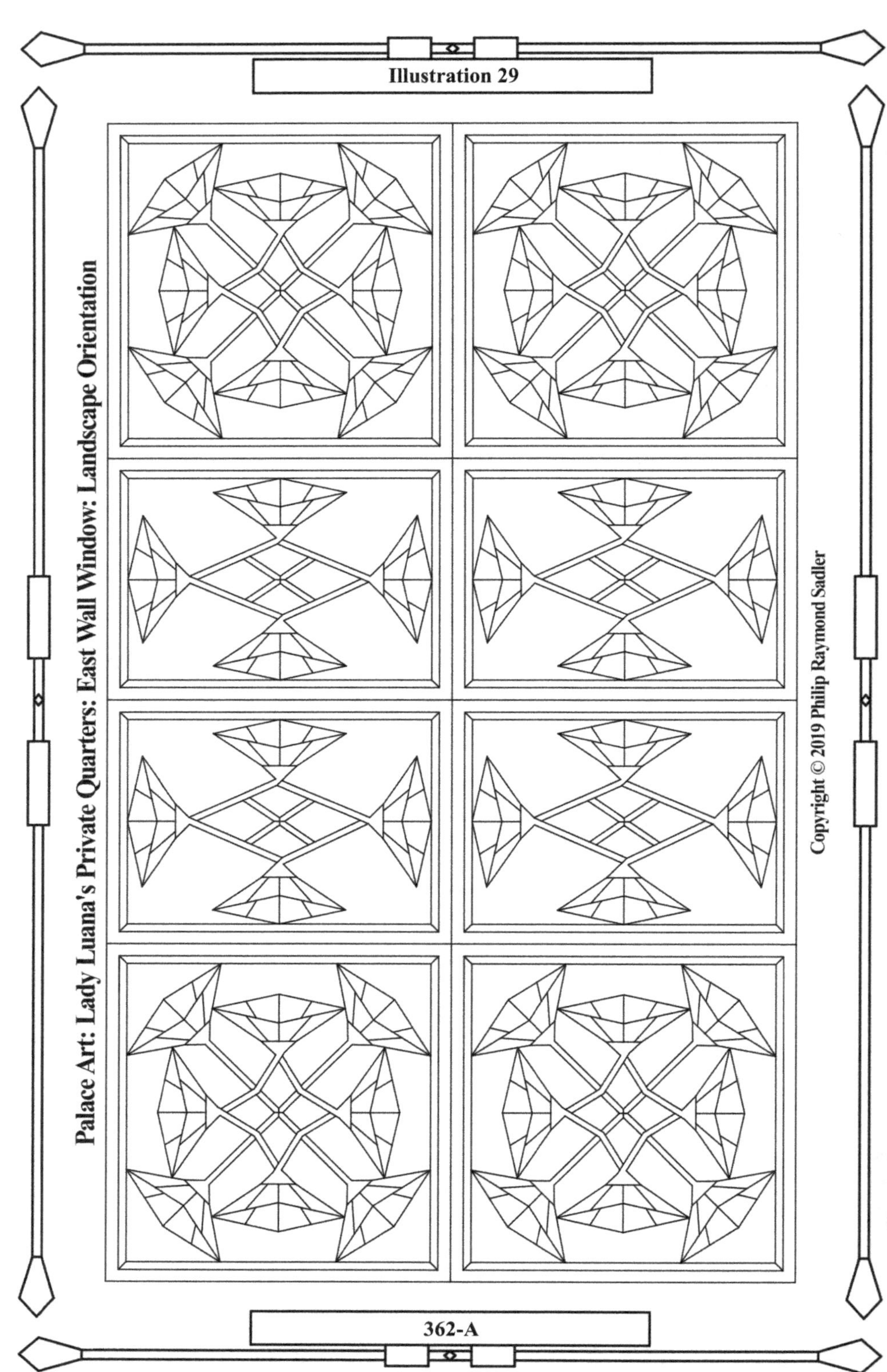
Illustration 29
Palace Art: Lady Luana's Private Quarters: East Wall Window: Landscape Orientation
Copyright © 2019 Philip Raymond Sadler
362-A

Illustration 30

Palace Art: Lady Luana's Private Quarters: West Wall Window: Landscape Orientation

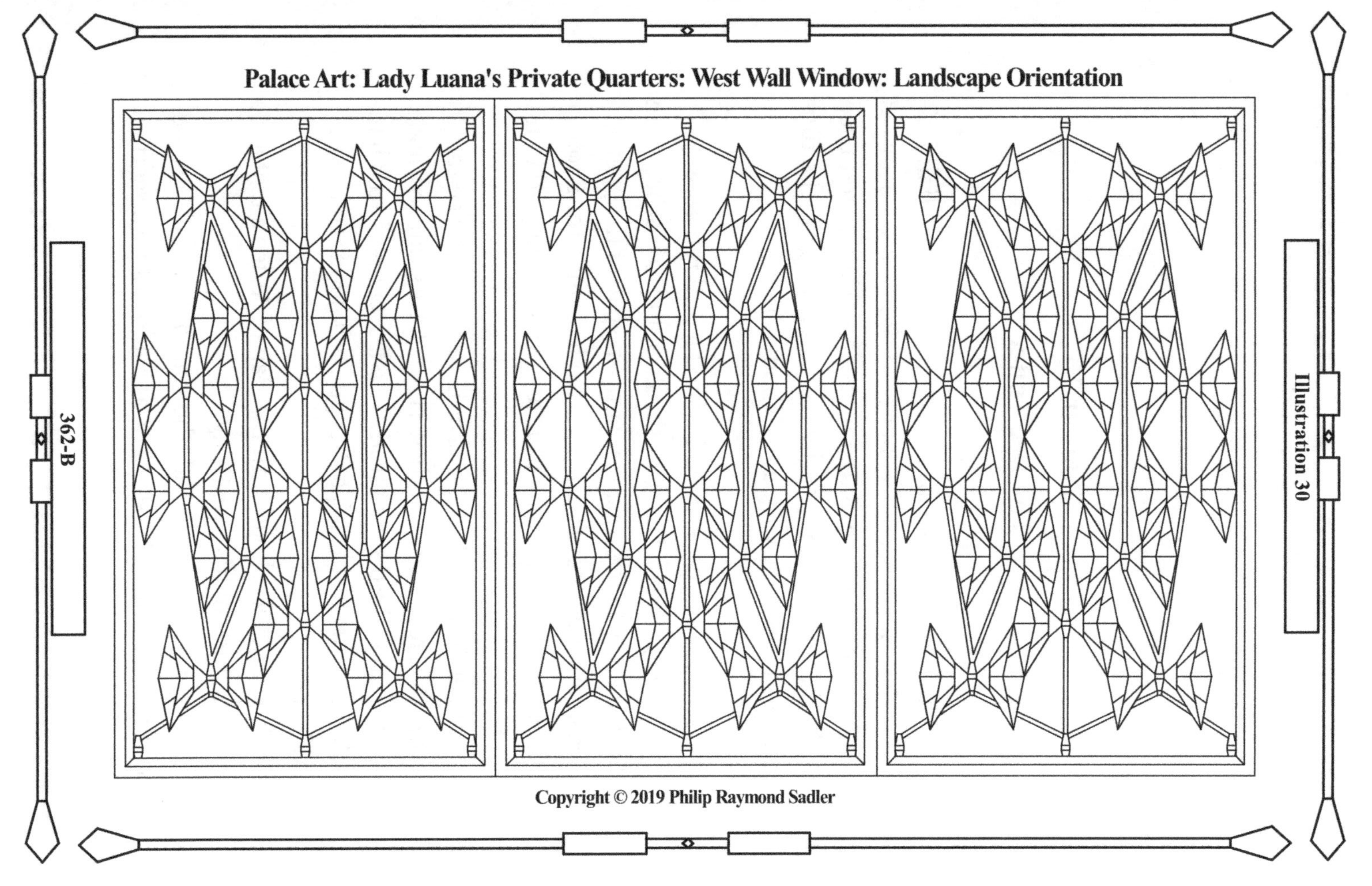

Chapter 15
The Pretender

The ivory radiance of the cooling cavern wall illuminated Nigel. He used his energy to right the overturned tank of Enhancer, levitated himself astride it, and used a similar force to propel the conveyance along the tunnel. He lit his way with a blue body sheen.

The cooling cavern wall issued a dull red glow.

Arden groaned. His right shoulder and side ached from his impact with the wall. He sat up in spite of the pain and began untying himself using his teeth to undo the knots at his wrists. He tossed the rope aside and struggled to his feet.

When he did not see Nigel or his evil tank, Arden started down the great psychically hewn tunnel. He stumbled, and it hurt to draw the deeper breaths needed, but he forced himself on. He ran with all his strength, will power and love for Aldora.

The tunnel echoed with the slap of Arden's footsteps and the rasp of his breathing.

Nigel was so far ahead, the sounds the tank's wooden wheels against the stone floor could not be discerned.

Arden had to be wary that he did not crash into one of the walls in the darkness. He did not believe he could continue after a collision, and the injury that would result to his sore ribs. He drew his sword and held it out in front of himself, waving it side to side, as a barrier detector.

Avery placed his palms to Galen's temples.

Guthrie held Galen's hands against the sides of Durward's head.

Avery spoke to his Elves in Elf Tongue. They began forming a single spiral line around the War Party. They placed their palms to each other's temples until they were all linked to Avery, Galen and Durward.

Psychic energy from the joined Elves began flowing into Durward.

Guthrie felt a painful tingling and was forced to draw his hands away.

Galen's hands did not fall from Durward's temples. It was as if magnets held them fast to an orb of iron.

A white light coalesced around the end Elf standing at the back of the cavern of rainbow stone and spread along the spiral of Elves until it engulfed Avery, Galen and Durward.

Durward's chest heaved, and he gasped a deep breath.

Galen's chest rose, and his eyes flew open.

Durward came awake.

"Enough!" Avery warned his Elves.

The ivory shine flowed backwards along the spiral

line. When it reached the last Elf, the glow faded out.

Durward and Galen stood up, unsteadily.

"For the *second* time, I have been drawn *back* from the *embrace* of the *Ethereal*," Durward said.

"A *unique* experience," Galen agreed. "Bless *you* and your *Elves* for your *intervention*."

"We could do *no* less, and *you* would have done the *same*," Avery said.

"*Where* is Nigel?" Durward asked.

"He has escaped through the cavern wall," Guthrie said. "My arrow shattered against his invisible shield."

"And *Arden*?" Galen asked.

"He leaped through the egress Nigel fashioned, just before Nigel sealed it," Guthrie said with worry. "He was struck by Nigel's magic, but I do not know how badly hurt he is. The way he *fell*, I *fear* he is *dead*."

"We were wrong," Durward said, with deep regret. "You should have shot when you first wanted."

"The Master's personal shield would have protected him," Aubrey said, insultingly. He was bound with ropes, hand and foot, and sitting against some rocks on the left side of the cavern. "The Master *will* return with *Aldora*, and you *all* will *die*!"

"*You* shall not witness it!" Avery promised. "What do my people say for this traitor?"

"Vincibility!" some shouted, angrily.

"Old age!" some suggested.

"Banishment!" some insisted.

"Show no mercy!" others shouted, irately.

"Place the Pretender into the hard Mother Stone as he and Nigel did to you!" one of the nearer Elves said. "*Banished*, he might *still* do us *harm*! In the *stone*, he will be *lifeless*, a threat *never* again!"

"Aye!" Avery said.

Aubrey had feared such might be his untenable fate. He sought the feeling within which spoke of Nigel's magical aid and was relieved to discover the Wizard's boon was still comfortingly there. He should be able to draw enough energy.

Avery raised his hands to his temples as he prepared himself to revoke the Pretender's invincibility.

Aubrey sparkled forth an energy beam.

Avery reeled back from the blow but steadied himself.

Aubrey sparkled forth another power beam.

Avery flinched. He placed a safeguard around himself to prevent Aubrey from binding his throat with strangling energy. "So," Avery said to his people, "the *Pretender* has played *sleeper* with his *might*. We do *battle* then, *Aubrey*?"

Aubrey thought forth a continuing red heat beam.

The searing energy smashed into Avery's clear shield. The barrier misted and began to fade. Avery was shocked. The power Nigel allowed Aubrey was great, for any Master to cede to a slave. Avery coursed additional power into his shield. The more Avery strengthened his barrier, the hotter Aubrey's beam became. Avery fell to his knees, gasping for air in his hot shield.

"*Strike* Aubrey!" Zadok urged Durward.

"It is *forbidden*, by Elf *Law*, to *intercede* for *either* vier," Durward said, with frustration. "The *battle* for *King* must be by the *contestants*, alone. *Anyone* who *interferes*, is *suffocated* by the *Elves*."

Aubrey broke his ropes by psychic force. He stood up and began moving closer to Avery, like a snake approaching a hypnotized bird. Aubrey staggered back, then flew into the air, landed with a thud against the left wall, and slid to the floor. His breath was knocked from him, and his heat beam was interrupted by his astonishment.

Avery stood up and struck blow after magic blow into Aubrey where he sat. They could not hurt the Pretender with his invincibility, but Avery could withdraw that protection from Aubrey now that King Avery was no longer under attack. If Avery were forced to slay evil Aubrey, the King would do so with a quick energy strike, not by painful suffocation.

"*If* you *yield*, Aubrey," Avery said, "I shall *revoke* only your *invincibility*." He kept Aubrey swaying left and right with his psychic blows. "You shall have age *protection* and *banishment*, instead of *death* or *suspended* life within the Mother Stone."

Aubrey caught his breath. "I *spit* upon your *mercy*, *false* King!" he screamed, with hatred and rage. "As long as I live, I shall not yield! *I* was *fated* to be *King* of the Elves! Not *you*! You *will* regret that you have ever *dared* opposed me!"

Avery sighed sadly. He concentrated and removed invincibility from Aubrey.

The Pretender shrieked in horror. His eyes looked wild, then they slitted, as do the eyes of a cat about to pounce.

Avery surged his mystical power to strike the magic execution blow.

Aubrey ghosted through the stone wall behind him.

Arden fell to the tunnel, panting. He could not continue to run for some time. He had covered five miles, at least, but there were thirty between him and Aldora. Perhaps ten between him and Nigel. The Dark Wizard would reach the Castle long before him. Arden felt more frustration now, than when the Shadows had him bound and half smothered in the Gray Fort.

If only his horse were there. Or Durward. Or War Serpent. Perhaps is father could travel fast enough to catch Nigel. To try to delay him.

Aldora, Arden thought. Aldora! If only you could *hear* my thoughts and *flee* into hiding!

Avery turned to his Elves. "Where, *then*, is my Queen?" he said. "Where *is* Elatiella?"

One of the female Elves stepped forward with tears sliding down her cheeks. "We do not *know*, dear King," she said. "Nigel led her away to this old cavern before he summoned us here. We have not *seen* her since. Sadness has *befallen* us, and we *fear* that she is *perished*."

Avery clenched his hands at his sides, turned toward the War Party, and started trembling.

The rage on the Elf King's face caused Durward to

step back.

"*If* your *son* has *slain* my *Elatiella*, not *even* the joined power of *you* and *Galen* will *prevent* me from exacting *revenge*!" he screamed. "Even if it means *Man* and *Elf* be *enemies*, forever!"

"Galen?" Durward pleaded.

Galen threw his hands up and circled where he stood, seeking signs of the Elf Queen. "*Nothing*!" He said. He started toward the cavern wall where Nigel had passed through. Then dodged to his left to where Aubrey had ghosted into the stone. He stopped in front of the boulders against which Aubrey had been set by the Elves. "*Here*!" he shouted. "*Yes*! *Here*! The traces of Nigel's and Aubrey's magic *disguised* her *Essence*! She *is* here! *Behind* this boulder! *You* will have to move it, *Durward*!"

"How *can* our *Queen* be *there*?" the Elf woman asked. "*There* is *not* enough *space*?"

"He has *placed* her *into* the Mother Stone!" Avery realized with hope.

Durward grasped the boulder with his mental force, pulled it over onto its flat side, and away from the wall.

Elatiella *was* imprisoned within the rainbow stone. A thin ring crown of silver adorned her long black hair. Her smooth oval beautiful face was vacant of emotion, but her green eyes expressed great sadness. She wore a flowing purple velvet dress which hid her sandals.

Guthrie's guards drew their long swords and placed them around the image of the Elf Queen.

Durward fused the blades, bent their hilts upward,

and drove the swords into the stone with his mental energy.

There was a pleasing trilling sound. The image of the Elf Queen stirred, and a feeling of joy filled the cavern. Elatiella stepped out of the stone, onto the boulder.

"My Queen!" Avery rejoiced.

The Elves cheered with jubilation that their beloved Queen was alive and back among them.

Avery reached up.

"I knew my King would not fail to prevail against Dark Nigel," Elatiella said, proudly, "and release me from the Mother Stone."

Avery lowered her to the floor.

"Nigel has *yet* to be *defeated*, my love, and it is by the *grace* of good *Durward*, that you are free," Avery said.

"You have my *gratitude*, great Magician," Elatiella said.

"I regret and apologize for my son's acts," Durward said, sadly.

"Nigel brings *no* shame down on *you* or *Inessa*," Elatiella said.

Durward was grateful for her words, but did not agree. He unbent the hilts of the swords, separated and cooled the blades, freed them from the stone, one at a time, and returned them to the soldiers.

"Aubrey will join your Nigel somewhere along Nigel's tunnel," Avery told Durward. "We must *break* through the cavern wall."

Durward stepped to the rear wall of the cavern and raised his hands.

Galen placed his palms to Durward's temples and the men knelt on the stone floor. Avery put his hands to the sides of Galen's head. Elatiella placed her hands to the sides of her husband's head. Avery's Elves did likewise to each other until they were all joined to Elatiella in a long zigzag line.

The white light developed around the end Elf and traveled swiftly to Durward's hands. As he sent the glow forth, he turned it red and formed it into a square half as large as the one Nigel had fashioned.

Guthrie noted this. Even with the combined magic of the Psychic Elves, Durward was still half matched to Nigel. Guthrie was assaulted by the fear that they would never best the Dark Wizard.

The wall square turned red, then blue, then white-hot.

Durward ended the heat beam and put force against the square, slowly bending it back.

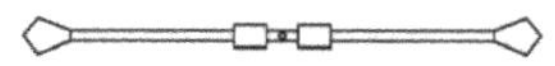

Arden forced himself to his feet and stumbled farther along the dark tunnel. He was still breathing hard. His feet and legs felt like stiff metal. He was a man possessed by love, mission and despair. His thoughts were almost chaotic, yet, for a moment, he realized this was how Nigel felt; how he agonized. He knew pity and compassion for him, but stifled it.

A feeble reflection of blue light on the wall to his left caught Arden's attention. The glow came from behind. He sheathed his sword and pressed his back against the left wall. The shine became more distinct and vaguely man shaped. Someone was—gliding—toward him.

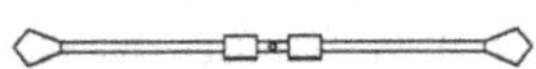

Aubrey came into focus.

Arden felt rage firing through him, giving him strength.

The Elf passed beside the Crown Prince.

Arden attacked with fury, forgetting about Elf invincibility.

Aubrey screamed in pain and fell out of the air, gasping. He grasped his scratched throat and writhed on the stone floor. For five hundred years, he had never experienced pain. He was horribly aware of it now.

Arden shook his head, managing to clear his thoughts a little. He bent over Aubrey.

The Elf tried to scoot away. His pain prevented the use of Nigel's energy, except for the blue glow, which was an unavoidable side effect of the transmission of Nigel's power to the Elf.

Arden grasped the Elf's wrist and held him firmly. "I see Avery has revoked your armor," Arden said. "I will not harm you again *if* you will help me to reach Nigel, *swiftly*."

Even through his pain, Aubrey's mind worked schemes. He would act friend to Arden, then hand the boy over to Nigel for a handsome magical reward.

Arden helped the Elf up but kept a steady, painful, pressure on the Elf's wrist.

"I *know* you *hope* to *betray* me," Arden said. "You will *die* if you do. For *any* disobedience you *offer*, you will *hurt*." Arden squeezed the wrist harder.

Aubrey cried out. The constant ache prevented him

from utilizing Nigel's magic. Without that, he could not perform in whatever way Arden needed. If he failed to do so, Arden would hurt him more. Arden would not cease the pain because that would allow Aubrey the opportunity to attack with psychic force. Aubrey's mind flooded with hopelessness.

"You *have* Nigel's *might* aiding you," Arden said, harshly. "*Levitate* us! *Draw* us *quickly* down this tunnel, as you were *just* doing!"

"I *can't*!" Aubrey said, desperately. "Your *hurting* me *blocks* my *using* the *magic*! I *swear* it!"

Arden waved his sword. "I dare not release you, Elf," he said, shakily. "I can not move more quickly than you. I must render you senseless." He raised his sword hilt to knock the Elf unconscious.

"*No*!" Aubrey screamed. "The *pain* will *kill* me! *Please*! Let me *go*! I'll *help* you! I'll *take* you to Nigel by *gliding*! I won't *fight* you!" Aubrey frantically tried to pull away despite the pain.

Arden gripped the wrist more firmly.

Aubrey cried out.

Arden increased the pressure until the Elf hung limply from his hand. He shook the Elf to see if Aubrey was faking. He slapped the Elf across the face. Aubrey did not respond.

Arden decided Aubrey could not keep silent to such pain if he were conscious, so he laid the Elf gently on the stone floor.

Arden sheathed his sword, wondering if he could manage to tap into Nigel's force through Aubrey. He placed his palms to Aubrey's temples as he had seen Galen and Durward do to each other. Arden closed his eyes, thinking of Nigel's might.

The silence in the tunnel was like a weight slowly crushing them. Nothing was happening.

Arden startled. Deeper blue energy began crackling around him. It coalesced on his hands. He felt warmth, similar to that which Galen's hands emanated when he was performing healing. The heat turned into a tingling, which covered Arden. His weariness ebbed away, and his mind cleared.

Aubrey began trembling. In a few moments, he lay still.

The tingling centered itself in Arden's solar plexus. He held his breath and moved his hands away from Aubrey's temples. The tingling remained in Arden's abdomen. He sighed with relief.

Aubrey stirred and groaned. After a moment, he opened his eyes. When he saw Arden, he sat up and thrust his hands at the Crown Prince Designate.

"I *possess* the *energy* Nigel *intends* for *you*," Arden said softly. "You would be *wise* to *remain* in the tunnel *until* Nigel is *slain*. *Then*, you should *leave* over one of the mountain ranges, to the Great Wilds. *Avery* will not *allow* you to *live* in *Indwin* any longer."

Aubrey sought within him the sensation which spoke of Nigel's magic boon. It was horribly absent. He sat in shock, glaring at Arden.

Arden stood up and faced down the tunnel. He recalled

the Elf's words:

"I'll *take* you to *Nigel* by *gliding*!"

Arden thought of floating inches above the tunnel floor. He felt weightless, then arose. He leaned forward a bit, and began gliding along the tunnel. Nigel's broadcast power would serve him well.

"*Please*!" Aubrey screamed in terror. "*Take* me *with* you! I can *harm* you no *longer*! Please, *Sire*! I *can't* be here *alone* without my *magic*! My *invincibility*! *Please*! Prince Arden!"

Arden stopped gliding. He did not want to have to worry about the machinations of the malevolent Elf, but could not bear to hurt him anymore.

He placed Aubrey in a trance, enveloped him in a beam of invisible force, lifted him a few inches above the floor, wove a blue body glow around him, and began gliding them down the dark tunnel, speeding ever faster toward the Castle, Aldora and Nigel.

The square of hot stone was fully bent back from the opening.

"Enough!" Durward shouted.

The red glow became soft white. It traveled back to the end Elf and vanished.

Durward cooled the portal.

Guthrie waited impatiently, then led his guards over the bent flap of stone, into the great tunnel.

Durward issued his ivory light after them. It pierced the murky dark far into the distance reflecting off the rainbow stone.

"Arden *must* have *survived* Nigel's *blow*!" Guthrie said excitedly, "and is chasing after Nigel. We will meet him as we travel."

"Join the end of the column," Durward ordered Guthrie and his guards, in a tone that brooked no argument or disobedience. "We shall utilize *magic* transport."

The white glow sprang up around the last guardsman. It traveled along the twisting line of Elves, to Durward. The group became weightless and lifted into the air. They glided through the opening, into the tunnel. As they sailed down the passageway, they were enveloped by the bright blue of Durward's might. They gathered speed, until the air was roaring past them.

Guthrie felt giddy for a moment. Durward had never been able to use the force of anyone who was not psychic. Now, he drew on Guthrie and his guardsmen. Durward's power must have increased during his breaching of the wall of the cavern. He was levitating almost a third of the population of the Elf Caverns at high speed and with little effort, another feat he could not muster before. He might now be equal to Nigel. *Equal*! Guthrie forced his excitement down and turned his expert attention to the tunnel ahead, searching for signs of Arden.

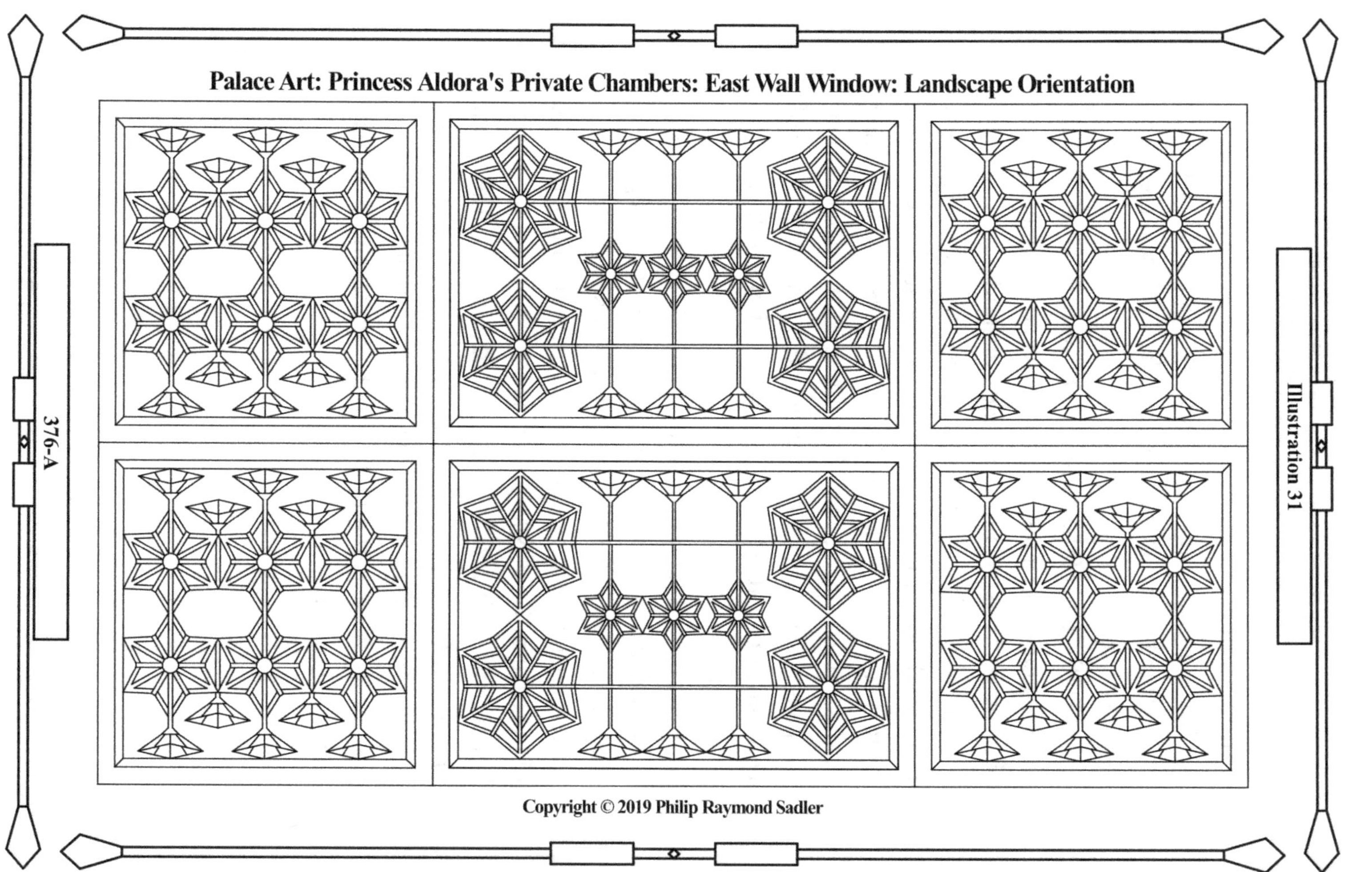
Palace Art: Princess Aldora's Private Chambers: East Wall Window: Landscape Orientation
Illustration 31
376-A
Copyright © 2019 Philip Raymond Sadler

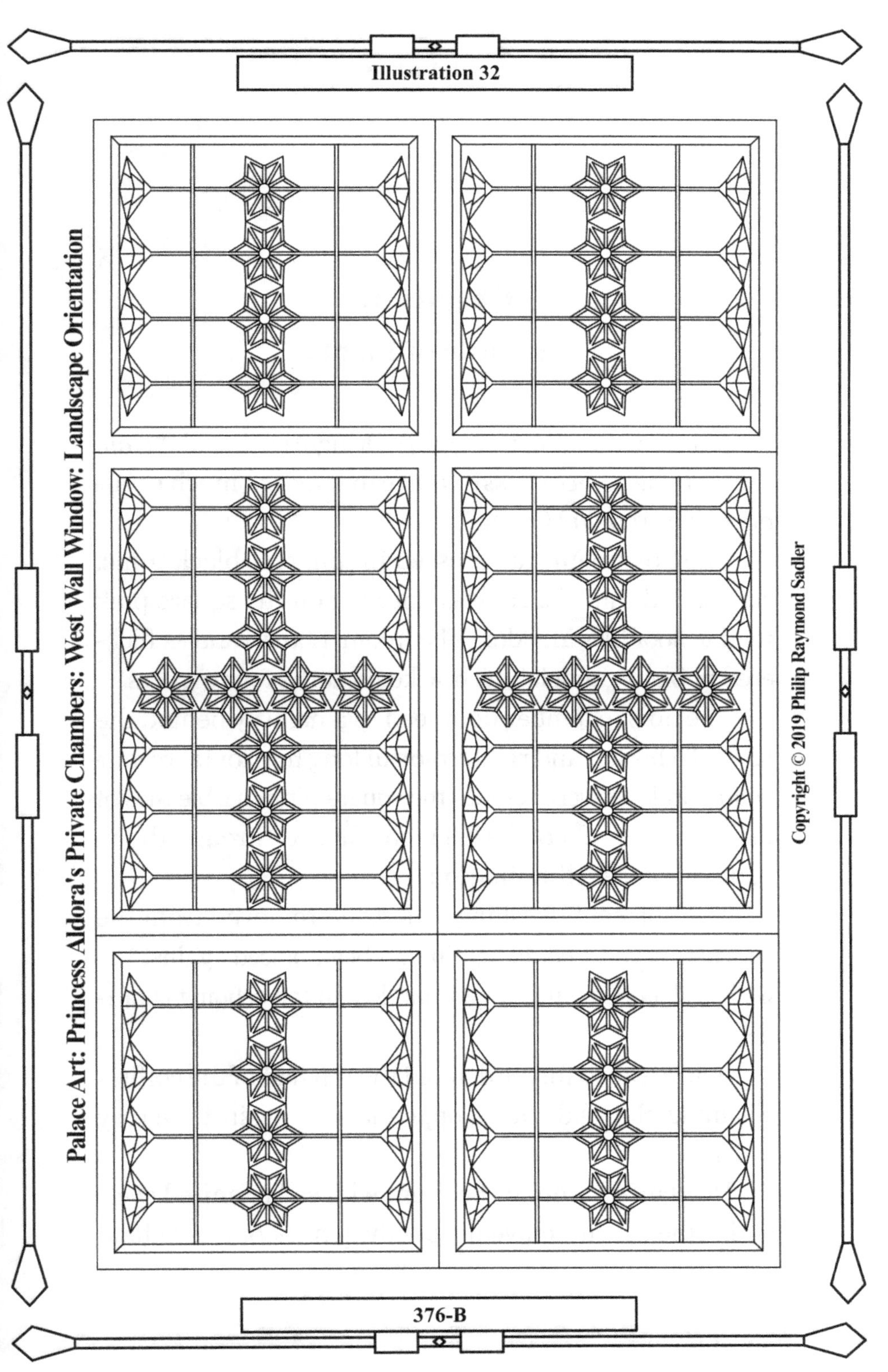
Illustration 32
Palace Art: Princess Aldora's Private Chambers: West Wall Window: Landscape Orientation
Copyright © 2019 Philip Raymond Sadler
376-B

Chapter 16
A Battle of Lights

"*How* can I *bear* this *grief*?" King Alaric said. "*How* can *Fate* be so *heartless*? *How* can it *ask* so much of *Aldora*? Of *Angela*? Of *me*?"

The Sovereign was dressed in funereal-black tunic, slacks, and sandals. He was kneeling on the square pink marble floor tiles in Aldora's bedroom. Ebony candles flickered in black candelabras bracketed at the four corners.

The open chamber door lead to a hallway behind the King. To his left and right, colorful long horizontal rectangular windows were set into the square pink marble tiles of the walls. The light of the full moon filtered through them, adding meager illumination.

The normal furnishings had been removed from the bedchamber. An ebony coffin had been placed against the wall, and looked small lonely and lost in the echoing chamber.

Alaric leaned forward, lifted the top half of the coffin's gleaming black lid, and propped it open against the rosy wall tiles.

He glanced around the room with sad agonized eyes, noting the upward movement of the pink floor tiles behind him.

There was the sound of masonry cracking.

Several rows of the large rosy tiles flipped up and back, forming a square opening.

Preceded by his blue psychic glow, Nigel levitated out of the breach, bringing his tank of Enhancer vertically with him. He settled the conveyance onto the floor and turned his wild eyes to inspect the silent bedchamber. He froze at the stark grief on Alaric's haggard pallid face, then saw the ebony casket. His heart thudded crazily and his psychic aura vanished. "*Who is it*?" he shouted hoarsely, knowing but not wanting it to be true.

"*Aldora*!" Alaric screamed, with acrimony. "*You* have *starved* her to *death*, you *monster*!" He started to attack Nigel, but the Wizard's scream of anguish shocked him like a physical blow.

Nigel dropped to his knees beside Alaric, staring into the coffin at Aldora's pale drawn face.

Alaric controlled his rage. He inspected the tank and the tube connecting the conveyance to Nigel's pale arm. The King realized their purpose, and reached for the hose.

The automatic psychic shield which jealously guarded Dark Nigel, flung the Sovereign back across the room and against the wall. Alaric tumbled to the floor in front of the hall doorway, losing his breath and striking his forehead on the stone squares. Unconsciousness took charge of the noble King.

Nigel reached into the casket. He lifted Aldora tenderly and gazed at her ashen face. Tears flowed to his soiled cheeks. "To no *avail*," He whispered tonelessly. "To no *avail*. All *wasted* effort. *Useless* suffering. To lose *my* life while I *love*, is not *ugly*. To *lose* the *one* I *love* while *I* yet *live*, is *torture*. *Torture*." He settled Aldora into her coffin. "*Galen*," he mumbled, the wildness returning to his gaunt face. "*Galen*, with *my* power, will *draw* her *back*. Bring her *back* to *life*. *If* she *returns*, I *shall* leave. *Die*. *Death* is *better*, than to hurt *her* again. *If* she will not *return*, I will *die* to join *her*. *Galen*!" he implored. He stood up, spun around and drew the tank of Enhancer toward the hole in the floor.

There was a flash of blue below.

Arden soared into the room and hovered in midair. He saw Nigel, and instinctively attacked with his new psychic energy.

The tube connected to Nigel jumped like a snake. Dark Nigel's protective force kept the hose intact and affixed to the Wizard's forearm.

Nigel's jealousy, hatred and rage canceled out all else. He struck Arden with a glowing ball of might.

The Crown Prince Designate exploded toward the wall to the left of the hall door. Arden managed a weak shield, just in time. The pink blocks cracked behind him with his impact against them. Arden hovered before the shattered wall and hurled an orb of force at Nigel's chest.

Nigel absorbed the blow, latched onto Arden with four beams of power, and pulled with all his psychic might.

Arden's arms and legs were snapped to a spread eagle position and his joints began to ache. He tried to draw more of Nigel's power, but there was no response. Nigel had set a limit for Aubrey, and this limit held for Arden. The pain in his joints became worse. Arden sent all his might into his shield. The ache lessened, for a moment.

Nigel sensed this and directed an invisible blow to Arden's chest.

The strike weakened Arden's safeguard. The pain in his joints increased. A blow vibrated him. Then another. A heat beam began to play over his shield. It was like being too close to a campfire. His facial hair began to singe, and more pain crept through him. He cried out, and strained to find added power.

Nigel hurled Arden against the ceiling and the floor with resounding thuds, cracking the ceiling and floor tiles.

In spite of his safeguard, Arden was stunned.

Nigel increased the red heat beam on the man who had not long ago been his beloved childhood friend; his jealousy canceling out his memories of those happy idyllic times.

Alaric came to. He struggled to his feet, drew a dagger from a sheath on his hip, and sliced savagely at the tube between Nigel and the tank. The dagger caused sparks, and flew out into the hallway.

Nigel psychically picked Alaric up and tossed him into the dark tunnel.

Nigel pinned Arden against the floor and steadily increased the heat force on him.

Arden's shield began to deteriorate; fissuring and sparking. Soon, he would be baked to death.

Nigel twisted Arden's arms opposite to his legs and

pulled against the weakening safeguard.

Arden desperately tried to muster more strength from Nigel. There seemed to be a greater response. Then there was nothing within Arden to indicate the presence of Dark Nigel's power working through the desperate Prince. To Arden's horror, his blue shield was no longer around him. He was at the unlikely mercy of the insane Wizard!

Nigel's red heat beam ended and the Crown Prince Designate was released from Nigel's psychic grip.

Arden fell to the floor on his face just short of plummeting into the breach in the tiles, and lost his breath.

Nigel was suspended in midair. A look of disbelief and frustration was frozen into the Wizard's wild features. His blue safeguard was gone, and his breathing was almost unnoticeable.

In the hallway outside Aldora's chambers, hidden by an invisibility shield, SaCee stood with a block of clear crystal on the palms of her hands. She held this toward Nigel.

A black mass about the shape and size of the egg of a fowl emerged from the Dark Wizard's forehead.

Although it struggled mightily, this essence of evil was drawn inexorably into the clear crystal block wherein it would be imprisoned for eternity.

SaCee was angry with herself because it had taken her this long to comprehend why a sweet shy and polite child like Nigel had suddenly developed behavioral problems. These extreme symptoms could not have been based solely on jealousy, or unrequited love.

SaCee had searched her memories until she recalled the final time Nigel, Aldora and Arden had stolen away from the Citadel and ridden their steeds to her Crystal Clear Mountain to see if they could find her.

Her mountain recorded all things which occurred without and within itself. SaCee could review these archives from any location. Today, she had done so to verify her suspicion of the secret of Nigel's illness.

On all previous occasions, Aldora, Arden and Nigel had failed to discover a way into her mountain, but on this day, and through Durward's astute tutoring, Nigel had managed to shut down the shield that disguised and blocked access to the main cavern.

Aldora and Arden became fascinated by a section of the cavern wall that flickered with intricate beautiful and unique multi colored designs.

Jealous of Aldora's obvious affection for Arden, Nigel wandered more deeply into the cavern. He took a side tunnel which led to a dark chamber blocked by a second energy shield. It required more concentration and will for Nigel to switch off this barrier.

When Nigel entered, the ceiling emitted a soft white light, and he became disappointed. He saw thousands of two foot high, clear crystal poles arranged in rows. He could fathom no reason why they should be hidden behind a protective shield. When he turned to leave, he bumped into one of the poles. A black orb flashed out of the top of the pole. Nigel thought it sailed over his head. When he spun around to look for it, the orb was nowhere in sight. He shrugged and

exited the chamber.

The ceiling went dark and the shield returned to block the entrance.

Nigel was halfway into the main cavern when Durward and Guthrie entered and angrily bade the children to return home. They were forbidden to approach the Crystal Clear Mountain.

SaCee frowned. The columns in the dark chamber contained the evil essences of the Southern Demons of Darkness that she had vanquished long before Nigel's birth. An unpleasant act which she had been forced to perform to preserve the Elves and the people of Indwin. She had imprisoned the demons in their energy form inside the crystals because the demons could not be slain and removed from the world, except with the aid of the Ethereal, and it had vehemently refused to assist SaCee in this.

Nigel's burgeoning knowledge and command of the principles of Mind Magic had inadvertently released one of the demons. It had entered Nigel and had begun to poison the hapless child's mind. The demon's ability to magically disguise itself had caused Galen to mistake its vile essence for an irreparable birth imperfection that had caused a defect in Nigel's personality.

SaCee gazed at the block of crystal in which the evil essence swirled. This was her remedy for that tragic event and condition. She would re-enforce the prisons of the rest of the demons so only the Ethereal could release them.

SaCee miniaturized the crystal block until it was the size of a pebble and dropped it into a pocket of her dress.

A white glow appeared in the breach in the floor of Aldora's chambers.

Durward floated into the battle damaged room. He alighted on the floor and gazed at Nigel with hope on his old exhausted and battle lined face. Although he did not understand how, he had negated Nigel's might, and more incredibly, had reversed the harm perpetrated by his Enchantments.

Zelam River flowed its life giving waters throughout thirsty, grateful Indwin. Vegetable and grain fields were green and golden, and ready for harvest. Windy Hills Orchards were lush with Honey Apples; ripe for the traditional picking. Sheep and cattle grazed on the long grasses surrounding the fragrant Orchards.

Though Durward could not see these remarkable things, he could sense them to be true. It was as if he were a part of the rustling Orchards. Of the lowing cattle, the bleating sheep, and the strutting goats. Of the grains and vegetables. Of the sparkling Zelam River.

The Magician noticed Aldora in her coffin. His sense of hope, joy and accomplishment vanished. Tears welled and he swiftly turned to Arden.

The Crown Prince Designate was lying on the floor and gasping for air. His mind was fogged by pain from his battle. He had not seen the casket.

Durward lifted a hand toward Arden to place him to sleep, but paused.

A blue gleam colored the breach in the floor.

Galen and Alaric levitated from the tunnel, riding on Durward's energy, and settled to the pink tiles.

"Aldora *slumbers* by *drugs*," Alaric said firmly to Durward and Arden. "When she heard sounds of tunneling below her room, we laid this trap for Nigel. We hoped his *grief* would make him *vulnerable* long enough for me to kill him. Do not *fret*, Arden, she will *awaken* soon."

Galen placed his hands to Nigel's forehead.

Durward floated the Healer, the tank of Enhancer, and the Wizard into the tunnel.

Galen would couple with the Enhancer and the Psychic Elves for the healing of Nigel and Aubrey.

"With Galen's help, Nigel will be able to deal with his love for Aldora without becoming deranged again," Durward said. "*All* of Aldora's fervent *prayers* for my son have been *answered*."

"As have ours," King Alaric said, squeezing the Magician's shoulders.

Arden struggled to his feet. He placed a hand against the wall, steadied himself for a moment, and stepped to the coffin. He lifted the rest of the lid and slipped Aldora into his arms.

"Take her to Queen Angela's rooms," King Alaric said. "Our loved ones are awaiting us there. Tell the hall guards to go forth and spread the word. Nigel's *War* is *ended*, and *Nigel* has returned *home*."

Outside Aldora's room, SaCee smiled, ended her invisibility and, heeding the call of the Ethereal, flashed down the hallway and up several flights of stairs to the Observation Tower. She raised her green staff into the air, sent forth her white energy and released from the pseudo stone, the people of Indwin who had been possessed by Nigel.

SaCee flashed from the Observation Tower to the grass outside the Citadel. She raised her green staff into the air, emitted her white energy, and liberated Zolazar and his Elves from the pseudo stone.

The Supreme Commander and his army could feel they were freed of Nigel's influence. They looked at SaCee with puzzlement.

Zolazar approached the Seer with his hands out.

"Nigel's War has *ended*. King Avery, Queen Elatiella, and many of your people await you and your army in Alaric's castle," SaCee said. "Not as *victors* over Indwin, but as Indwin's *friends*. Fear not for your *progeny*," she said, her voice carrying to each member of the army. "I *shall* free them from the Mother Stone *before* I return to my Crystal Clear Mountain."

Zolazar and his army cheered, then gasped with wonder as SaCee flashed out of sight toward the North and the Elf Caverns.

www.ingramcontent.com/pod-product-compliance
Lightning Source LLC
Chambersburg PA
CBHW060807030726
47503CB00002B/383

9780934370462